Cabin

5

P. L. Wellisley

Cabin 5

Cover design by P. L. Wellisley

ISBN: 979-8-9994875-2-0

Printed in the United States of America

First Edition

Note to the Reader

For the reader that's been broken. You are not the weight of your past…you are the courage it took to survive it. This story contains sensitive material related to abuse and emotional distress. Please take care of yourself while reading.

"Hey, RaeRae." His voice is gentle and warm. The same voice that talked me through scraped knees, science projects and every middle school heartbreak I swore I'd never survive.

I can't even say hello before the tears come harder and my voice cracks. "I did it."

There's a pause. A quiet breath on the other end. "I know, sweetheart, and I'm so damn proud of you."

He tells me it's going to work out. That being single isn't a bad thing. That strength sometimes looks like chaos and uncertainty. He would know.

My mom died just after I was born from an infection after her C-section. I never knew her, but Dad made sure I knew who she was. He used to tell me stories about her, how kind she was, how quick to laugh, how she opened her heart and home to anyone who needed a place to land. I clung to those stories like a map, building a version of her in my mind that felt real enough to miss.

When I was younger, I'd ask why he never remarried. He'd just smile and say, "They weren't good enough for you." It wasn't until I was older that he told me the rest. Every woman he brought home met me first. And if I didn't light up, if I didn't show interest or affection, he knew she could never truly be a mother to me. So eventually, he stopped looking.

I wipe my cheeks with the back of my hand. "What am I going to do, Dad? I don't know how to be alone."

"You start over," he says gently. "You figure out who you are and enjoy being whoever the hell you want to be. Take the time. Breathe. Heal. But most importantly, RaeRae, don't ever settle for less than you deserve again."

"Thanks, Dad. I love you."

"I love you, too."

We hang up with a promise that I'll visit soon. And I know he'll come see me. He's always wanted to visit Cranberry Ridge.

It's a six-hour drive back. I'm halfway there when my phone rings again, cutting off the audiobook I was using to fill the silence. Jacob.

His name flashes across the screen, and for a moment, I freeze. I almost don't answer. I want this divorce to be peaceful, no drama, no screaming, just closure. But old habits die hard. So, I answer carefully.

"You actually left." His voice is quiet, but not soft. There's a sharpness beneath it, anger simmering just below the surface.

"I told you I was going, Jacob. This isn't new."

"You didn't have to leave like that."

What he means is without permission, without asking. Without staying long enough to take one last blow to my self-worth.

"I left the way I had to," I say calmly. "You just didn't believe I actually would."

"We're just separated. It's not over yet. We can still fix this." His voice sharpens, desperation threaded with denial, the kind that used to trap me in circles until I forgot which way was up.

"I have to go," I say firmly, already reaching to end the call.

"Okay, babe. I get it." His tone smooths over, practiced and polished. "Take your time, we'll talk soon, yeah?"

I hang up without answering.

The rest of the drive is silent. No audiobook. No music. Just the hum of tires on asphalt as the trees thicken and the world narrows into something slower, quieter. Safer.

By the time I pull into the gravel driveway of cabin five, the sun is low, painting the lake gold. It's small and temporary, but it's mine for now. I kill the engine and sit there for a moment, Dad's words echoing in my mind. '*Be strong. Be happy. Don't settle.*' I can do this. I will do this. And I know Kinsley will be there every step of the way.

1

Emotional Support Donuts

Raelynn

I've been holed up in this cabin long enough. Two weeks of hiding. Two weeks of going through the motions like I'm still living the life I left behind. But I didn't leave everything just to keep pretending I'm still Jacob's wife. The divorce isn't final yet, but the legal separation is. It should feel like freedom, but most days, it just feels sad, that maybe I failed. I suppose that's how he wanted it.

Jacob was my high school sweetheart. For a while, it was good, safe, familiar, the kind of love that felt invincible. But everything changed when he became a police officer. Somewhere along the way, the uniform became a wall between us. He grew controlling and critical, like the badge gave him permission to reshape me into someone smaller. We were together for fifteen years, and for the last ten, I let him make every decision, from what I wore to who I could spend time with. I told myself it was love, but it was just fear.

I still feel like I'm living that life. I wash the dishes right after breakfast. I make dinner at 5:00 p.m. sharp. I wake up early and make the bed. I still wear the clothes he picked out, safe colors, modest cuts, things that made me blend in. I'm done. I didn't come here to keep being that version of myself. I came here to start over, and that starts today.

I jumped in the shower for the first time in over a week. Depression is no joke. It creeps in slowly, makes you forget how long it's been since you felt clean, felt normal, felt like yourself.

I rummage through my clothes until I find the black yoga pants I wasn't allowed to wear in public. I pair them with a soft hoodie, comfort over control. I pull my long, wavy hair into a high ponytail and swipe on a little makeup. Just enough to feel like I tried. Just enough to feel like me. When I glance at my reflection in the mirror, I freeze for half a second. I look like my mother.

I've only seen pictures, but I have her blonde hair. My dad's brown eyes. I'm short like she was at five foot three. I stare at myself for a moment, letting the weight of that settle. Then I take a deep breath and lift my chin.

It's nearly 3:00 p.m. when I plop onto the couch, remote in hand, flipping aimlessly through TV channels. I'm not really watching, just letting the noise fill the silence. The cabin creaks with the afternoon breeze, and somewhere outside birds chirp.

Then there's a quick knock at the door. Before I can even stand, the door creaks open, and Kinsley lets herself in. Kinsley's been my best friend since grade school.

She's already halfway inside before she says anything. "Hope you're not naked."

I snort. "Not today."

She grins as she kicks the door shut behind her, a reusable shopping bag dangling from one arm. Her auburn hair is twisted up in a clip. She's wearing those worn-in jeans on her perfect little body that make her look effortlessly cool.

Kinsley is also starting over but in a different way. She's here for love and I'm here to escape. Kinsley moved in with Miles and I moved into cabin five. Just like always, we're in this together.

She takes one look at me on the couch and raises an eyebrow. "You do own real clothes."

I roll my eyes but smile, tugging at the hem of my hoodie. "Don't get used to it."

She tosses the bag onto the kitchen counter and turns to face me, already looking suspicious. "Too late. I was hoping you'd be up for something today."

I arch a brow. "Something like…?"

Without answering, she reaches into the bag and pulls out two bottles of wine. "Well, I figured we could start with this." She sets them on the counter. "And then we could finish with this." She pulls out two bottles of whiskey, flashing me that devilish smile.

I chuckle, shaking my head. "You planning on dragging my secrets out of me or just knocking me unconscious?"

"Either way, we're bonding."

Just as I start to push off the couch, there's another knock at the door. I glance at her, eyebrows raised.

"You expecting someone else?"

"Maybe," she chuckles.

I cross the room and open the door to find Naya standing there, her dark hair pulled into a messy bun and a massive white pastry box balanced in her arms. The gold lettering across the top reads The Sweet Spot, her bakery back in town.

"I come bearing sugar and judgment," she says cheerfully, pushing past me.

I blink. "Did you bring the chocolate one?"

"And carbs. And maybe too much frosting." She sets the box beside the wine like we're about to throw the most unhinged book club meeting in history.

Kinsley whistles low. "This is starting to feel like an intervention."

"But with snacks."

I close the door and head straight for the pastries like a woman on a mission. "I'm gonna need a gym membership after this," I mutter, lifting the lid on the box.

I didn't know Naya well when we first met. She came by to see Kinsley right before our trip to Seattle for my legal separation.

It's impossible not to like her. Somewhere between that day and now, she became one of the few people I can really be myself around. The kind of friend who shows up with pastry boxes and never lets you lie to yourself.

"Same," Kinsley says, eyeing a glazed lemon tart. "But I'll happily risk the muffin top."

Naya snorts. "Please. We all know I bake to avoid my feelings and then give the leftovers to people I love so they gain the weight instead. It's a system."

We all burst out laughing as I reach for a cinnamon sugar donut. Kinsley pops open the first bottle of wine with practiced ease and starts pouring into mismatched mugs from my tiny kitchen cabinet.

"To sugar, wine and bad decisions we can blame on each other." She hands out drinks like a priest with communion.

Naya raises her mug. "Amen."

The three of us settle around the low coffee table, a storm of crinkling wax paper and pastry crumbs. There's no music playing, no deep confessions yet, but it feels like something real is starting. Like maybe healing doesn't always begin in silence, it begins with laughter and raspberry-filled cookies.

I lean back, licking frosting from my thumb. "God, I forgot what it felt like to just…live."

"You're allowed to enjoy things again, Rae," Kinsley says softly.

The lump in my throat catches me off guard. I take a sip of wine and reach for another donut, hiding behind sugar.

"So," Naya says, mouth full of apple tart, "who's ready to talk crap about Jacob?"

We all groan, but the kind that turns into laughter again. Loud and messy and long overdue. We sit and talk about the deep stuff, grief and guilt, freedom and fear, until the wine is gone and the tears dry up. Kinsley wipes her face on a napkin, green eyes still shining but softer now, like something heavy just let go.

Naya stands, stretching out her five-foot-five athletic frame, and heads into the kitchen. "Alright, enough emotional detox. It's time we toast to new starts."

She reappears with three plastic cups and the whiskey. Then she flicks on the radio, and classic rock fills the room with something wild and free. Before I can blink, Naya's pulling me to my feet, her grin infectious. Kinsley's already spinning barefoot across the living room, shoving the coffee table aside to make space. She does a dramatic dip with a throw pillow like it's her dance partner and winks at me.

I watch them, my best friend twirling around the room, and Naya laughing, bouncing on her toes. For a moment, I just stand there, caught in the stillness while everything else moves around me.

Starting over. It sounds simple when other people say it. But I know the truth of it. I know what it costs. The ache of leaving, the fear of becoming someone new, the way it makes your chest tight and your steps uncertain. But watching them, these women who refuse to let me drown in my own doubt, I realize how badly I want it. Not just to feel better, but to actually be better. To laugh without flinching. To wake up and not feel the weight of approval pressing down on me. To finally build something that's mine.

"Hell yes," I say, just as Naya hands me a glass.

We throw back the shots with a single, chaotic cheer, no real words, just the sound of three women reclaiming themselves. Kinsley doesn't even pause before pouring another round.

"To all the exciting things waiting ahead," she toasts, her voice wobbling with hope.

We clink cups again and dance between gulps, hips swaying, hair loose, laughter louder than the music. It's not graceful, and it's definitely not coordinated, but it's free. Maybe that's what starting over really looks like. It's not perfect. It's just possible.

We're halfway through another song, Kinsley using a spatula as a microphone and Naya twirling like a tornado, when there's a sharp knock on the door.

Naya gasps like it's Christmas morning. "Judy!" She squeals, skipping toward the door.

She swings it open, and there she is, Judy, wearing jeans, a cardigan, arms full of bags and that trademark smile showing off her dimples. The one that always makes me feel like everything's going to be okay.

Judy is Miles' aunt and in her late sixties, but she doesn't look a day over fifty. Judy lives just a few cabins down, tucked into cabin one like the matriarch of some small, rugged kingdom. She's been checking in on me every couple of days since I arrived, always showing up with food I didn't ask for and a pat on the back I didn't know I needed. She never pried, never pushed, just made sure I knew someone was close by if I wanted to talk or eat.

Before she can say a word, Kinsley charges forward, grabs her hand and pulls her inside. "You're not just dropping by. You're joining."

"I...what in the world..." Judy starts, glancing around at the empty wine bottles and pushed-back furniture.

I'm already pouring her a glass of whiskey, handing it over with a chuckle. "You don't get to judge us, not until you've had a drink."

Naya throws an arm around her shoulders. "C'mon, Judy. One drink won't kill you."

"All right, all right." She relents with a chuckle. "But just one, and I brought real food." She eyes the mess of cookies, tarts and donut crumbs littering the coffee table.

That gets another round of cheers.

While Judy sets down the bags she's carrying, Kinsley starts unpacking them with a dramatic gasp. "Oh my God, are you kidding me?"

She lays everything out on the kitchen island like it's a holiday feast. Whole roasted chicken, creamy mashed potatoes, green beans glistening with butter and golden dinner rolls that are still warm.

We all rush the food like we haven't eaten in a week, laughing with our mouths full, grabbing forks and making little mountains on our plates. No one bothers with napkins. It's glorious and messy and perfect.

Judy excuses herself for a moment, stepping out onto the porch with her phone. We don't pry, just keep eating and laughing while Kinsley tries to convince Naya to take her fifth bite of mashed potatoes like a shot.

When Judy comes back inside, she's already smiling. This time, when Kinsley refills her glass, she doesn't argue. She throws the shot back like a champ.

We all cheer like it's the Olympics. Just like that, Judy's one of us, cackling, swaying, singing along, letting Naya spin her around like they're at a barn dance.

We're a wild mess of tears and laughter, sticky with sugar and whiskey warmth, but it feels like the most alive I've been in years. And watching Judy belt out lyrics with one shoe off and a donut in hand? Amazing!

By now, we're all good and drunk, the kind of drunk where everything is hilarious and nothing hurts. Kinsley is doubled over at Naya, who's trying to teach Judy how to twerk, and bless her heart, she's giving it a valiant effort. I nearly choke on my whiskey when she throws her hands in the air and yells, "How do your knees even bend like that?!"

Naya is crying she's laughing so hard, clutching her stomach as she slides down the wall.

"You're gonna break a hip!" Kinsley wheezes between gasps.

"I've got strong hips, thank you very much," Judy declares, adjusting her cardigan over her curvy figure like she didn't just try to drop it low in orthopedic shoes.

We collapse onto the floor in a tangled pile of limbs and crumbs, breathless and high on joy. Someone turns the music down and for a second the room goes soft, quiet in that warm, heavy way that only happens when the chaos settles just enough for the feelings to sneak in.

"I really needed this." My voice is thick, and no one asks me to explain.

Kinsley reaches over and laces her fingers through mine. "We all did."

Judy sighs, content. "Maybe I'll regret this in the morning. But right now?" She raises her glass, nearly sloshing it. "I'd do it all again."

We all toast again. Because why not?

The night spins on in slow, sweet spirals, more dancing, more stories, more food eaten with our fingers straight off the island. For the first time in a long time, I'm not thinking about yesterday or worrying about tomorrow.

Our words start to slur, laughter bubbling up for no good reason, everything tingling with that warm, woozy glow of too much whiskey and not enough water.

Then there's a knock on the door. We all freeze like we've just been caught in the middle of a heist. Judy squints toward the sound, swaying slightly. "Well, who could that be?"

"I hope they're hot." Naya sighs dramatically.

I burst out giggling. "Yeah. Hot. Preferably tall, possibly shirtless."

Kinsley stumbles toward the door, arms out like she's bracing for a hurricane. "I got it, I got it," she says, nearly tripping over her own foot.

That just makes us laugh harder, wild, wheezing belly laughs. Judy is wiping her eyes, muttering something about how we're a menace to society, and Naya's already leaning in, whispering, "Please be hot, please be hot."

Whoever's on the other side of that door has no idea what kind of madness they're about to walk into.

2

Good with Hoses?

Reed

The station was quiet today, just the way I like it. No sirens screaming down Main Street. Just a slow, easy shift. A fender bender outside the grocery store. A false alarm from burnt toast in Mrs. Clayton's kitchen, again. And a raccoon tripping the motion sensor at the high school. I spent most of the afternoon doing equipment checks and sweeping out the engine bay. Slow days don't happen often, but when they do, I take them.

When my shift ends, I pull on my sweatshirt, toss a few see-yas to the crew and step out into the evening air. The smell of cut grass hangs in the breeze, and I let myself breathe it in for a second before heading to my truck.

The drive home takes all of two minutes. My brick ranch sits on two flat acres off a gravel road. It has two bedrooms and a wide front porch. I bought this place five years ago, not long after making lieutenant. It's not fancy, a single-man's setup, leather couch, big TV, weights in the garage, a stack of firewood by the back door.

The second I step inside, there's the familiar sound of tiny paws scrambling across hardwood.

"Hey, Fifi."

Eight pounds of curly-haired enthusiasm barrels toward me, tail wagging so hard her whole-body wiggles. She's brown with big soulful eyes that still have a little nervous shelter-dog edge in them. The name came with her, Fifi, and I'd meant to change it. But she answers to it, and I have to admit, it's worth keeping just to see the looks I get when I call her that.

I open the fridge and stare into the void. A few sad condiments. Half a lime. One lone beer can standing like a soldier. I let the door fall shut and sigh.

Yeah, I'm not shopping tonight.

Ten minutes later, I'm pulling into the Fireside Lounge, the local bar and grill, where half the town comes to eat, drink and gossip. The place smells like grilled meat, spilled beer and pine cleaner.

I sit at the bar, catching Tess' eye. She's a pretty blonde, crooked smile. "Hey firefighter. The usual?"

"Unless you feel like living dangerously and surprising me."

"Oh, I can do that." She winks and disappears into the kitchen.

I laugh and lean back, pulling my phone out to call my brother, Miles.

"Hey, you busy?"

"Just wrangling chickens. You?"

"Just ordered food. Wanted to check in about cabin two."

He sighs. "Yeah, it's toast. Tree came straight through the roof. Judy says it's gotta come down."

"I figured. You thinking this weekend?"

"Might work. Luke's back in town Friday, so we could get it done after that. I'll give him a call."

Luke is one of our best friends, always has been. He lived with us through high school after things got rough at home. At this point, calling him a friend doesn't really cover it. He's family.

"Good. We should probably loop in Dylan, too. He's got that new saw he won't shut up about."

Miles chuckles. "Man loves his tools."

"He owns the hardware store and the construction company. He has to talk about tools. It's basically his whole brand."

We talk a little longer, about lumber costs, who'd bring beer, and whether Luke would actually show up on time.

Just as I hang up Tess returns and sets a plate in front of me. "Dangerous enough for you?"

I look down at the massive burger and mountain of fries. "You nailed it." I shoot her a wink and a smile.

"Don't flirt with me, fireman. I already know you." She waves a hand at me like she's shooing off a stray dog.

She's not wrong. I do like to flirt. Maybe too much. Yeah, I've got a bit of a reputation in this town, but I've earned it fair and square. I'm upfront with the women I meet; I warn them right out of the gate. No sleepovers. I don't want to settle down yet. I like the single life. Doesn't mean I don't enjoy a little back-and-forth, though.

"You wound me, Tess." I press a hand to my chest like she's just shattered my poor, fragile heart.

She rolls her eyes and tosses a rag over her shoulder. "Save it for someone who hasn't seen you work the entire dining room like a politician on election night."

"Politicians kiss babies. I don't."

"Mm-hmm. You kiss plenty." Tess spins and heads down the bar to check on another customer.

I chuckle under my breath and go back to my burger, finishing it off in a few big bites. By the time I wipe my hands and toss some cash on the bar, the place is buzzing with the usual dinner crowd. I nod to Tess on my way out.

The moment I get into the driver's seat, my phone starts ringing. Judy's name flashes across the screen.

"Hello, Aunt Judy."

"Hello, Reed, sweetie," she says in that sing-song voice she uses whenever she's about to ask for something. "I could use a strong man's help."

"Stop buttering me up," I chuckle. "I'll do it."

She giggles, like she's been caught. "Will you swing by Floyd's farm and pick up the pumpkins I ordered? I need them for the firehouse Halloween fundraiser. I want to start carving them soon."

"Yeah, sure. I'll pick them up now and bring them by."

"Oh, perfect. Thanks, honey."

I hang up, shaking my head with a small smile. Judy's been pulling this "strong man" routine since I was sixteen, and it still works every time.

Judy's been living on my brother's land in cabin one ever since my mother passed. She sort of stepped into the role of cabin manager and acting mother for everyone around here, whether they asked for it or not. The thing is nobody minds. Everyone loves her. Which is why I find myself driving ten minutes out of town instead of going home like I'd planned.

I pull into Allen Farms, the big wooden sign out front faded and crooked. The place has been around forever, and so has its owner, Old Man Floyd. He's pushing eighty now and mean as a badger on a good day. Doesn't care who he offends.

I hop out of my truck and I'm greeted with Floyd's signature scowl.

"Hey, Floyd," I call, heading toward the massive pile of pumpkins stacked near the driveway.

"Hey yourself," he grumbles. "Hurry up and get your pumpkins before they kill my lawn."

I can't help but chuckle. Classic Floyd, never a hello, just straight to the point.

"Yes, sir," I say, mostly to amuse myself.

Floyd stands there for a second, arms crossed, like he's making sure I don't screw it up somehow. Then he huffs and turns toward the house, muttering something under his breath.

By the time I toss the last pumpkin in the truck bed, Floyd's already vanished into the house. I slam the tailgate shut and climb back into the driver's seat, brushing pumpkin dirt off my hands.

The drive to Judy's only takes about ten minutes, but my mind drifts to the upcoming fundraiser, and why on earth Judy needs this many pumpkins. There must be twenty or so rolling around back there.

The firehouse Halloween fundraiser is in a little over a week. It's an annual thing we do to raise money for coats for kids before winter hits. This year's fundraiser promises to be bigger than last year. I know there are a few new things in the works, but Chief's been tight-lipped about the details. Which, honestly, has the whole department on edge.

Last year, Chief's "big idea" was to have us dress up as superheroes and host a haunted obstacle course for the kids. Sounds innocent enough, right? Except my cape got caught in the bouncy house fan, and I spent ten minutes flailing like an idiot while parents took pictures. If Chief's planning something bigger this year, we're all screwed.

I pull into the long drive leading to the cabins, the same road that winds past the Davison family farm. The property's surrounded by the Colville National Forest. A small lake sits nestled in the center. The Miles farm borders one side of it, the cabins lining the other.

I ease the truck to a stop and back up close to Judy's place. I hop out and head up to her porch. I knock once on her door and let myself in; Judy never locks it. "Judy?" I call, stepping inside. No answer. I step back out and make a slow lap around the outside of her cabin, but she's nowhere to be seen.

I pull my phone from my pocket and call her. It rings twice before going to voicemail. "Alright," I mutter, scrolling to Miles' number.

"Hey."

"Yeah, hey. Is Judy with you? I tried calling her, but she's not picking up."

Miles chuckles. "She's probably over with the girls at cabin five. Why, what's up?"

"She asked me to pick up the pumpkins for the firehouse fundraiser."

"Give me a minute, I'll head over, help you unload them and then we can track her down."

"Alright. Thanks."

While I wait, I wander over to cabin two to check out the damage from the storm. Miles wasn't exaggerating, there's no saving it. The tree came straight down through the middle of the roof, like some giant decided to split the place in half. The side windows are shattered, the frame cracked and leaning, and inside, everything's soaked through and starting to smell like mildew.

A few minutes later, I glance over my shoulder to see Miles pulling in, his truck kicking up a little cloud of dust behind him.

He steps out of his truck, tugging the brim of his hat. Miles is thirty-three, two years older than me, and stands 6'2" to my 6'4". We both have walnut brown hair, but his eyes are dark brown while mine are golden. He gives me a nod, and together we start unloading the pumpkins, stacking them near Judy's cabin. When we're finished, we fall into step along the dirt path toward cabin five.

"Kinsley's been gone a while." His tone is casual as if he's commenting on the weather. "Which means we can expect one of two things when we get there."

I arch a brow. "Yeah? What's that?"

He smiles. "Either they're all sitting around in cabin five sad as hell, having some emotional heart-to-heart that'll make us wish we'd brought tissues..."

"Or?" I prompt, already bracing for it.

"Or they're drunk off their asses, probably loud enough to scare off half the wildlife, and acting like Raelynn's porch is a damn karaoke bar."

I snort. "Knowing Judy, it could be both."

Miles chuckles, shoving his hands in his pockets. "That's the scary part. You never really know with her."

As we step closer, he jerks his chin toward the soft glow coming from cabin five's windows. "But I'd put my money on sad tonight. Raelynn's in there with them."

"Raelynn?"

"Yeah. Kinsley's best friend. She's staying for a while, trying to sort her life out." Miles' voice drops just enough for me to catch the weight behind his words. "She split from her husband a few weeks back. Divorce isn't final yet, but it sounds like it was...bad."

"Bad how?"

He shakes his head. "The controlling kind of bad. Kinsley didn't give me details."

"That explains the emotional heart-to-heart option." I glance at the porch, half expecting to hear muffled sobs or laughter already. "What about the drunk karaoke bar version?"

Miles' smirk returns. "That's where Naya comes in. If there's a bottle of wine open, she's instigating something. Trust me."

I huff a quiet chuckle, imagining the scene inside. "Alright then. You're saying we might need tissues or earplugs."

"Exactly."

Miles knocks on the door, three solid raps that echo. For a moment, there's silence. Then, laughter. Loud, cackling laughter that sounds like it's coming from at least three different women. Something crashes inside, maybe furniture, maybe a body, it's hard to tell.

I glance at Miles. "That doesn't sound sad."

"Nope," he says flatly. "Sounds like whiskey not wine."

It feels like forever before anyone comes to the door. Just as I'm about to ask if we should knock again, the door flies open so fast it nearly smacks the wall behind it.

Kinsley stands there, her smile stretched wide across her face. Her hair's a little mussed, her cheeks flushed pink, and her eyes are glassy enough to tell me whiskey is definitely involved.

"Perfect timing!" Her voice is warm and a little too loud. The words slur together just enough to make me bite back a chuckle.

Miles folds his arms. "How much timing we talkin', baby? One glass or three?" He tries to suppress a smile but fails.

She waves a dismissive hand and leans against the doorframe. "Don't be dramatic. Two…ish."

Before he can answer, Judy barrels in like a heat-seeking missile. "My boys!" She wobbles slightly as she crosses the tiny living room. "Come give your favorite aunt some love."

I barely have time to brace before she's grabbing my face in both hands and pressing a wet kiss to my cheek. Then she moves on to Miles, who takes it like a pro.

"You've been drinking."

"Just a sip," Judy lies, her voice warm and unconvincing.

Naya snorts into her glass. "You missed the first act. But don't worry, there's still time for an encore."

Then she cuts her eyes toward the kitchen, where a short blonde woman is standing stiffly, one hand fiddling with her ponytail, the other clutching a half-empty glass.

"Go on, Rae," Naya encourages, her voice low and teasing. "Be polite. Introduce yourself."

The blonde, Raelynn, shoots her a look that's equal parts panic and defiance. But then she squares her shoulders and steps forward. She's wobbly but determined, her wavy hair bouncing behind her.

"Hi, I'm Raelynn." She sticks her hand out toward me. Her cheeks are pink, her brown eyes sharp in a way that catches me off guard.

I take her hand, surprised at the firmness of her grip. Her skin's warm, soft and smells faintly of vanilla and wine.

"Reed," I say, keeping my tone even though I catch myself staring.

Her eyes do a quick once-over, bold despite the slight wobble in her knees. A slow grin spreads across her face.

"Sooo...you're the fireman."

"That's me."

"Well, Hotshot." The words roll off her tongue like she's testing how they feel. "You gonna stand there all-night smoldering, or are you gonna come in and make yourself useful?"

For a second, I can't tell if it's the liquor or pure guts making her so bold. Either way, it's cute as hell.

Miles chuckles beside me. "Careful, Raelynn. His head's already big enough."

She shrugs, still holding my gaze like she's not the least bit sorry. Her lips curve into a sly little grin. "They say firemen are good with hoses, think you càn live up to the hype?"

For a second, my brain short-circuits.

Miles coughs loudly behind me, and Naya lets out a scandalized howl.

"Raelynn Nicole Newberry!" Kinsley gasps, half-horrified and half-amused.

But Raelynn doesn't backpedal, even when Kinsley uses her full name. She just grins wider, eyes sparkling with mischief. "What? I'm curious."

I arch a brow, the corner of my mouth tugging up. "Careful, Raelynn Nicole Newberry. You might start a fire you can't put out."

Her eyes go wide for a split second before she bites her bottom lip and giggles, swaying slightly on her feet.

"Reed!" Kinsley shrieks, half-laughing, half-scolding.

Miles groans beside me. "God help us all."

But Raelynn doesn't seem the least bit rattled. "I like him!" She points at me with her glass.

I chuckle, shaking my head as she spins and stumbles back toward the kitchen, Naya hot on her heels and Kinsley following behind. I hear Raelynn whisper loudly, "What? He's hot."

As soon as the women disappear, the cabin goes blissfully quiet except for the faint clinking of glasses.

"Jesus," I mutter, dragging a hand over my jaw.

Miles smirks at me. "Don't say it."

"I wasn't gonna say anything."

"Uh-huh."

But I can't help it, the thought creeps in anyway. She's cute. Way cuter than I expected. There's something about that messy ponytail, the flush in her cheeks, and the spark in her eyes that I can't stop replaying. And the mouth on her…God, if she weren't drunk, I'd have half a mind to see what else I could get it to do. But she's drunk. She's still getting over her ex, the last thing she needs is me adding to the mess.

When the shenanigans start up again in the kitchen, Miles blows out a sigh. "We need a plan before this turns into an all-night babysitting gig."

"Agreed."

"You take Judy, I'll deal with Kinsley and Naya. If I can pry the bottle from Naya's death grip, that is."

"Fair."

Miles quietly peeks into the kitchen, shooting me a look that says 'be ready'. It takes a few minutes, but eventually Miles corrals Kinsley and Naya out the door, one arm around each as they giggle their way out.

"Good luck."

"Pray for me," he mutters back.

I glance back inside to find Judy leaning against the couch arm, her eyes already drooping. "Alright, Aunt Judy." I tug the throw blanket off the back of the couch and drape it over her shoulders. "Let's get you back to your cabin."

"Such a good boy." She pats my chest before she rests her head against my arm as I ease her toward the door. I stop when I spot Raelynn curled up on the couch, one leg tucked under her.

She's out cold, soft snores escaping her lips. Her glass abandoned on the coffee table.

Shaking my head, I grab another blanket and tuck it around her. Her ponytail has half fallen out, little waves framing her face. Even asleep, she's adorable. She's gonna be mortified when she remembers all this tomorrow. And yeah, I can't wait to see her again, if only to tease her about every second of it. She doesn't strike me as the type who normally throws out bold, flirty one-liners to strangers. Not sober, anyway.

"Reed, you coming, honey?"

"Yeah," I say softly, glancing at Raelynn one last time before stepping away.

Judy hooks her arm through mine, leaning into my side as we step out the door. "You're such a good boy."

That's twice she's called me a good boy.

I chuckle as we head down the path. "Don't spread that around, I've got a reputation to protect."

3

Key Lime Redemption

Raelynn

My mouth tastes like death. No, worse than death. Like something crawled in there and threw a party before dying a slow, horrible death on my tongue. I groan, rolling onto my back as my head protests with a dull throb. The inside of my mouth is desert-level dry, and my tongue feels glued to the roof like it's been superglued there overnight. *What the hell happened last night?*

Bits and pieces come back in slow, painful flashes. Kinsley and Naya showing up with two bottles of wine and two ill-advised bottles of whiskey. Judy barging in halfway through, declaring she was "still young enough to twerk" and proving, very definitively, that she was not. So much laughter my ribs still ache. And then Miles showing up to break up the fun like some overgrown hall monitor.

I groan again and press the heels of my hands into my eyes, trying to force the memories to cooperate. The faint smell of cedar and pumpkin drifts in from somewhere, along with the sound of birds outside. Finally, I manage to peel myself off the couch. My ponytail is hanging by a thread. My sweater is half twisted around my body like I fought it in my sleep and lost.

I shuffle to the kitchen in search of water and redemption. There's a folded piece of paper propped on the counter in Kinsley's neat, looping handwriting.

To-Do List:

1. Shower. I'm sure you smell bad.
2. Drink some water.
3. Grab your stuff and head over for breakfast.
4. You owe Hotshot an apology.

I blink. Hotshot? Who the hell's Hotshot? And then, like a bad movie montage, the memory slams into me.

"They say firemen are good with hoses, think you can live up to the hype?" My own voice. Bold. Tipsy. Flirty.

The heat rushes into my face so fast it's like I'm standing in front of an open oven. Oh God. Hotshot. The fireman. Reed. I flirted with him. No, worse than that, I teased him about hoses in front of his brother and Judy and Kinsley and Naya. And he, oh God, he smirked at me like he was actually amused.

I drop my forehead to the counter with a groan. "Kill me now."

For a split second, I consider skipping breakfast. Pretending I overslept or came down with some sudden, mysterious illness. But then my stomach growls loudly enough to echo in the cabin. Dammit. Kinsley is a fantastic cook. I can practically smell the bacon and fresh coffee already. I'm too hungry to stage a full retreat. Which leaves me with one option: the walk of shame.

I grab my bag, pull my hair into a bun and splash some water on my face. It doesn't help. I still look like someone who lost a fight with a bottle of whiskey. I grab my sweater off the hook and step out the door.

The trail crunches under my shoes as I make my way around the lake, and every step closer to the farmhouse feels like a step closer to my own public execution. Reed's probably sitting at the kitchen table right now, coffee mug in hand, wearing that perfect smile and waiting to roast me alive. I hope not, but if he does, I probably deserve it. Who knows what else I did to make a fool of myself. *Hotshot.* God, even the nickname makes me want to crawl under the nearest log and stay there until winter.

The thing is, I remember him. Way more clearly than I should, considering how much whiskey was involved. He's tall. Definitely over six feet, six-four, maybe, because I remember having to tilt my chin up to meet his eyes. And those eyes…light brown, almost gold. Warm in a way that felt a little dangerous. His hair was cropped short in a clean crew cut. His shoulders, God, those shoulders. The sweatshirt he was wearing last night fit snug across the broad span of them, sleeves pushed up just enough to show strong forearms and tattooed tan skin. He looked solid, like someone who could carry you out of a burning building without breaking a sweat. Not that I need to be carried anywhere. Or think about him carrying me. Or think about him at all.

If I had an ounce of dignity left, I'd turn around right now. I'd crawl back into bed, sleep off the hangover, and let Kinsley bring me a plate of eggs later with a side of "you embarrassed yourself in front of a literal firefighter" pep talk.

By the time the farmhouse comes into view, my stomach is growling like a wild animal, and I'm already rehearsing excuses in my head in case Hotshot is lurking inside. Before I can even set foot on the porch, the front door swings open and Kinsley steps out, squinting against the morning light.

"Did you get my note?" she asks, one brow arched, eyes scanning me from head to toe.

"Yes, I got your note. And no, I didn't shower. I want coffee first. So, if I smell bad, blame yourself. You're the one who provided the whiskey. Live with it."

Kinsley's lips twitch, and then she laughs, the sound warm and just a little too loud for my throbbing head. "Fair enough." She holds the door open for me. I take a deep breath and step inside, whispering a silent prayer: "Fingers crossed he's not here."

The house smells incredible, coffee, bacon, something sweet and cinnamon-laced. My stomach growls again, louder this time. Then I see Kinsley properly in the kitchen light. "God, you look awful."

Her auburn hair is sticking out in every possible direction, and her sweatshirt is inside out. There's a faint smudge of mascara under one eye, like she tried to wash her face and gave up halfway through.

"Thanks," she deadpans, running a hand through her tangled hair. "You're no beauty queen either."

I open my mouth to reply, but then…"Oh no."

Naya stumbles into the kitchen from the hallway, still wearing the oversized Cranberry Ridge T-shirt she must've borrowed from Miles. Her ponytail is barely hanging on, and her eyeliner is smudged so badly she looks like a raccoon who lost a bar fight.

She freezes when she sees me. "Why is it so bright in here?" She groans, shielding her face with one hand.

"I look worse than you do."

She points at me with her other hand. "You're lying. No one looks worse than I do right now. I can feel it."

Before I can argue, a low chuckle comes from across the room. Miles is standing at the stove, one hand wrapped around a coffee mug, the other flipping something in a skillet. His dark hair is still a little damp from a shower, his plaid shirt rolled up at the sleeves. And of course, he's smiling.

Not just smiling, grinning. At us. At the three disasters standing in his kitchen. One holding her head (Naya). One shielding her eyes (Kinsley). And one…you guessed it…with shame written all over her face (me).

"Morning, ladies." He chuckles shaking his head.

I want the floor to open up and swallow me whole.

The sound of the front door opening makes all three of us flinch. Judy breezes in like last night never happened, looking fresh as a daisy in her crisp white blouse and pressed jeans. Her hair is perfectly curled, not a strand out of place, and her lipstick is a flawless shade of berry pink. Even her pearl earrings catch the light like they've been polished.

"Good morning," she sings, setting her oversized leather purse on the counter.

All three of us stare at her like she just descended from the heavens.

"You've got to be kidding me," Kinsley mutters, rubbing her temple.

Even Miles looks a little thrown, his brow raised as he flips bacon in the skillet.

Naya squints. "How? How are you not dead? Are you…are you a good witch or a bad witch?"

Judy giggles, the sound light and breezy. "Oh, sweetheart, I'm the best kind of witch, the one who knows a recipe that'll fix that little hangover of yours."

Before any of us can protest, she's already moving. She sidesteps Miles, who's still blinking in surprise, and grabs three empty glasses from the cabinet. Then, to our collective horror, she reaches into her massive purse and pulls out a glass bottle filled with a swamp-green liquid so thick it clings to the sides like motor oil.

"My stomach just rolled," I whisper.

Naya is still squinting. "Is that green?" Naya and Kinsley are already shaking their heads in sync, their faces pale.

"Oh, no. Nope. Absolutely not," Kinsley says firmly.

Judy ignores her, unscrewing the cap and pouring the sludge into each glass with the care of someone handling a vintage wine. The smell that wafts up isn't as bad as I expected, herbal, citrusy even, but it's still green. Thick, suspiciously green.

"Girls, trust me." Judy slides a glass toward each of us. "It doesn't just cure hangovers. It's like hitting the reset button on your entire body. You'll thank me."

"Or curse you." I look at the glass like it might bite me.

"Bottoms up," Judy chirps.

The three of us exchange wary glances. This feels like the kind of moment where we should be holding hands, making a blood pact and hoping we survive.

"Together?" Naya asks.

"Together."

We all shrug, take a deep breath and throw the drinks back.

"Oh my God!" Naya's eyes go wide. "That's, actually good?"

"Wait, what?" Kinsley blinks in surprise. "It tastes like a key lime pie smoothie."

My eyes widen as the flavor hits me, too. Sweet and tart, creamy but bright, with just the tiniest hint of ginger at the end. I expected swamp water, but this is delicious.

Judy smiles knowingly, screwing the cap back on her bottle. "Told you. You're welcome. Give it fifteen minutes."

We're all sitting around the table now, plates piled high with eggs, crispy bacon and thick slices of Judy's cinnamon swirl bread. The green hangover cure really was magic. I can feel life trickling back into my limbs, the pounding in my head fading with each bite of food.

Miles leans back in his chair, mug in hand, watching us with that faintly amused smirk. "So, what's on the agenda for today?"

"I've got to stop by the bakery. My mom's filling in for me, and I need to drop off the new menu cards for her." Naya's voice is still scratchy but improving.

Kinsley perks up, poking at a slice of cantaloupe on her plate. "That works out perfectly. Rae, why don't we head into town after? There are a couple of empty buildings I've been meaning to check out. One might be perfect for your salon, and there's another that caught my eye for my law office."

My fork pauses midair. "Really?"

She nods. "Really. You've been holed up here long enough. Let's get you back into the world."

My heart gives an unexpected little kick of excitement. "I can't wait to get back to work." I love my job, and the chance to start over? To build something that's mine from the ground up this time? That's kind of thrilling.

Miles smiles, swirling his coffee. "Two powerhouse women opening businesses in the same small town? Sounds like Cranberry Ridge won't know what hit it."

"It's perfect." I ignore the little flutter in my stomach at his teasing tone. "We'll keep each other accountable. She'll make sure I don't work myself into the ground, and I'll drag her out for wine when she forgets life exists outside a courtroom."

Miles offers to clean up so we can get ready, waving us off with his coffee mug like we're wayward teenagers. "Go on, town won't wait forever."

Back at the cabin, I pause for a moment on the porch, breathing in the crisp morning air. The lake is still, a faint wisp of fog curling off its surface. Pine needles crunch under my boots as I step inside, feeling a little lighter than I did earlier. I'm grateful for a few things: Judy's magical hangover elixir, Reed not being at breakfast and the chance to finally start really living again.

The hot water of the shower feels like heaven, washing away last night and replacing it with something like clarity. I pull on a soft knit sweater in a warm oatmeal shade and my favorite dark jeans, tucking them into a pair of brown knee-high boots. A quick curl through my hair leaves it in loose waves, parted down the middle.

Gold hoops catch the light as I fasten them in place, and I finish with just enough mascara and eyeliner to feel polished but not overdone.

When I step outside, the chilly air bites at my cheeks, but it's invigorating instead of harsh. Kinsley is already waiting in the driveway, her sleek new SUV purring softly. She told me earlier she couldn't keep the rental from her vacation any longer, and Miles' truck was, in her words, "basically a monster truck."

I open the door and climb in, the car warm and smelling faintly of leather. Kinsley looks gorgeous, as usual. Her auburn hair is sleek and straight, makeup done in the same simple, understated way as mine. She's wearing a black leather jacket over a fitted red top, faded jeans that mold perfectly to her legs.

"You clean up nice."

I chuckle softly. "Coming from you, that means something. You look annoyingly perfect right now."

She smiles, adjusting her sunglasses. "You ready?"

I take a deep breath and glance out at the winding road ahead. A little thrill of excitement runs through me. "Yes."

We spend several hours bouncing between the realtor's office and the bank, juggling conversations with loan officers and signing what feels like an endless stack of paperwork. The building I picked is small, but it's got good bones and potential. It sits right next to the yoga studio and only a block away from Naya's bakery, The Sweet Spot, which feels like fate. The exterior needs a facelift, peeling paint, cracked trim, but the price is good, and I can already picture the fresh white siding, big windows and my salon's name in sleek lettering over the door. Kinsley found her office space on the edge of town, closer to Cranberry Ridge Grocery. Hers doesn't need much beyond fresh paint and new flooring, but I can tell she's already envisioning it filled with light and lined with tidy shelves of case files. By the time we've wrapped up, the sun is dipping lower in the sky, and our shoulders ache from the weight of decision-making. We both made offers. Now…we wait.

4

Chief's Grand Plan

Reed

I should've stopped by Miles' place this morning. Not for the food, but for the entertainment. The three of them must've been hurting after last night: Headaches, regret, the whole nine yards. And Raelynn, I'd give anything to see her face when it hit her. The memory of what she said and that flush creeping up her neck. Bet she couldn't look me in the eye if she tried. Yeah, I missed my chance. I could've sat there with my coffee, watched her try to act normal, and asked if she wanted some ibuprofen just to see if she'd glare at me. It would have been a great start to my day.

I smile as I steer the truck toward the firehouse. The early morning sun glints off the hood, and the cool air streaming through the cracked window smells faintly of pine.

The Cranberry Ridge Firehouse comes into view up ahead, all brick and white trim, three wide garage bays lined neatly in a row. The red doors gleam in the sun, freshly washed. Chief Sanford's been on a kick about appearances lately.

I ease the truck into the lot and park in my usual spot near the side entrance. The moment I step inside, the familiar mix of scents hits me, faint smoke clinging to turnout gear, motor oil from the trucks and stale coffee from the pot that's probably been burning since last night's shift. It's a grounding smell, one that says home as much as work.

The three wide bays stretch out to my left, sunlight streaming through the high windows and glinting off polished chrome. The engines sit lined up in perfect formation, every hose coiled tight, every tool in its place. Even the floors are spotless.

In the corner of the common room, I spot Tommy slumped in a chair long thin legs stretched out, his curly blonde hair sticking up like he lost a fight with his pillow. Leo and Jose are perched nearby, sipping coffee and trying to look awake.

Jose's short but solidly built. His black hair falls in soft waves. Next to him, Leo looks every bit the seasoned veteran. He's taller, broad-shouldered, with a frame that's still strong despite the years on him. His dark brown hair is shot with just enough gray to make him look distinguished.

I laugh and call out, "Tommy, you look like your wife made you sleep on the couch again. What'd you do this time? Don't tell me she caught you with your hand down your pants like a teenager."

The guys erupt in laughter, Tommy flipping me the bird without lifting his head from where it's cradled in his palm.

"Better a hand than nothing at all, Davison," Leo fires back with a chuckle. "At least Tommy's got a warm body in his house. You? Your right hand must be filing for workers' comp by now."

The table howls, and I shake my head, grinning. "Careful, old man. You're talking big for somebody whose blood pressure spikes if he even thinks about standing up too fast."

Jose nearly chokes on his coffee. "Leo? Please. The only thing he's popping these days is Tums. Ain't no way he's getting it up without a team of paramedics standing by."

"Damn straight." Tommy lifts his head just enough to join in. "And speaking of paramedics, Leo, how's your girl doing? Or does she need me to stop by later and show her what a real man looks like?"

The room goes silent for half a beat before everyone bursts out laughing, even Leo, who tosses a crumpled napkin at Tommy's head.

"Yeah, yeah. Keep talking Tommy," Leo laughs. "Your mom didn't seem to mind when I had her screaming my name last night."

The room explodes and I can't stop the laugh that punches out of me.

"Jesus Christ," I manage between breaths. "That's low, even for you."

Tommy's wheezing now. "Low but effective. He just wrecked your whole family tree, bro."

Before Leo can bask in his victory, the sound of boots on concrete cuts through the laughter.

"Sounds like I walked in on story time." Chief Sanford strolls in with his coffee cup in hand. His lips twitch like he's trying not to smile. "Whatever it was, I'm not sure I want to know."

The guys straighten instinctively, but the tension doesn't last long.

"Morning, Chief."

"Morning," Sanford replies. He gives the group a once-over, eyes lingering on Tommy's bedhead. "You all done solving the world's problems over here, or should I give you another five minutes to roast each other?"

Jose snorts. "We're good, Chief."

"Good." Sanford sets his cup on the counter and claps his hands together. "Then let's roll into checks before the coffee wears off. Gear first, then trucks. I'll take the bay floor. Try not to make me regret trusting you with the important stuff."

We all start to stand, chairs scraping as we move to get to work, but Chief Sanford raises a hand.

"Hold up. Quick announcement. This afternoon, the rest of the crew will be reporting in for a meeting. I want everyone there. We're going over this year's fundraiser and an idea I've come up with."

"What kind of idea, Chief?"

He smirks. "You'll find out at three. Try not to lose sleep over it, Davison."

A few of the guy's chuckle, and Sanford waves us off. "Alright, get to work before I think of something worse to make you do."

"Yes, Chief," we say, scattering toward the bays.

The guys scatter to their stations, and the usual rhythm takes over, gear checks, radio tests and making sure the rigs are stocked and spotless.

By mid-morning, the quiet doesn't last.

First call: Two-car accident on the highway. Minor injuries but enough chaos to keep us busy for an hour.

Second call: Another fender bender at the edge of town. This time, no injuries, just two angry drivers screaming at each other while we directed traffic.

Then came the weird ones. A senior citizen busted out of the assisted living center and was found cruising down Main Street on a motorized scooter, singing at the top of his lungs. Took three officers and half a box of donuts to convince him to pull over. And just when we thought we'd seen it all, dispatch came through with: "Single-vehicle incident. Car...up a tree."

Jose had stared at the radio like it was broken. "Up a tree? Did she say up a tree?"

But sure enough, some poor kid had tried to take a corner too fast and launched his compact sedan into a pine. Took a tow truck and a chainsaw to get it down.

By the time we rolled back to the station, it was nearly three. Chief Sanford was already waiting in the meeting room, flipping through a folder with his glasses perched low on his nose. The rest of the crew is there, too, spread out around the table, their conversations quieting as we filed in.

Chief Sanford closes the folder and stands, taking off his glasses. "Alright, listen up. We're only adding two new things to the fundraiser this year." That earns a few nods and murmurs around the table. He pauses just long enough to get their attention. "The first is a donation box for a 'Kiss the Fireman' booth."

A couple of the younger guys let out loud whoops, slapping the table like it's the best idea they've ever heard. A few groaned in unison, and more than one is already shaking their heads slowly, muttering about how their wives would murder them if they even thought about it.

"Relax," Sanford says. "It's volunteer-only. I'm not about to make anyone do it, so if you don't want to sign up, you're off the hook. Nobody's sleeping on the couch over this thing."

That earns a round of laughter, though Tommy mutters under his breath, "Too late for me either way."

"Do we have four volunteers?" Sanford scans the room.

Six hands shoot up immediately, the younger guys grinning like they'd just been handed free beer. Mine wasn't one of them.

Don't get me wrong, I like kissing women. Hell, I've been accused of liking it a little too much. But I choose the one. Always. I might have a reputation in this town, but I do have standards. Random lips for the price of a donation? Not my thing.

"Aw, come on, Davison. What's the matter? Afraid your lips will fall off if they touch someone who isn't hot enough?" Jose smirks across the table.

The table explodes, a few guys smacking the wood like it's the best line of the day.

I shake my head, fighting a grin. "Nah. I just don't like standing in line and handing out samples. You know me, I only cook for one."

That earns a round of "oohs" and a couple whistles.

"More like he's scared some poor girl will fall in love and never leave him alone." Tommy laughs.

"Exactly." I lean back in my chair. "Do I look like I've got time for another restraining order?"

That gets the guys laughing even harder until Sanford clears his throat, still fighting a smile.

"Alright, alright, enough. Let's save the flirting for the booth, gentlemen."

He gives the room a once-over, then his eyes land squarely on me.

"Davison, I've got a feeling this next one is perfect for you."

The guys immediately start snickering, a few muttering my name like they already know trouble is coming.

I raise a brow. "Perfect for me? That's never a good sign, Chief."

Sanford smirks and continues, "We're adding a sealed bid auction this year. Winner gets to have a date with a fireman. Only one winner, and the department's footing the bill."

A ripple of noise shoots around the table, but I just lean back in my chair, grinning.

"Yes," I say without hesitation. "What could possibly go wrong?"

That gets a few howls and some raised eyebrows.

"Called it," Sanford says, pointing at me with his coffee cup. "I knew you'd be game for this one."

"Of course he is. It's basically a date. That's Reed's natural habitat." Jose slaps Leo on the back, laughing.

"Better than kissing booth roulette." That earns a round of chuckles and a few groans from the married guys.

"That settles it then." Sanford claps his hands together. "Reed will be the prize for the sealed auction."

The room roars in laughter and whistles, a few guys calling out things like, "Better bring your A-game, Davison!" and "Hope she likes cocky firemen!"

"And as for the kissing booth," Sanford goes on over the noise, "a sign-up sheet will be hanging on the bulletin board by the end of the day. Volunteer only, gentlemen. I'll assign the rest of the kid-friendly stuff before the event. For now, you're free to get back to work. Meeting adjourned."

Chairs scrape as the guys stand, still snickering and throwing jabs my way as we file out.

As I'm about to follow the guys out, Sanford calls my name. "Davison. Office."

The room bursts into a chorus of "Ooooh!" and "Ahhh!" like we're back in high school and I just got sent to the principal's office.

I chuckle, shaking my head. "Settle down, children."

Still smirking, I follow Sanford into his office. He steps behind his desk and lowers himself into the chair, motioning for me to shut the door.

I do, leaning against the frame. "So, what's my sentence, Chief? Dish duty for a month?"

Sanford pins me with a look that's equal parts amusement and warning. "Two things, Reed."

I raise a brow. "Alright."

He holds up a finger. "One, do not sleep with the winner. Do you hear me? Under no circumstances do we need some crazy, love-struck woman banging on the bay doors at two in the morning because you broke her heart."

I can't help but grin. "You wound me, Chief. What makes you think I'd let it get that far?"

Sanford's expression doesn't budge. "Because I know you, Davison. You've got a history of making bad ideas look fun."

I smirk. "Okay, Chief. No sleeping with the winner. Got it. What's the second thing?"

Sanford leans back in his chair, folding his arms. "Tell your Aunt Judy thanks for the great ideas. This should bring in a lot of money for the kids this year."

Of course. Judy.

"Sure thing, I'll let her know."

Figures she'd have her hands in this. Somehow, Judy's managed to worm her way into every corner of this town, baking pies for charity, organizing events and now influencing the fire department's fundraiser. Hell, I wouldn't be surprised if she'd pitched the kissing booth idea with a straight face and convinced Sanford it was wholesome. I shake my head, letting it go. That's Judy for you.

By the time I step out of the Chief's office, my shift's over. The guys are already packing up and heading out, and the place has that quiet hum it gets when the day slows down.

As I pass the bulletin board, I can't help but laugh. The sign-up sheet for the kissing booth is already covered in names, more than ten guys scribbled down.

"Idiots," I mutter, still grinning as I push out the door.

Sliding into my truck, I pull out my phone and call in a large, extra cheese, pepperoni and jalapeños pizza.

"Pickup in twenty? Perfect."

The drive home is quick, and I swing by the pizza place on the way, the smell filling the cab so thick my stomach growls. By the time I'm kicking off my boots at home, I'm ready to eat half the box in one sitting.

I let Fifi out into the yard, grab a slice and flop down on the couch. She comes bounding back in a few minutes later and curls up against me, her little body warm and soft.

As I lean back, my thoughts drift to Miles. Poor bastard. I can only imagine what he's enduring if the girls are still at his place. Hangovers, sass and whatever chaos Judy's stirring up. Or maybe they're all fine, and I'm the one sitting here curious like an idiot.

I grab my phone off the coffee table, swipe to Miles' number and hit call. Let's see how bad it really is.

Miles answers on the second ring, his voice calm. "Hey."

I squint at the ceiling, already suspicious. "Hey. So... how's it going over there? The girls still alive, or did you have to call in reinforcements?"

"They're fine."

"Fine?" I sit up a little. "You're telling me four women who were absolutely trashed last night aren't currently curled up on your couch begging for death?"

"Nope."

I blink. "No hangovers? No regret?"

Miles huffs a quiet laugh. "Nope. Judy made them her 'magic potion' this morning."

I pause. "Her what?"

"Yeah. Some ginger-lime thing she swears cures hangovers. I didn't believe it either."

"And?"

"And..." Miles lets out a slow breath. "It worked. They're walking around like nothing happened."

I lean back, staring at the ceiling. "You're kidding me."

"Wish I was."

"Damn." I shake my head. "Next time I go out, I'm calling our aunt."

"Yeah," Miles says dryly. "So am I."

We're both quiet for a second, thinking about why in hell Judy never gave us this "magic potion."

"Alright, I'll let you get back to whatever you're doing."

"I'll see you tomorrow, Reed."

"See ya tomorrow."

I end the call and toss my phone onto the cushion next to me. Fifi shifts in her sleep, and I scratch behind her ears, still shaking my head.

"Magic potion," I mutter. "Figures."

Tomorrow, we're taking down cabin two. Honestly? It could be fun. And Judy's promised us lunch, which means it's worth showing up for.

5

Freedom and Fire Hoses

Raelynn

The sharp ding of a text message pulls me out of sleep. I groan and roll over, fumbling for my phone on the nightstand. The screen glows too bright against the dim room, and when my eyes focus, my stomach drops.

Jacob: I can't wait until you get this out of your system. I miss my wife. Call me.

I stare at the words for a long moment, my thumb hovering over the reply box. But I don't respond. I set the phone face down and push myself out of bed. The sheets are warm where I've been curled, but I make the bed anyway, tucking the corners tight like I'm trying to straighten out more than just the blankets. The silence in the room feels heavy, but I shove it aside and head for the shower. The hot water pelts my shoulders as I stand there, letting it soak into my skin, my hair, my bones. My mind keeps circling the same question over: *How can he still think I'd come back?*

After everything, years of him controlling every detail of my life, from what I wore, to who I spoke to, he still believes I'll slip right back into that role. Like leaving was a phase I just need to "get out of my system."

He doesn't miss me. He misses the version of me he molded, the one who was too tired, too small, too scared to fight back. But that's not me anymore.

When I step out of the shower, I wrap a towel around myself and head for the kitchen. The house is quiet, filled only with the soft creak of the floorboards beneath my feet.

I move on autopilot, pulling eggs from the fridge, sliding bread into the toaster, slicing strawberries and cantaloupe. Before I know it, a plate is sitting on the counter: eggs, toast, fruit. Jacob's favorite. I freeze, staring at it. *What the hell am I doing?*

The sharp scrape of the plate against the counter breaks the spell. I carry it to the trash and dump the whole thing in with a satisfying clatter. The smell of toast and fried eggs clings to the air, but I don't care. He doesn't get to live here anymore, not in my head, not in my habits.

Back in the bedroom, I yank the neatly tucked sheets loose and mess up the bed I'd made just minutes ago. The smooth perfection of it had felt too much like the old me, tight, suffocating, controlled.

Standing in front of the mirror, I press my palms flat against the dresser and stare at my reflection. My hair is damp and curling around my face. My eyes are a little tired, but alive in a way they weren't before.

"You're not with him anymore," I whisper to the woman staring back at me. "You're free. The life you want? It's yours now. Sketch again. Laugh again. Live on the wild side for once. Be reckless. Be happy." I take a deep breath and let it out slowly, the weight on my chest lifting just enough for my shoulders to ease. "Be free." The words hang in the air like a promise. I step back from the mirror, the words "be free" still echoing in my head like a challenge.

In the kitchen, I grab a bowl and pour cereal, the kind with little marshmallows. It feels almost rebellious to eat something Jacob would have rolled his eyes at. "Sugar for breakfast?" he'd say, like I was a child. *Good. Let it be childish.*

I sink onto the couch, pulling my knees up as I crunch through spoonfuls of technicolor sweetness. It tastes like Saturday mornings and cartoons, like me, before everything got so heavy. By the time the bowl's empty, my fingers are already itching. I need paper. Charcoal. Something to drag across a page and bring to life.

Jacob's voice creeps into my head, "*Sketching is a waste of time, Raelynn. You're not going to sell it, so what's the point?*"

I shake it off. *The point is, it makes me happy, you controlling ass.*

I put on a pair of dark jeans and a soft forest green sweater, slipping my feet into leather ankle boots. My hair falls in loose waves around my face, and a swipe of mascara makes my brown eyes look almost bright again.

When I catch my reflection, I almost don't recognize her. Not because she's polished, but because she's smiling.

I'm halfway down the path when Judy's door creaks open across the way.

"Well, hello, Raelynn," she calls, stepping out in a crisp flannel shirt and dark jeans. Her gray hair is perfectly curled, and there's a twinkle in her eye like she's been waiting for me to appear all morning.

"You're up early."

"I am." I smile faintly. "I thought I'd head into town. Stop by Crafty Cottage and maybe The Second Chapter bookstore."

Judy lights up, clasping her hands together. "That sounds wonderful! Crafty Cottage is my favorite place. Watch out, you'll lose hours in there."

"That's the plan."

"Good girl." She gestures toward the porch where a massive pile of pumpkins sits stacked in a haphazard pyramid. "When you get back, would you like to help me carve these pumpkins? I'm trying to get ahead for the firehouse fundraiser."

My lips twitch into a smile. "I'd love to. I haven't carved a pumpkin since I was a kid."

Judy beams. "Perfect. How does eleven sound?"

"I'll be here."

"Wonderful. Have fun in town, sweetheart."

"Thanks, Judy."

As I climb into the car and start the engine, excitement bubbles through me, not nervous excitement, not fear, but the kind that feels light, almost fizzy.

I'm going to buy a sketchbook. I'm going to draw again. And for the first time in years, I don't care if it's a "waste of time."

The drive into town feels… good. The radio's cranked up, windows cracked just enough to let in the crisp fall air. Somewhere nearby, someone's burning leaves, and the earthy, smoky sweetness drifts into the car. God, I love that smell.

Crafty Cottage sits on the corner of the block, painted soft white with big windows showcasing jars of paintbrushes, stacks of sketchbooks, and colorful yarn. A chalkboard by the door reads:

"Pumpkin Painting Kits, 15% Off!"

Next door, a small art studio with tinted windows, Studio Indigo, catches my eye. I think about going in but shake my head. Not today.

From here, I can see the building I hope will be my salon, Naya's bakery down the street, and just past that, the Main Street Café with its white bistro tables stacked neatly outside and a For Sale sign in the window. The Second Chapter, a used bookstore, sits next to it, bright and impossible to miss with its blue, red and yellow siding.

I push open the door to Crafty Cottage, and the soft tinkle of a bell greets me. The air smells like cinnamon and wood shavings. Inside, shelves of sketchbooks line one wall, canisters of charcoal and pencils neatly arranged on tables. Paints spill across a rainbow-hued display.

Jacob's words creep into my mind… *'Sketching is a waste of time.'*

I take my time strolling the aisles, letting my eyes skim over rows of sketchbooks and neatly stacked pencils. A small, compact sketchbook catches my eye, perfect for slipping into my purse for quick ideas on the go. Further down, I spot a larger leather-bound one. It's heavier, the kind of book that feels like it should hold something important. I add it to my basket without overthinking. At the charcoal display, I choose a pack of soft sticks for shading and another one for compressed sharp lines. Nearby, I grab special wipes for cleaning smudges off my fingers, a kneaded eraser, a blending stump and a sharpener designed for delicate tools.

By the time I reach the register, my basket feels like a quiet rebellion, every item a small step back to myself. I walk out the door with what feels like a mix between pride and contentment.

I step inside The Second Chapter and am greeted with the familiar scent of old pages. The shelves are crammed full, books stacked in every direction like a cozy labyrinth. Though a spicy romance would be my usual choice, I head straight for a wooden sign that reads "Art & Creativity."

A slim hardcover catches my eye, 'Advanced Drawing Ideas.' It's filled with prompts and techniques to push my skills further. Perfect. At the counter, a woman in leopard-print bellbottoms and a matching headscarf beams at me as she rings it up.

"Great pick, sweetheart. That one's magic."

"Thanks." I smile and tuck the book into my bag before heading back out into the warm morning air.

I tug at my sweater as I walk, already feeling the heat creeping in. *It's unusually warm for this time of year. I should've worn a T-shirt.* But this is Washington, tomorrow it'll probably snow.

The Main Street Café is just a few doors down, and the aroma of espresso calls to me. I pop in, order a quick iced latte and wrap my fingers around the cool cup as I step back out.

The Sweet Spot sits just across the street, its big windows glowing with warmth and the smell of sugar drifting out every time the door swings open. I pull the door open, and the little bell above it jingles cheerfully.

"Raelynn!" Naya's voice rings out from behind the counter, bright and warm as the scent of cinnamon and fresh bread greets me.

"Hey," I smile and walk up to the counter.

"Look at you, out and about early."

"I figured I'd make a morning of it." I glance toward the window. "Picked up a few things in town… sketchbooks, charcoal. It feels good to get back into it."

Naya's face lights up. "That's amazing! And Kinsley told me about your offer on the building down the street. You're really going for it."

"It's a little terrifying," I admit, "but exciting, too."

Naya leans on the counter. "Sounds like you're finally letting yourself breathe."

"Yeah…it feels strange, but in a good way. Like I'm remembering who I was before everything got so heavy."

"That's the best part, you get to choose what comes next."

I glance down at the bakery display case. "Speaking of next…Judy asked me to help carve pumpkins later. I haven't done that since I was a kid."

"She invited me, too. And I think Kinsley's coming."

"Then I'll bring the sweets."

Naya chuckles as she moves behind the counter. "Dangerous offer in a bakery."

"Surprise me with a variety."

She pulls out a box. "You got it, I'll make it good."

We say good-bye and I practically skip to my car. I take my time driving back enjoying the scenery. Oranges, yellows and reds make the road feel like I'm driving in a kaleidoscope. Even though the leaves are dying, I couldn't feel more alive.

I drop my bags on the kitchen island and head straight for the bedroom. I'm looking forward to time with my friends and the nostalgia of carving pumpkins. Digging through my drawer, I pull out a gray fitted V-neck T-shirt that reads: "Flirt First, Ask Questions Later." I shrug as I pull it on. Normally, I only wear this as pajamas, never in public. But today? I don't care. It's just the girls.

Outside, tables are lined with newspaper, each one set with a large bowl for pumpkin guts and clusters of carving tools spread out like little surgical kits. A few candles flicker in mason jars, their soft glow dancing against the fall air.

Naya waves at me from the far end of the table setup, a pumpkin nearly as big as her torso sitting in front of her. "There she is! We were about to send a search party."

Kinsley grins, wiping her hands on a dish towel. "About time. We saved you the best pumpkin."

"Best or biggest?" I ask, laughing as I step closer.

"Both," Naya teases. "Consider it a challenge."

Meanwhile, Judy is flitting between tables like a woman on a mission, arranging bowls and passing out extra spoons. There's a little pep in her step, and her smile is brighter than usual, like she's thriving on the sight of us all gathered here, laughing and ready to make a mess.

We all get to work on our first pumpkins, carving away as the speaker plays a soft country playlist in the background. Two minutes in, the sound of tires crunching on gravel pulls my attention up. Two trucks with empty trailers rumble down the drive.

"What's going on?" I ask, wiping pumpkin juice from my fingers.

"Oh, I must have forgotten to mention." Judy smiles brightly. "The boys are tearing down cabin two today."

Before I can even process that, the deep rumble of a motorcycle fills the air. I freeze. A tall, broad-shouldered man in a fitted black T-shirt pulls in behind the trucks, tattoos twisting down one arm like inked vines. When he pulls off his helmet, my stomach drops. Reed.

Panic flutters in my chest. I haven't seen him or talked to him since the other night when I made an absolute ass of myself. He catches my eye for half a second, a slow smirk tugging at the corner of his mouth as he sets his helmet on the bike seat.

Oh God.

Dylan and Luke climb out of the trucks behind him. I met them once a couple weeks ago when everyone was pitching in to help Kinsley. Dylan is all easy grins and dimples, while Luke's quieter, his blue eyes sharp like he's always sizing up the room.

Reed greets the other guys with a casual slap on the shoulder as Miles walks up, motioning toward the tables. It's only then I realize the three of us, me, Kinsley, and Naya, are openly staring at them like we've forgotten how to function.

"You girls need a napkin to wipe the drool?" Judy asks, her voice full of innocent mischief.

All three of us drop our heads and laugh, caught.

Naya shakes her head with a grin. "They're hot, sure. Nice to look at. But I've known them way too long for it to be anything more than eye candy."

Kinsley snorts. "Speak for yourself."

I keep my head down, cheeks burning, praying Reed didn't notice the way my eyes lingered on him.

The three of us settle back into our pumpkins, but we're not really carving anymore. Not with that gun show happening twenty feet away.

The guys have pulled out sledgehammers and saws, their voices carrying faintly over the sound of wood splintering and metal tools clanking. I can't make out what they're saying, but it's obvious they're close, laughing easily, moving like they've done this a hundred times before. The rhythmic thunk of sledgehammers striking beams fills the air. Then the buzz of saws as they slice through old siding. Every few minutes, one of them hauls heavy planks to the trailers, muscles flexing under the strain.

And then, God help us, they start pulling off their shirts. Sweat glistens across lean, tanned shoulders and abs as they move in the late morning sun. We're all silent for half a beat.

"This," Naya says, her voice low and reverent, "might be the hottest thing I've ever seen."

I can't even argue. It's like some absurdly perfect lumberjack fantasy come to life. Just as I'm trying to compose myself, Naya cups her hands around her mouth and lets out a sharp whistle.

"Woo! Take it off, boys! Looking good over there!"

"Naya!" I hiss, horrified, my eyes going wide as I swat her arm.

She giggles, completely unbothered. "What? I'm giving them encouragement."

Kinsley is doubled over, giggling so hard she nearly drops her pumpkin carving knife.

Reed pauses mid-swing, glancing over his shoulder with a slow, amused grin. "Careful over there, ladies. I'd hate to have to grab the hose to cool you down."

Reed's golden-brown eyes flick briefly in my direction, his grin deepening.

Kill me now.

The words I'd slurred at him the other night crash back into my head like a freight train. *'They say firemen are good with hoses, think you can live up to the hype?' I want to crawl in a hole and die.*

Kinsley claps a hand over her mouth, trying to muffle her giggling, but it's no use. Naya is nearly in tears, clutching her stomach as she wheezes. Even Miles, standing nearby with his hands on his hips, is enjoying the show.

I duck my head, pretending to be fascinated by the crooked triangle eyes I'm carving, praying no one notices the heat crawling up my neck. *Maybe if I sit really still, they'll all forget I exist.*

6

Sledgehammers and Side-Eyes

Reed

The sun is warmer than it should be for October, baking down on my shoulders through my black T-shirt as the road winds in front of me. This might be one of the last good days to take the bike out before the cold sets in, and I'm determined to enjoy it.

The matte black cruiser hums beneath me, steady and smooth, the kind of machine built for long roads and quiet escapes. The ride out here has always been one of my favorites, long empty stretches with barely any traffic. As I ease off the throttle and make the turn onto the long drive leading to the cabins, the trees close in, golden leaves spinning lazily in the breeze. The lake glitters between the trunks, the surface so calm it looks painted.

When the clearing opens up ahead, the old cabins come into view. Trucks are parked to the side, trailers empty and waiting to be loaded. And there, in the yard by Judy's cabin, four women are bent over pumpkins.

I catch sight of her first. Raelynn. She's sitting closest to cabin two, her ponytail falling forward as she carves, shoulders drawn up in concentration. Even from here, she's a damn good-looking woman, simple jeans, a T-shirt. She pulls your eyes like a magnet.

My grin spreads under the helmet before I can stop it. This day just got a hell of a lot more entertaining. The memory of her flushed cheeks the other night comes roaring back. The way she'd leaned in too close, words slurred with whiskey and just enough sass to make me want to grin and growl at the same time.

Yeah. She's probably still mortified about that, and I'd be lying if I said I wasn't planning to remind her. Not in a cruel way. Just enough to see her squirm. I'm not even off the bike yet, and it's already a win-win. I get to break stuff and give her a hard time at the same time.

I kill the engine and swing a leg over, the kickstand scraping against the packed dirt as I set the bike steady. The helmet comes off with a soft click, and I rest it on the seat, raking a hand through my hair to shake out the heat.

When I glance up, three pairs of eyes are fixed on me from across the yard. Raelynn's the first to look away, her cheeks pinking as she ducks back over her pumpkin like it suddenly needs all her attention. The corner of my mouth curves. Cute.

"Morning, boys," I call as I stride over to where Miles, Dylan and Luke are standing near the trailers. "What's the plan? We tearing this thing down like a bunch of cavemen, or you three gonna get fancy with it?"

Dylan tosses a sledgehammer from one hand to the other like it's nothing. "Fancy? Hell no. This is pure smash-and-haul. I'm here for the destruction."

"Sounds like a good morning to me." I flex my fingers, already itching for the weight of the hammer.

"You look way too excited about breaking stuff," Luke says.

"Worried?"

"Hell no!" Dylan cuts in. "Reed's probably been waiting all week to hit something without paperwork involved."

"Damn straight, This is therapy. Cheaper than a shrink, and I don't have to talk about my feelings."

Miles shakes his head with a low chuckle. "Just try not to put a hole in one of the trailers while you're at it, alright?"

"No promises. Depends on if Dylan keeps running his mouth."

Dylan barks a laugh. "Go ahead and swing at me. I'll just duck and let you eat dirt in front of the ladies."

Luke lets out a low whistle, jerking his chin toward the porch. "Speaking of, don't look now, but we've already got an audience." I don't look. Not yet. I already know they're watching.

We don't waste time standing around. As soon as the plan's laid out, the four of us split off, Miles and Luke tackle the north wall while Dylan and I head south. The first swing of my sledgehammer sends a deep crack through the air. Rotten wood splinters, a chunk breaking loose and landing with a satisfying thud. Dylan winds up for his turn.

It doesn't take long for the October sun to start working on us. Warm for this time of year, the air sticks like honey and sweat trails down my back. After a few more swings, my shirt clings like a damp rag. I yank it off and toss it onto the trailer hitch without thinking.

That's when I catch movement on the lawn. Raelynn's standing out front with Naya and Kinsley, pumpkin carving tools dangling uselessly from her fingers. Her ponytail sways as she shifts her weight, trying and failing, to keep her eyes off us. Every time her gaze flicks our way, she jerks it back down like she's been caught stealing. A grin pulls at my mouth. *Damn, she's pretty when she's flustered.*

Around me, boards groan and splinter. Miles and Luke peel siding from their wall with calm precision, muscles working as they haul beams to the waiting trailer. Dylan's already shirtless, his arms gleaming in the sunlight as he swings like he's trying to prove something.

Then Naya's voice cuts through the air. "Woo! Take it off, boys! Lookin' good over there!"

This is my chance. I sling the sledge over my shoulder and glance toward the girls. "Careful out there, ladies," I call. "I'd hate to have to grab the hose to cool you down."

That does it. Raelynn freezes like a deer in headlights, her face going crimson as her carving tool slips from her hand. She gives a small shake of her head and presses her lips together, like she's willing herself not to die on the spot.

Kinsley cracks first and nearly drops her pumpkin. Naya's doubled over beside her, shoulders shaking.

Miles glances over and shakes his head with a knowing grin. He doesn't need the backstory, he already knows.

Luke frowns, looking between us. "What's with the hose?"

Dylan snorts. "Yeah, did I miss a joke?"

The girls lose it all over again, Raelynn covering her face with both hands.

I chuckle and swing the sledge down hard, the beam groaning as it gives. "Don't worry, Raelynn," I call across the lawn. "If you ever need a demonstration, I'm happy to show you how well I handle the equipment."

Her head snaps up so fast I almost laugh again. But this time, she doesn't look away.

Raelynn squares her shoulders, eyes narrowing as her cheeks burn. But she fires back, her voice steady despite the flush on her cheeks. "Hope your equipment's as impressive as your ego."

For a beat, I freeze mid-swing. Damn. A slow grin spreads across my face.

"Looks like she's not gonna take your crap today." Dylan laughs.

"She's got more bite than I thought," I admit, gripping the sledge tighter as I watch her turn back to her friends with a small, triumphant smile. And hell if that doesn't make her even more interesting.

We work for another hour, the rhythmic thunk of tools and the occasional scrape of nails filling the air. Every now and then, my eyes flick toward the lawn where the girls are gathered, laughing as they set their pumpkin creations in a row like some kind of harvest display.

I don't let myself stare. Not really. Just enough to catch Raelynn tossing her hair back, her shoulders still squared like she's proud of putting me in my place.

Before I can dwell on it too long, Judy's voice cuts across the yard, warm and commanding.

"Alright, you animals! Drop the tools and wash up. Lunch is ready."

"Please tell me there's food for an army," Dylan mutters, rubbing the back of his neck.

"You know Judy," Miles says with a smirk. "There's probably enough for three armies."

We trail toward the long table Judy's set up on the lawn. Sure enough, it's covered edge to edge with sandwich fixings. Stacks of bread, rolls and wraps filled the table alongside platters of meats, cheeses and fresh veggies. Bowls of chips and pickles round it out like a full-on deli spread.

"Looks like a damn sandwich shop exploded," Luke mutters under his breath.

"Better than any shop I've been to."

"Hands off until everyone's here!" Judy wags her finger. "Go wash up, all of you. Don't make me chase you with the spray bottle."

"Yes, ma'am," Dylan says with mock seriousness before heading toward the spigot by the side of the cabin.

Raelynn's standing there alone, her hands brushing pumpkin seeds off her jeans . Her ponytail's starting to fall loose, a few strands clinging to the side of her flushed face.

Instead of following Dylan, I veer toward her. Maybe I can get another rise out of her. Hell, half the fun is seeing how fast she blushes. But before I can even open my mouth, she glances up at me, her brown eyes steady and sharper than I expected.

"I was going to apologize for being so crude the other night," she says coolly, crossing her arms. "But you seem to like it."

"You know what?" I lean a little closer. "You're not wrong."

Her lips twitch like she's fighting a smile, but she doesn't break eye contact.

I hold her gaze for a moment, then smirk and turn toward the spigot. Walking away feels good, like I've kept the upper hand without saying another word.

At the pump, Dylan glances over as he rinses his hands. "What was that about?"

"Nothing," I say easily, letting the cold water wash away sawdust and sweat.

The girls sit together on the lawn, laughing as they eat, while the guys and I eat fast, already thinking about the work left to finish.

Back at cabin two, hammers swing and boards groan as we pull it down piece by piece. Across the yard, more pumpkins take shape, orange rinds and seeds scattered like confetti.

By late afternoon, the trailers are full, and Judy's porch is lined with jack-o'-lanterns.

Engines rumble as the others pull out.

"Reed," Judy calls. "Can you help fold the tables and haul them inside?"

"Sure thing."

The sun dips lower, shadows stretching long across the grass. Then the screen door creaks open. Raelynn steps out, her ponytail swaying as she pauses on the porch.

"The dishes are done."

"Thank you, sweetheart." Judy smiles. "Saved me a chore."

She leans against the doorframe, watching as I stack the last of the folding chairs. "Got plans tonight, Raelynn?" Judy asks.

Raelynn shakes her head. "No. Just a quiet night, I guess."

Judy glances my way. "What about you, Reed?"

I shrug, wiping my palms on my jeans. "Probably just take the bike out for a ride before heading home."

"Oh," Judy says, thoughtful now. She looks back at Raelynn. "You ever been on a motorcycle?"

Raelynn hesitates. "No, I wasn't allowed to..." She catches herself too late, her lips pressing together like she wishes she could pull the words back.

My brow pulls tight, but I don't say anything.

Judy gives a little shrug and a kind smile. "Well, it's a nice evening for a ride. Maybe Reed can show you what all the fuss is about?"

I nod without hesitation. "Sure. If you want, I'll take you for a spin."

It's not about wanting time alone with her, though the thought does cross my mind. It's about the way riding makes you feel: The wind, the open road, the quiet that settles your thoughts. And something tells me she could use that.

She glances at me, hesitating. "I don't have a helmet." Her voice quieter now.

Judy waves a hand like it's nothing. "I'm sure Reed has another one back at his place." Her eyes flick to me. Waiting.

"I do." Then I glance toward the road. "If you're serious, I'll grab it. But only if Judy agrees to watch my dog. She's been home alone long enough."

"Of course, I'll spoil her rotten until you're back."

Raelynn exhales, biting her lip for half a second before her shoulders drop. "Okay. I'll go."

"Grab a sweater." I pull my keys from my pocket. "I'll be back in a few minutes."

She glances toward her cabin like she's not sure if she's really going to follow through. But then she gives a small nod and walks toward the path.

I watch her go. She's scared. I can see it in the tight set of her shoulders and the way her arms fold across her middle. But there's something else there, too. Determination.

The bike growls to life under me as I swing a leg over and snap my helmet in place and head down the long drive.

At the house, I cut the engine and step into the garage. The spare helmet sits on a shelf, and I tuck it carefully into the side bag of the bike before heading inside.

"Fifi," I call softly.

Her tiny paws click against the hardwood as she comes trotting around the corner, tail wagging furiously.

"C'mon, girl. You're going to Judy's for a bit."

I scoop her up, open the hall closet, and pull out the world's smallest helmet, black with a pink bow on top and a little chin strap. "You're going to hate me for this," I mutter, buckling it under her chin.

Fifi blinks up at me like she's already plotting my murder.

"Yeah, yeah." I chuckle as I clip her harness to my chest. "You'll forgive me."

Stepping back outside, I settle onto the bike and adjust Fifi's position before firing up the engine. The road back to Judy's is quiet, the autumn air warm against my arms as I ease the throttle forward. Fifi loves the ride. The second the engine hums beneath us, she presses into my chest like she was born for it. The helmet, though? That's another story. She keeps pawing at the strap like I've strapped a bowling ball to her head.

"Quit it, drama queen."

As the cabins come into view, I spot Raelynn and Judy standing together near the porch. They're close, Raelynn with her arms folded, Judy's hand resting lightly on her shoulder. It looks like they're in the middle of one of those quiet heart-to-hearts Judy's so damn good at.

I cut the engine, the silence swallowing up the space around us. Both of them glance up and the second their eyes land on Fifi with her tiny helmet and her big brown eyes blinking out from under it, they both burst.

"Oh my gosh, look at you, Fifi!" Judy croons, her voice going soft and high as she crouches down.

"You're the cutest little biker girl I've ever seen." Raelynn giggles wide as she pulls out her phone. "Hold still, sweetie. This needs a picture."

I watch as Raelynn snaps a photo, her face lighting up with something easy and unguarded. The sound of her laugh carries across the yard, warmer than I've heard it all day.

Something shifts in my chest. I didn't plan on offering her this ride, not really. But now that I'm here, with her standing there with those damn eyes, I can't help wondering what she'll be like on the back of my bike. Nervous? Bold? Both? I can't wait to find out.

7

The Ride That Woke Me Up

Raelynn

My heart thuds a little harder as Reed swings his leg off the bike and walks toward us, Fifi still strapped to his chest in her ridiculous helmet.

I force myself to look away, but it doesn't help. He's all dark jeans and a fitted black T-shirt, tattoos stretch under one sleeve. He unclips Fifi's harness and passes her to Judy, who takes the tiny dog like she's just been handed a priceless treasure. I don't think I've ever seen Judy this happy; someone really ought to get her a dog of her own.

As she heads toward her cabin, she glances back with a bright smile. "You two have a great time!"

"You ready?"

I nod before I can talk myself out of it. "Yeah. I think so."

Truth is, I've never been on a motorcycle in my life. The thought makes me nervous, but there's something else, too, excitement maybe.

Reed reaches into the side bag and pulls out a sleek black helmet. "Here."

I take it from him, turning it over in my hands like it might bite me.

"Let me help."

Before I can respond, he steps closer, close enough that I catch the faint scent of sawdust and pine. He takes the helmet gently, and slides it over my head, careful not to pull my hair.

"Chin up." He fastens the strap beneath my jaw. His fingers brush against my skin, and I swear I stop breathing for half a second.

"There." He gives the helmet a little tap. "Perfect."

I let out a nervous laugh. "Do I look like I know what I'm doing?"

He smirks. "Not even a little, but that's fine. I'll show you."

Reed steps back to the bike and pats the seat behind him. "You're going to swing your leg over like this." He demonstrates slowly, then holds out a hand to steady me.

I hesitate, my pulse racing.

"Relax, Raelynn. It's easier than you think. Just take my hand."

I do, and the warmth of his palm against mine is grounding in a way I don't expect.

"Now swing your leg up and over."

I follow his instructions, a little clumsy but somehow landing on the seat behind him.

"There you go." He glances back at me with an approving nod. "Natural."

"Ha. You're lying."

"Maybe a little." His grin deepens. "Alright, scoot closer."

I scoot closer, the leather seat warm beneath me as my knees brush against his jeans. And then it hits me, I'm practically wrapped around him. My hands hover awkwardly for a second before I settle them lightly on his sides, my palms brushing against the firm muscle under his T-shirt.

Oh God.

He's solid. Not just strong, ridiculously strong. I swallow hard, my heart thudding for an entirely new reason now. This felt like a fun little adventure five minutes ago, but now? Now I'm fully aware of every single inch between us, or lack of inches. The warmth of his back. The way his shoulders stretch his black T-shirt.

"Don't overthink it," Reed says suddenly.

Is he talking about the ride or the fact that I'm spread out behind him?

"Too late, I'm already mentally drafting my obituary: 'Woman goes flying off the back of local fireman's motorcycle, tragically dies in a gray T-shirt with questionable flirting advice on it.'"

"That's one hell of a headline."

"Think the town paper will print it?" I grip his sides a little tighter as the bike rocks slightly under his shift.

"Probably, but relax, I'm not going to let anything happen to you."

The engine rumbles to life beneath us, a deep growl that sends a thrill through me.

"I'll take it slow, and if at any point you want to stop, just tap my shoulder. Deal?"

I nod, even though he can't see me. "Deal."

"Good." His hand comes to rest briefly over mine on his side, warm, reassuring, before settling back on the handlebars. "Hang on, Raelynn."

The second we start to roll forward, my panic spikes. Without thinking, I throw my arms all the way around him, plastering myself to his back and burying my helmet between his shoulder blades. My eyes squeeze shut so tightly it feels like I'll never be able to open them again.

I can feel him vibrating under me, and it takes a second to realize… he's laughing.

"You okay back there?"

I make a sound somewhere between a squeak and a groan.

"Raelynn…Are your eyes closed?"

"Yes!" I squeak out, my voice muffled against his back.

I can practically hear the grin in his voice. "We're only going five miles per hour. You can open them."

"Not helping," I mumble.

"You're fine. I promise."

Okay. I trust him. He's a firefighter, for Christ's sake. He wouldn't let something happen. Right? But then it hits me, *oh no.* I should've asked him how long he's been riding. What if this is new for him?

I crack one eye open…He's right. I could probably walk faster than we're going.

"How long have you been riding?" I blurt out, my voice tight, before he has a chance to pick up speed.

"About three days. Why?"

Panic slams into me, and I feel my grip tighten around him like a vice.

"What?" The word squeaks out. "Three days?" Before I can launch into a full-blown meltdown, I feel his chest shake as he laughs.

"I'm kidding, Raelynn." His voice is deep, amused. "I've been riding since I was a teenager."

I let out a strangled sound, half relief, half frustration. "Wow. That's hilarious. You'd be laughing a lot less if I hurled us both into a ditch from sheer panic."

"You want to go faster, or should I keep us creeping along like a golf cart?"

"Oh, shut up. We can go faster…but not too fast."

He chuckles again; it somehow steadies the little flutter of nerves in my stomach.

As the bike eases forward, I can't help noticing how effortless he makes it all seem. The way his hands rest on the handlebars, relaxed. The way he leans slightly into the curves. Reed is so easy, laid back in a way that feels foreign to me. I wish I had a little of that. A little of his comfort in his own skin, his sense of adventure. Instead, I'm clinging to him like the cautious rule-follower. But right now, I feel equal parts terrified and a little exhilarated. And if I'm being completely honest with myself…it's kinda hot. I mean, here I am, wrapped around a gorgeous man on a motorcycle. His back is solid under my hands. There's an easy strength about him, the kind that doesn't have to try, it just is. The low rumble of the engine runs through him, and the heat of his body seeps into mine, making it impossible to tell if my racing pulse is from fear or something else entirely.

Hold it together. He's just a guy… a ridiculously hot guy on a motorcycle, but still.

"You're doing good," Reed calls back over the soft growl of the bike. "I'm going to pick it up a little now, alright?"

"Okay." My voice comes out higher than I intended.

The bike surges as he twists the throttle, and I can feel the wind start to whip harder against us. It rushes past my helmet, tugging at the strands of hair peeking out, cool but not unpleasant.

The road ahead stretches between rows of trees, their branches arching overhead in a fiery canopy of golds and reds. Leaves tumble lazily across the pavement, catching in little eddies before settling back down. There are no other cars, no sounds but the steady hum of the engine and the wind slipping past us. Open fields roll out on either side, dotted with fences and the occasional weathered barn.

I feel him accelerate, the bike responding with a smooth surge of power, but this time, I'm not scared.

"This is amazing!"

I see him nod, just enough to let me know he heard. Then, to my shock, his hand slips off the handlebars for a second, reaching back to pat my leg. The gesture is small, simple…but somehow it sends a rush of warmth straight through me. My grip on him loosens, because I trust him. That little touch feels like reassurance, like a quiet "I've got you." And maybe, just maybe, I believe him.

We keep riding, the sun dipping lower as the world around us shifts into gold. The air cools slightly, and my nerves fade with every mile. Eventually, I'm only holding on with one hand, my other resting in my lap as the scenery blurs by.

The bike begins to slow, the engine humming softer as Reed eases us off the road and into a scenic overlook. The view opens wide, rolling hills brushed with autumn colors, river catching the last light of day like liquid fire.

He brings the bike to a stop and looks over his shoulder. "I'll hold it steady. Step off the same way you got on."

I slide off carefully. Reed kicks the stand and cuts the motor. Then he pulls off his helmet. And thank God he can't see my face through mine, because the sight of him like that, hair mussed, golden light hitting his sharp jaw and easy grin…he looks like he just stepped off the cover of a romance novel. And there's a very real possibility I have drool on my face.

I fumble awkwardly with the helmet strap, my fingers not quite cooperating. Before I can get it undone, Reed steps closer.

"Here."

His hands lift, and I freeze as his fingers brush just beneath my chin. His fingers are warm against my skin as he works the strap loose with slow, careful movements. The helmet slides free, and suddenly I'm hyper-aware of everything. The way the breeze hits my flushed cheeks. The fact that my hair is probably a wild disaster from the ride. The way he's still standing close, looking at me with that calm, unreadable expression.

His jaw tightens slightly, and then he steps back. "Come on. I'll show you why I stopped here."

I follow him a few steps to a weathered white wooden fence, its paint peeling from years of sun and rain. Beyond it, the land drops away into a small cliff, and the view steals my breath.

Below us, a wide river winds lazily through the valley, its surface catching the last rays of sunlight like molten gold. The trees along its banks are set ablaze with fall color, against the rich green pines scattered among them. The whole scene is so still it feels like a painting. Leaves swirl gently in the breeze, some breaking free and drifting down to the water below.

"I'd love to sketch this one day." My eyes trace the way the river curves.

Reed glances over at me, surprise flickering across his face. "You sketch?"

"I…did," I admit, a little sad. "A long time ago."

"Hey." The word is gentle but firm, pulling my attention back to him.

He steps closer, and I have to tilt my chin up to meet his gaze. The sunlight catches in his eyes, making them seem warmer somehow.

"You don't need permission to do what you love, Raelynn."

The thought of the sketchbook back at the cabin sends a thrill through me. "I'm going to. I bought a sketch book this morning."

I catch a flicker of a smile, but he stays quiet. Instead, he turns back toward the view, resting his arms on the top rail of the fence.

I follow his gaze for a moment. "Alright, your turn, what keeps you busy when you're not saving the world?"

He huffs a quiet laugh, his expression thoughtful. "A little bit of everything, I guess. I'm kind of an adrenaline junkie."

"Adrenaline junkie?" I arch a brow.

"Yeah." He glances at me. "Riding my bike, skydiving, bungee jumping, anything outdoors. Hiking, camping, rock climbing. And…I've got a pilot's license."

I blink at him, surprised. "You fly?"

"Not as often as I'd like, but yeah. Single Engine Air Tanker mostly, used for fighting wildfires. One day I want to learn how to fly helicopters."

"Of course you would. You're basically a walking adventure brochure."

He chuckles.

I turn back toward the view, drinking it in one last time. *How nice would it be,* I think, *to live a little like him? To let go of fear and just… breathe. Have a little adventure for once.*

Reed straightens beside me. "We better get going." His voice breaks through my thoughts. "It'll be dark on our way back."

We both slide our helmets on, the air between us shifting as we step away from the fence. Reed leads us back to the bike.

The ride home feels different somehow, even though we're retracing the same road. The sun has dipped lower, and this far from town, there are no streetlights, just the glow of the bike's headlight cutting a path through the dark.

I'm so relaxed, I stretch my arms out wide and lean back slightly. For a moment, I close my eyes and just feel it, the freedom, the quiet thrill of flying down an empty road on the back of his bike.

When I open them again, that peaceful bubble pops in an instant. A deer steps out of the trees, its body illuminated in the headlight. My arms fly down, wrapping quickly around Reed's torso as my heart jumps into my throat.

"Reed!" I shout, my voice muffled by the helmet.

He jerks the handlebars sharply to the left, the bike swaying dangerously as the tires hit loose gravel on the shoulder. The rear wheel fishtails slightly before he steadies it, his body leaning expertly into the movement.

My arms are still locked tight around him, my pulse thundering in my ears as the deer vanishes in the darkness behind us. The bike steadies, but I'm shaking so hard I can barely catch my breath.

Reed reaches down with one hand and wraps it over mine where it's gripping his chest like a lifeline. His fingers anchoring me in place as he eases the throttle back and slows the bike to a crawl.

"It's okay." He looks over his shoulder, his voice calm.

The bike rolls to a stop on the dirt shoulder. We don't get off. We just sit there, the dark pressing in around us. Reed pulls off his helmet and hooks it on the handlebar. Then he glances back at me, his brows drawn tight, concern etched in his face.

"Raelynn." He reaches up to undo my helmet strap. I let him slip it free, and the second the helmet's off, cool air rushes against my damp skin.

I look away quickly, hoping he won't notice the sting in my eyes, the tear threatening to fall.

"Hey, look at me. You're okay." His thumb brushes over my knuckles where his hand still covers mine. "We're okay. You did everything right."

A small sound escapes me, and I try to look away again, embarrassed.

But Reed doesn't let me. Instead, he presses my palms against the steady rise and fall of his chest.

"Feel that? Heart's still beating. We're fine."

The warmth of him grounds me, pulling me out of the spiral in my head.

"We're safe, Raelynn. You're safe."

My body gives a little shudder, the last of the adrenaline slipping away, and I nod against the lump in my throat.

"Take a minute. No rush. We'll ride when you're ready."

His calmness is infectious. Slowly, I feel my whole body start to relax, the knot in my chest unraveling. *He's right, we're fine.*

I sit up a little taller, drawing in a deep breath. "Okay," I say, my voice steadier now. "I'm ready. Just…maybe keep the wildlife encounters to a minimum on the way back? I'm not sure I can handle a moose."

"Deal. No moose. I'll even try to avoid squirrels if it'll make you feel better."

"Good." I give him a mock-serious nod. "My nerves are officially tapped out. One more surprise and you're carrying me home."

Reed smiles as he slides his helmet back on. "Noted. Maximum caution. But just so you know, boring isn't really my specialty."

"Oh, trust me. I've noticed."

By the time we ease back onto the dark road, the tension has melted away. This time, I don't dare let go. My arms stay wrapped snugly around Reed's waist, my head resting lightly against his back. And it strikes me how…different this feels.

Reed is reassuring in a way I'm not used to. He didn't snap when I panicked. He didn't make me feel ridiculous for holding on too tight or letting fear creep in. He just…understood. That kind of patience isn't something I've known for a long time. Now that I'm finally starting to find myself, to understand how I deserve to be treated, a part of me wishes we could just keep going. Turn around, ride until morning, and let the world fall away for a little while longer.

8

Losing My Edge

Reed

Riding down the cabin drive, I can't stop replaying the way she'd clung to me after that deer stepped out, her body trembling, her small hands gripping my chest, and the way she'd called out my name. Even though I know she's not fragile, there's still this part of me that wants to wrap both arms around her and keep the whole damn world from getting too close.

"Hey, you okay back there?"

She lets out a small laugh. "Are you kidding? I'm great."

Her words hang in the air for a moment, and I can't help the corner of my mouth from tugging up. "Glad to hear it."

When the bike rolls to a stop in front of the cabins, I keep my eyes on the handlebars a moment longer, letting the engine settle before cutting it.

"Thanks for the ride." She slips her helmet off and hands it to me.

"Not a problem." My voice comes out even, though I can feel the tension in my jaw. I swing my leg over and step off the bike, then hold out my hand to help her down. Her small hand slips into mine, and I notice it's still trembling. She knows I can feel it, too, because she gives me a soft smile.

"Okay, that was a little intense with the deer, but really…I'm fine."

"Are you sure?" I ask, still holding her hand.

She nods, but before I can stop myself, my other hand lifts, fingers brushing a loose strand of hair across her forehead. The movement feels natural, easy, and I catch myself lingering a second too long before dropping my hand. For a moment, I freeze. *What the hell am I doing? This isn't me. I don't get caught up like this.*

I clear my throat and let go of her hand, forcing my voice to stay steady. "Good. I'm glad."

She gives me a small smile, hesitating, like she's unsure what to say next, and I busy myself placing her helmet into the side bag, deliberately avoiding her gaze.

"Good night, Reed."

"Night, Raelynn."

I look up just in time to see her walking away, her hand brushing through her hair as she reaches her cabin. I let out a slow breath and turn on my heel, heading across the yard. I shake my head, trying to clear the thought. *Why do I feel this pull to protect her?* I don't catch feelings. That's not me. Never has been. Yet here I am.

At Judy's place, I give the door a soft knock before pushing it open. Fifi meets me at the door, her tiny tail wagging like mad.

"Hey, wigglebutt." I crouch to scoop her up.

By the time I stand back up, Judy's beside me, moving as quietly as ever. "How'd it go?"

"It was fine." I shrug, not giving her any more than that.

Before she can press, I glance toward the kitchen. "Did you cook this late?"

"Yes. For Fifi."

I huff a quiet laugh, shaking my head. "You cooked…for the dog?"

"She's special. Sometimes it's worth a little extra effort for the ones who need it."

The words don't register as anything more than her usual Judy-isms, but for some reason, the image of Raelynn flickers through my mind, her smile when she climbed off the bike, the soft laugh she gave when she said she was fine.

"Why? Do you need something? Are you hungry?"

"No. I don't need anything. Thanks for asking."

"Alright then." Judy pats my arm and presses a kiss to my cheek before turning back to her chair. She picks up a book from the side table, settling in with a content sigh. I linger a second, watching her flip to the next page, calm as ever.

"Night, Judy."

"Night, sweetheart. Be careful driving," she murmurs, already lost in her story.

The drive home is quick. Once the bike's parked in the garage and locked up, I carry Fifi inside. I toe off my boots and head for the shower. The water hisses as it warms, steam curling around me while I strip down. Then I pause. Four faint crescent-shaped nail marks curve across my chest, the ghost of where Raelynn's hands had clutched me tight when the deer darted out.

I can laugh about it now, but in the moment, all I'd thought was: *Is she okay?* I step under the spray, letting the hot water pound my shoulders, willing it to wash away more than just dirt and sweat. *Let it go, Reed.* By the time I shut off the water and step out, steam curls around me like a heavy fog. I drag a towel across my skin, knotting it around my waist as I head for the bedroom.

The room is simple. King-size bed against the far wall, functional dresser, nightstand with an alarm clock and a charging cord. No pictures. No clutter. Just the way I like it.

I pull on a clean pair of boxers and flop onto the bed. Fifi hops up behind me, circling twice before settling in. The second my head hits the pillow, I'm out.

***

The blare of my alarm drags me back to consciousness what feels like minutes later. I scrub a hand over my face, forcing myself upright, and head for the bathroom. Ten minutes later I'm dressed and standing in the kitchen, waiting for the coffee pot to finish gurgling out the first cup of the day.

Fifi pads in yawning so hard her whole body shakes. "Don't give me that look." I pour coffee into a travel mug. "You've got the good life. All naps and treats."

I grab my keys and head for the door. "Try not to shit on the floor while I'm gone, okay?"

The rain is coming down in sheets by the time I pull into the firehouse lot, the wipers working overtime. *Great.* Rain always means a busy day. Slick roads. Fender benders. The occasional idiot who thinks they're invincible in a pickup. I cut the engine, grab my coffee and jog through the downpour to the side entrance.

We start the morning like always, gathered in the meeting room while Chief Sanford runs through the day's schedule. It's routine, the calm before the storm I know won't last. As soon as the meeting wraps, the front door swings open catching my attention. A familiar voice calls out, cheerful and warm.

"Well, don't you boys look handsome this morning."

I glance over to see Judy standing there, a big white box from The Sweet Spot balanced in her arms. She stops by a few times a month with treats for the crew, and like clockwork, the guys light up when they see her.

"Judy!" Jose greets, striding over to relieve her of the box. "You're the best."

77

The room breaks out in cheers as everyone crowds around to greet her.

"Hey, Judy!"

"Lookin' good as always!"

Half the crew leans in for hugs or kisses on the cheek. I can't help but chuckle. Judy eats this shit up, smiling like she's holding court. Truth is the guys adore her.

Jose carries the box to the meeting room table like it's sacred, popping it open to reveal two dozen donuts. Within seconds, everyone's got one in hand, even the chief, who's already halfway through a cinnamon twist.

Judy makes her way over to me, pats my shoulder and presses a kiss to my cheek. "What are you up to today?"

She flashes a knowing smile, then turns her attention to the room like she's about to make an announcement. "I was hoping," she says sweetly, "I could get a couple of you strong, young men to stop by my place and grab the carved pumpkins for the fundraiser." Before she even finishes, half the room raises their hands.

"I'll go!"

"Me too!"

"Hell, I'll carry the whole pile myself."

Judy laughs, clearly delighted. "Well, aren't you all just the sweetest things?"

"You're good," I murmur to her.

She winks. "I know."

"I swear, you could get these guys to haul your whole house across town if you asked nicely enough."

She pats my arm, amused. "Maybe I'll test that theory one of these days."

Turning back to the room, she calls out, "Tomorrow morning sound okay?"

A chorus of "Yes!" rings out.

"Perfect." Judy leans in to kiss my cheek again before heading for the door. "Take care of yourself, Reed."

"Always." I watch her wave to the guys as they shout their goodbyes.

The crew's still crowded around the table, grabbing second donuts and swapping jokes when the sharp wail of the alarm cuts through the room. The calm is over.

Downed power lines. Three traffic accidents. One bad enough we had to cut a guy out of his crumpled sedan while the rain came down sideways. One small kitchen fire, thankfully contained before it spread beyond the stove.

By the time we roll back into the station, soaked to the bone and smelling like wet gear and smoke, it's not even noon. And I know the day's nowhere near over.

When my shift ends, it's almost six. The rain has finally let up. The clouds are still thick and heavy overhead, but at least I'm not getting soaked through to my socks as I make the drive home.

Halfway there, my phone buzzes in the cup holder.

"Yeah?" I answer, not bothering with a hello.

"Hey," Luke drawls on the other end. "You alive after that shift?"

"Barely. What's up?"

"Dusty's. Tonight. Six. You in?"

I smirk. Dusty's Delightful Diner, is the least delightful place in town, but their burgers are worth the flat soda. "Yeah, I'm in."

"Good. I'll call Miles, see if I can drag him out of his little love spell long enough to eat with us."

"Good luck with that." I snort. "You'll probably have to pry him off Kinsley with a crowbar."

Luke laughs. "Wouldn't be the first time. I'll call Dylan, too."

"Sounds like a plan."

"Alright. Six o'clock."

"Later."

I hang up just as I pull into the driveway. Inside, I make a quick change of clothes and praise Fifi for not leaving me a surprise on the floor before letting her out.

Five minutes later, I'm pulling a ball cap low over my head as she trots back in. "I've got the day off tomorrow," I tell her, grabbing my keys. "So, you and me, we'll hit the park first thing. Then I'll even take you to the ice cream shop for one of those fancy pup cups you love." She tilts her head like she understands every word.

The drive across town is quick now that the rain's stopped. The streets are still slick and glowing under the streetlights as Dusty's neon sign flickers faintly in the distance.

Dylan's already inside, chatting up the hostess when I step through the door.

"Hey, man." He grins. "Was starting to think I'd have to eat alone."

"Wouldn't want to deprive you of my company."

Before we can get too far into it, the door opens and in walks Miles with Luke right on his heels.

"Holy shit. She actually let him out?" Dylan chuckles.

Luke laughs. "Yeah, I wasn't sure if Kinsley would give him a permission slip, but here he is."

I smile. "Careful, Miles. Does she know you're out here unsupervised?"

Miles shoots us a look as he slides into the booth. "Laugh it up, assholes. At least I've got someone waiting for me at home."

"Ouch," Dylan clutches his chest in mock pain. For the next couple of hours, we eat and toss childish insults back and forth like it's a sport.

"So, where's Kinsley tonight?" Dylan leans back in the booth as he polishes off the last of his fries.

Miles smirks into his drink. "She said she was going to stay in. Raelynn's sketching, and she didn't want to bother her."

I have to stifle a smile at that. The thought of her doing something she loves. Before I can sink too far into that image, Luke's voice cuts through. "When's the fundraiser again?"

"Saturday."

"You all coming?"

"Yeah, wouldn't miss it."

"Same," Luke adds.

Miles shrugs. "Kinsley's making me go, so I'll be there."

The table chuckles at that as we all stand, tossing a handful of bills down for the waitress before heading for the door.

The drive home is quiet, the roads still slick but empty. I shouldn't be thinking about her. But I can't help it.

Raelynn on the back of my bike, her arms locked tight around me.

Raelynn drunk and sassy.

Raelynn sketching.

Raelynn looking up at me with those wide brown eyes.

Damn it. She's hot.

I don't do relationships. That's not me. But maybe she doesn't need that. Maybe what she needs is a rebound. Someone to remind her she's still desirable, still wanted. *I could do that.* I smirk to myself as I turn down my road. I'll flirt with her. Keep it fun. Nothing serious.

I step through the door and kick it shut behind me, the house quiet except for the soft jingle of Fifi's collar as she trots out of the living room to greet me.

"Hey, Girl." I bend to rub her tiny head.

I head straight for the bedroom, stripping off my hat and tossing it on the dresser. The bed looks damn good right now, and I waste no time crawling in.

As my head hits the pillow, I tell myself, "I've got this under control." Raelynn? She's beautiful, yeah. And sweet. And clearly still trying to figure out who she is. But I know how to keep things simple. I close my eyes, but her laugh from the other night slips into my head. The feel of her arms wrapped tight around me on the bike. The way her eyes softened when she talked about sketching. I shift on the mattress, dragging a hand over my face. *This isn't dangerous right*? But it sure as hell feels like a slippery slope.

9

New Keys, New Pages

Raelynn

I wake to the sound of my alarm, groaning as I smack it quiet. I stayed up way too late sketching last night, but I couldn't stop. There was this itch in my fingers to finish.

Rubbing the sleep from my eyes, I drag myself to the bathroom for a quick shower. By the time I've toweled off and done my hair, I feel a little more alive. A swipe of mascara, a hint of blush and I pull on my favorite distressed jeans and a fitted navy long-sleeve top.

Kinsley, Judy and I are having an early lunch today, and for the first time in a while, I actually feel excited to go.

In the kitchen, I pause by the counter where my sketchbook lies open. My lips curve into a smile as I run a thumb gently across the page. It's the sketch I'd finished last night, Reed's bike, parked by the overlook, the river and trees behind it. The scene feels alive, like I'd poured every ounce of my restless energy into the charcoal lines.

This is what I want to keep doing. Sketching the things that make me happy. The things that make me feel alive. My phone buzzes on the counter, pulling me out of my thoughts.

Kinsley: Bitch, you have GOT to see this. I'm out by my car.

I grab my jacket and slip it on before stepping out the door and immediately freeze.

There are about eight firefighters crowded around Judy's cabin, carrying carved pumpkins to their trucks. The sleeves of their Cranberry Ridge Firehouse hoodies are pushed up, forearms flexing as they juggle stacks of bright orange pumpkins.

Kinsley stands by her car, waving at me with a grin that says she's been watching the whole show. I force myself to pull it together and walk toward the driveway, my eyes sweeping the small crowd, half-expecting, and hoping to see Reed among them. He's not. And I don't know why that leaves me with a strange little pang.

"Well don't you look lovely," Judy calls as I approach, that familiar twinkle in her eye.

"Thanks." I laugh, tugging at my jacket.

Unfortunately, my arrival doesn't go unnoticed. All eight firemen turn at the same time, curious eyes sweeping over me in unison. My cheeks heat instantly.

One of them, his hoodie labeled Jose, steps forward with an easy smile. "You must be Raelynn. I'm Jose."

He's cute in a boyish way, dark wavy hair falling over his forehead, but I can't summon even a flicker of interest. Before I can respond, Judy swoops in like a protective hawk, lightly smacking Jose on the shoulder. "Shoo, you. Go help Leo with the last load."

Jose chuckles as he backs away, hands raised. "Alright, alright."

I can't help but laugh. Kinsley and I hang back, watching as the guys finish loading the pumpkins. Judy beams the whole time, clearly in her element, chatting with the crew as they work.

When the trucks finally roll away, the three of us pile into Kinsley's car.

"So… how'd the sketching go?" Kinsley asks as she pulls out of the driveway.

"Good. Really good, actually. I finished one last night."

"That's amazing. You'll have to show us later."

From the passenger seat, Judy glances back at me. "Raelynn, would you like to come with me to the fundraiser on Saturday? It's for winter gear for the local kids in need."

"I'd love to go."

Kinsley lights up. "This is perfect! I'll call Naya and see if she wants to join us. I'm sure Miles would rather hang with the guys anyway."

Judy chuckles. "Good thinking. The more, the merrier."

I settle back against the seat as the car winds through town. We pull into the lot at the Fireside Lounge. It's a mix of bar and restaurant, pool tables tucked into the back corner, an unlit dance floor and stage off to the side, a couple of dartboards on the far wall and a long wooden bar stacked with every kind of liquor imaginable.

This time of day, it's quiet, just a few locals scattered at tables and one older man nursing a beer at the bar. We slide into a booth near the front windows, sunlight filtering in across the polished wood table.

Judy's already chatting as we settle in, her hands animated. "The chief says this year's fundraiser is going to be the best one yet. He's got a few surprises planned, and I think it's going to pull in more donations than ever."

"That's great." Kinsley smiles, flipping open her menu.

Before I can respond, a waitress stops by, balancing a tray of glasses for another table.

"Morning, ladies. Can I get you started with drinks?"

"Coffee, please," Kinsley and I say almost in unison.

"I'll have a sweet tea." Judy smiles warmly.

"Perfect. I'll be right back with those."

I pull my phone from my bag to check the time, but it buzzes in my hand, screen lighting up with an unfamiliar number. My brows pinch together. I hesitate for half a second, then swipe to answer.

"Hello? Yes…it is. Yes. When?"

Across the table, Kinsley's eyes narrow, clearly picking up on my short, tense responses. Judy leans in slightly, trying to catch any clue from my expression or tone.

"Okay…yes, I can be there. Thank you. Bye." I lower the phone slowly, still gripping it like I'm not quite sure it's real. My heart is racing, but my brain hasn't caught up yet.

I turn to Kinsley, wide-eyed. She immediately reaches for my arm. "What is it?" she asks, her voice laced with concern.

"I…I got the building," I breathe out. "I was approved."

There's a flash of stunned silence.

Judy exhales with a soft, happy sigh just as Kinsley practically leaps from her seat.

"You what? Rae, that's amazing!" Her hands fly to her mouth before she leans across the table to hug me.

I laugh, a little shaky, still half in disbelief. "I can't believe it."

Judy beams, eyes shining. "Oh honey, of course you did."

"When can you sign the papers and get the keys?" Kinsley's eyes sparkle with excitement.

"Anytime," I say, still a little dazed. The words feel strange in my mouth, like they don't belong to me yet.

"Well then, let's go." Judy slides out of the booth with surprising speed for someone her age, her smile wide, dimples on full display. She tosses enough cash on the table to cover our drinks and a tip.

"Wait, right now?" I blink at her, trying to keep up.

"Yes, right now." She's already sliding her arm into her jacket. "This calls for a celebration, and I want to see this place for myself."

Kinsley giggles, grabbing her purse. "You heard her. Lets go."

By the time we pile into Kinsley's car, Judy is practically buzzing with excitement, talking a mile a minute about paint colors and potential layouts.

"Judy, I haven't even signed the papers yet," I protest weakly, though I can't help smiling.

"Details, honey." She waves dismissively. "This is your time. You've earned it."

As Kinsley eases the car out of the parking lot, I lean back against the seat, my hands twisting in my lap. It feels wild, how fast everything is moving. Just a few months ago, I couldn't have imagined starting over like this. And now? A building. A blank canvas for a future that's entirely my own. *This is actually happening.*

The drive is short and when we pull up, my heart lurches. The realtor is already standing by the door, a folder in one hand and a key in the other, waiting with a polite smile.

"Oh God," I whisper, staring at the building.

Kinsley reaches over to squeeze my hand. "You've got this, Rae."

Judy pats my knee with a grin. "Let's go make this official."

"Congratulations, Raelynn," The realtor says as we step out of the car. "You're officially the owner."

"This is happening." My hand flies to my mouth.

"Don't move." Judy's already pulling out her phone.

Kinsley smiles, looping her arm through mine. "You're glowing, Rae. Smile like you just landed your dream life, because you did."

I laugh, as Judy snaps picture after picture of me holding the keys, of Kinsley hugging me, of all three of us standing in front of the door like we're celebrating a national holiday.

"Okay." Judy lowers her phone. "Go on and unlock it, sweetheart. A moment like this deserves a grand entrance."

I step up to the door and notice a flyer taped to the glass. Reading it over, it says: **Congratulations on the new building. I'd love to talk about the possibility of purchasing it for more than your original investment. Please give me a call (555) 013-2498. – Bradley Manchester.**

I pass the note to Kinsley, and she reads it. "Looks like you had an offer in before someone else. I knew this was a great location."

She hands the paper back, and I wad it up, dropping it into the trash can on the sidewalk.

Kinsley laughs. "That's right. Don't sell your dream to anyone."

The key turns in the lock with a satisfying click, and when I push the door open, the scent of wood and faint cleaning supplies hits me. The space is wide open, tan tile floors stretch across the room, the white walls catching the light from the front windows. Above us, the industrial-style black ceiling gives it a modern, edgy feel. Off to the back is a small hallway leading to a bathroom, a large walk-in storage closet and an office.

"It needs a good scrubbing, a fresh coat of paint and maybe a facelift to give it more personality, but nothing major." I spin around to take it all in.

"You know what? I should call Mel. She's really good at painting and organizing." Kinsley claps her hands and pulls out her phone.

Just then, Judy perks up. "You're going to need an inspection, too. Let me take care of that for you. I'm sure they won't mind stopping by for me."

I laugh, shaking my head. "Judy, I think you can get just about anyone to do anything for you after what I saw this morning."

Judy giggles, already heading for the door as she waves her phone. "You're not wrong, honey."

Meanwhile, Kinsley's already scrolling her contacts and tapping a name. Within seconds, she's got Mel on speakerphone.

"Hey, Kins! What's up?" Mel's cheerful voice fills the space.

"Hey, you're on speaker, and guess what? Raelynn was just approved for the building we've been talking about. We're standing in it right now."

"No way! Rae, that's amazing!" Mel's voice bubbles with excitement. "Congratulations!"

"Thanks, Mel."

Mel and I have only met a couple of times, but I liked her instantly. She's one of those people who radiates warmth, her energy bright and infectious. Always smiling, always ready to jump in and help. With her sun-kissed skin, amber-brown eyes, and chestnut hair that falls in effortless waves, she's the kind of gorgeous that turns heads.

"Mel," Kinsley jumps in, "do you think you could come help us get this place cleaned up and painted? We could really use your magic touch."

"I'd love to! When?"

Kinsley looks at me for an answer.

"The fundraiser's this weekend, so how about next weekend?"

"You can stay at the farmhouse with me. We've got two spare rooms," Kinsley adds.

"That's perfect!" Mel says, her excitement practically crackling through the speaker. "I've been wanting to come visit anyway. This is going to be so much fun!"

"The other line's ringing, I've gotta run. I'll see you both next weekend!"
We call out our goodbyes and thanks before the line goes quiet.

Judy steps back through the door, beaming. "The inspector will be here in ten minutes, and pizza should be here in five."

"You ordered pizza? You're a godsend."

"You really are. I swear I might've passed out otherwise."

Judy smiles, hands on her hips. "Well, we can't have that, can we? Big day like this calls for proper fuel."

My phone buzzes in my bag, and I pull it out to see a text message from Jacob. The second I read his name, my whole body stiffens.

Kinsley notices instantly. "What's wrong?"

"It's Jacob," I murmur. "He texted me."

Kinsley's expression hardens. "Raelynn, do not respond. Not today. This day is for you to enjoy."

Judy steps up, resting a comforting hand on my shoulder. "Kinsley's right, honey. It's nothing you can't take care of another day."

I draw in a deep breath, pushing back the creeping anxiety. "You're right. The asshole can wait."

A few minutes later, the pizza delivery guy shows up, and Judy heads to meet him at the door. As she turns back toward us, she smiles. "If we're eating on the floor, one of you girls is helping me back up."

Kinsley and I answer in unison, giggling. "Of course."

Judy lowers herself to the floor with surprising ease, and we all join her, cross-legged on the dusty tile. The smell of melted cheese and pepperoni fills the air, making my mouth water.

Then the door swings open. In walks Reed. And now my mouth is watering for an entirely different reason. He's wearing faded jeans, a solid black hoodie, and a ball cap turned backward. I don't know what it is about a man with his hat like that, but it sends a sharp little ping straight to my stomach. I know he catches me staring because the moment his eyes meet mine, he gives me a quick wink.

Heat creeps up my neck, and I force myself to look away, but it's too late. Kinsley catches the whole thing. She elbows me under the guise of reaching for a napkin, giving me a look that clearly says, "What was that wink about? And what's going on?" With everything moving so fast right now, I'm not sure what's going on today. But today so far has been amazing and it might have just gotten a little better.

10

Inspector Hotshot

Reed

Fifi stares at the tennis ball like it personally insulted her. "Come on, girl. You're a dog. This is in your DNA." I give the ball another toss. It bounces once, twice, and rolls to a stop a few feet away. Fifi doesn't budge. "You're supposed to fetch." She flops down and rests her chin on her paws. I drag a hand over my face and let out a low laugh. "Alright. Guess it's on me." I walk across the grass, pick up the damn ball and toss it again. Nothing. *I'm officially playing fetch with myself. Great.*

Out of the corner of my eye, I notice I've drawn a crowd. A small group of women is standing near the park benches, dogs in tow, whispering and trying not to make it obvious they're staring.

"Oh my God, he's so patient," one says, her voice carrying just enough for me to hear.

"The dog's cute, too," another one chimes in.

"What dog?" a third woman murmurs, and I nearly choke back a laugh.

I shake my head, pretending I didn't hear.

"Okay. I see how it is." I crouch down, slipping a hand under her small body. "Alright, I get it. It's time for that pup cup I promised."

She doesn't move, but her tail gives a tiny wag like she's accepting my surrender. With Fifi tucked under one arm, I head to the truck and set her in the passenger seat. The second I climb behind the wheel and start the engine, she perks up like she knows exactly where we're headed.

By the time I pull into the drive-thru at the ice cream shop, she's practically vibrating with excitement. When I pull up to the window, Fifi loses her damn mind. Her whole body wiggles as she tries to crawl out the window to get to the pup cup.

"Whoa, easy there," I laugh, trying to hold her back. "This isn't a smash-and-grab."

The girl behind the counter giggles. "She's adorable."

"She knows it."

The second I peel the lid off, Fifi lunges at it, nearly knocking the whole thing into my lap. I end up holding the cup while she demolishes it in record time, her tiny pink tongue smearing ice cream across her nose.

My phone buzzes on the console. I glance down. Judy. I hit speaker and keep wiping Fifi's sticky little face. "Hi, Judy."

"Hello, honey. Are you busy?"

"No, why? What's up?"

"Perfect." Her tone is all rainbows and unicorns. "Can you stop by Raelynn's new building to give it an inspection?"

I pause, my brow pulling tight. "New building?"

"Oh yes. She put in an offer on a place, and she got the keys today."

That catches me off guard, but not in a bad way. "Huh. Good for her. I was going to run a few errands today."

"Oh well," Judy says breezily. "I suppose I could ask Jose. He seemed quite fond of Raelynn when they met this morning."

My jaw tics before I can stop it. "No. I'll be there in ten. Let me just drop off Fifi. Send me the address."

"Sending it now, sweetheart."

"Fine. But you're making dinner," I counter.

"I'll order pizza."

"Perfect. I'll see you in ten."

The call ends, and I glance down at Fifi, still sprawled across my lap with her tiny paws resting on my arm.

"Let's get you home."

My phone buzzes again with Judy's text, the address lighting up the screen. I know exactly where this is, prime spot right in the middle of town. Figures she'd land something like that.

I head home, dropping Fifi off and slide back behind the wheel. Raelynn won't be alone. Judy and Kinsley will be there, too. It's still the perfect setup to test the waters, see if that spark she showed the other night is still there. It should be simple. A little teasing. A little push to see how much I can make her blush before she fires back with that sharp tongue of hers. Except it doesn't feel simple. Not with her. This isn't supposed to matter. But there's this pull to see her, to watch her eyes light up, to hear what kind of sass she's packing today. I scrub a hand down my face and mutter under my breath. "Keep it light, Reed. Don't make it complicated."

I park the truck and glance through the front windows. The place looks empty, but Judy said they'd be here. Pushing the door open, I step inside and see the three of them sitting on the floor surrounding a pizza box, laughter still lingering in the air.

My eyes find Raelynn instantly. She freezes, her brown eyes wide as she looks up at me. For a split second, it feels like the air tightens between us. I flash her a quick wink, and the reaction is immediate, a soft pink rolls up her neck as she ducks her head, trying to hide her smile.

Judy waves me over. "Reed! There's plenty of pizza left, grab a slice."

I cross the room, but instead of dropping down beside Judy like she clearly expects, I plant myself right next to Raelynn. Her breath hitches faintly, and I have to bite back a grin.

"You're here for the inspection?" Kinsley's eyes flick between the two of us.

"Yeah," I say smoothly. "I had some free time."

I grab a slice of pizza from the box, as I lean back against the wall. Raelynn shifts slightly beside me, her thigh brushing mine for half a second before she tucks her legs under herself.

Judy turns my way. "So, Reed, how long does an inspection usually take on a place like this?"

I take a bite of pizza. "Depends. If there aren't any major issues, a couple of hours tops. But if I find something that needs a closer look, it could run longer."

"Perfect." Judy dabs at her mouth with a napkin. "That gives Raelynn time to pick out paint colors, and Kinsley and I can run to Cranberry Ridge Grocery for cleaning supplies."

Kinsley leans back, smiling. "Oh, we're doing this today, huh?"

"Why not?" Judy replies. "No time like the present."

Out of the corner of my eye, I see Raelynn shift, her fingers brushing a loose strand of hair behind her ear as she gives Judy a look somewhere between amused and nervous.

I lean back against the wall, chewing slowly as my eyes flick toward Raelynn.

"What's wrong, Sunshine?" My lips curve up. "You afraid to get a little dirt under those pretty nails?"

Her head snaps up, brown eyes narrowing slightly. "I'm not afraid of a little dirt."

"Good. Because this place has plenty to go around."

Kinsley bites her lip, trying not to laugh.

"Well then, it's settled," Judy says, patting Kinsley's knee. "Let's go."

Kinsley glances down at her half-eaten slice and shrugs. "Okay."

Judy's eyes soften as she looks over at me. "Reed, sweetheart, come help me off this floor. I can't feel my legs."

I chuckle, already standing, reaching down and hoisting her up with ease.

Judy pats my shoulder. "You're a good boy."

"Don't let that get out."

Kinsley reaches down and swipes another slice from the box clearly not done eating as she and Judy head for the door.

"We'll be back soon."

The moment the door clicks shut behind them, I turn back and take my seat on the floor.

"Finally," I lean back on my hands. "Thought they'd never leave."

That earns me a blink, a quick flicker of surprise in her eyes before she covers it with a scoff. "You're full of it."

"Maybe, but you're still sitting here. Guess that means you don't mind too much."

Her lips twitch. "Or maybe I'm just too polite to leave mid-slice."

"Ah," I nod, pretending to be serious. "So, it's the pizza keeping you here, not me?"

"Obviously." She pops the last bite of her crust into her mouth and brushes off her hands.

"Good to know. Guess I'll have to step up my game if I'm going to compete with mozzarella and pepperoni."

This time, she laughs. "Good luck with that, Hotshot."

The nickname makes me chuckle, the memory of her saying it the first time, tipsy and bold, flashing through my mind. She has no idea how much that stuck.

As she stands, she looks down at me with a spark in her brown eyes. "Where should we start?"

"With you telling me if you're actually going to help, or if I'm about to put on a show for you."

She crosses her arms, cocking her head. "Depends. Is this show worth the price of admission?"

I huff a quiet laugh and push to my feet. "Stick around, Sunshine. You might get a free preview."

Her eyes light up.

"Come on, Let's start in the closet."

She falls into step behind me, eyeing the narrow door at the back. "So…is there a fire hazard in the closet?"

I glance over my shoulder with a cocky grin. "Only if you count me."

That earns me an eye roll. I glance into the closet, then turn back to her with a smile. "Ladies first."

She squares her shoulders and steps past me. It's a big walk-in, easily large enough to hold a washer and dryer. I follow her in and scan the space.

"Don't see any major problems in here." I rest my hand on the wall. "But you're going to need a smoke alarm and an extinguisher."

She pulls out her phone and starts tapping a note, her brow furrowed in concentration. "Anything else?"

"Nope." I step past her to the door, my hand brushing against hers in the tight space. I catch her freeze out of the corner of my eye.

Grinning, I move into the office across the hall. "You coming?"

"I'm coming."

"Two of my favorite words," I say under my breath, just loud enough for her to hear.

Her sharp inhale and muffled laugh make my grin widen as I crouch to check the baseboards. I stand and run a hand along the edge of the doorframe, checking the latch before moving to the windows. Thorough. That's the key here, stay focused. Except focus is a hell of a lot harder with Raelynn standing across the room.

Jesus. That navy shirt hugs her just right, soft fabric stretching across her large chest in a way that's impossible to ignore. And those jeans? They're doing dangerous things to my concentration, clinging to her hips and ass. I drag my eyes away, clearing my throat. *Get it together, Reed.*

I check the outlets along the baseboard, anything to keep my mind and my damn hands busy.

"Raelynn."

She looks up from her phone where she's still typing notes. "Yeah?"

"Come here a sec."

She crosses the room, her steps quiet on the tile. When she stops beside me, I point to an outlet near the floor. "See this?"

She leans in slightly, her brows drawing together. "What about it?"

I step closer, close enough that my chest brushes her back as I bend slightly, reaching past her to point at the cracks in the cover plate. "The casing's loose here, and there's a tiny burn mark around the edge. It'll need to be replaced."

I feel her shift, not away, but subtly leaning back into me, like she's not even aware she's doing it. I swear I can feel the tiniest tremor in her shoulders.

"Okay." Her voice is softer now. "I'll put it on my list."

I straighten to full height again. "Good idea."

"What's next?" I ask, my voice lower now as she turns. We're standing face to face, and for a second, neither of us moves.

She tilts her chin up, her lips quirking with amusement. "You're the expert. You tell me."

I chuckle, shaking my head as my eyes sweep her face. "Careful, Sunshine. You keep looking at me like that, and I might start thinking you're impressed." My eyes lock with hers. "I do know what I'm doing…and I'm damn good at it."

She doesn't break eye contact. Then she steps back, slipping out from between me and the wall, her fingers brushing the doorframe as she walks toward the hall. At the door, she pauses and glances over her shoulder, a smile playing at her lips.

"Let's hope you're as good at inspections as you are at running your mouth," she says sweetly. "Otherwise, I might have to call someone else."

The words hit. I just blink, caught between surprise and an unfamiliar edge of jealousy. She's gone before I can come up with a comeback, her laugh soft and teasing as it drifts down the hall. I follow a step behind, eyes tracing the sway of her hips, heat curling low in my gut. *That smart mouth of hers, God, she doesn't even know.*

11

Caught in the Act (Almost)

Raelynn

This is getting intense. He makes me nervous, really nervous. But I'm not backing down. I saunter toward the bathroom. At the door, I pause and hold out my hand, gesturing for him to go ahead. My brain screams at me not to follow him into such a small space, not with the heat already building between us. But my body doesn't listen. I step inside just as he turns, his eyes locking with mine. It's bold, maybe reckless, but I hold his gaze anyway, a silent message. *I'm not backing down.*

He moves slowly, reaching past my shoulder. I don't budge, even when he leans in closer, his presence filling the small space. My back presses against the cool wall, every nerve in my body on high alert as his arm cages me in. My pulse pounds in my ears. I'm painfully aware of the heat rolling off his body. His eyes stay locked on mine, like he's waiting for me to flinch. His hand skims the wall, searching blindly until his fingers find the switch. He flicks it. Nothing. He leans inches closer; I can feel the warmth of his breath just under my ear. "You need a light bulb."

The tension snaps like a rubber band, and I burst out laughing, the sound surprising even me.

He straightens with a deep laugh, the sound rumbling low in his chest. "Put it on your list." He grins as he spins to check the rest of the bathroom.

I step into the doorway, giving him space, though my eyes can't help but follow him as he moves. *That was alarmingly hot. Play it cool, Raelynn.*

"Everything looks good in here." He turns back toward me, his gaze skims over me once, with intention. I know what he's doing, and as hard as I try, I can't stop heat running through me.

"I was thinking the same thing. But I'm not the professional." My eyes sweep over him taking him all in. Broad shoulders, strong hands, that backward hat doing criminal things to my self-control.

His eyes catch mine mid-scan. He tilts his head slightly, lips tugging into a wicked half-smile.

"Stop undressing me with your eyes, Raelynn."

My jaw drops. Heat burns my cheeks as my brain scrambles for a comeback, but I've got nothing. Because he's not wrong.

He steps past me with a low chuckle, leaving me standing there in the doorway like an idiot. My jaw snaps shut as I blink after him. *Oh, no! He does NOT get to have the last word. Not like that.*

I push off the doorframe and follow quickly behind him as he strides along the long wall in the main room, scanning the outlets like he didn't just toss a verbal grenade my way. "You know, I'll stop undressing you with my eyes, if you stop undressing me with yours."

He glances over his shoulder with that maddening smirk still in place. "Can you blame me?"

I open my mouth, but before the words can form, he stops abruptly and spins. I barely have time to react before I walk straight into him.

"Oof," I gasp, my face nearly colliding with him. I catch myself with my hands pressed to the hard plane of his chest, but I don't move.

His fingers glide under my chin, his thumb resting lightly as he tilts my face up to meet his gaze. We just stand there, the air charged and heavy. I can feel a burn low in my stomach as his eyes flick down to my lips. Instinctively, I bite my bottom lip between my teeth.

"Raelynn," he growls. His thumb brushes my lip and gently pulls it free.

He's so close. Too close.

But before either of us can move, the front door swings open with a sharp creak.

"Raelynn?" Judy's voice calls but then stops abruptly.

I stiffen, heat flooding my cheeks as Kinsley and Judy freeze in the doorway, wide-eyed.

Shit.

I shove Reed back, harder than I mean to, and he steps back with a flicker of surprise. My pulse is hammering so hard it feels like it might burst. My hands are still in the air like I'm caught red-handed, and I swear I can feel the blood drain straight from my face.

"No… no, it's not… it wasn't…" I stammer, my voice breaking as I turn towards them.

Next to me Reed snickers, and somehow that makes it a hundred times worse.

I drop my hands with a groan, shaking my head as I spin on him, whispering sharply, "You're not helping."

Judy's eyes soften as she steps fully into the room, breaking the heavy silence. "It's alright, honey." Her tone full of warmth like she's trying to soothe my frayed nerves. "No explanations needed. We didn't see a thing."

"There's nothing to see," I blurt out, my voice pitching higher as I flail for some kind of defense and fail miserably.

Kinsley glances between us, taking in the scene before slowly nodding. "Okay, okay," she says, drawing out the words like she's trying to convince herself. "I believe you."

Except I can tell by the look in her eyes…even she doesn't believe her own damn words.

I drop my head with a groan, completely giving up on defending myself. There's no salvaging this.

That's when Reed, finally, throws me a bone. "Where are the cleaning supplies you two have been gone two hours to get?" His voice cuts through the awkward air.

I turn to glance his way, ready to thank him for bailing me out. And this smug son of a bitch winks at me.

Throwing my hands in the air, I turn on my heel. "I'll help get the supplies out of the car." I'm desperate to put some space between me and this whole circus.

"I'll help, too," Reed says quickly, already moving before I can stop him.

At this point, I've got nothing left. I'm just riding the chaos out.

Fuck.

The four of us step out the door, and I freeze when Kinsley pops open her trunk.

"What did you buy?" My voice is full of shock as I take in the mountain of bags and boxes crammed inside. "And why is there a mini fridge back here?"

Kinsley shrugs. "Judy said it'd be nice to have while we're cleaning and painting. We had to drive out of town to get it."

Reed steps up, grabs the mini fridge like it weighs nothing and swings it over his shoulder. Then, because apparently he's not human, he hooks a few more bags in his free hand.

I quickly spin away. If I look too long, I know I'll start this whole thing back up, and I'm not sure I could play it cool a second time, not that I did the first time. I wait until Reed walks away before turning back to grab a few bags. Kinsley and I step inside with the rest, setting them down near the counter.

His voice is smooth like nothing happened. "Is there any more?"

I keep my response short and quick. "No."

"Good." He straightens, that maddeningly confident look. "I'm going to finish the inspection." His eyes lock on mine, and the corner of his lips curves into a smirk. "Care to join me?"

I can't with him, I think to myself, fighting the ridiculous heat surging up my neck for the hundredth time today.

"I'm sure you can finish this up on your own." I cross my arms and do my best to sound unaffected.

He tilts his head just slightly, like I've amused him. "Oh, I could," he says lazily. "But where's the fun in that?" He gestures toward the back with a little tilt of his chin. "C'mon, Sunshine."

"Fine," I huff, falling into step behind him.

Once we're in the room and out of sight of the others, I lean in and whisper sharply. "Stop it. You're making me look bad."

His eyes catch mine, a flicker of something unreadable in them before his mouth curves into that lazy, cocky grin. "Baby, you could never look bad."

"Oh my God, stop complimenting me. This is not the time." I scowl trying to convince him I'm serious. *But am I really?*

He steps closer, voice dropping low enough to send a little shiver racing down my spine. "Then give me a time, Raelynn."

That's it. I'm done. Shaking my head, I spin on my heel and march out of the room, leaving him standing there…laughing.

As I stomp back into the main room, Kinsley and Judy are busy unpacking bags in the middle of the floor, chatting like nothing's amiss. Reed saunters in a moment later, moving slow, smug as ever, as he finishes up his inspection. I kneel down, focusing hard on unpacking cleaning supplies, determined to ignore him. I try, God, I try, but I can't stop myself from sneaking a quick peek over my shoulder. He catches me. *Of course he does.*

When he finishes, he strolls over and stops in front of me. I'm already kicking myself. I look up and immediately know I've made a mistake. Here I am. On my knees. In front of him.

Before he can get a single word out, I jab a finger at him, heat rushing to my cheeks. "Don't you say a word."

"Didn't say a thing." He throws his hands up in faux defense, but that gleam in his eyes tells me he's thinking plenty. His lips curve. "That's an image I'm gonna hold on to all damn night."

I scramble to my feet. "Reed Davison, you're ridiculous!"

He chuckles darkly, straightening to full height, his hands slipping casually into his pockets.

"Not my fault you keep handing me the material," he says, voice rich with amusement.

"Go home, Reed." My hands are planted on my hips in my best attempt at looking unbothered.

Judy steps into the room, breaking whatever invisible tension is hanging in the air.

"I'm done here. I'll see you later, ladies."

"Okay, sweetheart. Do you work tomorrow?" Judy steps up to him and pats his arm.

"Yeah, the firehouse fundraiser's in a couple of days. We've got to get everything set up."

Judy taps her chin. "Hmm. Maybe I'll stop by and bring you lunch." She steps forward with her usual warmth and presses a kiss to his cheek. "Thanks for coming out, honey."

I swallow my pride as I force the words out. "Thanks for helping me."

His eyes flick to mine, his grin as maddening as ever. "Anytime."

Just like that, he's gone, leaving my stomach in knots and my brain screaming at me to not watch him walk out the door… but, of course, I do anyway.

Kinsley steps into the room, glancing around like she's mentally checking off a list. "Okay, what's next?"

"I think we can call it a day."

"We got a lot done today." Judy pats me on the back with agreement.

We gather our things and step out the door. I lock it behind us and pause for a moment, taking a step back to look at my soon-to-be salon. Pride swells in my chest, pushing away the exhaustion as I let the sight sink in. *This is really happening.*

We pile into the car and make the five-minute drive back to the cabin. The ride is quiet, and my thoughts are still spinning.

When Kinsley pulls into the drive and cuts the engine, I already know what's coming. I'm going to have to explain myself, in detail.

We all step out, stretching stiff muscles. Judy turns to me with that soft, glowing smile that always makes my heart swell. "I'm so proud of you, honey."

I blink fast, trying to hold back the sudden rush of emotion. "Thank you, Judy."

I pull her into a hug, and she squeezes me tight. Kinsley smiles and wraps her arms around both of us.

When Judy heads for her cabin, Kinsley and I walk in silence toward mine. The second the door shuts behind us, she spins on me, her eyes narrowing. "Alright." Her voice sharp with curiosity. "Tell. Me. Everything."

"There's nothing to tell, really," I say with a shrug, trying to sound casual even though my pulse still hasn't settled. "He flirted…like he did when we carved pumpkins. But that's all."

Kinsley gives me a look but glances at her watch and sighs. "I promised Miles I'd make him chicken parmesan for dinner."

I smile faintly. "We can talk about this later."

"Damn right we will." She smirks, but her voice softens as she steps closer. We hug at the door, and she squeezes me tightly. "I love you."

"I love you, too. And thanks for today."

"You're welcome."

Once she's gone, I close the door and lean against it for a second, letting the silence settle over me like a heavy blanket.

I make myself a quick sandwich in the kitchen, then grab my sketchbook and charcoal before collapsing onto the couch. Between bites, I flip to a fresh page and start sketching.

At first, it's the empty salon, the wide windows, the tiles, the blank walls that feel full of possibility. But as my hand moves, the lines shift. Shapes form. And before I even realize it, I'm sketching Reed. Him standing in the middle of the salon, ball cap turned backward, hands in his pockets.

I pause, staring at the image taking shape under my fingers. My stomach flips, heat blooming low as I drag the charcoal across the page. *Why am I drawing him? It's just because he was there so long today,* I tell myself. He did the inspection. And even though he flirted nonstop, he was helpful. *That's all this is.* But even as I tell myself that, my fingers keep moving, sketching the way the light might fall across his jaw, the faint smirk on his handsome face. And if I'm being honest with myself…it was nice. Nice having someone flirt with me, to feel wanted, even if he was just joking around.

12

Stay Out of My Head

Reed

I wake up tired and already in a mood, the kind that clings no matter how much coffee I throw at it. Should've gone to bed earlier, but instead, I'd stayed up staring at the ceiling, running circles in my head about Raelynn.

"Flirting means nothing. Just a little fun. That's all it is." I mutter the words as I set Fifi's bowl down and let her out into the yard. She sprints across the grass. I envy her. She doesn't overthink. She just runs.

By the time I'm showered, dressed and halfway through my first coffee, I'm telling myself today will be different. No distractions. No thoughts of her.

The firehouse lot is already packed when I pull in. The whole crew's here, trucks lined up like they're on parade. Some guys are unloading tables and tents from the rigs while others wrangle boxes of supplies inside.

Tommy falls in step beside me. "Looks like we're late."

"Or everyone else is just too eager."

Inside, Chief Sanford's standing front and center, clipboard in hand, calling out assignments like we're heading into battle.

"Listen up! Tomorrow's fundraiser is gonna be our biggest yet, so let's make sure this place looks sharp. Five of you will handle runs if any calls come in; the rest are setting up."

He starts rattling off names and jobs. "Chase and Darren, dunk tank. Eric and Shane, you're on cider and donuts. Nolan and Pete, ring toss game."

Tommy nudges me. "Bet you five bucks we get stuck with garbage duty."

"Wouldn't be the worst thing."

"Reed, Tommy," the chief's voice cuts in. "You two are giving tours. Take the small groups, answer questions and keep it interesting. Sell the place a little."

Tommy grins. "Tours. That's practically VIP duty."

I grunt, unamused.

"Oh, and Reed," the chief adds with a pointed look. "You remember you're the prize for the sealed auction. Keep that charm turned on."

"Now…the moment you've all been waiting for." The chief pauses for dramatic effect, his eyes scanning the room. "The kissing booth."

That gets everyone's attention. Half the room perks up like dogs hearing a can opener.

"The lucky gentlemen are…" He draws it out on purpose. "Leo, Jose, Mason and Carter. You're it."

The room erupts into cheers and laughter. Leo pumps a fist in the air like he's just been drafted into the NFL.

"Hell yeah!" Jose grins wide. "Told you this face was money."

"I'm not even mad about it," Carter says, flashing a cocky smile.

Mason leans back in his chair, arms crossed and smirks. "Ladies of Cranberry Ridge better bring cash."

"Settle down, Casanovas," Chief Sanford says dryly, though there's a faint hint of amusement in his tone. "Remember, it's for charity. Keep it clean-ish."

Everyone splits into groups and starts setting everything up. Tommy and I are cleaning the inside of the station for the tours when I look up and see Miles walking in through the open bay door.

"What the hell are you doing here?" I say flatly.

"What, no warm welcome?"

I grunt, going back to wiping down a counter. "Didn't expect to see you here, that's all."

He saunters closer. "You look like shit, by the way. Rough night?"

"Just tired."

"Damn. You're crankier than usual. That bad, huh?"

"Nothing's bad," I snap.

Miles tilts his head, eyes narrowing slightly. "Does this have something to do with Raelynn?"

"Why would it?" I shoot back, too fast.

Miles' smirk widens. "Because Kinsley saw you two standing pretty damn close yesterday."

"It was nothing. I was doing an inspection." I keep my tone even.

Miles gives me a look, all amusement and no belief. "And does this inspection involve you standing chest-to-chest with her?"

I smirk. "So what? I flirted. Big deal. I flirt with plenty of women, Miles. Don't make it sound like I'm picking out curtains."

Miles chuckles, shaking his head. "Well, for the record, Kinsley said if you hurt her friend, she'll bury you in the cornfield behind the farmhouse."

That actually makes me laugh. "She said that?"

"Word for word."

"Tell her she's adorable. But she doesn't need to worry." I lean back on my heels, smirk locked in place. "Raelynn's a grown woman, and I'm not breaking any hearts here. I know what I'm doing."

Miles raises his hands. "Don't say I didn't warn you."

"Noted."

Miles lowers his hands and gives me a look that's half amused, half knowing. "Alright, man. I'll see you tomorrow."

"Yeah, See you then."

"Try not to scare off too many people with that mood."

I let out a short laugh. "No promises."

He smirks over his shoulder before disappearing through the open bay door.

The moment he's gone, I blow out a breath and drag a hand down my face. I need to get my shit together. She's in my head way too much for my own good. That laugh, those big brown eyes, the way she looked up at me yesterday like she wasn't sure whether to slap me or...*Damn it.* I need to stay away. At least enough to get her out of my system. I grab the rag again and go back to wiping down the counter, trying to scrub away more than just the grime. *Stay busy. Don't think about her. Don't...*

The sound of squeaky shoes on the freshly cleaned floor makes me glance up and see Judy walking in the door. I let out a low groan. *You've got to be kidding me. Not another interrogation.*

But I paste on a smile as she strolls in, her tote bag swinging on her arm.

"Hi, honey," Her eyes are already sparkling. "I brought you lunch. Are you hungry?"

"Starving," I toss the rag on the counter and lean in to peek into her bag. "What've you got?"

She laughs, holding it out of my reach. "I made your favorite. Beef stew."

"That sounds perfect right now." I grin and lean down to press a kiss to her cheek.

"And I brought you cornbread."

"You spoil me, you know that?"

"I know." She wraps her arm through mine as we walk toward the break room.

The room is blissfully empty. I pull out her chair, grab two spoons from the drawer before sitting across from her. We eat in easy silence for a few minutes, the smell of her stew filling the air. It's rich, hearty and exactly what I needed after the morning I've had.

Halfway through my bowl, I lean back and glance at her. "You know…I was just messing with Raelynn, right? There's nothing going on. She wasn't wrong yesterday. It really wasn't anything."

Judy doesn't even blink. She waves her hand brushing away the thought. "Oh, I know, honey. You enjoy the single life. There's nothing wrong with that."

"Exactly." I point my spoon at her with a grin. "See? You get it."

"Of course I do. Eat your stew before it gets cold." Judy takes a sip of her water. "So, did the chief decide who's the prize for the sealed auction tomorrow?"

"Yeah," I say with a small laugh. "That'd be me."

Her lips curve into smile. "Well, I suppose I'll have to put in a bid then. How could I pass up a date with one of my favorite boys?"

I grin. "Hope you win. At least then I know I'll be eating with a beautiful lady."

Judy chuckles, swatting my arm as she stands. "Well, whoever wins that bid tomorrow is going to be one lucky girl."

I shake my head with a soft laugh. "Guess that's up for debate, but I'll try not to disappoint."

"I better get going. Still have a few things to do before tomorrow."

I give her a quick hug. "See you tomorrow."

"See you tomorrow, honey," she says, smiling as she heads for the door.

I spend the next hour helping Tommy stack chairs along the wall and hauling extra tables out of storage for the cider stand and donut table. After that, I check over the outdoor setup, making sure the ring toss station isn't missing any pieces and the banner for the fundraiser is secured tight across the bay doors. By the time everything's in place, the station's quiet again. Most of the crew has already clocked out for the day.

I head for my locker in the back and Jose's already there, tossing his hoodie into his duffel. "Hey, I thought I saw Judy a few hours ago. Did she happen to have anyone with her?"

I shake my head as I spin my combination. "No. Why?"

He shrugs. "Just wondering, that's all. See ya tomorrow, Reed."

"Later." I watch him sling his bag over his shoulder and head out.

I grab my keys and shut the locker, but the question sticks in my head. Who the hell was he expecting to see with Judy? Then it hits me. Raelynn.

I head out to my truck, the thought gnawing at the edge of my mind. *So what? What do I care if he's got his eye on her? She's not mine.* I grip the steering wheel tight as I start the engine. Doesn't matter. It's none of my business.

By the time I pull into the driveway, my knuckles ache. The house is dark except for the porch light, and Fifi's already waiting at the window like she's been on watch all day.

I step inside and she bolts to me. "Hey, trouble." I crouch and scoop her up. "You're the only girl I need," I tell her with a dry laugh. "Let's go outside." I set her down in the yard and watch as she darts off. The cool night air does nothing to clear my head.

A few minutes later, I head for the garage, flipping on the light. The faint hum of the bulb fills the space as I stalk toward the weight rack, stacking plates onto the bar with a loud clang. I don't even bother warming up. My muscles are already coiled tight, my blood running hot. Jose. His easy grin. That casual tone. And her. Soft brown eyes, flushed cheeks, lips parted in that shy smile she doesn't even know drives me crazy. The way she bites her bottom lip. Now I can't stop picturing her, laughing at something Jose says, tilting her head up as he leans down, his hands sliding around her waist like he's got the right. *He does, because I don't care.*

I grip the bar and push it off the rack, muscles straining as I press it upward. Again. And again. The image won't leave my head. Jose's mouth on hers. Her fingers curled in his shirt. That soft sound she made when she clung to me on the bike except this time it's for him. "Fuck!"

I slam the bar back into place, chest heaving. Sweat already beads at my temples, running in hot trails down my neck and across my shoulders. I drop to the floor for push-ups, driving down hard, then pulling myself back up with sharp, controlled precision. Each movement burns, but it's not enough.

I crank out another set, arms shaking, veins bulging as I push through the burn. Sweat drips down my chest, soaking my shirt until it clings. With a grunt, I drop the bar into place and yank off my hoodie, tossing it aside. Heat rolls off my bare skin, but it doesn't burn out the thoughts. The image of someone else, anyone else, getting her? It lights me up all over again. I shove the bar up with a guttural sound, jaw tight enough to crack. *She's not mine.* The weights slam back onto the rack. I sit up, forearms on my knees, chest heaving.

"I DON'T CARE!" I shout into the empty garage.

The sound makes Fifi jump, her tiny body stiffening as she stares at me from where she's curled up in the corner.

"Shit," I mutter, dragging both hands over my face. "It's okay, girl." I crouch down, scooping her up. "You're fine. I didn't mean to scare you."

She licks my jaw, her little tail wags hesitantly. I press a kiss to her head and carry her inside, flicking off the garage light on the way.

Inside, I set her on her bed and head straight for the shower. The hot water hits my shoulders like a sledgehammer, as I brace my palms against the tile. *I wonder what she's doing right now?*

"Damn it! I'm going to fucking bed!"

13

Raising Funds and Heart Rates

Raelynn

I swipe on a layer of ChapStick and press my lips together, leaning closer to the mirror. Cream sweater, dark jeans, brown boots that click just right on pavement. My hair's pulled back with a claw clip, the kind I always reach for when I need something quick but decent. Short gold hoops, light makeup, thin tan jacket. Clean. Polished. Like I tried, but not too hard.

Except I did try. I've never second-guessed an outfit this much in my life. But Cranberry Ridge is my home now, the town where I'm opening a salon. A place where word spreads fast and people remember what you wore, how you looked, who you talked to. And sure, I want to make a good impression. But if I'm being honest, I also want to look good for Reed. Even though he's already seen me with full-blown helmet hair. And not the bouncy, voluminous kind, the tragic kind.

Still, I don't want to give him another reason to flirt or poke at me. I already know how fast he can turn a smirk into a full-body blush. *I shouldn't like it. I don't like it…I kind of like it.*

I step outside and breathe in the crisp morning air. The sun's out, but it's doing absolutely nothing to take the edge off the cold. Judy and Naya are already out on the porch, bundled up in their coats and rocking slowly in the chairs.

Naya glances over and grins. "Any colder and I'm gonna need a fireman to sit on."

Judy snorts. "Lord help us."

All three of our heads turn when Kinsley's SUV pulls into the drive. She hops out like a woman on a mission, a drink carrier balanced in one hand. "Hot chocolate for the ladies," she calls, lifting it like a trophy.

"My hero." Naya snatches one before Kinsley can even finish passing them out.

Judy claps her hands once and pushes up from her rocker. "Alright, girls. Let's go support the kids."

We all pile into Judy's car, Kinsley riding shotgun, me and Naya in the back with our hot chocolates in hand.

Naya turns to me as we pull out of the driveway. "By the way, congrats on locking down the building."

"Thanks. Mel and I spent all day yesterday on video chat picking out equipment and shelving units. Pretty sure we maxed out my brain and maybe my credit card."

"I can't wait to see Mel again." Judy looks in the rearview mirror at us.

"Me too," Kinsley says. "She's smart, loyal and pretty much good at everything."

"I'll be there next week to help clean. I'm bringing donuts for the breakfast and whiskey for lunch." Naya holds up her cup.

Kinsley's head snaps around. "Those are my favorite."

Naya nudges me. "I'm so excited a salon's finally opening up here. I better be your first customer."

As we roll into town, Judy flicks on her blinker. "I've got VIP parking. I'm allowed to park behind the station with the crew."

Kinsley and Naya say it in unison. "Of course you do."

We all laugh as Judy turns into the firehouse drive. A firefighter standing near the entrance gives her a wave and moves the rope blocking off the lot, clearly recognizing her.

We step out and walk around the side of the building to where all the excitement is. The driveway in front of the station is buzzing, music playing, the smell of popcorn in the air, and kids darting between booths with painted faces and sticky fingers. Some are butterflies, some are superheroes, all of them hyped up on sugar and freedom, donuts in hand.

Kinsley scans the scene and nudges Naya. "Did you supply all the donuts?"

Naya grins. "Yeah. I made them and dropped them off last night, about thirty dozen. But I had help from my mom."

Judy beams at her and pats her shoulder. "You're such a good girl."

Naya rolls her eyes, but she's clearly pleased.

Kinsley steps closer to me. "Where should we start?"

"The food truck."

Kinsley raises her cup. "Now you're speaking my language."

We head toward the food truck, the smell of fried batter growing stronger with every step. The line's short, and the handwritten chalkboard menu promises corn dogs, popcorn and something called "firehouse chili."

Kinsley squints at the menu and points. "Skip the chili. I've had it, it'll make your nose bleed."

"I'm getting a corn dog and popcorn."

"Same."

"Make that three," Naya says, eyeing the golden corn dogs through the window. "I skipped breakfast for this."

As we get in line, Judy slows her steps.

"I'll catch up with you girls in a minute." She waves us ahead. "I ate before I left."

She slips into the crowd, gone before any of us can say a word.

We eat standing around a tall table, chatting between bites about the crowd and what to do next.

"I say ring toss next," Kinsley says, brushing crumbs off her sweater.

Naya grins. "Okay, but I'm calling donuts after that."

I nod. "Yes" I point a knowing finger at her.

As we finish up, Judy reappears with a big smile. "You girls ready?"

Together, we walk toward the line for the ring toss, weaving through the crowd.

Naya glances around. "Where's Miles?"

Kinsley shrugs. "He's around here somewhere with Luke and Dylan."

Judy chimes in, not missing a beat. "I saw them in the long line for the dunk tank."

As we reach the back of the line, there's a table with a large wooden box marked with a handwritten sign that reads: 'Donations.' There's a narrow slit in the top, and as we step into line, each of us drops in some cash without a word.

When we finally reach the front, Judy grins and waves. "Hello, Nolan. Hey there, Pete."

Both guys light up when they see her, each leaning in for a hug like she's the mayor of the town.

"Alright, ladies." Nolan rubs his hands together. "It's simple. Land three rings on a bottle and win a prize."

We each take a turn, throwing with various levels of confidence and technique. And the three of us walk away with absolutely nothing, cracking up over how much we suck.

"I think I hit a guy in the foot." Naya's still laughing as we walk away. "That counts for something, right?"

"Well, at least you hit something. Kinsley didn't even hit a bottle." I toss my arm around her shoulder. "We might not have aim, but we've got spirit."

"Spirit doesn't win stuffed animals."

Judy snickers, her arms full of stuffed animals.

We round the corner to the next booth. This one smells like cinnamon and sugar. A folding table is set up beside a stack of hay bales with baskets of donuts and a cooler of cider behind it. Another wooden donation box sits front and center.

I inhale and smile. "Now this is the prize I came for."

We do the same as before, drop a few bills into the donation box and each grab a donut and a cup of cider. The cinnamon sugar sticks to my fingers, and the cider's warm enough to thaw my face. As we stand and eat, Judy stops every kid passing by and hands out all her stuffed animals until she left empty handed.

As we walk toward a small tent set off to the side, I slow down, eyeing the crowd inside. It's mostly women. "What's this?" I squint toward the sign taped to a folding table.

Judy strolls up beside me like she's been waiting for the question. "Sealed bid auction, you fill out a piece of paper with your contact info and the amount you're bidding. Seal it in an envelope and drop it in the box. They go through them later and find the highest bidder."

"What are we bidding on?"

Judy smiles sweetly. "Oh, a date with a fireman."

Kinsley immediately raises her hands and steps back. "I'm out. Miles would murder someone."

"Yeah, I don't think I want to do this. How about we just slip some cash in and skip the rest?"

"Done," Naya says, already reaching for her wallet.

But Judy? Judy takes her time. She leans over the table, carefully filling out the card with a pen she brought from her purse. Then she slips her envelope into the box with a satisfied little smile. "Let's hope I win. All these boys are so nice."

We step out of the tent and head toward the larger one across the lot. The line is wrapped around the side, nearly to the street. Judy glances at it and then at us. "I need to use the bathroom. I'll be right back."

We take our place at the end of the line, bundled in our jackets and holding our cider cups.

"What's this line for?" Naya asks, peering ahead.

Kinsley and I both shrug. "No idea. Judy's the expert here."

"Well, whatever it is, it sounds like fun in there."

We hear the laughter, cheers and clapping echo from inside the tent. We finally reach the doorway, still completely clueless, but we drop our money in the donation box anyway. Judy finally makes it back just as we step through the tent flap.

"What is this?"

The woman in front of us turns around, grinning. "It's the Kiss a Fireman booth." Her smile spreads like she's been waiting all day for this.

"Yeah…I'll just watch." Kinsley starts backing up a step.

"Come on, Raelynn," Naya says, nudging me with a wicked smile. "Let's show these men a good time."

I open my mouth to protest, but before I can get a word out, Judy and Kinsley both start cheering for me. Loudly. Like, draw-a-crowd loudly.

I roll my eyes, already laughing. "Fine. I'll do it."

They keep clapping like I just volunteered as tribute. I laugh and step up on my toes to see who's behind the booth. One of the guys looks vaguely familiar, broad shoulders, messy dark hair and an easy smile. Wait. I remember him. He was one of the firemen who came by Judy's place the other day to pick up the carved pumpkins. I think his name is Jose. *He's cute enough,* I think to myself, adjusting my jacket like that'll somehow make me more prepared.

"I should've brought mints." Naya checks her pockets. "And maybe a travel toothbrush."

"Chapstick check." I reapply quickly.

"Thank God none of you ate onion rings today." Kinsley grins.

The line shifts forward, and Judy casually digs into her purse. "I have mints." She holds them out like a magician revealing a trick.

We each take one, and she pops one in for herself. The three of us just stare at her.

"Wait." I narrow my eyes. "Did you put in money, too?"

"Yes." Judy winks. "It's for the kids."

We all burst out laughing. I turn as the line moves again and freeze. He's standing off to the side, just behind the booth, arms crossed over his chest like he's supervising the whole operation. Reed.

He's wearing turnout pants with heavy black boots and red suspenders slung loose over a fitted navy T-shirt that reads: 'Cranberry Ridge Fire Department' across the front. He hasn't seen me yet, and I don't say anything. I just stare, caught somewhere between how do I get out of this and why does he have to look that good?

I turn back around quickly, face warm, and lean toward Judy. "Do you have another mint?"

She hands one over, and I mumble my thanks, just as the line shifts again.

Suddenly, it's really hot in here. I fan my face and mutter, "Thank God for deodorant."

Naya laughs. "Why are you so nervous? It's just a kiss."

Kinsley glances over my shoulder, and her mouth drops open.

My eyes lock with hers instantly. "What?"

Naya looks between us. "What's going on?"

Kinsley starts laughing. "It's Reed."

"So what?" Naya shrugs. "He's cute. And it's just a little peck."

"You're right." I stand a little taller. "It's just a peck."

He might just be watching.

I turn back to look…and sure enough, he sees me. A small smile plays at the corner of his mouth.

Or maybe he's not.

14

Kissed Her Like No One Was Watching

Reed

It's barely afternoon, and Tommy and I are already on our twentieth tour. We've been switching off to keep the line short, one of us walks the group, the other stays back helping kids try on gear and making sure nobody wanders off or licks something they shouldn't.

Tommy comes around the corner with the latest crew, a blur of sugar-high kids in plastic fire hats. "You're up."

I nod and motion to the next group of six. "Alright, let's head in."

We move through the usual loop, past the trucks, into the breakroom, down the hall where the lockers line both walls and into the bunk room. Just long enough to make it interesting, short enough to keep things moving. Back in the bay, the kids light up when they see the gear table and the open truck door.

One of them tugs on my sleeve. "Do you get to drive the firetruck?"

"Yeah, when it's my turn and nobody beats me to the keys."

He stares up at the cab like it's a rocket ship. "That's so cool."

I give the kid a high five, and his group heads out through the bay door, chattering and waving as they go. I turn back, expecting another set already lined up, but for the first time all day, we're down to one group. Just one. Progress. I'm about to call them forward when Judy pokes her head into the bay, smiling and holding something in her hands.

"Hi, sweetheart. Sorry to bother you, but the kissing booth sign just gave out on us. It tore clean down the middle." She holds it up, and sure enough, the thing's split like someone got a little too enthusiastic.

I take it from her. "Yeah, I can fix it."

Turning to the waiting group of kids, I nod toward Tommy across the bay. "I'll be right back. Tommy'll get you started."

Then I follow Judy toward the office, sign in hand, already hunting for duct tape in my head. In the office, I lay the torn sign flat on the table and start smoothing the edges. It's a clean tear, right down the middle. I open the drawer, find a roll of duct tape and start flipping the sign over to patch the back.

"What are you doing in the kissing booth anyway?"

"Oh, the girls and I thought it would be fun. You know, spice things up a little."

I nod, focused on lining up the edges, trying not to make it obvious when I glance up. "Girls?"

"Oh yes, Naya, Kinsley."

Don't say it. Don't say it.

"…and Raelynn."

My hand freezes for half a second, the strip of tape sticking halfway to the table. I keep taping, but slower now. *She can kiss whoever she wants. What do I care?* Still, my jaw ticks as I smooth the last piece across the back of the sign.

"So," I say, voice a little too even, "how'd it go?"

"Oh, we're still in line," Judy says, like it's no big deal. "It was wrapped around the tent, but I'm sure by now the girls are already inside."

I press the tape down hard. *It's just a kiss. For charity. No big deal.* That's what I keep telling myself, anyway. I stare down at the sign, jaw tight. I don't care. *I don't.* Except my grip on the edge of the sign says otherwise when I remember Jose's in the booth.

I clear my throat and straighten up. "I'll take this back for you."

She pauses, then shrugs. "Alright, if you're sure."

"Yeah," I grab the sign and step around the desk. "Go join the girls. Have a good time."

Judy flashes me a grin as she heads for the door. "Okay, wish me luck." She practically skips out, humming to herself like this is the highlight of her day.

"See you later." I don't wait a minute longer. I've got a sign to deliver and absolutely no reason to care what's happening in that tent. None at all.

I step into the bay and catch Tommy's eye. "I'll be right back."

He nods, already waving the next group forward. "All good."

I make my way across the lot, stepping around hay bales and weaving through groups of women still lined up outside the tent. Judy wasn't lying, there's a lot of them. The line wraps halfway around the side, everyone bundled up and buzzing with energy.

When I reach the entrance, the women closest to the front all turn to look at me. It's like someone hit pause on the whole scene. They part like the Red Sea, eyes wide and hopeful, watching every step I take as I reattach the torn sign.

One bold woman leans in, smiling. "Are you working the booth?"

Every woman near the entrance perks up, waiting for an answer.

I chuckle, shaking my head. "No, ma'am. Just fixing the sign."

A collective groan ripples through the group as I step away.

And because I can't help myself, I round the side of the tent and slip in through the back entrance, behind the booth. I linger in the corner, out of sight, eyes scanning the crowd.

Then I see her. She's laughing with her friends, head thrown back, completely at ease, beautiful and carefree. I step back, staying in the corner, not wanting to draw attention to myself.

The booth is chaos in the way only small-town fundraisers can be. Four guys are working it, two I know too well. They're making spectacles of themselves, playing it up for every squeal and laugh they get. Some kisses land on the cheek, but most? Right on the lips. I watch them take turns, one after another, puckering up and quietly calling dibs like it's a game.

My jaw clenches. I tell myself to do nothing. Just stand here. Just watch. That's it.

The line moves at a steady pace, laughter and clapping filling the tent, and I know Raelynn's getting closer. I glance up to check and our eyes lock. A flush of pink rises in her cheeks, spreading fast, and she turns away.

The girls finally step up to the front, and I stay where I am, arms crossed. Close enough to see, far enough to pretend I'm just here for booth maintenance.

Naya steps up first, fearless as ever. Zero hesitation. Kinsley backs away, making it clear she's not in line, cheering the girls on from the sidelines. Raelynn stands just behind Naya, trying to play it cool, but I can see she's flustered. She shifts her weight, presses her lips together, eyes darting everywhere but forward. Judy's at the end of the line, casually chatting with the woman behind her like this is just another day at the market.

The guys in the booth start bickering over who gets to kiss Naya, voices overlapping like it's a damn auction. Before any of them can settle it, Mason steps forward. And Naya? She grabs him by the front of his shirt and kisses him hard. No warning. The crowd erupts. She pulls back with a wink. "Thanks." Mason stumbles back, his face the color of a tomato, looking like he forgot how legs work.

Raelynn steps up next, and now the booth is down one guy, Mason still recovering somewhere off to the side. The three left standing start calling dibs before she even reaches the table.

Before I can stop myself, I step forward. "Don't bother, guys. I got this one."

They start to protest, but I'm not listening. My eyes are locked on Raelynn. She stiffens slightly as I approach, her gaze flicking to mine. I watch her swallow.

"Are you afraid, Sunshine?" I ask, voice low, lips showing the barest hint of a smile.

"No. I'm not afraid," she says, steady as ever.

I step closer and lean down, my eyes locked on hers. She lifts her chin, just a little.

"How about now?" I whisper.

The entire tent goes still, silent, waiting for the show.

She blinks a few times. "No," she says again, but softer this time.

I reach up slowly, cupping her face, letting my fingers brush along her jaw. Her breathing picks up, and I swear you could hear a pin drop in here.

My eyes drift down to her full, pink lips. I lean in, just enough. "Are you sure?"

Her breath catches. "Yes."

I close the space between us and press my lips to hers, soft, slow. Testing the waters. Giving her a way out if she wants it. She doesn't take it.

I part my lips first, brushing them against hers with a quiet exhale. An invitation. She lingers for a second, and then her lips part in return, just enough. That's all it takes. My tongue grazes the seam of her mouth, gentle, teasing, and she opens to me. The kiss deepens. It's not rushed. It's not wild. It's slow and hot. She leans in closer, her fingers curling into the front of my shirt, and I slide my hand to the back of her neck, holding her there. The crowd erupts in the background, hooting, clapping, cheering, but it barely registers. Because right now, all I can feel is her. The softness of her mouth. The way she moves against me. The way she tastes like heat and mint. Everything else fades. Just her lips. Just this moment. And damn if I don't want more. Which is exactly why I force myself to slowly pull away.

Raelynn's eyes flutter open, dazed and dark. She drags her tongue across her top lip like she's trying to chase the taste of me, and then she takes a slow step back.

I straighten, the spell breaking just enough for reality to crash back in. That's when I hear it, some woman in the crowd blurting out, "Can I be next?" followed by another laughing, "I'll pay double if it comes with that."

I glance toward the booth, jaw tightening, and without thinking, I reach down and grab Raelynn's hand. Her fingers slip into mine. I don't say a word. I just walk away quickly, pulling her out of the tent with me, away from the noise, the eyes, the commentary. Because I need air not an audience.

I don't stop until we're around the side of the tent, tucked between two trailers where no one's watching. I let go of her hand, immediately regretting it, but I need a second. *That was stupid. Bold, reckless, unplanned. And I liked it way too much.*

My pulse is still racing, and the taste of her is still on my lips. I shouldn't want more. And now I've got to find a way to play this off. I glance over at her, trying to get my damn expression under control. "You think we put on a good enough show?" My voice is casual. Cool. Almost smug. It's a complete lie. But I run with it.

Raelynn lifts a brow, arms crossing as she leans back against the side of the trailer. "Yeah, we sold it."

"For the kids," I add, matching her tone.

She smirks. "Obviously."

We both seem to agree it meant nothing. It was just a kiss. But my pulse is still thudding in my ears, and I can still feel the way she melted into me. I say nothing. Just shove my hands in my pockets and pretend I believe it, too.

Raelynn jerks her thumb over her shoulder. "I better catch up with the girls. I'm sure they'll have plenty to say." She turns to go, tossing me one last look. "Have fun at the kissing booth."

And because I can't keep my damn mouth shut, I call after her, "I wasn't assigned to the booth."

Fuck…Why did I say that? She's already walking away, but I see the corner of her mouth lift. I turn the opposite direction before I say something even dumber. I shove my hands deeper into my pockets, willing the memory to fade, but it doesn't. Not even close. It plays on loop in my head the whole walk across the lot. By the time I step into the bay, I've almost convinced myself it wasn't a big deal.

There's no one in line, and Tommy is sitting near the door waiting for more kids to show up. My phone buzzes in my pocket. I answer without looking.

"Yeah?"

Luke's voice is as dry as ever. "How'd the kiss go?"

I freeze, one boot halfway off the ground. "What?"

"You and Raelynn."

"How the hell do you know about that?" My phone dings. I pull it away from my ear and check the screen.

Cranberry Ridge Community Board: Kissing Booth Fundraiser Highlight of the Day!

And right there, front and center, a photo of me kissing Raelynn. Hands in her hair. Her fingers in my shirt. Lips locked. Full-on moment.

"It was for charity. You know. The kids."

"Sure."

"I'm serious. I was fixing the sign and I just…look, it happened."

"Mmhmm."

"Why is that even up there?"

"Someone in line took it. Posted it with the caption 'Cranberry Ridge's Finest.'"

I drag a hand down my face. "Can you take it down?"

"I could."

"Luke."

"But I'm not." He laughs.

I blow out a breath, half a laugh, half a groan. "You're an asshole."

He doesn't deny it. "We're over by the dunk tanks. You should head this way."

"I gotta make sure everything's still running smooth here first."

We hang up and I slip my phone into my back pocket, glancing toward the bay doors. From this angle, I can still see the edge of the tent. Still feel the heat of her mouth on mine. I exhale, shake it off, and head back to check on Tommy.

"You busy?"

He looks up from the gear table and shakes his head. "Just had the one group after you left."

"Cool. Well, since it's quiet, I think I'll head over to the dunk tanks. You care?"

"Not at all." He leans back, props his feet on the opposite chair like he's settling in for a vacation.

"Alright. Call me if you do get busy."

He waves me off, already pulling out his phone. "Will do."

I step out and make my way across the lot. I almost turn back around when I see her. Raelynn, standing with the girls, watching the guys, all crowded around the dunk tanks. Judy spots me instantly and starts waving me over. *Great.* Now I can't back out without looking like a complete chicken shit. All because I kissed her. Once. For charity.

"Did you come to work the dunk tank?"

"Nah, just came to check on things."

I step up beside Luke. He's already chuckling. "They just got here," he says under his breath.

"You could've warned me."

He chuckles. "And miss this?"

I jab him in the arm and turn back around. *It's fine. I've run into burning buildings. This is nothing. Have fun with it. Easy enough, right?*

15

Too Smug to Stay Dry

Raelynn

I step around the corner of the tent, still trying to level my heart rate. His words echo in my head. *"I wasn't assigned to the booth."* Then why was he there? Did he show up just to get a rise out of me? To mess with my head? Because if that kiss was just a joke to him, he's a hell of an actor.

The way his lips moved against mine, firm, unhurried, just rough enough to make my knees go soft. The way he took his time, like he wanted to make damn sure I wouldn't forget it. Spoiler alert…I won't. It wasn't some quick, showy peck. It was heated. Intentional. And hands down the hottest kiss I've ever had. Maybe it was my nerves that made it feel so intense. Or the fact that there were dozens of people around, and he kissed me like none of them existed.

I kissed him back. Worse…I wanted to. And now I have to walk up to the girls and pretend it didn't matter. They're going to be relentless. I already know it. They'll want the story, the details, the play-by-play. I'll have to laugh it off. Brush it aside. Say it was for the fundraiser. That it didn't mean anything.

Naya spots me first. "Girl…that was hot!"

"That was for charity," I blurt, hoping to cut it off before it starts.

Kinsley's hand settles on my shoulder, soft, supportive, and absolutely not letting me off the hook.

"Really," I say quickly, taking a step back. "It was just for show."

And thank God for Judy. She smiles, completely unfazed. "It was so nice of you to put on a show for a good cause."

Mercifully, the girls let it go. Kinsley glances toward the dunk tanks. "Let's go meet up with the guys."

"That's a great idea." Anything to distract them.

When we reach the dunk tank, the firefighter inside is still bone dry, clearly loving every second of it. He's tossing out insults like candy, trying to rile people up just enough to miss.

"Wow. I almost felt a breeze. Almost."

"You sure you're not aiming for the moon?"

"Do you even know where the target is, or should I draw you a map?"

Dylan and Miles are standing off to the side, deep in conversation about strategy like this is the World Series and not a dunk tank fundraiser.

I'm mid-eye-roll when I catch movement. Judy is waving someone over with that familiar bright smile. I turn automatically, then immediately turn back. My pulse kicks up when I see Reed walk up and stop next to Luke.

And because I can't help myself, I glance over at him. Hands in his pockets, watching the guy in line throw and miss, like nothing happened. Like he didn't just kiss me ten minutes ago. I shove it all down. No more overthinking. No more squirming. If he can act like nothing happened, so can I.

The guy in front of us misses all three shots, each one farther off than the last. The firefighter lounging in the tank sits up straighter, grinning as he gestures toward the table of balls.

"Okay, ladies, step right up. You get three chances to make me swim."

Kinsley bounces forward like she's heading into a dance-off. Miles trails behind her, giving her tips like he's some kind of dunk tank expert.

"Look at those little arms," the guy in the tank calls out. "No way she's hitting anything but air."

Kinsley rolls her eyes, fires off her first throw and misses by a mile. The next two aren't much better. We cheer like she knocked him straight into the water anyway. Naya steps up next, calm and focused. She narrows her eyes like she's lining up a sniper shot, but her throws are just wide. And then it's my turn.

Reed steps up beside me, eyes on the tank, voice just loud enough to carry. "Don't worry, man, she'll miss. She's still a little shaken from that kiss earlier."

I can't believe he just said that! I turn slowly, facing him head-on, ball still in hand. "If you're so sure I'll miss, you get in the tank."

That smug grin twitches.

The people around us go quiet for half a second, then there's a ripple of laughter and a few "ooohs" from the crowd.

"Aw, you afraid to get your hair wet, Hotshot?"

He doesn't flinch. "Not worried."

Then he steps around the table, casually pulling his shirt over his head like this is just part of the show. He walks toward the tank, boots thudding on the wooden platform. He kicks them off one by one, then peels off his turnout pants, revealing worn jeans underneath. The firefighter in the tank grins, climbing out like he's thrilled to be off the hook. "All yours, man."

Reed doesn't say anything. Just climbs up, sits back on the seat, and rests his arms on the rails. "Whenever you're ready," he calls down, easy and smug. "Try not to choke."

The girls cheer behind me, clapping and laughing, fully invested.

"Come on, Rae!"

"Sink him!"

I square up, aim and let the first ball fly. It misses, just wide.

Reed chuckles from above, leaning forward with that cocky grin. "Was that supposed to scare me, Sunshine? Because I've seen toddlers throw harder."

I shake my head, reaching for the next ball. "That was just a warm-up."

I throw. The ball smacks the target dead-on.

"Shit…" That's all Reed gets out before the seat drops and he vanishes with a massive splash.

The girls lose it, jumping up and down, screaming. The guys are doubled over, laughing as Reed surfaces, hair plastered to his forehead, blinking water out of his eyes, surprised. And from the way he looks at me, maybe a little impressed.

I smile, toss the last ball back onto the table. And because I can't help myself, I call out to him. "Clearly that kiss wasn't as good as you thought."

Luke grabs a towel from the railing and tosses it at him. Reed catches it, dries off one arm, then slings it around his neck. I watch as he walks toward me, water still dripping from his hair, eyes locked on mine. Steam from the cold air rises off his bare chest. I turn to face him, waiting for whatever he's about to say. I'm not backing down.

He stops, water still dripping, a crooked smile pulling at his mouth. "Alright, I'll admit it, that was a hell of a throw. Didn't think you had it in you."

I smile sweetly, tilting my head. "Maybe you shouldn't have acted so cocky before you ran your mouth."

Kinsley bounces up beside me. "Yeah, Reed. Don't you know Raelynn played softball in high school?"

Laughter breaks out instantly. Miles groans dramatically, Dylan claps way too loud and Judy covers her mouth like she's trying not to laugh.

Luke just smirks and mutters, "Rookie mistake."

Dylan leans in, grinning. "You cold, man? Or are your nipples always that aggressive?"

Reed barks out a laugh, rubbing a hand over his chest. "Stop looking at my nipples, Dylan. My eyes are up here."

I try not to stare, but it's hard when the man's literally dripping and dragging his palm across his chest like that. *Definitely not helping.*

Reed takes it with an impressed smile, then turns to head back toward the firehouse. "I need to get changed." He doesn't say anything else, but I catch the glance he tosses over his shoulder before disappearing into the crowd.

Kinsley claps her hands together. "Okay, now that we've publicly humiliated Reed, who's up for the haunted house tonight?"

"Ooh, yes," Naya says, then winces. "Actually, ugh. I can't. I've got orders to prep at the bakery for tomorrow. I'll be up half the night elbow-deep in cinnamon rolls."

Judy pats her arm. "You girls go have fun. I'll be in bed by eight. Haunted houses are for young people."

Miles shrugs. "I'm in."

"Sure." Dylan says.

Luke grins. "Yeah, I'll go."

Kinsley looks at me. "You good with that?"

"Definitely."

After the fundraiser winds down, the guys scatter in their own directions, saying they'll meet us later at the haunted house. The girls pile into Judy's car, and we head to the other side of town for food. We end up at Dusty's Delightful Diner, a retro little spot with checkerboard floors and spinning stools. We each order a messy burger and split a basket of curly fries between us. It's loud with laughter, the kind that bubbles up easy when you're full and still riding the adrenaline high of the day. Kinsley reenacts Reed's splash with over-the-top flailing arms. I throw a crumpled napkin at her laughing. If I'm honest, hitting that target was better than winning the championship game my senior year. After dinner, we head back to the cabins.

"I've got to head out," Naya says as we climb out of Judy's car. "Have fun tonight."

"Wish you were coming."

Naya waves as she climbs into her car. "Scream loud for me."

Judy turns toward her porch. "You girls go scream yourselves silly. I'll be in bed with a heating pad and a romance novel."

Kinsley grins. "I'm gonna run home and change. Give me twenty?"

"Twenty," I agree, practically skipping to my cabin.

Inside, I glance at the couch and freeze. My sketchbook's open to the last drawing I did…Reed, standing in my salon. I stare at it too long, then remember the kiss. The way he touched me. The way I kissed him back. How, for one reckless second, I didn't want it to stop. And the guilt hits hard. Because I'm still married. Technically. And even though I've made up my mind, even though I know I'm done…really done, I still feel it. That tight, awful twist in my chest. I shouldn't have wanted more. But I did. And I do.

I scrub a hand over my face and head into the bedroom. *I will not let this ruin my night.* I quickly change into a hoodie and boots, throwing my hair into a ponytail in case I need to run. I step out the door just as Kinsley's pulling back in. I slide into her car, and we pull away.

She doesn't waste any time. "So…what's going on with you and Reed?"

"Nothing. We're just friends. He flirts. It's nothing, really."

She glances over. "What about that kiss?"

"It was just a kiss. Nothing more." I know she doesn't believe me. But she lets it go.

We pull into the haunted house parking lot, headlights washing over a crooked wooden sign that reads: The Butcher's Wake. The paint's half-faded and one corner's dangling like it gave up years ago. Kinsley leans forward, squinting through the windshield. "The line looks short."

We step out of the car just as another set of headlights swings into the lot. Miles, Luke and Dylan pull in next to us and climb out.

Dylan grins. "Everyone ready?"

I open my mouth to answer, but then I see him. Reed. I should've known he'd be here. And a little part of me, just a little, is glad he is. He walks toward us, one hand in his pocket, gray hoodie, distressed jeans, black sneakers. Seriously, this man could wear a paper bag and still look good.

Kinsley leans over. "The sign says only two at a time." Miles immediately steps up beside her, slinging an arm around her shoulder like he's claiming his spot.

Dylan eyes Reed with a grin. "I'll keep you safe, Raelynn. You can go with me."

Kinsley laughs behind me, and before I can roll my eyes, Luke chimes in. "Oh no, I'm holding her hand through it."

Reed's jaw ticks. "Yeah, that's not happening."

Dylan and Luke both laugh. "You pick, Raelynn," Dylan says.

And before I can stop my stupid legs, they walk me straight to Reed's side.

16

She Chose Me. I Chose a Mistake.

Reed

I'd like to think I'm surprised she chose me but I'm not. I lean down, bringing my mouth close to her ear, lowering my voice just enough for only her to hear.

"So, you did like the kiss."

She elbows me in the side, hard enough to make me chuckle, but doesn't say a word. It's too dark to see if she's blushing, but I'd bet anything she is.

Kinsley and Miles are in front of us, practically wrapped around each other like the haunted house is an excuse to make out. Behind us, Luke and Dylan are already talking shit.

"You start screaming like a little girl, I'm leaving you in there," Luke says.

Dylan snorts. "You better not try and hold my hand."

Raelynn huffs out a quiet laugh beside me. I peek down and catch her smiling, shaking her head as she listens to them banter. *Damn it*. She's so damn beautiful. I quickly face forward when the line shifts.

The place is falling apart in the best way, boarded windows, lights flickering above the entrance, casting shadows across the warped siding. Somewhere inside, metal clatters hard against metal, followed by a chorus of screams. Then laughter. Then more screaming.

Kinsley and Miles are next in line when a woman in a white butcher's apron, covered in blood, bursts out from the entrance and lets out a guttural scream. It scares the shit out of both Kinsley and Raelynn. Kinsley jumps a foot in the air. Raelynn lets out a small scream and leans into me hard.

I laugh, I can't help it.

She immediately sidesteps, shoving my shoulder. "Shut up. That scared the crap out of me."

Kinsley and Miles step up to the entrance.

I lean in, keeping my voice low, just for her. "If you get too scared…you can hold onto me."

She turns to me slowly, eyes locking on mine. "I know."

We stay like that for a few seconds, until we finally remember where we are and turn back. Kinsley and Miles are gone. We step up to the entrance, and Raelynn starts rubbing her hands together, grinning like a kid on Christmas morning.

"This is it," she says, giggling.

I shake my head, chuckling. "You're way too excited about this."

From inside, we hear Kinsley scream, then again, louder this time, and the sound fades deeper into the house. Then the door swings open with a creak, and thick smoke billows out across our feet. A low, cryptic voice slithers through the fog. "Welcome to The Butcher's Wake…Step inside, if you dare."

She takes a deep breath as we step forward. It's pitch black the moment we cross the threshold. The door slams shut behind us with a loud bang. Raelynn jumps, slamming right into me, and this time, she doesn't move away.

All we can see is the faint glow of another door ahead with a crooked sign above it that reads: Ring the doorbell. She reaches up to press the button. The second her finger touches it, something crashes on the other side. The door swings open with a violent creak. Raelynn squeals and jerks her hand back, practically stepping on my foot. I have to bite back a laugh.

Inside, a flickering light swings overhead, casting jittery shadows across the room. Two large butcher tables sit under the light, stained and cracked, with ropes dangling from the ceiling. Fake limbs and mangled body parts hang above, swaying gently like some kind of sick wind chime. Somewhere in the dark, we hear the soft plink…plink of blood dripping onto metal.

Raelynn reaches for my hand as we step fully into the room. I glance down at our fingers just as something launches from behind one of the tables, a masked figure covered in gore, dragging a fake axe behind him with a metallic screech. Raelynn lets out a sharp gasp and squeezes my hand tight. I step a little closer, guiding her through.

We turn the corner into a narrow hallway, barely wide enough for one person. Raelynn goes first, still holding my hand behind her back like a lifeline. Her shoulders are tense, her steps careful. She's so focused on what's ahead, she doesn't notice the tiny door by her feet slide open. A pale hand shoots out and grabs her ankle. She screams at the top of her lungs and spins, practically climbing me like a ladder. I burst out laughing, instinctively wrapping my arms around her. She tucks herself under my arm, clinging tight as we exit the hallway together.

We step into the next room, and it's colder, like walking into a giant walk-in refrigerator. Metal shelves line the walls, each stacked with grimy plastic bins labeled: Intestines, Livers, Hearts. The air smells like rust and something sour. The door clicks shut behind us. Then we hear it…the lock.

A burst of cold air rushes past us, and the light overhead cuts out completely. Raelynn screams and buries her face into my chest, arms wrapping around me tight. I hold her closer, guiding us forward through the dark, toward the faint glow coming from underneath another door ahead.

She peeks out, just barely, trying to see what's going on. That's when the lights flash back on, bright, harsh and fast. Three bloody butchers stand around us in a triangle, masks twisted into grotesque smiles, cleavers dripping red. They start chanting, all at once, loud and jagged: "Liver! Heart! Tongue!"

She doesn't scream this time. She sucks in a sharp breath, squeezes her eyes shut and throws herself back into my chest. I press my lips to the top of her head and hold her tighter.

As the three figures step back into the shadows, I walk us through the next door. We're standing in what looks like a warehouse, wide open space, dim lights, pallets stacked high with boxes marked in red. Some have fake blood dripping down the sides like something's trying to leak out.

I pause, checking her face. "You okay?"

She nods and peeks out, letting out a shaky wheeze. "Is it almost over?"

I chuckle. "Yeah. We're almost done."

She sighs, half laughs, and slowly peels herself off me. The second she starts to relax, a huge man in a blood-stained apron steps out from behind a stack of boxes. Jagged fake teeth fill his mouth, and he lets out a roar as he yanks the cord of a chainsaw. It growls to life with a deafening roar. Raelynn jumps, wide-eyed.

I grab her hand, grinning. "Run, Sunshine!"

She laughs, and we take off toward the glowing red EXIT sign at the end of the room, our footsteps echoing through the warehouse as the chainsaw roars behind us.

We run out into the cold night, still laughing, still holding hands. We stop just outside the door, adrenaline still pumping.

Raelynn's cheeks are flushed, eyes bright. She's laughing as she says, "That was so much fun."

I chuckle. "You didn't even open your eyes."

She smiles. "Didn't have to. I knew you wouldn't let anything get me."

That one hits harder than I expect. I search her eyes, and for a split second, everything feels heavier. Real. Too real.

"No," I say quietly. "I wouldn't."

The weight of it settles. I swallow the lump rising in my throat and step back, letting go of her hand.

"Come on. Kinsley and Miles are probably waiting."

We round the corner, and Kinsley bounces up to Raelynn, already grinning. The two of them start giggling, voices overlapping with breathless energy. I run a hand through my hair, looking anywhere but at her. Luke and Dylan stumble out of the exit behind us, still laughing and shoving each other.

We all head toward the parking lot, everyone recapping loudly about their favorite scares. Kinsley swears she almost peed her pants, Dylan is insisting he never screamed, and Luke is calling him a liar. At the edge of the lot, I turn to face them, still avoiding her eyes. "I've got work in the morning. I'll see you guys later."

A chorus of goodbyes follows me, casual and loud. Just as I turn, my eyes flicker her way. She doesn't say anything. She just looks away.

I make it to my truck without looking back. I yank the door shut, hard, the slam echoing through the cab. *Why do I care who she went in with? Why did I feel like I needed to protect her? Why does it matter? Why do we keep running into each other?* Hell, I've known Naya for years and don't run into her this much. This makes no damn sense.

I pull into my driveway, headlights sweeping across the porch. I head inside, barely kicking off my boots before stripping down for a quick shower. When I walk into the bedroom, Fifi's already curled up dead center on the bed. I climb in beside her, scrubbing a hand down my face before turning off the lamp. I stare at the ceiling, the darkness no quieter than my thoughts.

***

I slam my hand down on the alarm, crawl out of bed and head straight for the coffee pot. Fifi trots to the door. I let her out, barely awake, and head into the bathroom, digging through the cabinet for aspirin. My head's pounding. Too many thoughts. Not enough sleep.

I get dressed, more determined than ever to forget about her. Today's about staying busy. No distractions. No wandering thoughts. Which means a full day of desk work, report writing, the shit I usually avoid at all costs. But right now, it's better than letting my brain keep chewing on things. Twenty minutes and five peptalks later I walk out the door.

I pull into the station lot and head inside. The second I step through the door, I know something's off. There's too much laughing coming from the back bay.

I glance up. There it is. Hanging from the rafters above the bullpen is a giant, blown-up photo of me and Raelynn. At the kissing booth. Mid-kiss. It's not even a flattering angle, but the image is clear enough to catch every damn detail, my hand in her hair, the way she leans into me. I stop in my tracks.

Jose grins from across the room. "You didn't tell us your charity work came with benefits."

Tommy leans on the counter. "Hey, man, that's a textbook rescue, quick response, solid grip, full mouth-to-mouth."

I shake my head, laughing. "That's why I got the promotion and you didn't. I always get the job done."

Just then, Chief walks in, glances up at the photo, then at me. He doesn't say a word, just shakes his head with a sigh and keeps moving. "Morning meeting in five," he calls over his shoulder.

We gather in the briefing room, the usual rundown, shift changes, equipment checks, upcoming events. I mostly zone out, jotting notes I don't need, trying to ignore Tommy smirking at me from across the table.

Chief glances down at his clipboard, then looks up at me.

"Davison. The winner of the sealed bid auction is meeting you out at Holland Farms. Noon. Hayrides, corn maze, the whole deal."

I sigh. "Do we know who the winner is?"

He shakes his head. "Still sorting through the entries. It doesn't matter, just show up, it's for charity and be friendly." He starts to walk away, glances up at the photo and looks back at me. "But not too friendly."

The guys burst out laughing again.

I shake my head, grab my notes, head to my desk and turn my back to the damn photo.

By lunch, I've managed to knock out half the paperwork. My eyes are on fire from staring at the screen so long. I stretch, trying to work the tension out of my shoulders, then catch a glimpse of the photo again. Nope. I'm not eating lunch here. I grab my jacket and head to my truck without saying a word.

My stomach's been growling for the last hour, so I head to the sub shop in town. On the way, I pass Raelynn's salon. She's standing out front, smiling at some guy in a tailored suit.

I don't know who he is. Don't care. She's not my girlfriend. I don't want a girlfriend. I keep driving.

The sub shop's slow, thank God. I walk in, order my usual without looking at the menu and wait by the door. A few minutes later, I've got my sandwich in hand and I'm heading back toward the station.

I hit the same street again. Glance out the window. Shouldn't have. She's still outside, but closer to the door now. Still talking. I look away.

I eat my lunch in the truck with the windows cracked, radio low, and my brain still trying to argue with itself. *She's not mine. I don't care.* Except I do. And I hate that I do.

When my lunch is over, I head back inside. The photo's still hanging there. Still mocking me. I drop back into my seat and try to focus, but it's slower now. Harder to concentrate. Every time I blink, her face flashes behind my eyes. It's ridiculous. I've got reports to finish. A checklist on my desk. Calls to follow up on. But all I can think about is her.

By the end of my shift, I've only managed to get through half of what I planned. I grab my things, toss my jacket over my shoulder and head out the door. Two minutes later, I'm pulling into the Fireside Lounge.

I grab a spot at the bar and order a tall beer. I sip my beer, letting the quiet settle in, trying to figure out how the hell to stop wanting her. To stop thinking about her. To stop wondering who the hell that guy in the suit was. I'm in deep, when a group of women walks in, loud, laughing and dressed up. They take over a stretch of the bar a few seats down from me. I don't pay them much attention at first. Then it hits me. Maybe what I need…is to get back in the game. Clear my head. Hell, maybe I just need to get laid.

I glance over. A couple of them are already looking my way. One's a brunette with dark eyes and a confident smile. She holds my gaze a little too long. So, I throw her a grin. Nothing over the top, just enough. Then I wait. It takes less than a minute before she gathers the nerve to walk over.

"Hi," she says, voice flirty. "You here alone?"

I gesture to the empty stool beside me. "Take a seat."

She does, crossing her legs and leaning in. I order us a round, and we settle into casual conversation. Soft touches pass between us. Her fingers brush my arm when she laughs. Mine rest a little too long against her knee when I lean in to hear her better.

After a couple more drinks and a whole lot of flirting, I glance over at her.

"Wanna get out of here?"

She smiles. "Sure."

I toss some cash on the bar and stand, holding out my arm. She loops hers through mine and waves to her friends. She giggles as we step out the door.

We start walking toward my truck. And that's when it starts. She's not Raelynn. Her laugh's too high. Her perfume's too strong. She doesn't look at me like she sees something real, just like she sees a good time. And maybe that's exactly what I asked for.

As we get closer to my truck, she leans into me, her body warm against mine. Now I'm actively trying to convince myself to go through with it. It's easy. She's here. She wants this. No strings, no pressure. Exactly what I thought I needed. We round the front of the truck, and I open the door for her.

She turns toward me with a smile, but something in my chest tightens. It's not excitement. It's not heat. It's…wrong. I let out a breath, rubbing a hand over the back of my neck.

"Wait, I'm sorry…I can't."

Her smile falters. "Why?"

I shake my head. "You've been great. Really. I just…" I can't say it. Not without saying her name. "I'm not in the right headspace."

She nods slowly, the flirtation fading from her eyes. "Okay. Thanks for being honest."

She doesn't seem mad. Just disappointed. And honestly, so am I.

I shut the truck door gently and step back as she heads back toward the lounge to join her friends.

Then I climb in, start the engine, and sit there for a second. *Goddamn it, Raelynn.*

17

No Sale. No Chance. No More.

Raelynn

There's a little adrenaline still buzzing from last night, but in the best way. No stress. No heaviness. Just excitement. Mel will be here in two days, and today I'm getting the salon cleaned up before the fun begins.

I head into the kitchen, still in my pajamas, and fire up the coffee pot. While it brews, I spot my sketchbook open on the table where I left it last night.

It's a quick sketch of the haunted house, just a rough scene of Reed and me running toward the exit. It's from behind, both of us mid-stride, smoke curling around our legs. His hand is reaching back, holding mine.

I keep thinking about the way he looked at me when I said I knew he wouldn't let anything get me. The way he went quiet. And how he left not long after. Not rude or awkward. Just...quick.

I head back to my room to get ready. Leggings, an oversized sweatshirt and a headband to keep my hair out of my face, perfect for cleaning. I toss my hair up in a messy bun, grab my bag and head for the door. Today's going to be productive. And I'm ready for it.

I stop at the post office before heading to the salon, needing to finally set up the official mailing address for the business. It's quick, just some paperwork and polite small talk with the clerk behind the counter. When I unlock my PO box, a thick stack of envelopes spills out. I carry everything out to the car and drop into the driver's seat, flipping through the pile. Bills. Flyers. Junk. Then I see them, six identical envelopes, all from the same address. All with the same name. Bradley Manchester. The name scratches at the back of my memory. Then it clicks. The flyer on the salon door the day I got the keys.

My stomach knots as I tear one of the envelopes open, wondering what could be so important he had to send six of the same letter. The paper is thick, professional, printed on a company letterhead. My eyes skim the first few lines.

Ms. Newberry,

I've attempted to reach you on several occasions with no response. I understand you've recently acquired the property at 231 Main Street in Cranberry Ridge, and while I'm sure you're quite busy, I'd appreciate the courtesy of a reply.

Congratulations, by the way. It's a promising location. I'd like to speak with you directly regarding a time-sensitive offer. Please contact me at your earliest convenience so we can arrange a meeting.

Regards,

Bradley Manchester

Manchester Commercial Group

He's trying to sound polite. Professional. But there's a current under the words, something impatient and annoyed. Like he's not used to people ignoring him.

Six letters. That's not just persistence. That's pressure. I refold the letter and sit back in my seat, staring through the windshield. I don't need to reach out. I'm not selling. And I won't be pressured. I toss the letter onto the passenger seat and drive off. Rounding the corner, I park in front of the building. The street's quiet. Bright sun. Crisp air.

I unlock the front door and step inside, locking it again behind me without thinking. No one's here. No distractions. Just me and a to-do list. I toss my bag on the counter, roll up my sleeves and get to work. I start in the office, scrubbing the walls. Some of the scuffs won't budge, and halfway through, I realize I've been scrubbing the same spot over and over without making much progress. Because I started thinking about Reed. Again. The way his voice dropped when he leaned in at the haunted house. The way he said, "If you get too scared…you can hold onto me." He meant it. I could feel it in the way he held me.

I reach for the broom. *Focus, Rae, you need to get this list done today.* I'm halfway through the office when a loud knock jolts me upright. I slowly peek toward the front door. A tall man in a crisp navy suit glances around like he's taking inventory of the place. He doesn't look threatening. Just…confident. His blonde hair is slicked back revealing his bright blue eyes. Too polished for Cranberry Ridge.

I wipe my hands on a rag, walk to the door and crack it open.

He offers a practiced smile. "Raelynn Newberry?"

"Yes?"

He extends his hand. "Bradley Manchester. Do you have a moment?"

I toss the rag just inside the door and step out, pulling the door mostly closed behind me. No way I'm trapping myself in an empty building alone with a stranger. "What can I help you with, Mr. Manchester?"

His smile slips just a bit. "Call me Brad." He smiles as he clasps his hands loosely in front of him. "I just wanted to say, congratulations. The place is great, perfect location, and you clearly saw that before most people even realized it was on the market. Impressive, really. You moved fast."

I blink, caught a little off guard by the compliment. A slow smile tugs at my mouth, pride slipping through before I can hide it. "Thank you. It felt like the right fit."

For a second, it does feel good, being seen. Being acknowledged for something other than just surviving. He nods like he's genuinely impressed, then glances past me toward the building.

"I can see you've already started working on it. That's great. But I'll be honest, Ms. Newberry, I'm here because I'd like to make you an offer."

I shake my head in understanding; my smile fades a little.

He meets my eyes, tone still polite but edging toward persuasive. "I'm prepared to double what you paid. No strings, no delays. Just a clean sale."

I straighten, that flicker of pride shifting into something else entirely. "I'm sorry you came all this way, but I'm really not interested in selling."

Bradley's smile tightens again, like he expected resistance but not refusal. "I'm sure with the amount I'm willing to pay, you could find a better suited building elsewhere."

I take a small step back, closer to the door. "I'm not interested in moving. But thank you for the offer."

He nods once, but the glint in his eyes doesn't soften. "How about I let you sleep on it? I'll reach back out. I'd hate for you to make a fool's mistake and pass up an offer like this."

That's it. I open the door, cool air rushing in. "Have a good day, Mr. Manchester." Then I walk inside, shut the door and lock it behind me. I don't look back, not right away. Not until I reach the office and glance toward the front window. He's still there. Standing on the sidewalk, staring up at the building like he's already imagining his name on the deed. He pulls out his phone and casually snaps a few photos before finally turning and walking away.

Did that asshole just call me a fool? I already know his type, slick suit, polished smile and just enough charm to cover up the fact that he's used to getting his way. He'll be back. I know it. But I'm not going anywhere.

Thanks to him, I'm already behind on my to-do list. I turn away from the window, tie my hair back tighter and grab the broom again. But as I scrub, sweep and wipe down every inch of this place, my thoughts drift back to everything that's changed. I'm sketching again. I'm standing in my own damn salon, in a town I actually like surrounded by friends who make me laugh more than I have in years. It's not perfect, but it's mine. And somehow, Reed's been tangled up in all of it.

By the time I check the last thing off today's list, it's already dark outside. I lean against the counter, feeling both accomplished and completely confused.

Reed's been involved in just about every part of this new life, helping with the inspection, showing up at the haunted house, hanging out with our friends. Hell, he's even made it into my sketchbook. And with all the time we've spent together, I still can't figure him out. He flirts, then pulls back. He's sweet and protective, then suddenly disappears. Why?

My stomach growls, yanking me out of my Reed-induced spiral. I pull out my phone and order a well-deserved burger and fries from the Fireside Lounge.

I grab my purse, lock the door behind me and decide to walk. It's not far, and maybe the cool night air will help clear my head. Main Street is quiet as I make my way down the block. I round the corner and step into the parking lot just as the lounge door swings open, and I freeze.

Reed is walking out with a woman on his arm. She's laughing, her hand resting casually on his chest as they head toward his truck.

I don't wait to see anything else. I turn quickly, hoping he didn't notice me, and pull out my phone, canceling my order with a few quick taps. Yeah, I'm not confused about Reed anymore. I know exactly what kind of man he is. He flirts with me, then fucks other women. Acts like he cares, then walks out with someone else on his arm. Maybe that's all I ever was to him…a charity case. Yeah. Confusion gone.

When I reach my car, I'm so mad I can barely see straight. And it's not at him. He doesn't owe me anything, no commitment, no explanation. I'm pissed at myself. For letting him in. Into my thoughts. My life. My damn sketchbook. Like an idiot, I let myself wonder.

I pull into the cabin driveway and do my best not to slam the door. By the time I reach the front door, I'm done. No more Reed.

I head straight for the kitchen, make a quick turkey sandwich, and eat it standing up. When I glance over at the island, my sketchbook is open to the page of me and Reed in the haunted house. I slam it shut. I swallow the last bite of my sandwich and my pride and hit the shower. By the time my head hits the pillow, I'm too tired to care.

***

I start the morning with a bowl of cereal, standing at the kitchen counter. I don't want to think about last night. About Reed. Or the way my stomach twisted when I saw him with someone else. Today, I'm keeping busy. That's the plan. No room for spirals.

After making a quick to-do list for today, I pull on a pair of jeans and a soft tee, brush my hair into a straight ponytail. Dab on a little mascara. Then I grab my favorite jacket and slip it on before heading for the door, clutching my list, ready to get my hands dirty at the salon again. But when I step outside, Judy's standing near my car.

"Oh, honey," Judy says, concern tightening her voice. "I was just about to come get you."

"What's wrong?"

She points toward my car. "Looks like a bear tried to get in last night."

My stomach drops as I hurry around to the driver's side. The window's completely smashed in.

I let out a slow breath, doing my best to rein in the flood of emotions pressing against my ribs. "Perfect." I crinkle my to-do list in my hand and shove it into my pocket.

Judy, sweet as ever, gives my shoulder a reassuring pat. "Don't worry. We'll get it fixed."

It's fine. I can keep myself busy here, maybe even cook dinner tonight. I glance at the shattered window and sigh. "Do you think you could follow me to the repair shop and bring me back?"

"I sure can. Let me grab my keys." She walks off, and I carefully open my door. Glass is scattered all over the seat, sparkling like sharp confetti.

Judy returns with her keys and a folded towel. "Here. Put this down, we don't want you getting little cuts all over your bottom."

I chuckle. "No, we don't." I lay the towel across the seat and carefully slide in.

I follow Judy into town, freezing my ass off the entire drive. The heat's on high, but the wind whips right through the broken window, stealing every bit of warmth. We pull into a small glass repair shop, and I'm in and out in less than ten minutes with a promise that the window will be fixed by 5:00 p.m.

I slide into Judy's car. "Thanks for helping me."

"Oh, you're welcome," she says with a warm smile as she pulls out of the lot. A second later, she glances over at me. "I feel a headache coming on. Think you could do me a favor?"

"Sure. Anything." And I mean it, I adore this woman.

"Well," she begins, "I won a little contest to spend the afternoon at Holland Farms. They've got all kinds of fall activities, and I'd really hate to let it go to waste."

I smile. "You know what? I'd love to."

This is perfect. A few hours of pumpkins, fresh air, and cider? Yeah, exactly what I need to keep "him" out of my head.

Judy glances at the clock on the dash. "Well, it starts in ten minutes. I'll drop you off."

"Perfect. Thanks."

A few minutes later, we're pulling into Holland Farms. The lot is already half full, families and couples filing through the decorated entrance lined with hay bales, corn stalks and carved pumpkins.

"Someone from the contest should meet you at the gate," Judy says as she slows to a stop.

I open the door and step out. "Thanks again. I really appreciate it."

"Oh, you're welcome, sweetheart. Call me when you're ready." She gives me a wave and shifts into drive.

I shut the door and turn toward the entrance. That's when I see Reed. Standing just inside the gate, hands tucked into his pockets, eyes scanning the crowd.

My heart skips. "No, no, no."

I whirl back around to wave Judy down, but her taillights are already disappearing down the drive.

I turn back around as he strides toward me with that stupid, cocky smirk.

Damn it.

He stops right in front of me, hands still in his pockets. "Couldn't get enough of me, Sunshine?"

"Don't flirt with me, Reed," I snap. "What are you even doing here?"

"I'm meeting the winner of the sealed auction, date with a fireman."

My stomach drops. "Did that winner happen to be Judy?"

He shrugs. "I wasn't told who, just told to be here."

I huff. "Judy won some contest, but she's got a headache and couldn't make it, so she asked if I would."

His smirk widens. "Looks like it's you and me then."

Son of a bitch. This is not how I wanted to stop thinking about him. How in the hell do I keep ending up in these situations with him? It's like the universe is playing some twisted joke and apparently, I'm the punchline.

18

Cornstalk Confessions

Reed

This morning, I told myself I was done with the back-and-forth.

Last night, I could've taken that girl home. Hell, I almost did. But I didn't. Because the truth is, I'm tired of pretending I don't care. I'm tired of trying to convince myself that Raelynn Newberry isn't already under my skin. I might as well stop fighting it. And now here I am, standing in front of her at Holland Farms. She's staring at me like I've just ruined her whole damn day.

"I mean it, Reed. Stop flirting with me." She plants her hands on her hips, standing her ground like she's ready to wrestle me into submission if she has to.

I chuckle. "Come on, Sunshine. Let's go have some fun."

She exhales like she's already regretting her life choices. "Fine. But stop calling me that."

I grin, already planning not to.

We walk through the gate NOT close and she's doing her best to keep it that way. Just to test the waters, I inch a little closer.

She side-eyes me, then veers left, widening the gap again.

I laugh. "So, what do you want to do first?"

She stops just ahead, taking in the rows of booths and signs scattered across the farm, hayrides, cider stands, corn maze, petting zoo, and toward the far end pumpkin smashing.

She points. "Let's do that first."

I grin. "Pumpkin smashing? You got a lot of pent-up rage you need to work out?"

"Maybe," she says, already walking.

"Alright then, lead the way, Sun…"

"Don't."

I snap my mouth shut, a smile growing as I follow after her.

When we reach the pumpkin smashing field, I pay for both of us. She doesn't even wait, already marching toward a pile of sad, misshapen pumpkins with a sledgehammer in hand. I jog to catch up.

She zeroes in on a lumpy one the size of a beach ball, plants her feet and swings hard. The pumpkin splits with a loud crack, chunks flying in every direction. She exhales, long and slow, like she's been holding it for days.

I grab my own sledgehammer and take a swing. The pumpkin under me doesn't stand a chance, it implodes, seeds and guts flying everywhere. I glance over just as she picks up her hammer again and starts wailing on the already-split remains of her pumpkin. She doesn't stop after one swing. She hits it again. And again. Each slam sending orange pulp flying, seeds sticking to her shoes. By the fifth swing, there's nothing left but stringy mush and a crater in the grass.

"Jesus," I mutter, watching her chest rise and fall.

She wipes her brow with the back of her arm, barely looking at me. "What's next?

I raise a brow. "Maybe something a little less violent?"

She doesn't answer, just tosses the sledgehammer to the side and starts walking.

I follow, still grinning, and say probably the worst thing I could've picked in that moment. "How about the corn maze? Get some alone time."

She stops short and spins on me, stepping in close, so no one else can hear, but still just sharp enough to slice through my stupid smile.

"I am not a charity case, Reed," she whisper-shouts, her eyes blazing.

She turns on her heel and walks off toward the maze. I follow, silent for once, my grin long gone. We don't speak again until we're standing at the edge of the corn maze.

"Raelynn." My voice is quiet, brows pinched. "Why would you say that?"

She doesn't look at me. "It's nothing, Reed. Come on. Let's get this done."

She steps into the maze, and I follow, no clue how I'm supposed to fix something I don't even understand. We walk in silence, our shoes crunching over broken husks, while I rack my brain trying to figure out what the hell is going on.

"Raelynn," I say finally, voice low. "Talk to me. Tell me what's wrong."

"It's nothing, Reed."

"It's obviously something."

She spins around to face me, cheeks flushed. Her mouth opens like she's about to say something, but then she stops, eyes flicking to the group approaching behind us. We step aside, letting them pass. She tries again, but a second group turns into the path, laughing too loud, walking too slow. Frustrated, I grab her hand and lead her off the trail, deep into the corn. We push through the stalks until I find a small clearing where some of the corn's already been trampled down.

I stop and turn to face her. "There. No more interruptions."

She crosses her arms, guarded. "Reed, really. It's fine. I understand."

"Well, that makes one of us." I shake my head. "Why the hell would you think I saw you as some kind of charity case?"

She lets out a huff, arms still crossed, eyes fixed on the ground. "What else am I supposed to think, Reed? You flirt with me. You say these sweet, stupid things that make it hard to breathe. You volunteered to kiss me at the fundraiser. You held me through the haunted house…" Her voice wavers, but she keeps going. "And then last night, I saw you walking out of the bar…with some woman on your arm." She shrugs, like she's trying to make it no big deal, but her voice tightens. "And it's fine. We're not together. I get that. But I don't need your pity."

I take a step back, shocked. "Raelynn, it's not what you think."

She shakes her head, backing away. "I know what I saw. And it's fine. It's none of my business." Her voice is calm, but I can see it in her eyes, she's already bracing to leave. To shut me out.

And panic claws at my chest because she's got it wrong, and if she walks away now…

"Don't," I say, voice urgent. I step toward her. "Don't walk away, Raelynn. You don't understand."

She huffs and drops her arms to her side. "Then make me understand."

"I didn't go home with her."

Raelynn's eyes narrow, her voice flat. "Reed, I know what I saw." She shakes her head, stepping back again. "But it's fine. We're done here."

I step forward. "Fine. You want the truth?"

She doesn't say anything, just watches me, guard up, lips pressed tight.

"Yes," I admit. "I was going to take her home. I went to the bar looking for anything, anyone to get you out of my head. But when we got to my truck…" I shake my head. "I couldn't do it."

Her voice is quieter now, almost a whisper. "Why?"

I take one more step, close enough to feel her warmth. "Because she's not you."

Her face softens, eyes searching mine. "Reed," she whispers, almost like a plea.

I close the space between us. "Do you understand now?"

She doesn't answer right away, but she doesn't move either. Her lips are parted slightly like she wants to say something, but instead, she just nods.

I lean in, my lips hovering just above hers, our breaths tangled in the inches between us. "I want to hear you moan my name while I take my time ruining you, Raelynn," I murmur, eyes locked on hers. "And I've been dying to since the damn inspection." I let the words hang there, my thumb tracing her bottom lip. "Tell me to stop, Raelynn. Say the word. Or don't and let me show you exactly what you do to me."

She doesn't say a word. Instead, she leans in, just enough for our lips to touch. That's all I need. I close the distance and kiss her. No hesitation, no holding back. Just weeks of want, crashing into a single breath. Her lips are soft, but the way she kisses me back? Fierce. Like she's just as starved as I am. I slide my hand into her hair, tilting her head to deepen the kiss, and her fingers bunch the front of my shirt, pulling me closer, until there's no space left between us. She exhales against my mouth, and I swear it lights me on fire. My hand trails down the curve of her back to her waist. I lift her effortlessly, and she wraps her arms around my neck, legs around my waist. I know she can feel it, what she does to me.

She moans into my mouth, and I just about lose my damn mind. I grip the back of her neck, tilt her head, and drag my lips along her jaw, tasting her skin, breathing her in. Her breath hitches when I reach up and guide her jacket zipper down, slowly. Her fingers slip into my hair as she gasps my name.

I return to her mouth, claiming another kiss, deep and unrelenting, then drop to one knee and lower her gently into the crushed corn husks. Our bodies align, perfectly flush, heat rolling off us in waves. She slides her hands down my back. And when I press my hard cock between her thighs, her head falls back, and her nails dig into my back, just enough to pull a groan from deep in my throat. I reach down, dragging her shirt up inch by inch, revealing black lace stretched across her beautiful chest.

I bend low, pressing my lips just above her waistband, then kiss and suck my way up her stomach. Her body shudders under my touch, breath catching with every inch I claim. When I reach the edge of her bra, her hand slowly lifts, cupping my face. I look up and meet her eyes, wide, glassy, her chest rising and falling fast. Her lips are parted, pink and swollen, when she whispers, "We have to stop."

I stop. Close my eyes. Try to steady my heart rate. I have never wanted anyone more than I want this woman. When I open my eyes, I can see she's trying to collect herself, too, lips still parted, cheeks flushed. Gently, I lower her shirt back down and press a soft kiss to her stomach, then her lips, before pulling myself off her.

I help her to her feet, cupping her face and kissing her again. "I'm gonna need a minute," I whisper against her mouth.

She laughs into the kiss. "Okay."

I force myself to let her go and take a few steps back, dragging a hand down my face. If she touches me again, even once, I'm never getting this hard-on to go away.

After a minute, once I'm sure I can speak again without embarrassing myself, I glance over at her.

"So," I say, keeping my voice light, "does this mean I'm allowed to flirt and call you Sunshine again?"

Her lips twitch into smile. "Maybe."

I grin. "I'll take it."

She tilts her head. "Why do you call me that?"

"Because you're Raelynn. Rae of sunshine."

She rolls her eyes, but I catch the smile she's trying to hide. "That's terrible."

"Tacky? Yes." I step closer and press a kiss to her forehead. "But it's true."

Then I hold out my hand. "Come on. We still have to find our way out of this maze."

She looks down at it for a second, then slips her fingers through mine.

Thirty minutes, seven wrong turns, and at least one group of eight-year-olds sprinting past us later, we finally stumble out, laughing.

We sip cider, pet a half-dozen goats, feed the chickens and wander through the pumpkin patch swapping childhood stories, favorite colors and the worst food concoctions we've ever tried.

"I once put ketchup on watermelon," I admit, watching her nose scrunch in horror.

"That's disgusting."

"I was seven and unsupervised."

She shakes her head. "Mine's still worse. My cousin dared me to microwave a pickle wrapped in a fruit roll-up."

I pause, visibly disturbed. "And you ate it?"

"I was eleven and competitive."

We both laugh, sidestepping a crooked pumpkin vine.

A little while later, we each pick out a pumpkin and, of course, she chooses the biggest one in the patch. So now I'm carrying both while she happily sips her cider.

She pulls out her phone and sighs. "I've gotta go. My car should be ready."

"What's wrong with your car?"

"I woke up this morning and the driver's side window was smashed. Judy said it was probably a bear, so she followed me to the shop and drove me here."

"You want me to drive you to your car?"

She smiles. "Are you just trying to spend more time with me, Hotshot?"

I grin. "Can you blame me? Last time we were alone, I damn near rounded second. Thought I'd try my luck at a double."

She giggles, nudging me with her shoulder. "Are you flirting with me?"

"Yes. Aggressively."

We make our way to my truck parked near the entrance. I load the pumpkins into the bed, then step around and open her door. Before she climbs in, she rises up on her toes and presses a soft kiss to my cheek.

"Thanks for today."

"You're welcome," I murmur, watching her slide into the seat.

When we pull into the repair shop lot, her car's already parked out front, good as new. She unbuckles as I shift into park.

"What are your plans tomorrow evening?" I ask casually, glancing her way.

"I was just going to get a little more cleaning done before the girls and I start painting."

"Ah," I nod, trying to sound cool about it. "Well, I was thinking maybe we could have dinner. But since you're busy, maybe another time."

She turns toward me, smiling. "Dinner would be great after a long day of cleaning."

"How about I bring dinner to you?"

"That sounds perfect, actually." She leans over, her fingers brushing along my jaw. "Thanks again for today."

Then she kisses me, soft at first, but I'm already reaching for her, pulling her across the cab and into my lap. Her hands slide into my hair as the kiss deepens, that familiar pull low in my stomach tightening like a knot.

Without breaking the kiss, I reach for the door and swing it open, stepping out with her still in my arms. She giggles against my mouth as I set her gently on her feet.

I grin, brushing a loose hair back. "I'll carry your pumpkin to your car."

I place the pumpkin gently in her backseat, then give the trunk a light tap.

"See you tomorrow," I say, backing away with a grin.

She leans on her door, smiling. "Tomorrow."

I glance back one last time before pulling away. Every part of me wants to turn around, go back and finish what I started. But I won't pressure her.

The road home is quiet, but my head is anything but. This feels different. I've never wanted a woman like this before. Sure, I know how to treat one, but how do I not fuck this up? I nearly did, before it even started. All because I was trying to get her out of my head. *Stupid.*

She's holding back. I can feel it, like she's still waiting for the other shoe to drop. Still trying to decide if I'm safe. But today? She let her guard down. Not all the way, but enough to know she feels something, too. And when she's ready to stop fighting it…I'll be right fucking here.

19

Where Guilt Meets Want

Raelynn

The road winds ahead, quiet and familiar, but everything inside me feels different. Like he rewired me with every kiss, every laugh, every second I let my guard slip. I should be overthinking. I should be doubting all of it. But I'm not. Not about him.

What's eating at me isn't confusion, it's guilt. Because technically, I'm still married. My divorce papers are sitting in some courtroom queue waiting to be processed while I'm out here letting a man touch me like that. Wanting him to.

And then there's the part I really don't want to admit, the part that makes me feel like I missed some crucial memo on being a woman. I've had sex before. Plenty of times. But not once has anyone ever gotten me there. Every orgasm I've ever had was thanks to my own hand behind a locked door, quick and quiet. Never quite enough.

I'm parked in the driveway, engine off, hands resting on my lap. Porch light's on, cabin's dark behind it, but I can't seem to make myself get out of the car.

Because I know Reed knows what he's doing. I felt it. In the pit of my stomach. In the way my body responded. Every kiss, every touch, he was so confident. Like he wasn't guessing. Like he already knew exactly how to undo me.

And that scares me. Because what if I'm not good at it? What if I freeze? Or get in my head? What if he sees the cracks I've worked so hard to patch over and realizes I'm not nearly as put together as I pretend to be?

I grab my bag and head for the cabin. The second I step inside, I know I need to talk to someone, get all this out of my head before it explodes. But Kinsley's not the right person for this. I already know what she'll say. She'll tell me to stay away, that she's afraid I'll get hurt. And if I call Naya, she'll just tell me, "Girl, fuck him. Have a good time." Neither of those is what I need.

I drop my bag by the door and head to the kitchen. I turn on the oven, toss in a frozen pizza, then open the fridge and grab a bottle of wine. I pour myself a giant glass, no shame and take a long sip then grab my phone. And I call the only person who won't try to talk me out of it…or into it.

Mel answers. "Hey."

"Hey. Are you busy?"

"Not at all. What's up?"

"Okay, so…it's kind of a long story. You might want to grab some wine."

"Ohh, it's one of those talks." I hear her clinking around, drawers opening, and then the soft pop of a cork. "Alright. I'm ready. Spill your guts."

I do. I tell her everything. I don't leave out a single part, from the night I made an ass out of myself calling him "hotshot" like I was in some low-budget rom-com, to today in the cornfield where I damn near let him take me apart, stalk by stalk.

I tell her how I feel about him. How it's not just attraction, it's more, and it terrifies the hell out of me. And how nervous I am about my ability to please him. About the fact that no one's ever really pleased me. That every orgasm I've ever had was solo. And then I drop the biggest one. "I feel guilty," I whisper. "Because I'm still married."

There's a long silence on the other end. I sip my wine and wait, stomach in knots, wondering if even Mel can make this part make sense.

"I completely understand all your reservations," she says, her voice soft. "And you are not wrong to have them. But let me address each one, okay?"

"Okay."

"First…the cornfield? Hot!" She laughs.

"Second, Reed sounds amazing. I mean, the man clearly wants you. And you wouldn't be calling me about this if you didn't want him, too. So, let's not pretend this is one-sided."

She pauses just long enough for it to land before moving on.

"Third, you're legally separated, Rae. You have no reason to feel guilty for wanting to be happy again. And as far as the legal side goes, it's not an affair. Not with the paperwork in place. Besides, we should have a date for the final hearing soon."

"So, what I'm saying is…do whatever the heck makes you happy. And don't hold back. Because if you do, if you let fear or guilt stop you, you're gonna end up with regrets. And honestly? You've had enough of those."

"You're right," I say quietly. "And I know it. I do. But it still feels like I'm sabotaging myself. Like there's this little voice in my head constantly making me question everything I do."

Mel doesn't hesitate. "That's not your voice, Raelynn. It's his. Don't let Jacob control you anymore."

Her words hit hard. Because she's right. That voice in my head, the one that tells me I'm too much, not enough, that I'll ruin a good thing before it even starts, it's his. It always has been. I stare down at my half-empty wine glass. "Thanks, Mel, I needed to hear that."

"You deserve more, Rae. You deserve to be happy. And if Reed does that, then lean in. Don't run from it."

"I'm trying."

"I know you are. And I'm proud of you."

We stay on the line a little longer, not saying much. When we finally hang up, I set my phone down and take a deep breath.

Then I grab a slice of pizza, top off my wine and curl up on the couch with my sketchbook.

I should write Book of Happiness on the cover, because that's what it's become. Every picture I've drawn in here is exactly that. A moment I let myself be happy.

I flip to a blank page and start sketching. The pumpkin patch takes shape first, then the corn maze in the background. I get as far as outlining a crooked vine before my eyelids grow heavy. The charcoal slips just a little in my fingers, my hand going still. I fall asleep like that, pizza crust on the table, wine glass half-full, sketchbook open in my lap.

***

I wake up early and clean up the mess from last night. After a quick shower, I throw on black leggings and a fitted t-shirt. I take my time getting ready, hair down in loose waves, pulled back with a headband, a little more makeup than I'd normally wear for a cleaning day, but…I want to look good when Reed shows up with dinner.

I pack a sandwich for later and, because I'm extra, grab two throw pillows to sit on when he stops by. Once I've got everything I need, I make a last-minute decision to tuck my sketchbook under my arm so I can finish the drawing I started last night.

I'm loading the last of my things into the car when Judy steps outside.

"Hi, sweetheart. Are you heading to the salon?"

"Yeah," I say, shutting the hatch. "Trying to get more cleaning done."

"That's nice, honey." She tilts her head. "So…did you have a good time at the farm yesterday?"

"I did. Thanks for letting me take your place." That's all I'm saying. There is no way I'm telling her that her nephew laid me down in a cornfield.

Judy's lips curve into a smile. "Maybe when you have more time, you can tell me all about it."

"Sure. Absolutely," I lie, forcing a bright smile.

I slip into the driver's seat before Judy can fish for more details and head out.

When I pull up, the first thing I see is another note taped to the salon door. I don't even have to read it to know it's from Bradley Manchester, again.

I rip it off the glass, shove it into my jacket pocket and head inside without looking at it.

After I finish unloading and putting things away, I lock the door and finally pull the note from my pocket.

Raelynn Newberry,

I've reached out multiple times regarding this property, and I urge you not to waste any more of my time. Opportunities like this do not wait. Contact me immediately so we can move forward before the window closes.

-Brad

I crumple it up and toss it straight into the trash. This guy's an ass, clearly used to getting his way. But not this time. I'm not selling.

I spend the next several hours scrubbing the main room, the same room I plan to have dinner with Reed. By the time I'm ready for lunch, I've got it more than halfway done. Feeling pretty good about it, I grab my sandwich and sketchbook, then settle cross-legged on one of the pillows. I eat while I work, shading in the last of the corn maze and pumpkins, losing track of time until an hour's gone by.

A loud knock on the door makes me jump, my heart lurching into my throat. When my head snaps up, I see Bradley standing there and I know he saw me. No chance of hiding now. With a sigh, I set my sketchbook aside and peel myself off the floor. This guy is really starting to get on my nerves. I unlock the door and crack it open.

"Raelynn, it's a pleasure to see you again," he says, but the words aren't warm, they're irritated.

"What can I help you with, Mr. Manchester?"

"I hope you've given my offer some thought," he says, his tone tightening. "And by now, I assume you're aware how stupid it would be to pass on it."

He can't be serious.

"I'm going to say this one last time, Mr. Manchester. I'm not interested. Have a good day."

I shut the door in his face, lock it and head straight for the office, out of sight. That's when I hear it, a loud bang, like he just slammed his fist against the door. I don't look, but I pull out my phone, ready to call for help if I need to. When the silence drags on, I peek out the door. He's gone. I'm pretty sure that grown-ass man just threw a temper tantrum outside my front door.

I'm not letting this ruin my day.

I walk out of the office and set my bag and sketchbook on the now-clean counter. Then I grab the broom, crank up some music on my phone and start dance-sweeping my way around the room.

Just as I'm about to use the broom as a microphone, there's another knock on the door.

I spin around, ready to tell Bradley where to shove it, only to see Naya grinning through the window.

I unlock the door and open it, still smiling from my impromptu broom performance.

Naya steps inside, her eyes flicking to the broom in my hand. "Wow. And here I thought you were opening a salon, not auditioning for So You Think You Can Sweep."

I laugh, leaning the broom against the wall. "Jealous of my moves?"

"Jealous? No. Mildly concerned? Absolutely." She pauses, giving me a slow once-over. "Also… why do you look so good to clean?"

I shrug, trying to play it off. "No reason. I just felt like it."

Naya snorts. "Uh-huh. And I wear heels to take out the trash."

I laugh and shake my head, moving toward the counter. "You're reading way too much into it."

She smirks, unconvinced. "What's going on, Rae?"

I huff. "Okay, fine. Someone's coming for dinner."

"Does this someone rhyme with 'need'… and have a jawline you could cut yourself on?"

I roll my eyes, but my lips twitch. "Fine. Yes. It's Reed."

Naya claps her hands like she's just won a prize. "Girl, I am living vicariously through you. Tell. Me. Everything."

I laugh and hand her the broom. "Only if we keep cleaning. I need to get this done."

"Deal," she says, taking it from me. "But don't think you're getting off easy. I expect a full play-by-play."

I grab a rag and start wiping down the wall while I tell her the whole story, every detail about what's been going on between us. I keep it surface-level, just the events, none of the messy feelings. That part can wait for another time. Throughout the whole thing, Naya gasps, lets out drawn-out 'wows'. She's grinning so big by the end, I'm half convinced her face might stay that way.

Naya leans on the broom. "So, what time?"

I pull my phone from my pocket. "It's 4:30. Reed didn't give me an exact time, but I'm guessing anytime now. Which is why you need to go."

She quickly hands me the broom and scurries to the door. "Call me tomorrow. I want the rest of the story." She blows me a kiss, and I chuckle as she skips to her car.

I quickly clean up my supplies and head to the bathroom to check myself in the mirror. Then I set the pillows on the floor and lean against the counter.

I can't just stand here looking like a desperate idiot. I grab my phone and start scrolling, pretending I'm deeply invested in the newsfeed I'm not actually reading. I check my email, open a weather app I don't need, even play with the brightness setting like that's somehow important right now. It's ridiculous, but it keeps me from pacing. I'm nervous and scared, and I can already feel my heart rate spiking. I don't know why, it's not like I didn't just spend time with him yesterday. But the truth about why I pulled away yesterday…that's the problem. What if I tell him, and he pulls away? Or worse…walks away.

20

No Coincidence, Just Judy

Reed

Today's my day off, and until I meet Raelynn for dinner, I decide to just stay home, maybe get some of my own cleaning done. I'm elbow-deep in laundry when there's a quick knock on the door and Miles lets himself in.

"Hey," he says, stepping into the kitchen and pouring himself a cup of coffee.

I hold out my mug, and he tops it off without missing a beat. "What are you up to today?"

"I just came to see what's up with you."

"What do you mean? Nothing's up with me."

He gives me a flat look. "Reed, cut the crap. You left the other night pretty quickly."

"Yeah, I had to work."

"I know you, stupid…stop pretending."

He's not wrong. He knows me better than anyone, and I know he's not going to back down.

I groan. "It's Raelynn. Okay."

"And?" He gestures for more.

"And what?"

"What about her?"

"Fine…we have a date tonight."

Miles' brows shoot up. "How did that happen?"

"I don't fucking know! Every time I turn around, she's there… I mean everywhere. And no matter how hard I tried, it kept happening. Then I started actually liking her. It's not just flirting. Now, I'm so fucked."

He laughs. Not just a chuckle, full-on grabs his stomach, slaps his knee, like I've just told the best joke he's ever heard.

"What's so funny, asshole? I'm serious, I don't know how this happened."

Miles wipes at his eyes, still grinning. "I know how this happened. And you're right, you are fucked."

"Okay. You want to fill me in?"

He pats my shoulder and starts walking toward the door. "You should visit Judy. And if I were you, I'd do it soon." He laughs as he heads out.

"What the hell does Judy have to do with this?"

He just waves over his shoulder. "Talk to Judy."

I stand there completely dumbfounded, staring at the door long after it shuts.

Why would I need to talk to Judy about this? Then it hits me. Judy must've won the damn date and sent Raelynn in her place. Did she do it on purpose? I grab my keys, slip on my shoes and head for the door.

Five minutes later, I'm walking up to Judy's door. I knock twice and let myself in. When she sees me, her whole face lights up. "Hello, sweetheart! You didn't have to work today?"

"No, I've got the day off."

"Are you hungry?" She opens her fridge.

I narrow my eyes. "No. I know you're up to something."

She blinks, all wide-eyed sweetness. "Me? What do you mean?"

"Don't start, Judy."

She shrugs, busying herself at the counter trying to dodge the question. "Coffee? I just made a fresh pot."

"Judy…"

She laughs, setting two mugs down on the table. "What exactly do you want to know, honey?"

"Did you win that date and send Raelynn in your place?"

"I did," she says easily. "I had a terrible headache."

"Did you tell Raelynn the date was with me?"

Judy's mouth twitches like she's trying not to smile. "It must have slipped my mind."

"Judy, you better start telling me everything you've done, or I'll start a petition to have you removed from the town council."

Her eyes widen. "You wouldn't."

"Don't call my bluff on this." I wouldn't actually, but it sounds good, and she believes it.

"Okay, fine." She sighs. "I might have given the two of you a little push. Is it working?"

"I want details."

"Okay…" She draws the word out. "When the girls and I had a few drinks, I sent you to get the pumpkins knowing you'd find me with Raelynn. And I knew when you boys were going to tear down cabin two, so I set up the carving tables with the girls and…"

"There's more?" I raise my brows.

"I suggested you take her for a motorcycle ride. Also, I knew you had the day off when Raelynn needed an inspection, so I called you. And when you said you had plans, I threw Jose in your face to make you jealous."

I'm actually shocked by her admission, but when she keeps going, I damn near fall out of my chair.

"When the girls and I were at the fundraiser, I excused myself to use the bathroom and grabbed the sign for the kissing booth. Tore it right down the middle. I knew if the girls saw what was waiting in that tent, they wouldn't have gone in. I also knew you wouldn't pass up the opportunity to have a little fun with her, so I made sure to bring the sign straight to you."

My mouth literally drops open. I quickly close it and lean forward. "And what about the date?"

"I overbid on purpose. And when the chief called to tell me I'd won, I told him I wanted to surprise you and asked him not to tell you. Then I convinced Raelynn I'd just won a contest and didn't want it to go to waste."

I pinch the bridge of my nose. "Tell me you didn't smash out her window to make sure she went?"

"Oh no," she says, all wide-eyed, "that was a happy coincidence." Then she smiles, clearly pleased with how perfectly it played right into her hands.

"Is there anything else?"

"Nope. Not unless there needs to be."

"There isn't. Because of you, I have a dinner date with Raelynn tonight," I admit.

"Oh, that's wonderful!"

"Yes, your twisted plan worked," I say, pointing a finger at her. "But no more. I can handle it from here."

"Okay, sweetheart," she says with a too-innocent smile. "I won't get involved anymore."

I stand and kiss her cheek, not believing for a second she's done meddling.

When I reach the door, I turn back. "Oh. By the way, I was bluffing. I wouldn't actually have you removed from the town council."

She plants her hands on her hips. "You're such a stinker, you know that?"

I chuckle. "I could say the same about you." Laughing, I head out the door.

I round the lake and head straight to Miles' place. He's in the barn, working under his tractor.

He glances up. "Did you talk to Judy?"

"I did."

"She's good, isn't she?"

"How did you know?"

He chuckles. "How do you think Kinsley and I got together?"

We both laugh.

"You need a hand down there?"

"No, I'm just about done."

"Alright, I'll see you around."

"Reed," he calls after me, "don't fuck this up."

"I don't plan on it."

When I get back to my place, I still have five hours before dinner, so I keep cleaning, then head into town for groceries. I take Fifi for a walk, and by the time we get back, I've still got a couple of hours to kill.

I jump in the shower, but my mind drifts straight to the corn maze, and how I almost blew it. Why was she even at Fireside that late? She must've placed an order, but I would've seen her walk in. Then it hits me.

I quickly finish, towel off, and wrap it around my waist. Grabbing my phone, I dial the Fireside Lounge.

"Fireside, this is Tess. Can I help you?"

"Hey Tess, it's Reed. I need a favor."

"What do you need?"

"Can you look up an order that was canceled two nights ago?"

"Yeah, if I have a name."

"It's Raelynn." I hear her tapping on the keyboard.

"Yeah, I see it. Why?"

"Can you make two of that exact order for around 4:30?"

"I can do that."

"Thanks. I'll see you then."

I head to the bedroom and finish getting ready, just jeans and a T-shirt, with a hoodie thrown over the top. Grabbing my keys, I tell Fifi to be good and head out the door, straight to the Fireside Lounge.

I grab the food and two minutes later, I'm pulling into the lot by the salon. Through the window, I see her leaning against the counter staring at her phone. She doesn't notice me. I push the door open. "You really should lock this door."

She jumps, a hand flying to her heart. "I thought it was locked."

I laugh, pull the door closed and twist the lock. "Clearly not, Sunshine."

She purses her lips, trying not to smile at the nickname. "Okay, Mr. Safety, I'll remember next time."

I chuckle. "You hungry?"

"Yes. We can sit on the pillows."

I follow her over, dropping down across from her. When I open the bag, I pause. "This might look familiar." I slide one of the containers toward her. "It's the same thing you ordered the other night and canceled."

Her expression softens. "How did you know?"

"I was thinking about how I almost fucked this up," I admit, "and how I didn't see you that night and why you were there. So, I called Fireside and asked if an order had been canceled. The waitress looked it up for me."

"That's…really thoughtful. Thank you." She shifts forward on her knees, crawling over to take the container, then settles back onto her pillow.

Watching her crawl… fucking hot.

"You're welcome."

We eat and talk about our plans for the weekend. When we're done, she stands and gathers up the containers, carrying them to the trash. I watch her for a moment, not bothering to hide it. When she turns around, she catches me staring.

"What? Do I have something on me?" She glances down at her shirt, searching for a spot where food might've dropped.

"Yes," I lie. "Come here, I'll get it." I stand up.

She walks over, still looking down, and when she's close enough, I tilt her chin up. She stiffens.

Our eyes lock. I lean down. "Are you scared?"

"To death."

I step back, feeling the edge of her nerves. I sit back down and slide her pillow closer until it's right in front of me. She takes a seat.

"Why are you scared?"

She covers her face with her hands. "I can't tell you."

I reach out, lightly tugging at her wrists until her hands drop. "Hey…you can tell me. I'm sure whatever it is, we can figure it out."

She shakes her head. "It's embarrassing."

"When I was a kid," I say, leaning in a little, "I had to go to the bathroom during class. I was wearing overalls, the straps twisted, and I couldn't get them off in time. I ended up peeing my pants. Trust me, you can't top that."

She laughs, shaking her head. "That is bad, but this is adult embarrassment. It's not the same."

"Raelynn. I would never judge you."

She sighs, dropping her head. "There's actually two things."

She can't look at me, and my heart breaks a little. I scoot closer and take her hands in mine.

I give her hands a little squeeze. "Start with the easiest one."

"I'm sure you know that I'm technically still married." She glances up briefly, checking my reaction.

"Yeah, I know. Miles told me, not in detail, just said you were getting a divorce."

"I have guilt…like it's wrong to do this." She gestures between us.

I let go of one hand and tilt her chin, making sure she hears me. "Sunshine, nothing about this is wrong."

She searches my eyes. "How do you know?"

"Let me ask you…do you like being with me?"

A faint smile hovers on her lips. "Yes."

"How often do you think about me?"

Her cheeks flush. "More than I'd like to admit."

"Do you trust me?"

Her brow creases. "Yes."

"Then there's your answer. Because I will never push you to do anything you're not comfortable with."

Her voice dips, barely above a whisper. "The problem is…I want to."

"Then what's stopping you?"

She buries her face in her hands again, voice muffled as she blurts, "I've never had an orgasm."

I go completely still, like I can't quite process what I just heard. "Never?"

She gives the smallest shake of her head.

"Not once?"

She drops her hands. "Oh God," she whispers.

I lean back, doing my damnedest not to let a smart-ass comment slip.

"I have," she finally admits, "but only by myself."

Fuck! She's making it damn near impossible to keep my hands to myself right now. Every cell in me is itching to show her exactly what it would be like to be with me.

21

My First Real One

Raelynn

I can't believe I just told him no one's ever given me an orgasm. He's not running, that's a good sign. But the way he's looking at me right now makes me question if I should've kept my mouth shut.

"Say something," I whisper. I can't take the silence much longer. I need to know what he's thinking.

He shakes his head, eyes never leaving mine. "When you're ready…I'll make sure you never say that again."

The way my body just reacted to those words tells me he's not lying. I swallow, embarrassingly hard, unable to get a single word out.

He chuckles. "Come on, Sunshine. Show me what you got done today."

He stands, pulling me up with him until we're chest to chest. His jaw tightens, and my pulse skips.

"Raelynn," he says it like a warning, but I don't move.

His lips brush mine first, testing, like he's gauging how far I'll let him go. I lean in, pressing my mouth to his, and the faintest groan vibrates against my lips.

At first, his kiss is slow, lingering, his bottom lip dragging against mine before he catches it gently between his. He releases it only to tilt his head, fitting our mouths together in a way that makes my pulse trip over itself. His hand slides to the small of my back while his tongue traces the seam of my mouth. I part for him without thinking. He deepens the kiss gradually, teasing at first, his tongue brushing mine in soft, tempting strokes. Then he presses in with more intent, coaxing, claiming, pulling me under. I answer him without hesitation, matching him, tangling my tongue with his. Heat pools low in my stomach, and I can't stop the soft, involuntary sound that slips from me, swallowed instantly by his mouth.

He pulls back just enough to whisper against my lips, his breath warm, "I want to show you how good I can make you feel."

"Show me," I breathe.

For a second, he just looks at me, weighing the choice between restraint and giving in. Then, without a word, he steps back and walks across the room. The absence of his touch leaves me dizzy. He flips the switch, and the room drops into darkness, my eyes straining until I can just make out his silhouette. I watch until he's right in front of me again.

"I want to show you," he murmurs, voice low enough to make my stomach flip, "but not with your eyes…with your body."

His hand finds my jaw, thumb brushing lightly along the curve of it before sliding up, threading into my hair. The gentle pull tilts my head just enough to bare my mouth to his, and my breath catches, my pulse thundering in my ears.

In the darkness, everything else comes alive. I hear the slow, steady sound of his breathing. The clean, warm scent of him, soap and cedar. His fingers slide deeper into my hair, the pads of them grazing my scalp in a way that sends shivers down my spine.

Every inch of contact feels amplified, each small movement sparking heat low in my belly.

Without breaking the kiss, he reaches down, finding the hem of my shirt. The fabric drags upward over my skin until he pulls it over my head, the kiss breaking for just a breath before his mouth finds me again, trailing along my jaw, down the curve of my neck to my collarbone. I moan into him, shivers prickling across the path his lips leave behind.

His hands follow, sliding down the length of my body, his thumbs brushing over my hardened nipples before skimming to my waist. He pauses there, as if giving me a chance to pull away. I don't. Instead, I reach for the bottom of his sweatshirt and push it upward. He steps back just enough to lift it over his head, tossing it aside. And does the same with the T-shirt underneath.

He catches my hands, flattening them to his bare chest. Heat radiates against my palms, the steady beat of his heart under my fingers. His hands slide down my arms, then over my sides, and the faint scrape of my nails digging in makes his chest vibrate with a low groan. His fingers tease along my skin until they reach my waistband. He hooks his thumbs there and slowly pushes them down.

He pulls me back in, his lips brushing over my shoulder, up my neck, before finding my mouth again. His arm wraps firmly around my back. I feel his hand unclip my bra, the lace falling down my arms. He draws me against him, and my hands slide up, looping around his neck.

He lowers me to the floor, the chill of it seeping through my skin in contrast to the heat rolling off him. He leans over me, one knee pressed tight between my legs, his weight balanced on his hands braced on either side of my head. The kiss breaks, leaving my lips tingling, every nerve lit under his shadow.

His voice drops. "You want this?"

"Yes." It's barely more than a whisper, my body trembling just enough for him to feel it.

He sits back for just a moment, grabbing both pillows. Then he reaches down, one arm sliding beneath me, lifting me. He tucks the pillows under my back, arching me higher, and a gasp slips out when his hands glide up the length of my legs. "Let me hear it again, Raelynn…do you want this?" he asks, his voice low, when his hands reach the edge of my panties.

A breathy, "Yes," slips out.

He slides them down slowly, lifting my legs one at a time to free them, then moves so both his knees are between my spread legs. He stops. "Let me feel how much you want this."

His thumb drags over my center once, and my whole body jerks into the touch. His name flies from my mouth, desperate for more.

"Mmm…you do want this," he rumbles, satisfaction in every syllable.

He bends low, his tongue tracing a slow line down my arched stomach. Two fingers push inside me at the same moment his tongue slides over my swollen nub. My head tips back, a moan breaking free as the pleasure crashes into me.

He starts slow, fingers stroking in a deep, deliberate rhythm, his tongue flicking in time. I can already feel my body tightening around him, the pressure building too quickly. *Keep it together, Raelynn.* He hums his approval, and the vibration sends a jolt through me. My arms shoot out desperately reaching for something to hold on to.

"Mmm, baby you taste so sweet." His breath is warm, his tongue flattens and his pace quickens.

My knees tense, holding tight around his head, clamping down as he pushes me closer until there's no holding back. "Oh God, Reed!"

My eyes roll back, my legs stiffen and shocks of pleasure tear through me. I scream his name as my body convulses, wave after wave breaking until I go limp. *Holy shit!*

He doesn't pull away immediately, easing me down from the high with slower strokes before sliding his fingers out. His mouth trails up my trembling body, kissing and tasting, until he reaches my lips. My chest is still heaving when I kiss him back, and I can taste myself on his tongue. He reaches down, pulling the pillows from under me, breaking the kiss to sit up. He lifts one of my legs, resting it on his chest, then picks up my panties and slides them back down my leg. My leg twitches under his touch, and he places a soft kiss to my thigh.

I touch his hand. "Reed…I want you to…"

He stops me with a shake of his head, his voice gentle but firm. "No, baby. This was for you, not for me."

He slips my other leg in and pulls the fabric up. My body shudders when the fabric reaches my sensitive center, but I lift my hips to make it easier. He shifts beside me on the floor, stretching out so we're side by side. His arm curls around me, pulling me into his solid chest. He presses a slow kiss to the top of my head, and I can hear the faint sound of his heart under my cheek.

"Why didn't you want to keep going?"

"I wanted to show you how good it can be…when it's just about you. Your pleasure. Your needs. And I want you to be one hundred percent ready before I show you more."

"I don't know how you're going to top that."

He chuckles. "Baby, you think that was good? Just wait until I'm inside you."

I kiss his chest and squeeze him. "Are you free tomorrow?" I laugh.

He hugs me back, smiling. "Anytime. I mean it…anytime."

I giggle.

"Come on, let's get you dressed. You still need to show me what you got done today." He stands and helps me to my feet, picking up my clothes. He slides my shirt over my head, his fingers brushing my skin in a way that makes me shiver, and I pull on my pants while he puts his shirts back on.

He walks over, cups my face in both hands and kisses me hard. Just as my body starts to lean into him, ready for more, he breaks the kiss and steps back.

"Shield your eyes."

I do, and a second later the lights flick on, blinding after so long. I squint until my vision adjusts, and when I finally look at him, my pulse jumps. He's staring at me from across the room, heat in his eyes.

"Jesus…you're beautiful after you come."

I feel the blush creeping up my neck. "Stop flirting with me."

He smirks. "Not a chance."

He walks over and takes my hand. "Okay, now that we've explored this room thoroughly, want to show me the rest?"

I swat his arm.

We spend the next hour walking around, talking about my plans for the place. He asks questions and listens to every word I say. When we step back in the main room, Reed's eyes land on my sketchbook sitting on the counter.

"You been drawing?"

"Yes."

He reaches for it, but I quickly snatch it up. He tilts his head. "What are you drawing, Raelynn?"

"Nothing. Just…things that make me happy."

Why did I just say that?

He takes a step closer. "And what makes you happy, Raelynn?"

"I'm not showing you, Reed." I back away, but he grins and follows. I pull the book behind my back, trying and failing to hide my smile.

He steps in, cups my face and kisses me. I melt into him, and while I'm lost in the feel of his lips, I let him slip the book from my hands. When he pulls back, he studies my eyes like he's looking for permission. I give a small nod. He opens the book, and my heart pounds. His eyes widen at the first drawing, his bike.

"Wow, Raelynn…this is really good." He flips the page. It's my building with him standing in the middle. His gaze lifts to mine. "It's me."

"Yes. The day of the inspection."

He turns another page and freezes. It's the two of us running through the haunted house. He flips to the last page, it's of the corn maze, him and I standing in the middle, locked in a kiss.

"This one I finished today," I lean in for a better look.

"Raelynn…these are art-studio good."

I'm shocked by his words. That's the exact opposite of what I've been told for the last ten years. He notices, leaning down to kiss me softly.

"Seriously. They're really good."

"You really think so?" I glance down at the page he's holding open.

"Yeah, I do."

"Thanks."

"Do I make you happy, Raelynn?" he asks, looking at the picture, then at me. "Is that why I'm in almost all of them?"

"Yes…but don't get a big head about it," I tease.

He chuckles. "Too late."

He hands me the book, and I flip to the page with his bike. I tear it out and pass it to him. "I want you to have this."

"Why?" he asks, taking it carefully.

"Because this was the day you made me feel alive again."

He sucks in a breath, then lifts my hand and brushes a kiss over my knuckles. "I'll keep it forever," he says quietly.

By the time we finish talking about my drawings, it's well after eleven.

He checks his phone. "I should go. I'm meeting the guys in the morning."

"Yeah, same with the girls."

"I think I should probably get your phone number," he says, glancing to the spot on the floor where he'd just worked me over.

I laugh, pull my phone from my pocket and hand it to him. When he gives it back, I read the contact info…Hotshot. I laugh again as he passes me his phone, and I put my number in before handing it back.

He looks at the screen and chuckles. "I thought you hated me calling you Sunshine."

"It's growing on me."

I throw my bag over my shoulder, turn off the lights, and we step outside. I lock the door, and he walks me to my car. He opens the door for me, bending to press a kiss to my lips.

"I'll see you later."

"Good night, Reed."

"Good night, Sunshine."

I climb in, and he shuts my door, tapping the roof before walking away. I watch him until he rounds the corner of the building.

I start the engine and pull away, the quiet of the drive giving my mind too much room to wander. Every nerve still feels lit from the inside out. I've never felt anything like that, my first real orgasm, and it was…mind-blowing. The way he touched me, the way he looked at me. And now I want him even more.

But he was right. I'm not one hundred percent ready. Not yet. And going further tonight wouldn't have been fair to him. By the time I pull into the cabin driveway, my thoughts are jumbled between wanting him and knowing I have to wait.

22

Her in My Sights

Reed

The alarm goes off before the sun's even thinking about coming up. I roll over, groaning, but there's no point in fighting it. It's hunting season, early mornings are part of the deal. I swing my legs over the side of the bed, the cold floor making me move faster toward the chair where I left my clothes out last night.

I get dressed quickly, pulling on my thermal camo pants and matching long-sleeve shirt, the fabric holding a faint scent of last year's woods. In the kitchen, Fifi's already waiting by the door. I crack it open, letting her out into the crisp morning air, then turn the coffee pot on, the drip echoing in the quiet house.

I glance over and see the sketch she gave me sitting on the table. I pause, fingers brushing the edge of the paper. My mind goes right back to last night. How she reacted to my touch and the way she moaned my name. I run my hand over my face. I wanted to go all the way with her. I think she might have let me, but I don't want part of her. I want all of her. I want her to give herself to me without hesitation, because when she does, I won't hold back.

Fifi barks outside, snapping me out of it. I shake my head, reminding myself I should be thinking about deer, not her. I grab my thermos, fill it, then pull on my coat and sling my rifle over my shoulder.

Outside, the air bites at my skin in that way only late fall mornings can. I call Fifi back in, give her a quick pat on the head and lock up before heading to the truck.

It's still dark when I pull onto Luke's long driveway, headlights sweeping over the perfectly trimmed lawn and the big white house with a four-car garage. I know Luke has money, but he doesn't flaunt it. He also doesn't talk much about what he does. I know it's something in security and computer technology. The garage light clicks on as I pull up, and the door lifts. Luke's waiting in the garage, coffee in hand. "Thought you overslept."

"Please. I was up before you even rolled out of bed."

He smirks. "You want one?" He holds up his mug.

I set my gear down just inside the garage, and we head into the house. His kitchen's huge, granite countertops, matching state-of-the-art appliances, the kind you see in magazines. He pours a mug and slides it across to me.

"Come on, I'll show you my new office."

That makes me pause. Luke doesn't normally talk about work. We head downstairs, and he stops in front of a sleek black door. Then, no joke, a red light scans him from head to toe. The door slides open with a hiss.

"Just stand here and let it scan you," he says. "You, Miles, Dylan and Judy already have access."

I step forward, the light sweeping over me. Inside is a wall of monitors, a massive desk planted in the middle.

"Holy shit, man."

He chuckles.

I turn, and the back wall stops me cold. It's lined floor-to-ceiling with bookshelves. In front of them, there's a small table with a chess set already in play. Only one monitor is active, and it's showing his property, camera slowly sweeping the grounds.

When the system catches movement, it zooms in, Miles' truck, clear as day. Then it zooms again, close enough to see his face. Text flashes across the bottom: **Miles Davison - Cleared for Entry.**

My jaw drops.

Luke pats my shoulder. "Come on. Dylan's coming down the road right now."

I glance around for the camera that's showing Dylan's location. "Where?"

He smirks, holds up his phone. "He texted."

I shake my head laughing, and we head upstairs, meeting them in the garage just as Miles' truck comes to a stop. Dylan pulls in one minute later. Both of them climb out lugging gear and thermoses.

"Morning, princesses," Dylan calls. "Hope you brought your A-game."

Luke grins. "Hope you brought a muzzle."

Miles laughs, pulling on his vest. "All right, let's pair up before it gets too light."

"I'm with Luke," I say immediately, grabbing my pack. "I like to actually see deer when I hunt."

"That works," Dylan says, clapping Miles on the shoulder. "Guess it's me and you. Let's show these two how it's done."

"Do you even know what a deer looks like?" Luke laughs.

Dylan pretends to be offended. "Talk all you want, pretty boy. I'm still the one bringing home the big one."

"Pretty sure that's what you said last year," I shoot back. "And all you bagged was a hangover."

We pull on our gear, the garage echoing with the sound of boots on concrete, rifles being checked and coffee being finished off.

Luke slings his rifle over his shoulder and jerks his head toward the treeline behind the house. "All right, ladies, let's move out."

The four of us step into the cold morning air, our breath fogging as we head across the yard. The path splits at the edge of the woods, Miles and Dylan veering left while Luke and I take the trail to the right, still tossing insults over our shoulders until the trees swallow the sound.

By the time Luke and I climb into the tree stand, the sky's just starting to lighten. He leans in, keeping his voice low so we don't spook anything.

"So… you and Raelynn, huh?"

I turn my head slowly toward him. "How the hell do you know about that?"

He smirks. "Did you see all those cameras in my office?"

My eyes go wide, mind flashing to last night and what he might've seen.

He chuckles under his breath. "Relax. Miles told me."

I exhale, shaking my head. "You're a dick."

He laughs, and that's the end of it. We sit there for hours, the woods quiet except for the occasional rustle of leaves. All I can think about is what Raelynn might be doing, and how I'd rather be anywhere with her than freezing my ass off out here.

By the time we finally call it, I'm starving and can't feel my feet. We climb down and take the trail back toward the house. Miles and Dylan are already there, leaning against the tailgate and throwing insults before we're even close.

Miles spots us first. "Well, look who finally decided to show up."

"Hope you enjoyed your nap out there," Dylan adds.

Luke snorts. "Hope you enjoyed missing every shot."

"Bold talk from a guy I didn't see drag anything in," Dylan fires back.

Luke waves them off. "Come on, let's get inside and warm up."

"I'm gonna head home." I sling my pack over my shoulder.

Dylan grins. "You going to see Raelynn?"

My head snaps toward Miles, who's already smirking. "You've got a big mouth."

He laughs. "Remember all the times you ragged on me for having a girlfriend? Payback's a bitch."

They all start laughing, blowing me exaggerated kisses and hugging themselves like they're in some romance movie.

I flip them the finger, still laughing as I climb into my truck.

When I get home, I let the dog out and head straight for the shower. The hot water does its job, thawing me out enough to feel my fingers again. I throw on a pair of jeans, a hoodie, and a ball cap, not bothering with my hair and grab my phone. I call Raelynn.

"Hello, Hotshot."

"Hey, Sunshine. Are you finished for the night?"

"Yeah, I just walked in the door. Why?"

"You hungry?"

"Starving. I haven't eaten since lunch."

"Perfect. I'm ordering a pizza. Give me twenty and I'll be there."

"Okay. See you soon."

"Soon," I say, hanging up and immediately placing the order.

I set down my phone, feeling something I'm not used to…relief. The kind that settles deep, knowing I'm about to see her. It's a weird feeling, one I've never had before, but there's no chance I'm staying away.

Twenty minutes later, I'm walking up the path to her cabin, pizza in hand. Just as I reach the door it swings open. I stop dead. She's got no makeup on, her damp hair hanging loose over her shoulders. She's wearing a tank top showing off her large, I-want-to-rub-my-face-in-them breasts, pajama pants and slippers.

I must be staring, because she frowns and plants her hands on her hips. "What?"

I give my head the tiniest shake. "You've never looked more beautiful."

Her cheeks flush, and she takes the pizza from me, ducking her head. "Thanks."

I follow her in and kick off my shoes. She sets the pizza on the coffee table, then heads into the kitchen for plates.

"You want a beer?" She glances over her shoulder.

"Please."

She comes back a moment later, handing me both bottles. I twist them open, pass one to her, and we each grab a slice after she flips the box open.

Her sketchbook is sitting on the couch, pages fanned out. I glance at the open page. It's another drawing of her salon.

"So, what made you happy today?" I ask, nodding toward the book.

She laughs. "I'll never tell."

I smirk. "Is it me? You wanna draw me like one of your…"

"Don't say it," she cuts me off, grinning.

"Are you afraid to see me naked?"

She chokes on a sip of beer, laughing. "That is not what I said."

"Didn't have to. I can read between the lines."

She shakes her head, smiling. "You are so full of yourself."

"Not full," I say, leaning in. "Just confident. Big difference."

Her eyes flick over me before she takes another bite of pizza. "Confident, huh? Pretty sure I could sketch you in ten seconds flat."

"Because you'd be too distracted to take longer?" I tease.

She tosses a crust at me. "Because it wouldn't take long to capture all that ego."

That sets us both off laughing. We finish the pizza, talking between bites about what she and the girls got done at the salon. I tell her about the guys finding out we had dinner together, and she laughs, saying it was the same on her end, except Kinsley was mad she was the last to find out.

We clean up the coffee table and carry our plates and bottles into the kitchen. She sets hers in the sink, and when she turns, she's right in front of me. I look down at her, and for a second neither of us moves. Then I bend, brushing my lips against hers. She makes this soft sound, wrapping her arms around my neck, and I don't think twice. My hands slide to her hips, and I lift her easily, her legs curling around my waist as I carry her back to the couch. I sit, keeping her in my lap. She stays right there, her hands resting against the back of my neck, eyes searching mine. I place a soft kiss on her lips before murmuring, "I have to go."

She nods, then kisses me again, lingering just long enough to make leaving harder. "Will I see you tomorrow?" she asks against my mouth.

"I hope so," I breathe into her lips.

She lifts off my lap and we both stand. She looks up at me. "Are you sure you don't want to stay longer?"

I focus on her, my chest tightening. "Sunshine, the last thing I want to do is leave. But I need you a hundred percent ready before I stay."

She nods in agreement, saying nothing, just taking a step back.

I lift her chin, my thumb brushing her jaw. "It has to be this way. If you're not at a hundred, you'll have regrets. And I don't want to be your regret, Raelynn. I want to be…" I stop myself, take a deep breath. "I have to go." I kiss her again and don't wait to find out if I've got any willpower left.

I leave without looking back. When I reach my truck, I stop with my hand on the door, the cold air biting at my face. Walking away from her tonight was harder than I thought it would be.

I climb in, start the engine and just sit there for a second. All I can think about is how desperate I was to see her today, how much I wanted to stay. Which is exactly why I need to stay away tomorrow. When she's one hundred percent ready, she'll come to me. Until then, keeping my distance is the only way to protect her…and myself.

23

Strong Enough to Stay Gentle

Raelynn

I'm up early and already dressed in my paint clothes; old sweatpants, an oversized t-shirt that's seen better days. My hair is pulled back in a loose braid, a little mascara, and that's it. No need to get fancy for a day of cleaning and painting.

The cabin is quiet except for the soft scratch of my pencil as I sit curled up on the couch, sketchbook balanced on my knees. I'm waiting for the girls to show so we can ride together, trying to distract myself with lines and shading. But all I can think about is him and how he's right. There's still a trace of guilt lingering, even though I know I shouldn't feel it. It's over between Jacob and me. He knows it, I know it. So why does it still hang over me?

A sharp knock at the door makes me jump, my pencil skidding across the page. Mel bounces in, all bright eyes. "Good morning!"

For half a second, I consider shoving her right back out the door and telling her to come back when she's in a shittier mood. But I don't, because as much as I want to roll my eyes, that kind of energy is…well, a little contagious.

"Morning. You want some coffee?"

"Nope. I threw back two energy drinks on my way over."

I grab my coat and we head out the door. Judy's waiting by the cars.

"Where's Kinsley?" I glance toward the farmhouse across the lake.

"That's why I needed two energy drinks," Mel groans. "Last night I was holding pillows over my head for hours, trying to suffocate myself just to drown out the two of them going at it all night."

I laugh. "And now you know why I'm staying in the cabin."

"Oh, you poor thing," Judy says, sipping her coffee. "Next time you come stay, we'll set you up in Cabin 4."

"I might have to take you up on that offer."

"Are we waiting for her?"

"No, she said she'd meet us there. Naya texted, she's on her way." Mel glances at her phone.

"Well, let's go then. We've got a salon to finish." Judy pats my shoulder. We pile into our cars and follow Judy out.

When we reach the salon, Naya's getting out of her car with a donut box tucked under her arm. She sighs. "I could've slept in today. I hope you know I love you."

Mel bounces past us. "We can't sleep in! You have the most energy in the morning."

Naya turns toward me, one eyebrow raised.

I lean in and whisper, "She had two energy drinks."

We both laugh. Mel doesn't need caffeine, she's naturally energetic.

I walk up and unlock the door, and we step inside, getting straight to work, setting up supplies, filling paint trays and taping off the main room. It's the last space left; the office, bathroom and walk-in closet were finished yesterday.

We're just about to start painting when Kinsley walks in. "Sorry I'm late. I got tied up this morning."

Mel smirks. "I bet you did."

We all burst out laughing.

Kinsley grins. "What? He missed me yesterday."

I keep quiet, because I think Reed missed me, too. He could've eaten at home. He could've stayed with the guys. But he didn't, he chose me.

Mel's voice cuts through my thoughts. "Okay, now that Kinsley's out of bed, let's get to work." She claps her hands, all fired up to get it done.

Naya turns on the radio and we dive in. Judy's wiping down windows while Kinsley, Naya and Mel roll fresh paint onto the walls. I'm on the floor painting the trim, the music makes it easy to keep moving.

"Raelynn, honey?" Judy calls, her voice light but carrying across the room. "I think you have company."

My pulse kicks up, a hopeful flutter starting in my chest. I turn toward the door, ready to see Reed. It's Bradley. Again. I groan. "This guy doesn't give up." I stand, and Naya turns down the music.

"What do you mean, he won't give up?" Kinsley and Mel ask almost at the same time.

I sigh. "This is Bradley Manchester. He's been sending letters and sticking notes on the door. He's stopped by twice. Last time, he got mad and hit the door. I thought I was going to have to call the police, but he left."

I start toward the front, but Judy says, "I'm sure he'll get the hint if I talk to him."

"Judy, I don't think that's a good…"

Before I can finish, she's unlocking the door. Kinsley and Naya are standing right behind her.

"Hello, Mr. Manchester," Judy says warmly. "What can we help you with?"

He looks her up and down. "I'm here to speak with Raelynn Newberry."

"I'm sorry, she doesn't want to speak with you." Judy keeps her voice polite.

He pulls off his sunglasses. "I'm not talking to some old lady about a property she doesn't own."

Naya and Kinsley pounce, voices sharp and fast. Naya's yelling about how he talks to elders, and Kinsley's shouting, "I'm a lawyer with a lot of friends! You better back off!"

I step forward and wedge myself between them. "You need to leave. And if you come back on my property again, I'll call the police."

I push everyone back inside, the girls still cussing him out, and lock the door.

"Unbelievable," Naya mutters, pacing like she's ready to march back out there.

Kinsley's face is flushed. "What is his deal?"

I press my palms to the counter, forcing a deep breath. "He's trying to get me to sell the building. Keeps acting like if he pushes hard enough, I'll cave."

"Not happening," Mel says, snatching her roller.

Judy glances at the door. "Let him huff and puff all he wants. We've got work to do."

The music kicks back on, and just like that, we're rolling paint again, only now with a little extra force behind every stroke.

Three coats of paint and a whole lot of dance parties later, we finally call it done. The only thing left is cleaning up the supplies, which I tell the girls I'll handle tomorrow. Judy had left a couple hours earlier, hugging me on her way out and telling me how proud she was of the progress.

By the time the rest of us are saying our goodbyes, it's nearly eight. Mel's leaving first thing in the morning, so I hug her a little longer. "Thanks for helping and organizing everything. You really are the best."

She grins and promises to come back once the salon's open. I pull Naya in next, thanking her for the donuts and for somehow turning the whole day into more of a party than work.

Then Kinsley wraps me in a tight hug. "This place already feels like you."

I watch the girls leave, then step back inside. I can already see it; large mirrors on the walls, three workstations, blow dryers, shampoo bowls and a cozy sitting area with books and magazines. It's almost done. All I need now is the equipment, which should be here in two days.

I grab my things and check my phone for maybe the tenth time in the last two hours. I was sure he would've called or texted by now, but nothing. I slip the phone into my pocket. I don't want to bother him if he's with the guys, but the silence still stings.

Stepping out, I lock the door behind me. The street is quiet as I make my way to my car. The whole drive home, I wonder what he's doing. I should be thinking about tomorrow and planning for the equipment drop-off, but I'm not.

Five minutes later, I'm walking through my front door, and I decide…I'm just going to text him.

Me: Hey, Hotshot. How'd the hunt go?

Three dots appear on the screen.

Hotshot: Didn't see a thing. How'd the painting go?

Me: It's all done. Just need to clean up tomorrow. Did you eat?

Hotshot: I did. Had dinner with the guys.

I type out an invitation, delete it, then type it again. My thumb hovers over the send button. Before I can talk myself out of it, I hit send.

Me: You want to stop by for a little while?

The three dots appear…then disappear, like he's still thinking.

Hotshot: I can't, Sunshine. I need you a hundred percent in. I don't ever want to push you into something you're not ready for…and I'm not sure I can be alone with you and not touch you. I'm sorry.

It stings, but I can't blame him. He's right, I need to figure this out.

Me: I understand. Maybe lunch tomorrow? Somewhere public.

Hotshot: Sure. Call me tomorrow and I can meet you somewhere.

Me: Good night.

Hotshot: Good night, Sunshine. Draw something happy.

I set my phone down, staring at the ceiling for a moment. I can't stop thinking about him and how much I wish the divorce was over.

I grab a quick shower, scrubbing the paint off until my skin feels raw. When I'm finally done, I pull on pajamas and crawl into bed early, hoping sleep will keep me from overthinking.

***

I wake up early and grab a quick bowl of cereal, eating it while I mentally run through the day. Once I'm done, I throw on a pair of jeans and a navy sweater, curl my hair and pin it back out of my face. A little mascara, a touch of blush, and I'm ready to go.

I grab my bag and keys, stepping out the door more determined than ever to get the salon finished. The cleanup should only take a few hours, and then, lunch with Reed.

First stop is the post office. I grab my mail and, of course, there are three more letters from Bradley Manchester. I don't even bother opening them. I just drop them straight into the trash on my way out.

When I pull up to the salon, relief washes over me. No note on the door. Maybe he finally got the hint. I grab my things and head inside, getting straight to work. I move from one task to the next without stopping, wiping down surfaces, stacking paint trays, folding drop cloths. The smell of fresh paint is still thick in the air, and each cleared space makes the room look more like the salon I've been picturing in my head for months.

Through the front windows, I spot Reed's truck pulling in. I wipe my hands on a rag and start toward the door, wondering why he's here. He said we'd meet somewhere for lunch. He walks up and pushes the door open a little harder than normal, his brow pinched. When his eyes land on me, he exhales like he's relieved, but I can tell he's upset.

I step closer. "What's wrong?"

His voice is firm. "Why didn't you tell me about Bradley Manchester?"

"What do you mean?" My chest tightens like I'm bracing for something that's not coming.

"Raelynn, a man has been harassing you, and you didn't think to tell me?"

I shift my weight. "I'm sorry. I didn't think it was a big deal."

He points toward the door. The sudden movement makes me flinch. Old habits die hard. Shame burns through me, and I have to look away.

Reed's expression shifts instantly, shock flashing across his face before he takes a step back. He turns away, and I feel it, a single tear slipping down my cheek.

When he turns again, his eyes are soft. He approaches slowly, like he's afraid of scaring me off.

I can't look at him. My focus stays glued to the floor.

"Raelynn, baby… look at me." His fingers are gentle as he lifts my chin.

"I'm sor…"

"Shhh," He cuts in, his thumb wiping away the second tear that falls, the touch soft. "I need you to hear me, Raelynn. Every word. I will never…ever…put my hands on you in anger. I will never give you a reason to pull away or flinch. I will not be the man who makes you feel small or unsafe. Not now. Not ever." His thumb traces my jaw like he's trying to erase every moment that made me react that way. "You're safe with me. Safe to breathe, safe to speak, safe to be exactly who you are without fear. Do you understand me?"

I try to answer, but my voice catches. The words knot in my throat. I nod instead, because if I open my mouth right now, the tears will win.

He draws me in, his body a wall of strength around me. I start to tell him I should have said something about Bradley, but he stops me gently.

"We can talk about it in a few minutes. Right now…I just want to hold you."

I press my face into him, taking in his familiar scent, the heat radiating through his shirt. Little by little, my heartbeat finds his rhythm, and I start to calm. His arms band tighter around me, an unspoken promise that nothing's getting past him.

He finally eases back, his hands sliding down to find mine. Without a word, he guides us both to the floor. We sit across from each other, knees nearly touching, his fingers wrapping around mine.

His thumbs trace little circles over my hands. "Okay," he says finally, "tell me what's been going on with Bradley."

I take a breath, eyes dropping to where our fingers are laced together. "He's been sending letters and leaving notes on the door. He's shown up here three times now. The last time, the girls freaked out on him because he wouldn't back off. Before that, he hit the door hard enough I thought I might have to call the police. But he left."

Reed's jaw locks, a muscle ticking in his cheek. His grip on my hands doesn't tighten, but I can feel the restraint in it, like he's holding back a storm. "Three times." He exhales slowly through his nose, the kind of breath someone takes when they're trying to keep from exploding. "That ends today. I don't care if it's a note, a phone call, or him breathing in your direction…you tell me."

I squeeze his hand. "Okay. You're right. I'll tell you every time, no matter what."

It's only then I realize, he wouldn't be here if I didn't matter to him. He came the second he found out, worry written all over him. And when he saw me standing here, whole and safe, the relief in his face said more than words ever could.

24

The Thin Line

Reed

I hold the door open for her, letting her step out into the cool air. She's smiling again, light on her feet like the conversation inside is already behind her. I wish I could shake it that easy.

It's not that she didn't tell me about him, it's that she didn't see it as a big deal. That's the part that makes my stomach tighten. Bradley Manchester might be a threat and he might not be, but I'm not the kind of man who's willing to wait and find out the hard way.

I follow her out, making sure the door's locked behind us, and try to keep my expression even. She doesn't need me hovering or making the whole day about him. I'll keep it in check. We've got lunch ahead of us, and I want her thinking about that instead.

"What do you feel like eating?"

She glances over with a little grin. "How about Dusty's? I could go for one of their bacon cheeseburgers."

"That works. Bacon cheeseburger it is."

The drive isn't long, but it's enough for my shoulders to loosen. By the time we pull into Dusty's, she's telling me a story about something Mel said yesterday, and I find myself more focused on the sound of her laugh than the name Bradley Manchester.

We make our way to a booth by the window. The waitress stops by a moment later, setting down two waters and sliding menus onto the table before heading off again.

"You're sticking with the bacon cheeseburger?"

"Yeah, just no onions."

"You don't like onions?"

"I like onions," she says with a little smirk, "but I don't want onion breath when you kiss me later."

I lean back, pretending to think it over. "Who says I'm going to kiss you later?"

She tilts her head, one brow lifted.

I cave first. "Yeah, you're right, no onions."

Her laugh bubbles out, and it's impossible not to smile with her.

We place our orders, no onions, and fall into easy conversation. Ten minutes later, the waitress sets our plates down. We eat slow, talking and laughing between bites, keeping the mood light. By the time our plates are clean, the check's on the table.

I drop cash, covering the bill and tip. We stand, and she leans up to press a kiss to my cheek. "Thanks for lunch."

I grin down at her. "Good call on the no onions." I brush my lips over hers in a quick kiss before we head back to the salon.

As we walk up, I glance inside. "What's left to do?"

She unlocks the door. "Not much, just the trash and turning off the lights."

"I'll help." I offer mostly because I don't want her here alone, but I keep that part to myself.

She grins. "Trying to spend more time with me?"

"Yep."

She pushes the door open, and I follow her in. We get busy collecting trash, moving around the room, when I spot something on her arm.

"Come here," I say, careful not to startle her.

She steps closer, and I flick a spider off her sleeve. "You had a spider on you."

The fact that it's already gone doesn't matter, she squeals, eyes wide. "Where is it?! Get it off me!" She starts smacking her arms and legs like she's on fire, darting around the room in a full-blown panic.

I laugh and cover my mouth trying to stop long enough to tell her it's gone. Finally I manage to get the words out. "I already got it."

She presses a hand to her chest like she's recovering from a heart attack. "Next time, say nothing. Ignorance is bliss."

That sets me off all over again. I hook an arm around her and pull her into my side. "So…you don't like spiders?"

"Hate them." She rubs her arm with a wince.

I chuckle again. "Did you hurt yourself?"

"Yes," she deadpans. "I just slapped the shit out of myself."

That's the straw that broke the camel's back. I lose it, bending over and clutching my stomach as I laugh.

She swats at me. "It's not funny."

But then her lips twitch, and she starts laughing, too, the sound mixing with mine until we're both doubled over like a couple of idiots.

The laughter fizzles out, leaving us both breathless and grinning. I take her wrist gently, lifting her arm to press a kiss to the spot she'd been rubbing.

Her eyes lock on mine, and the air between us shifts. I lean in, catching her mouth with mine, slow at first, tasting the smile still lingering there. Then I pull her closer, deepening the kiss until all the air between us is gone. My hand slides to the small of her back, urging her closer as I walk her backward.

She doesn't resist, her arm tightening around my waist as I guide her step by step until her back meets the wall. The soft thud sends a jolt through me. I angle my head, catching her lower lip between my teeth, and the quiet sound she makes shoots straight through my veins.

My hands slide up her body, over her hips and along the curve of her waist, fingertips brushing higher. I trail my mouth from her lips to her jaw, then lower, tasting the soft skin of her neck. She tilts her head just enough to give me more, and the faint sound she makes almost pushes me over the edge. When her hips shift against mine, she feels how hard I am. Her breath catches, a quiet moan spilling out as she presses closer, and I tighten my hold, not wanting to let her go.

And then her phone rings.

The sound cuts through the moment, sharp and out of place. We break apart, both breathing hard. She scrambles for her bag, pulls the phone free and sighs when she sees the screen.

"It's Mel." She hesitates for half a second, then presses the button to silence it. "I'll call her back."

Then she steps back into me like she doesn't want to lose the closeness we just had. I kiss the top of her head, my hands lingering at her waist. "Come on, let's get this trash taken out." I know I need to stop now, before we fall right back into it, because I'm holding on by a thread.

She steps back, just a little, and I catch the flicker of disappointment in her eyes. "Okay."

"When you get to one hundred percent, baby, you'll know what to do." I leave it at that, grabbing the trash bags. On my way past, I give her a quick swat on the ass and she lets out a surprised giggle, hurrying ahead to grab the door. I step outside, the blast of cold air hitting me like a reset, and for once, I'm grateful for it.

She flips the lights off and locks the door behind us. I toss the trash into the bin on the side of the building, then fall into step beside her, walking her to her car.

Leaning down, I press a kiss to her lips. "I'll see you tomorrow."

"Do we have plans tomorrow?"

I chuckle. "Not yet, but I'm sure we will."

She laughs. "We do seem to see each other almost every day, don't we?"

I grin at her realization but keep my mouth shut about the real reason…that Judy's been pulling strings since day one. I'll tell her eventually. Just not yet. I kiss her again. "Tomorrow," I say.

"Tomorrow," she echoes.

I wait for her to pull away before I drive off. Five minutes later, I'm home. I let Fifi out into the yard, then head straight for the bedroom to change into sweatpants and a hoodie. The garage is waiting, and so are the weights. I need something to burn off the tension knotted up in me.

I load the bar, settle on the bench and grip the steel. But my mind's not on the lift, it's on her. On the way she flinched earlier, and how it damn near broke something inside me. I'd give anything to erase whatever put that reaction in her.

Then the image shifts to her pressed to the wall, my mouth on hers, the heat between us rising until the phone cut in. The look in her eyes when we stopped…the disappointment. She's close. I can feel it. All she has to do is come to me, and I'll know. I'll know she's ready to give herself to me completely. Ready to push past the guilt that's been holding her back.

And then there's Bradley Manchester. The thought alone makes my jaw lock. He's been pushing her, harassing her, and it's a good thing for him he didn't show his face today. Judy said the girls gave him hell the last time he did, but even that's not enough for me. I won't sit back and wait for him to cross the line…because I am that line.

I pick up the bar and fall into a steady rhythm, pushing until my muscles burn and the cold air in the garage turns thick with my breath. The weights clank, echoing in the quiet, my mind running through every thought I've been trying to bury. An hour turns into two. Sweat drips down my back, soaking into my shirt, my grip starting to slip as my arms finally give out. I rack the bar with a hard exhale, chest heaving. For a minute, I just sit there, letting the ache settle deep into my muscles. When my arms won't take another set, I push up from the bench and head inside, the heat from the house wrapping around me as I close the garage door behind me.

I pull my hoodie over my head, tossing it into the laundry basket on my way to the kitchen. I grab a bottle of water, chug it in a few gulps and fill Fifi's bowl before heading for the bathroom.

The shower's set to cool, just enough to ease the tightness in my muscles. When I'm done, I wrap the towel around my waist and run a hand through my damp hair. In the bedroom, I swap it for clean boxers and gray sweatpants, wrap my towel around my bare shoulders, then head back toward the living room, the quiet settling in like a blanket.

I drop onto the couch, flick the TV on, and Fifi hops up beside me. I'm not really watching, just staring at the screen while my mind runs circles around her. Same as it has almost every night since I met her.

It's torture, wanting someone this much and not having them. I've never felt anything like it. I'd give this woman anything, and all I want in return is for her to let herself be happy. I drag a hand down my face, glancing at Fifi.

"She'll figure it out, right girl?" I mutter, like she might actually answer.

Deciding I've had enough, I click the TV off and start for my bedroom. I'm halfway there when a knock rattles the door. I glance at the clock, 9:30 p.m. My brow furrows. I turn back and pull the door open.

25

Until I Beg

Raelynn

The drive back to my cabin is quiet, but my head isn't. I keep replaying the day, the way my body betrayed me with that flinch, and how Reed's whole demeanor shifted in that instant. Not with anger at me, but protective. I know, without a doubt, he would never hurt me. The idea of anyone pressuring me had him on edge, and yet the way he handled me afterward was so careful, so gentle.

By the time I pull into my driveway, I feel lighter than I have in weeks. I step inside still thinking about the way he made me laugh, how easy it feels to just…be myself with him. I could tell Bradley was still somewhere in the back of his mind, but for my sake, he let it go.

I drop my bag on the counter, kick off my boots and head to the washer. A pile of laundry waits, and I start sorting it without really paying attention, still lost in the feel of Reed's playful smirk and the sound of his laugh lingering in my head. I grab the clothes from the dryer and drop the basket on the bed, hoping they'll magically fold themselves later. No such luck, but future-me can deal with it.

Flopping onto the couch, I pull my sketchbook into my lap. Normally, it's the easiest way to clear my head, but tonight I can't come up with a single thing to draw. All I see is him. Not the salon. Not my friends. Just Reed. The way his hands felt on me, the look in his eyes when my phone rang. With a sigh, I set the sketchbook on the coffee table and remember I still need to call Mel back.

She picks up quickly. "Hey, girl."

"Hey. How'd the drive back go?"

"It was good. Peaceful. Did you get the salon cleaned up?"

"I did. Thanks for helping me this weekend."

"You're welcome. But that's not why I called earlier."

I sit up a little. "Oh?"

"You should check your email."

"Why?" I ask, a little wary at the edge in her voice.

"Just look at it." She laughs.

I put her on speaker and pull up my email. I scroll through my inbox, not sure what I'm even looking for until I see it. An email from the family courthouse. My finger hovers over it before I open it slowly. My eyes scan the document, my voice dropping to a whisper. "It's the final court date."

"Yes," Mel says, her voice warm. "December 20th. An early Christmas present."

She chuckles, but I'm already exhaling, relief washing over me. "Oh my god. I can't believe it. This makes it so much more real."

"Go celebrate, Raelynn. Go and be happy. I'll notify Kinsley and start getting all the documents ready. You don't need to worry about a thing; Kinsley and I will take care of everything."

My throat tightens. "Thank you, Mel...for all of this."

"You don't need to thank me, but I'll take it. Talk soon, okay?"

We hang up, and I just sit there for a second, letting it sink in.

I stand unable to sit any longer and start pacing the floor, phone still in my hand, the urge to share the news with Reed pulling at me. My mind drifts back to earlier, how our kiss was interrupted and the words he said after. 'You'll know what to do,' he'd told me.

I think about all the times he's left the ball in my court, how it's always been up to me to take the next step. I told myself it was because of guilt. But it wasn't. It was me.

I've known for a while now that I want him, in every way, but I let fear stop me. Today, he showed me exactly who he is. Caring. Gentle. Strong. Playful and intense all at once. This man cares for me in a way I was afraid wouldn't last, afraid to let in. He asked me once if I trusted him, and I said yes, and it was true. What I didn't trust was myself because I made a mistake and married the wrong man who controlled me. But Reed is not that man. And I am no longer that woman.

I stop pacing. I need to see him. I run out the door and head straight for Judy's cabin. I knock until she answers. Her eyes widen when she sees my face and hears my uneven breathing.

"What's wrong?"

"I need Reed's address," I blurt out.

She doesn't say a word, just smiles and disappears inside. A minute later, she's back, pressing a slip of paper into my hand.

"Thank you," I say quickly, already turning to head back to my cabin.

I toss the paper into my purse and head straight for the shower. I scrub, wash, and repeat, buff and wax every inch of my body until the water starts to turn cold.

Wrapping a towel around myself, I wipe the steam from the mirror and get to work on my hair and makeup. When I'm done, I head to the bedroom and dig through my dresser for the perfect bra and panties, skipping right past the cotton and going straight for lace.

In the closet, I grab a fitted V-neck sweater and a pair of jeans, then pull on my knee-high boots. One last look in the mirror, my hair falls in soft waves past my shoulders, my mascara perfectly fanning my lashes. My jeans hug in all the right places, and my sweater shows just the right amount of cleavage. A quick spritz of perfume, and I grab my bag.

I slow my pace on the way to the car, not wanting to break into a sweat. Sliding into the driver's seat, I tap his address into the GPS and pull away.

That's when it hits me. Nerves flood my body. My hands start to shake. My pulse picks up like I just ran a marathon. I've never been this bold, just showing up at a man's house in the middle of the night. *What if he rejects me?* For a second, I think about turning back. *No, bitch. He wants you. Stop getting in your own head.*

The GPS says one mile away. I could turn back. I could run, hide, and pretend this never happened. But I won't, because deep down, I know this is what we both want. And I'm done holding myself back.

I pull into his driveway and spot his truck. The lights are on. My pulse kicks up, but I step out of the car anyway. I walk up the steps and knock.

The door swings open, and there he is bare chest, sweatpants hanging low on his hips. His jaw ticks, and I can't stop my eyes from tracing the way his arm flexes against the doorframe.

"What are you doing here, Raelynn?" His voice is low, guarded.

"You know why I'm here."

His gaze sharpens. "Say it."

I swallow, my heart pounding. "I'm one hundred percent."

He grabs me, pulling me so close. His lips hover just over mine, his breath warm against my skin. "Say it again."

"I'm one hundred percent," I whisper.

His mouth claims mine instantly, the kiss deep and fierce. My hand slides over the solid line of his chest, feeling every ridge of muscle. He wraps one strong arm around me, lifting me off the ground, our mouths never breaking.

He takes a step back, pushes the door shut with his free hand before setting me down, my back pressed to the wood. His lips trail down the edge of my jaw to just below my ear, each brush of his mouth making my knees weak.

"Do you trust me, Raelynn?" He pulls back just enough to look at me, his eyes dark with want, searching mine.

"Yes," I breathe. "I trust you."

His mouth curves into something dark. "Then I'm going to take my time with you, Raelynn… drive you right to the edge and keep you there until you're shaking, until you're begging me to let you come. And when you beg…" His voice drops lower, rougher. "…I'm going to fuck you harder."

A shiver rips through me. Heat pools low in my stomach, my thighs pressing together instinctively, from the sheer anticipation curling around every nerve. *God help me, I want exactly what he just promised. Every drawn-out second of it.*

"I want it…I want you."

He bends, brushing a soft kiss over my lips before catching my lower lip between his teeth. The sharp sting melts into heat. He pulls back, eyes locked on mine and turns toward the couch. He shoves the coffee table back just enough to clear space, then drops onto the cushions, legs spread in quiet command. One hand rests on his thigh, the other curling over the armrest.

"Come here, Raelynn."

The way he says it sends a pulse of heat through me, every nerve ending on high alert. I walk toward him slowly, my eyes locked on his. His tongue traces his bottom lip when I stop in front of him.

He grabs my hips and pulls me closer, his touch firm. His hands move down the curve of my hips, gliding over my thighs until he reaches my boots. One at a time, he unzips them, waiting for me to step out before tossing them aside.

His palms skim back up my legs, higher this time, and one hand drifts right up my center. The slow pressure makes my head tip back, a sharp breath escaping me.

"So sensitive," he murmurs, a low chuckle following. "This is going to be too easy, baby."

His hands stop at my waistband, fingers toying there for a second before he undoes the button and slides the zipper down.

"Open your eyes, Sunshine. I want you to watch what I do to you."

I force my eyes open, finding him looking impossibly good sitting there, completely focused on my body. My hand lifts to touch his face, and when his eyes meet mine, he stands, bringing our chests flush together. His mouth claims mine in a deep kiss before he pulls my shirt over my head and lets it fall to the floor.

He sinks back onto the couch, his mouth trailing down my body, each slow inch making my pulse race. When his lips close over my breast, he bites just enough to make me gasp, the sharp sting melting instantly into a rush of heat. His mouth moves lower, and I suck in a breath, every nerve strung tight in anticipation.

He leans back and hooks his fingers into my waistband, sliding my jeans down in one slow motion. When they hit the floor, I step out of them, the air cooler against my skin.

He sits back on the couch, eyes roaming over me, taking in the sight of me standing there in nothing but my matching black bra and thong. He doesn't say a word at first, just watches, his jaw ticking.

"Turn around."

I turn slowly, feeling the weight of his gaze on every inch of me. I've never felt this exposed, not just physically, but in the way he's looking at me. Like he's stripping away every last layer I've used to protect myself. It should make me want to cover up, but it doesn't.

"Take off your bra."

A tremor runs through me at the quiet command, but my hands stay steady as I reach back and unhook it. The straps slip from my shoulders, the fabric falling away, and the air rushes over newly bare skin, making my nipples tighten instantly.

"Good girl," he growls. "Now I want you to bend…and slide your panties down."

I reach for the thin lace at my hips, but his next command stops me in my tracks.

"Slowly, Raelynn."

I draw it down an inch at a time, feeling his gaze track every movement. The panties slide over my hips, down my thighs. Just as I reach my knees, I'm fully aware of the view he's getting. I feel his breath on my back and then a hand sliding between my legs. I freeze when his thumb presses inside me.

"Keep going, Raelynn," he growls.

I bend further, and his fingers glide over my swollen nub, sending a sharp pulse through me. I freeze again, caught in the sensation, unable to move as his fingers begin to circle, slow and deliberate.

"All the way down, baby."

I push past the sensation building and bend lower, reaching my ankles. The lace slips free, pooling at my feet. I start to rise, but his hand presses firmly against my back, holding me in place, keeping me bent just where he wants me.

His fingers start to circle faster, his thumb pressing into that soft, aching spot. The pressure builds so quickly it steals my breath, and I try to fight it, embarrassed at how fast my body responds to him.

He knows. I can feel it in the way he keeps me still, working me deeper. My body begins to tighten, that rush about to crest…then he stops. His hand slips from between my legs, leaving me aching.

His hand glides up my spine, gripping the back of my neck as he stands me upright and turns me to face him. His mouth comes close, his voice low. "You haven't begged yet."

His lips press into mine, his tongue tracing the seam until I open for him. His grip stays firm at the back of my neck while his other arm wraps around my waist, lifting me. My bare skin presses to the solid heat of his chest. I loop my arms around his neck, pulling myself tighter against him, my legs wrapping around his waist. The moment I feel his hardness against my spread folds, I grind into him without thinking. He groans into my mouth, the sound vibrating through me, then pulls back, his lips brushing under my ear.

"If you do that again, baby, I won't be able to control myself."

I'm about to test him, shifting to grind against him again, when his hands clamp around my hips, holding me still and pulling me just far enough away that I can't.

"You want it? Earn it baby, beg."

My mouth parts, ready to give him exactly what he's asking for, but I stop myself. I can do this. *I can hold off...right?*

26

She begged

Reed

She opens her mouth, and for a second and I think she's going to give in. Then she closes it, that stubborn streak flashing in her eyes.

I grin. "Careful, Sunshine." I tighten my grip on her hips. "You're playing a dangerous game."

Her legs are still locked around my waist, her body soft against mine, and I can feel the heat of her where we're pressed together. My jaw ticks. *If she grinds into me again, I'm done for.*

I turn toward the couch and lower her, but I don't dare put my full weight on her. I know if I do, she'll grind against me again, and I'm not sure I'd have the willpower to stop. My arms cage her in, holding me just above. I lean down, brush my lips over hers, then push back enough to take her in, laid out beneath me, legs spread, skin flushed, nipples tight and begging for my mouth.

I drag in a breath. "Fuck, you're beautiful."

I run my hand from the hollow of her neck down, gliding over the full swell of her breasts, my thumbs brushing the peaks, down through the warm valley between them. I keep going, over the flat plane of her stomach, her body arching into my touch chasing more.

I lean down, following the same path with my mouth, tasting every inch until I reach her nipple. I pull it between my lips, clamp my teeth lightly, and her whole body bucks into me as she grits out my name.

"Open your eyes, Sunshine. Watch me...watch me taste you."

She opens them, and I can see it, she's close to begging. I keep going, not taking my eyes off her. The moment I flatten my tongue over her sweet spot, her mouth parts and a moan slips through her teeth. One hand flies into my hair, the other gripping the couch. I lick and suck, flicking my tongue in a steady rhythm, giving her no chance to recover between waves of sensation.

Her legs start to shake, her body goes rigid, and I stop.

"No...please, Reed...please."

"Good girl." I lean up, kissing her. "Say it again, Raelynn, and I'll give it to you."

"Please," she breathes into my mouth, the sound raw and desperate.

I pull back from her and stand, her eyes following me as she curls her knees in tight, trying to ease the ache. Her breathing is still uneven, her gaze locked on me. I hook my thumbs into the waistband of my sweats and slide them down. My boxers strain against my hard cock, and her eyes drop, tracing the length of me. I take my time pulling my boxers down, slow enough to watch her swallow hard. I can see it in her face, she's a little intimidated by my size, but she's not looking away.

I lower myself between her knees, the heat of her wrapping around me before I even touch her. Leaning forward, I kiss her slow, letting it sink in what's about to happen. My hand wraps around my cock, guiding the head to her entrance. I pause, meeting her eyes. She pulls in a breath, bracing.

"Stop me if it hurts."

She nods, biting her bottom lip, and I can feel the tension coiled in her body.

I push forward, slow, the head of my cock meeting the tightest, hottest squeeze I've ever felt. Every instinct in me wants to drive in hard, but I grit my teeth and keep it slow. She's so tight I have to push a little harder, inch by inch, feeling her stretch around me, until I see it. The way her brows draw in, the small hitch in her breath. She's struggling to take all of me.

I stop, holding still, my hand sliding to her hip. "Breathe, Sunshine. Let me in." I keep my eyes on hers. "Take a deep breath."

The second she does, I drive into her fast and hard, burying myself to the hilt. She cries out, the sound a mix of pleasure and pain, and I still, letting her stretch around me. Her walls grip me like a vice, every muscle pulling tight.

When I feel her start to relax beneath me, I move slow, grinding my hips into hers. My mouth finds hers, swallowing her moans, each one pushing me to sink a little deeper, a little harder.

I keep the slow grind going, drawing it out, letting her body adjust. When her hips start to lift into mine, meeting my thrusts, I know she's ready. That little push, the way she chases me, is all I need.

I plant my hands on either side of her and drive in harder, deeper. Each thrust pulls the sweetest sounds from her, her nails digging into my back as I push us both closer to that edge. I give in completely, pounding into her, each stroke harder than the last. Her head tips back, eyes shut, body arching into me as she comes screaming my name. The way she tightens around me shreds the last of my control. I grind deep one final time, her body gripping me so tight it pushes me over. A raw groan tears from my chest, her name on my lips as I spill inside her, every pulse of release sending waves of heat through me.

Her body convulses beneath me, as I milk the last of our releases. Our breathing is heavy, chests rising and falling together, and I find her mouth, kissing her softly.

I lower myself over her for a moment, feeling the warmth of her against me, then roll us until she's on top. Her head settles under my chin, our bodies still pressed close, neither of us in a hurry to move.

I run my hand lazily up and down her back, feeling the way she melts into me. "You okay, Sunshine?" My voice is still rough from everything we just did.

She nods against my chest. "More than okay."

A slow smile spreads across my face. "Good. Because I'm not done with you yet."

She lifts her head and kisses me. "I was hoping you'd say that."

I chuckle. "Now who's flirting?"

"Me."

I wrap my arms around her, lift us both off the couch and toss her over my shoulder. My hand smacks her ass on the way to the bedroom, her laugh spilling over my back.

I toss her onto the bed, and she giggles when she bounces. Crawling up after her, I cage her in with my arms. "Round two, Sunshine… and this time, I'm not holding back."

Her eyes widen. "Oh my god! You were holding back?"

I laugh. "You have no idea."

And I show her, for hours, again, and again until neither of us has anything left to give.

After the last time, she curls on her side, head on my shoulder, her arm draped heavy across my chest. I pull the blanket over us, my body still humming.

I watch her sleep, thinking about how she showed up tonight, ready to give herself to me completely. I'd always thought it would feel strange, having someone sleep in my bed. I've never woken up next to anyone before. But with her, that's exactly what I want.

***

When I wake the next morning, I reach for her without opening my eyes, my hand searching the sheets. The bed's cold. I sit up, glancing around the room, empty.

Climbing out of bed, I pull on a pair of boxers and head into the living room. All her clothes are gone, the coffee table still shoved out of place from last night.

In the kitchen, Fifi sits by the back door, waiting. I let her out, then glance out the window. Her car is gone.

Running a hand through my hair, I scan the room for my phone, a tight knot forming in my chest. *Did I push her too far last night? Is that why she left without a word?* I call her, but it goes straight to voicemail. *It's fine. She stayed all night.*

Letting Fifi back in, I head for the shower. The water beats against my skin, but all I can think about is her, what she's feeling, why she left.

I finish up fast and head for the bedroom, pulling on jeans and a hoodie. I need to see her. I need to know she's okay.

Back in the living room, something catches my eye under the couch. I bend down and pull it free, it's her black thong. I shove it into my pocket. I grab my keys and head straight for her cabin.

I'm halfway down her road when I try her number again. Straight to voicemail. "Damn it," I mutter, gripping the wheel. *What did I do?*

When I pull into the cabin driveway, her car's there. Relief loosens something in my chest, but it's short-lived. I'm already out of the truck, striding toward the cabin.

Judy steps out from her porch. "Reed, honey…"

"Just a minute, Judy," I call back, not slowing down.

At her door, I knock, slipping a hand into my pocket, fingers brushing over the black lace there. The door swings open and Raelynn's standing there, eyes wide like she wasn't expecting me.

"Reed." She glances over her shoulder into the cabin at someone inside.

I don't bother asking. "Are you okay?"

Her brows pinch. "Yes, of course."

"I called you; your phone went straight to voicemail."

"Oh, sorry. My phone died."

"I was worried I hurt you last night. That's why you left without a word."

She shakes her head, pressing a palm to her forehead, and lets out a chuckle. "No." She steps aside, pushing the door open wider. An older man stands inside, moving toward us.

"Reed, this is my dad. Dad, this is Reed."

Heat crawls up the back of my neck the second I realize what I just said and who I said it in front of. *Perfect. Just perfect.*

Her dad steps forward, hand outstretched. "You must be the reason my daughter wasn't here when I showed up this morning."

"Yes, sir."

"Well, Reed, it's a pleasure meeting the guy who finally makes my daughter smile, even if I don't need to know the reason why." He chuckles.

I shake my head, mortified. "Understood, sir."

"You can call me Frank."

"Dad, can you excuse us for a minute?"

Frank chuckles. "Sure, hun. Take your time."

She steps out the door, and I take a step back as she closes it behind her. Her hand finds mine. "I'm sorry."

"Raelynn, you don't need to apologize to me…"

"Shh," she cuts in. "Yes, I do. I also owe you an explanation. I woke up to a text from my dad saying he was almost here. I didn't know he was coming. I panicked, grabbed my stuff and ran out the door. I tried to call, but my phone died, and when I got here, he was waiting. I'm sorry." Her eyes search mine like she's waiting for me to be upset.

I lean down and kiss her. "I was just worried, baby. That's all." I kiss her again. "Everything's fine. Spend time with your dad and call me later."

She grabs my hand again. "Stay. Stay with me. I can make breakfast."

I can't help the smile. "Okay, I'll stay, only because it can't get any more awkward."

She giggles, wraps her arms around my neck, and leans in to whisper against my ear, "I really wanted to spend the morning in bed with you."

Then she kisses me, slow and tempting, and my hands slide up her sides before I remember where we are. I drop them. "Raelynn…your dad is in there."

She laughs softly. "Then you better kiss me fast."

I cup her face and kiss her hard, pouring everything into it. When she steps away and turns toward the door, I can't help myself, just as she cracks it open, I smack her ass hard.

She bites back a squeal, shaking her head, trying not to draw her dad's attention. I chuckle under my breath and follow her inside.

Raelynn moves around the kitchen, making breakfast while her dad sits across from me, asking question after question. She's laughing quietly behind me, clearly enjoying watching me squirm.

I glance over my shoulder, and she's leaning over the counter, completely at ease. She slept in my bed, spent the night, and now I'm meeting her dad. The messed-up part? I like it. And even worse? I'm already imagining more mornings like this.

We eat, and the conversation eventually shifts to lighter topics, her salon, his plans. He explains he's only here for a quick visit, that he has business in Spokane in the morning, and thought he'd surprise her. *Mission accomplished.*

After a while, he stands. "I'll give you two some alone time and check out the sights in town before I head out."

Raelynn tells him to stop by The Sweet Spot to meet Naya, and that Kinsley would love to see him if he stopped by the farm.

He kisses her head. "I'm proud of you. I'll be back to spend more time when the salon opens." We shake hands. "Be good to my little girl, or I'll hunt you down."

"Dad," Raelynn hisses.

I chuckle. "You don't need to worry, sir."

He nods, eyes scanning me. "I can see why she likes you." He pats my shoulder.

"Oh my god, Dad," she groans.

He walks off with a wave. The door closes behind him, and Raelynn exhales like she's been holding her breath the whole time.

I lean back in my chair, grinning. "That wasn't so bad."

"You didn't see the look on his face when he figured out I spent the night with someone last night."

I reach for her hand, give it a gentle tug, and she comes willingly into my lap. My arms wrap around her waist, holding her there as she settles in against me. "Was it that bad?"

"Yes." She laughs. "I got a lecture until you knocked on the door."

I laugh with her. "We need to work on our communication skills, maybe make hand signals."

She swipes a hand across her throat. "Yeah, this means shut up."

I grin. "Got it. And this…" I kiss her. "…means" I kiss her again. "Charge your phone."

27

The Collision Course

Raelynn

He kisses me once before pulling back. "I've gotta get going, Sunshine. I've gotta work today."

I sigh but slide off his lap, letting him stand. He kisses me again, slower this time, like he's making it last, then heads for the door. His hand is already on the knob when he glances back, a smile playing on his face. "You got plans for lunch?"

"Nope. I'm free until the equipment comes in tomorrow."

"You wanna meet me at the sub shop in town? Around noon?"

"Okay…but only if you let me buy."

"Not a chance. But I'll let you try to change my mind." He winks.

He leans down, presses a kiss to the top of my head, and walks out, glancing over his shoulder once before disappearing out the door. I close the door and do a little shimmy on my way to the couch, grinning like a fool. Plopping down, I flip open my sketchbook, pencil in hand.

Happiness spills onto the page, him cupping my face, my hands tangled in his hair, our lips just about to touch. The lines blur into memory, and my cheeks heat. Last night flashes back in vivid detail. I never knew it could be that good, that intense. I find myself wondering if it's always like that…and somehow, I know it will be with him.

My pencil stills as my thoughts shift to this morning, him driving over just to check on me, worry written all over his face. That kind of protectiveness is rare. Then I laugh under my breath, remembering the look on his face when I pushed the door open and my dad was standing there, right after Reed had announced, in full volume, that he thought he'd hurt me last night. The mortified twist in his expression was priceless.

By the time I finish the sketch, it's a collage of last night and this morning, Reed with my dad, Reed standing at the door, Reed kissing me. Each image layered over the next, every line pulling me right back into those moments. It might be my favorite sketch so far.

I glance at the clock, it's nearly eleven. Closing my sketchbook, I set it on the coffee table and head straight for the shower. Ten minutes later, I'm blow-drying my hair, pulling it into a ponytail and swipe on light makeup. I pick yoga pants, the ones that make my ass pop, a sweatshirt, and sneakers, and I'm out the door with my keys in hand.

The drive into town feels lighter than air. I crank up the music, windows cracked, smiling so hard it almost hurts. Last night and this morning are still buzzing in my head. When I pull into the lot, his truck is already parked out front.

I park next to his truck, and the second he spots me, he's out and rounding the hood. I meet him there, and before I can get a word out, he's pulling me in for a kiss. I giggle against his mouth, grinning when he pulls back.

"You miss me, Hotshot?" I tease.

"What? No." His chuckle gives him away, and he brushes a kiss across my cheek. "I've got thirty minutes for lunch, Sunshine. Let's make 'em count."

We step inside and join the short line. He shifts to face me, that sly grin pulling me in. "By the way," he murmurs, slipping a hand into his pocket. When it comes back out, my black thong dangles from his fingers. "Think you forgot something at my place."

Heat rushes to my cheeks as I swat his arm. "Reed!"

I make a grab for it, but he's quicker, shoving it in his pocket with a grin. "Nice try, Sunshine, but that's staying with me."

I lunge for his pocket, but he's faster, catching my wrist.

"Uh-uh," he murmurs, eyes glinting. "You'll just have to earn it back."

"And how do you want me to do that?" I step in close, dragging my other hand down his chest, lower, just about to slip into his pocket.

His hand snaps around my wrist, stopping me cold. His mouth dips close to my ear.

"Careful, baby. You keep tempting me like that, I'll drag you out to my truck and fuck you across the seat before we ever make it to lunch."

I part my lips to say something, but the bell over the door jingles. I glance over my shoulder and freeze. Bradley.

Shit!

Every muscle in my body locks. I turn back to Reed, debating whether I should whisper it, but I don't get the chance. Reed's already looking past me, his eyes narrowing on the man behind me. The playful heat is gone, burned off in a second flat. Anger flickers across his face, and I don't have to say a word. He already knows who it is.

I touch Reed's arm, trying to ground him before this explodes. "Not here," I whisper, but of course Bradley has to open his big fucking mouth.

"Raelynn. I thought I saw your car outside."

I whip toward him, but Reed's already moving. He steps in front of me, his whole body coils tight, ready to swing.

"Bradley, right?" Reed steps closer, voice like steel. "I heard some shit about you, that I didn't like." His jaw ticks, eyes hard. "Stay the fuck away from her. Stay the fuck away from her salon. Because if I hear anything else I don't like..." he leans in, quiet but lethal, "...I'll make damn sure you regret ever stepping foot in this town."

Bradley smirks, trying to puff himself up. "I don't think you know who I am."

Reed steps in closer. "I don't give a fuck who you are."

Bradley's jaw works, but he takes a step back, eyes cutting over Reed's shoulder to glare at me. Then he turns and shoves his way out the door, the bell rattling in his wake.

Reed doesn't move until he's sure Bradley's gone, then he turns back to me. All that fury in his face eases, his hand brushing my arm. "You okay?"

"Yeah." I wrap my arms around his middle, needing the feel of him against me.

He holds me, then exhales like he's forcing the tension out of his body. "Good. Cause I'm starving."

I laugh, knowing exactly what he's doing, switching gears for my sake. He drapes his arm over my shoulder as we step up to the counter. We both order, and of course he pays, no matter how much I argue.

We sit at one of the small tables, talking about my dad and laughing about this morning. Then his phone buzzes, and he glances at it. "Oh, shit. I gotta go. I'm late."

We clean up quick and head for the door. He kisses me fast, then waits until I'm in my car before pulling out of the lot. I drive to Cranberry Ridge Grocery, my thoughts circling him. I don't even know when I'll see him again, and for a second I think about texting. Instead, I decide to wait.

Inside the store, I grab a few essentials, then swing by the post office. Sorting through the pile of mail, I don't even hesitate before dropping another letter from Bradley straight into the trash.

I pull out of the parking lot, still thinking about Reed, and I'm barely a mile down the road when a silver car cuts me off. My breath catches as I jerk the wheel to the right, slamming the brakes, but it's too late, my tires skid and the front end smacks hard into a tree.

The jolt stuns me more than it hurts. My hands are shaking on the wheel, heart hammering, when there's a sharp knock on my window.

"You okay?"

I blink up at the older man standing there. His voice is gruff, but not unkind.

I push the door open, my knees wobbly. "Yeah… I think so. A car cut me off."

"Seen it happen." He jerks his thumb down the road. "S.O.B. kept driving. Headed east."

I nod, still rattled. "I've never been in an accident before, so I'm not really sure what to do."

"Well, you call the authorities."

"Right." I fumble for my phone, dial the police and give them my location. When I hang up, I let out a shaky breath.

The man shifts his cap back on his head. "Name's Floyd."

"Raelynn." I take his hand, his grip firm.

"I'll wait by my car till they get here," he says with a grunt that sounds more like a habit than a complaint.

The adrenaline still buzzes in my veins. "Thanks, Floyd."

I circle around to the front of my car, wincing at the crumpled bumper and dented fender. It's definitely going to need a tow, but at least it looks repairable. I drag a shaky hand down my face, wondering how the hell my day went from good to bad that fast. A broken piece of my fender lies in the grass. I scoop it up and toss it into the back seat on top of my grocery bags, then lean against the passenger door to catch my breath. That's when I feel it, heat burning across my chest. I tug the collar of my sweatshirt down for a better look, and there it is: an angry red welt where the seat belt slammed against me. *Perfect.* I press my fingers over the tender spot and hiss under my breath. "Yep. That's gonna bruise."

I hear sirens in the distance and push off the car, waiting. The first to arrive is a police cruiser. An officer steps out and gives me a quick once-over.

"You hurt?"

"No."

"What happened?"

I explain about the silver car cutting me off.

"Did you see who was driving?"

I shake my head. "It happened too fast."

He nods, then asks for my paperwork. I dig through the glovebox, fingers fumbling a little, and hand it over.

"I'll call a tow, and I'll need to get a statement from Floyd."

Of course he knows Floyd by name. I'm not even surprised.

The officer comes back and tells me the tow truck should be here in five minutes. "You'll need to arrange a ride home."

I pull my phone from my pocket, staring at the screen like it might give me the answer. Reed's at work. If I call Kinsley or Naya, they'll both lose their minds. And Judy? The last thing I want is her parked on the side of the road with me.

So, I hit Miles' name.

"Hello?"

"Miles, I… got in a little car accident."

His voice sharpens instantly. "Are you hurt?"

"No, I'm fine. Just a couple bruises. But don't tell Kins. She'll panic."

He chuckles. "Don't I know it. Where are you?"

I give him the location, and without hesitation he says, "I'll be there in ten minutes," before hanging up.

I glance up and see cars already backing up down the road, most of them just nosy people slowing down to gawk. *Figures.* The tow truck finally comes crawling along the shoulder, lights flashing, moving slow thanks to the jam. It pulls in behind my car, and the driver climbs out mid-call, phone pressed to his ear.

"I've gotta wait for backup to get around all these cars," he tells me after hanging up.

"Got it. Thanks."

I go back to leaning against my car, trying to ignore the stares of passing drivers and wait for Miles to show up.

A couple minutes later, more sirens echo down the road. *Great.* An ambulance this time. The line of cars part enough to let it through, and it pulls up alongside. Two EMTs hop out and head straight for me.

"Anything hurt?" one asks.

"No," I sigh, "just shaken up."

"Protocol," the other says, already reaching for a cuff.

I roll my eyes but hold still while they strap it on and check my vitals. Before they even finish, another siren wails in the distance. *Oh, for fuck's sake.*

I glance over to see what's coming down the damn road now. The cars split, and my heart falls to my feet as a firetruck pushes through. Reed.

When it screeches to a stop, three men climb out. I spot him instantly. He turns, eyes scanning, and the second he sees me, he freezes. Worry flashes across his face, before he's jogging toward me.

The EMT barely has the cuff off my arm when Reed grabs a hold of me, hands firm on both my arms. "Are you hurt?" He steps back just far enough to scan me head to toe.

"I'm fine, Reed."

He doesn't hear me. He spins me around, checking my back, his voice cracking. "Raelynn, does it hurt anywhere?"

"Reed, I'm fine. Really."

But he's still searching me over, frantic. I reach up, laying my hand on his arm, trying to ground him. "I'm fine."

A voice cuts in. "She's fine, Reed. Dial it back."

We both turn and see Miles. Reed shoots him a hard look, then turns back to me, his chest still heaving. I touch his face softly, drawing his eyes back to mine.

"Reed, I'm fine."

He drags in a slow breath, panic slowly giving way as his focus locks on me. Then he pulls me against him, arms tight.

"You're shaking." He pushes me back just enough to check me over again.

"It's just adrenaline and maybe a couple bruises."

His jaw tightens. "How did this happen?"

"A silver car cut me off and drove away."

His teeth grind, rage flashing across his face, but before I can calm him again, a familiar voice cuts through the noise. *You have got to be kidding me.*

Kinsley barrels through the crowd, practically shoving Reed aside to grab my arms.

"Are you okay? What hurts?"

And I start the whole process again. I glare at Miles. "I told you not to tell her."

He just shrugs. "You know what she would've done if I hadn't?"

I sigh, nodding. "You're right."

Miles gently pulls Kinsley back, reassuring her I'm fine, and Reed steps in again, wrapping his arms around me.

"I've gotta help the guys."

I squeeze his arm. "Miles is driving me home."

His jaw works like he doesn't want to let go, but after a second, he nods. He kisses the top of my head, then jogs back toward the firetruck.

Miles steps in beside me. "You ready? I convinced Kinsley you'll need a bubble bath and soup. She's already on her way to the store."

"Why?"

"Because once that adrenaline spike wears off, your whole body's gonna ache."

I cringe, lifting my hand to show it's still trembling. "Great."

"Come on, let's get you home before that happens."

I follow him, but just before climbing in, I glance over my shoulder. Reed's watching me, eyes locked on mine. I blow him a kiss before sliding into Miles' truck.

28

CPR for a Bruise

Reed

Tommy's at the wheel, the siren off now, as I stare out the window, my reflection staring back at me. I can't get the image out of my head…Raelynn standing there on the side of the road with that damn cuff on her arm, her car banged up and sitting crooked against the tree.

For a second, I thought my knees were gonna give out when I saw her. All I could think was what if. What if she'd been trapped? Or seriously hurt? I drag a hand over my jaw, trying to get my head straight, but every thought circles back to her. How small she felt in my arms. How she kept trying to tell me she was fine when I could feel her shaking.

Tommy backs the rig into the bay and we climb out. He studies me a second. "We've only got a few hours left on shift. Why don't you go check on her?"

I stare at him, waiting the usual smartass comment. But there isn't one. He's serious.

"Go," he repeats. "I'll call if we need you." He claps my arm and heads inside.

I don't think twice. I head straight for my truck, pull out and drive past the spot where I saw her standing earlier. Debris still litters the shoulder, a reminder that it wasn't just some bad dream.

When I pull into her drive, I'm caught off guard by the lineup of cars, Kinsley's SUV, Naya's Jeep, Miles' truck. My shoulders finally ease, knowing she's not in there alone.

I step out and spot Miles leaning against the porch rail. He straightens when I walk up. "She's fine. Judy just left, but Kinsley and Naya are in there treating her like she's got head-to-toe injuries. Doesn't matter how many times Raelynn swears she's fine, they're not buying it."

I can't help but chuckle. "That bad, huh?"

Miles shakes his head. "Yeah, and I don't even know how Naya got here before us. Pretty sure Mel's already called her twice in the last twenty minutes."

I step closer to the door, hand halfway to the knob, when I hear Raelynn's voice from inside.

"Kinsley, I don't need to be spoon-fed! And for fuck's sake, Naya, stop fluffing my pillow!"

I bite back a laugh, leaning against the frame. She's outnumbered, poor thing doesn't stand a chance. For a second, I debate whether to go in and save her…or just stand here and enjoy the show.

I turn back to Miles. "You wanna help me out here?"

He just huffs. "Let's go."

I push open the door…and freeze.

Raelynn's curled up on the couch, blanket tucked to her chin, a washcloth draped across her forehead. She's surrounded by so many pillows it looks like they're trying to smother her. Kinsley's parked on the coffee table in front of her, spoon in hand. And Naya? She's standing over her, waving a trail of burning incense straight into Raelynn's face.

Raelynn squints, swatting at the air. "Now I've got smoke in my eye."

I chuckle under my breath. "Ladies, I'm trained. I can take it from here."

Kinsley jumps up like she's been waiting for the order. "Oh, thank God. She won't eat."

I drag in the deepest breath I can, fighting the urge to bust out laughing. "Let me have a look. You guys step outside for a minute."

Kinsley and Naya practically trip over each other getting to the door, and Miles pulls it shut behind them.

When I turn back, Raelynn's already tossing the blanket off and kicking pillows onto the floor.

I laugh. "That was intense."

She glares at me. "They already rubbed me down in essential oils, Reed."

I wrinkle my nose and laugh. "Is that why it smells like the perfume store at the mall in here?"

"I'm not kidding, Reed. I don't know how much more of this I can take," she deadpans.

I chuckle. "Let me try."

I walk over and crack the door open. Kinsley and Naya stop mid-step.

"Ladies, you've done a great job here. Whatever you did worked, she's already asleep."

They both sigh in relief.

"Okay, but she needs to be woken up every two hours in case she has a concussion," Kinsley warns.

I nod with the straightest face I can manage. "Got it."

Miles tucks Kinsley under his arm, steering her and Naya down the path. I close the door behind them, only to see Raelynn peeking out the window.

"Lock the door," she mutters.

I flip the lock, and the second it clicks, we both start laughing. But she winces and stops.

"What's wrong?"

"I'm just a little achy. But I didn't tell them that. They would've called an ambulance."

"Heat helps with that."

Her lips curve into a small smile. "Kinsley bought bubble bath."

"Sit, I'll run the bath."

I head into the bathroom, twisting the knobs and pour in a generous amount of soap. The scent fills the small space. Raelynn slips in behind me, quiet, then brushes a kiss against my cheek. "Thanks."

I lean forward, grip the hem of her shirt and slip it over her head. My hand fists tight in the fabric when my eyes land on the bruise across her chest from the seatbelt.

Raelynn follows my gaze, fingertips brushing it gently before she looks up. "Reed…it looks worse than it is."

I let her shirt drop to the floor and pull her against me, lowering my head to press the softest kiss over the bruise. I step back, letting her finish undressing. My eyes scan over her, not in the way that makes her blush, but checking for anything she hasn't told me. When I see nothing but that bruise, I finally turn and pull a towel from the cabinet.

"Can you grab two?"

I grab another and set them both on the vanity.

"That one's for you." She tilts her head at me, a spark in her eyes.

I smirk. "You trying to get me naked, Sunshine?"

"Yes." She giggles.

I toe off my boots and tug my shirt over my head. She sinks lower into the bubbles and exhales a quiet sigh, eyes fluttering shut. I finish stripping down and step into the tub behind her. She leans forward just enough for me to slide in, then eases back, settling between my legs with her head resting against my chest. I reach for the loofah, soak it in the water, and run it slowly down her arms, across her collarbone, then gently over the bruise.

We stay like that in silence until the water starts to cool. She finally sits up and turns slightly toward me. "Will you stay with me tonight?"

"Yeah, baby. I'll stay."

She stands, grabbing both towels. I follow her out, and she hands me one. I wrap it around my waist while she tucks hers snug around her body.

"I need to go get Fifi and a change of clothes."

"Okay. While you're gone, I'll make us some dinner."

She heads toward the bedroom, and I dry off and get dressed. Sliding my shoes on, I call out, "I'll be back in twenty."

"Lock the door behind you." She laughs.

I chuckle, opening the door. I turn the lock before closing it behind me.

I make the quick drive home, grab everything I need and scoop up Fifi. Twenty minutes later, I'm back. As I reach the porch, the door flies open and Raelynn grabs my arm and yanks me inside before I can knock. She shuts it fast and presses her back against it.

"Did Kinsley see you? She just called me."

I laugh. "No, I think you're safe."

I set Fifi down, and Raelynn bends, her voice soft and sweet. "Who's a good girl? You're a good girl." Fifi spins in a circle at the praise. I shake my head, grinning.

"Dinner smells good," I say, glancing toward the kitchen.

"I made steak fajitas." She beams and gestures at the counter. "Plates are ready."

"Damn, Sunshine, that was fast."

She giggles. "It's my favorite. Come on, you'll love it."

She hands me a plate piled with peppers, onions, and steak, plus another stacked with tortillas. She gathers all the toppings and two cold beers. Together we carry everything into the living room and spread it across the coffee table.

We eat, talking about the day and laugh over Kinsley and Naya's antics until we're both stuffed. After we clean up, I stretch out on the couch, making room for her. She curls into my side, flipping on the TV. I pull the blanket down over us and wrap my arm around her. Within minutes, her soft snores drift up against my chest. I close my eyes and let myself fall asleep with her there.

About an hour later, I stir. She's still out, breathing deep and even. Carefully, I slide out from behind her, then scoop her into my arms. She barely stirs as I carry her to bed. Laying her down, I slip in beside her. She curls into me instinctively, and I hold her close, listening to the rhythm of her breathing.

Today wrecked me in a way I didn't see coming. I've never lost it on a call before, not once. No matter what I roll up on, I keep my head. That's the job. But the second I saw her standing there on the shoulder...everything in me split wide open. I couldn't breathe until I touched her. Couldn't think straight until I knew she was really okay. That's not me. That's not how I work. And yet, she's the exception.

I brush a kiss against the top of her head, letting her warmth sink into me. I've got it bad for this woman. Worse than I ever thought possible. The weight of the day finally pulls me under, and I drift off with her in my arms again.

***

I wake the next morning, reach out and she's already gone. *Damn it. I just want to wake up next to her.* I throw the blankets back and head into the living room. She's in the kitchen, humming while she flips something in a pan. I don't say a word. I walk straight up, turn off the stove, and she spins around, surprised.

"You don't want breakfast?"

Still I say nothing. I just scoop her up, and she squeals as I carry her back to the bedroom. She's giggling when I lay her down and tuck her back into the blankets.

Her brows pinch. "Reed?"

I climb in beside her and pull her close before finally speaking. "Good morning."

She laughs, shaking her head. "What are you doing?"

"I wanted to wake up next to you. But this is twice now I've opened my eyes and you're already gone."

She giggles again, softer this time, snuggling closer. "Good morning."

I brush a strand of hair from her face. "How are you feeling? Anything hurt?"

She shakes her head. "Surprisingly, no."

I lean back a little. "What about the bruise?"

Her mouth tips into a half-smile. "It's turning purple, but it only hurts if I touch it."

"Show me." I need to see it for myself. I know she won't lie, but it gives me peace of mind.

She lifts onto her knees, pulls her shirt over her head, and my breath stalls when I realize she isn't wearing a bra. I have to bite back the urge to touch her. "Baby…you could've warned me."

She giggles. "What fun would that have been?"

I wink. "I'll finish making breakfast."

I grab her, roll her onto her back and lean over her. My eyes find the bruise, dark and spreading across her chest. I bend and press a soft kiss over it. She inhales deep, but not from pain. I trail up and kiss her mouth, slow, before rolling off the bed. "My years of training, tells me I have to do that every fifteen minutes." I wink. "I'll finish making breakfast."

She stays there stunned that I'm walking away. I chuckle and head out of the room. But then I hear her footsteps as she stomps into the living room. She doesn't say a word. I turn, and my chest tightens at the look in her eyes. She hooks her thumbs in her pajama pants and slips them down slowly, pausing just long enough to keep me locked in place. My eyes scan every inch of her, my hands twitching with the need to touch.

She slides her panties down one teasing inch at a time. My body jerks, heat rushing through me, and before she can test the last of my willpower, I cross the room, grab her by the waist and lift. She wraps around me instantly, lips on mine, until I pull back just enough to press a kiss to the bruise again.

"I'd love to have you for breakfast," I murmur against her skin. "But until that bruise is gone, we're fasting."

"It doesn't hurt." She runs a hand through my hair.

I lift my eyes to hers. "But I do, baby."

"Fine." She slides down my body with a wicked smile. "Maybe I'll just do it myself." She saunters toward the bedroom, stopping in the doorway to glance back at me, eyes daring me to follow. Then she disappears inside. I stand there shocked, deciding if I should follow. Yeah, there's no way in hell I'm missing this. I stride after her. "Raelynn, don't play with me."

Her giggle carries out from the room. When I step inside, she's fully dressed, head tilted with that smug little grin. "How do you like it, Hotshot?"

I chuckle, shaking my head. "That was evil."

Before she can get another word out, I rush her, scooping her into my arms. She laughs against my chest, kisses me quick and sweet. "I know." Pride laces her voice.

I set her down, and she pats my chest. "Now that you're done with your shenanigans this morning, I'll finish breakfast."

I chuckle, leaning in close. "My shenanigans have barely started, Sunshine."

Her eyes narrow, but the corner of her mouth gives her away as she fights a smile. I watch as she heads to the kitchen. *I could get used to this.*

I head to the bedroom and get ready for work. By the time I come back out, she's setting a stack of pancakes on the island. We eat together, talking about her plans for the day. That she needs a ride to the repair shop to check on her car and pick up a loaner, and after that, she'll be tied up with delivery drivers and install companies.

I tell her I'll stop in and bring lunch, and by the time we finish eating, I've only got forty-five minutes to get to work. She darts to the bedroom, and I clean up from breakfast. About twenty minutes later, she comes out in jeans and a hoodie, her hair pulled into a high ponytail, a touch of makeup brightening her eyes.

We climb into my truck, and I drive her to the repair shop. She leans over, kisses me, and says, "Go have a good day. I got it from here."

"I'll see you at lunch," I promise, waiting until she disappears inside before pulling away.

29

Promises

Raelynn

The mechanic wipes his hands on a rag. "Two weeks, give or take. We'll call as soon as it's ready."

Two weeks? Perfect. I force a smile and take the keys to the loaner. A little four-door sedan that smells like cigarettes and pine. But it's better than asking for rides.

I pull out of the lot and head straight for The Sweet Spot. If I'm going to bribe delivery drivers and installers into a long day of hauling equipment, donuts are the way to go.

The bell jingles when I step inside. The smell of sugar and bread wraps around me.

"Well, look who it is." Naya rounds the counter, grinning. "How are you feeling?"

"I'm good. Just a bruise from the seat belt."

Her grin turns sly. "So…did Reed spend the night?"

I laugh. "Yes… and no. Nothing happened."

Because he's acting like I'm glass, I think to myself.

Her jaw drops. "Wait…you're telling me you two haven't slept together yet?"

I dodge toward the display case. "I need two dozen donuts. The good ones. None of those plain cake imposters."

"I knew it." She grabs boxes, smug as hell. "You're dodging. Which means?"

I've been dying to tell someone, but I don't want everyone to know. I lower my voice, glancing around the room. "I'll spill, but only if you pinky promise not to tell a soul."

Her eyes light up, and she sticks out her pinky. "Promise."

I bite my lip, scanning the tables one more time. "We did. The other night."

Naya gasps, then quietly claps her hands like she's about to burst. "Oh my God!" She grabs my arm and yanks me toward the back. "Come on, we need privacy for this."

I glance around one last time before blurting it out. "First off, a man has never made me finish."

Naya's jaw drops, and for a second I almost stop there, but I can't. I've been dying to tell someone.

"But Reed…" I lower my voice, heat rushing up my neck. "He did. And not just once."

Her eyes go wide, but I keep going, spilling every perfect detail, leaving nothing out. By the time I'm done, both of us are fanning ourselves like we've been standing in front of a bonfire.

"Wow, Raelynn. That's fucking hot."

"Girl, don't I know it." I laugh, my cheeks still warm, but it feels good to finally say it out loud.

After a few more of her relentless questions, the bell over the door jingles. Naya groans, muttering about bad timing, and straightens up. "Back to work," she sighs, grabbing the donut boxes she'd started filling.

I take them from her with a grin, hugging her quick before heading for the door. "Thanks for the girl talk."

"Anytime."

I push out the door into the crisp morning air and stand there for a second, trying to remember what my stupid loaner car looks like. When I spot it, I climb in. One minute later, I'm pulling into the salon parking lot. I grab everything I need and unlock the door, leaving it open since the first delivery guy should be here soon. The donut boxes go on the counter with a sign that says: Help yourself.

I grab the window cleaner and a stack of rags, heading straight for the glass door. I freeze. The little hairs on the back of my neck stand up, that prickling feeling you get when someone's watching. My gaze darts to the parking lot, then down the sidewalk. Nothing. I glance back into the empty salon. Still nothing. I blow out a breath, shaking my head. I'm freaking myself out for no reason. Probably because I left the door unlocked. I flip the lock and feel a little better, going back to wiping the glass. Ten minutes later, the first delivery truck pulls up.

I spend the next couple of hours directing traffic, pointing out where I want everything set up and how I want it arranged. I'm mid-sentence with an installer, showing him where to hang the mirrors, when someone suddenly kisses my cheek. I spin, ready to throat-punch whoever it was, only to find Reed standing there, grinning at my shock.

I relax instantly and swat his arm. "You scared me. I thought I was about to have to kick someone's ass."

He chuckles. "You're so cute when you get feisty."

"Oh, shut up." I laugh.

"Sorry I'm late. Had a call just before lunch."

"It's fine. I've been so busy here I lost track of time."

He looks around the room, taking in the chaos. "It's really starting to come together."

"Come on, we can eat in my finished office." I clap my hands, grinning.

We weave around workers and ladders until we reach the office. Reed steps inside and glances around. "This is nice, Sunshine. You've got a good eye for this."

"Thanks." I shrug, not used to praise. But coming from him, it means so much more. "Come on, let's eat before you have to go back to work."

He opens the bag and sets out the containers on my desk. The smell of grilled chicken and warm bread fills the office. My stomach growls, earning me a raised brow and a smug grin from him.

"Guess I got here just in time."

"Don't get cocky." I steal a piece of bread before he can hand it over.

We sit side by side at the desk, bumping elbows as we eat. For a few minutes, the noise outside fades.

He watches me finish off my food, that quiet little smile resting on his face. "You look happy."

"I am." I lean in to kiss him when a knock on the door jolts us, and one of the workers pokes his head in asking about the shelving placement. I sigh and push up from the chair.

"What time are you going to be done?"

"I don't know. One of the drivers had a flat tire and is running late. He said it'll probably be after five."

"Well, if you want, I'll make dinner tonight at my place."

"That sounds good." I kiss him quick before hurrying out of the office to help direct the worker.

Reed winks at me as he heads out the front door.

Hours pass, and I'm still waiting on the last delivery. I busy myself sweeping and cleaning up their mess when that feeling hits again…the feeling that someone's watching. I cross the room to lock the door, but just as my hand touches the bolt, I see the delivery driver pulling up.

"Sorry I'm late," he says as he walks up.

"It's not a problem." I show him where the washer and dryer are going, and he gets to work. I half-expected him to have help, but it's just him. Two hours later, he finally finishes the install. When he leaves, I don't stick around to take it all in. I can do that tomorrow. I grab my bag, turn out the lights and step through the doors, locking them behind me as I go.

I drive straight to Reed's. When I pull in and climb out, he's already standing at the door.

I walk up the steps, and the second I reach him, he wraps his arms around me. "I was just about to come check on you."

"I know. I'm sorry it took so long. He didn't have any help with him."

Reed bends to kiss me, and I loop my arms around his neck. The kiss deepens quickly, and he walks us backward, pulling me inside and shutting the door behind us.

He pulls back a little. "Let's eat."

I huff. "Stupid bruise."

He chuckles, kissing the top of my head. "Come on, it's getting cold."

When I step into the dining room, I stop dead in my tracks. I expected pizza or burgers, maybe takeout at best, but no. He's made lasagna with breadsticks and a big bowl of salad. It's all laid out on the table with two wine glasses waiting.

He pulls out my chair then sits across from me as if he didn't just blow my mind. I catch myself staring, and he notices.

"What?" His smile pulls at his mouth.

"I can't believe you made this."

"It's not a big deal. I just followed a recipe I found online."

"Okay, I have to ask…how are you single?"

He smirks. "I didn't want to be in a relationship."

"Ever?"

"Nope."

"And now?" I glance down at my plate, then back up at him.

He leans back in his chair, eyes locked on mine. "And now…I'm looking up recipes."

"What does that mean?" I ask, my voice quiet.

"It means…I didn't want a relationship. But now I'm doing stuff I've never done."

I lean back in my chair, eyes searching his, because I don't know how to feel about his answer. Does he like this? Or does he resent it?

"This is new for me, too."

"You've been in a relationship. Hell, you're in one now."

He's not talking about us. He's talking about Jacob. The marriage I haven't legally ended yet.

I push back my chair and stand. "Excuse me for a minute."

He nods, but I can't bring myself to meet his eyes.

I walk into the living room, grab my bag and keep moving straight out the door. My chest tightens with every step, and by the time I slide into the driver's seat, I want to throw up.

Does he think I forced him into this…this so-called relationship? That I don't regret every day marrying Jacob? That I haven't been counting down the days until it's over? I grip the steering wheel, fighting the sting in my eyes. And I don't look back.

By the time I get home, the tears are hot and blinding. I toss my bag on the couch and pace the length of the room, replaying his words on a loop. 'You're in one now.'

He's right. On paper, I am. No matter how much I try to tell myself it's over, no matter how many times I remind myself Jacob and I are done, it doesn't change the fact that I haven't signed the final papers. Maybe I'm the one pushing too hard. Maybe Reed feels cornered and doesn't know how to say it. Maybe I've been selfish, pretending I'm free when I'm not.

I sink onto the couch, bury my face in my hands and whisper into the quiet room, "Why did I believe I was worth it?" The words taste bitter. I stand, stumbling to my room. I sink to the floor as a sob rips through me. I curl into a ball, arms wrapped tight around myself, like maybe I can protect myself from…the only person left to hurt me. Me.

The front door swings open, but I just lie there, trapped in my own head, unable to move.

"Raelynn?" Reed's voice echoes through the cabin.

Why is he here? I'm not worth it. I'm no one. The thought shreds me, and I cry harder, because I want to be. I wanted to be his.

I hear his footsteps cross the room, closer, until he's right beside me. I turn my face into the floor, hair falling over like a curtain.

"Raelynn." His voice is softer now, and then his hand brushes my arm.

"Go home, Reed," I whisper.

His hand falls away, the silence stretching before he finally says, "I'm sorry, Raelynn. Please."

My voice cracks as I choke out, "I'm not worth it. Just…leave."

His breath hitches, then comes out rougher. "Don't say that."

I flinch, but he keeps going, his voice tight, almost shaking. "You think I'd be here if you weren't worth it?

He lowers himself beside me. His hand finds my arm, firm but careful, and he coaxes me upright. My body resists at first, heavy with shame, but he doesn't let go until I'm sitting up, my face still turned away.

"Damn it, Raelynn," he says quietly. "Look at me." His hand comes up, cupping my face, thumb brushing my cheek as he turns me toward him. "Listen to me," he says, voice low but strained. "I shouldn't have said that. That's not how I meant it."

I try to look away, but his grip doesn't falter, keeping my eyes on his.

"You think I don't know what you've been through? You think I don't see how hard you're fighting just to start over? I want things I didn't even know I wanted. Because I want those thing with you."

I shake my head, still not believing him.

"Don't you get it?" His voice cracks. "You're already enough for me."

It isn't his words that break through, it's his eyes. The raw hurt there, the way he looks at me like it physically pains him that I can't see myself the way he does.

I reach for his shirt, gripping it tight, and then we crash into each other. His arms wrap around me, strong and steady, and I curl into him. Needing him.

After a while, he eases back just enough to brush a tear from my face. His gaze searches mine, silent, asking.

I nod.

He leans down and kisses me carefully, like he's afraid I'll break.

I pull back, wiping at my face. "I'm sorry I ruined your dinner." My voice cracks on the words, a sniffle slipping out.

"I don't care about dinner, Sunshine." His thumb still brushes my cheek. "But I need you to promise me something."

I shake my head, already agreeing before he even says it.

"Never walk away upset again. We can fix it…the two of us."

My throat tightens. "I promise." I kiss him softly, and we both stand. I start toward the bathroom, then pause and glance back. "I'm sorry."

He steps closer, brushing a strand of hair from my face before leaning in to kiss me gently. "No, Raelynn. I'm sorry. I shouldn't have said that. I know how hard it was for you to get past the guilt. It won't happen again."

I rise on my toes and kiss his cheek before turning back toward the bathroom. I've always known he would never intentionally hurt me, but I let my doubts blind me. Not anymore.

30

Postcard Perfect

Reed

I hang up the phone after ordering pizza and sink back in the chair, the quiet pressing in.

When Raelynn didn't come back into the dining room, I figured she just needed a minute. But when the minutes stretched on, I went looking. The living room was empty. I stepped outside and her car was gone. I spun, shoving my feet into my shoes, laces be damned. I knew she'd go home. Sliding into my truck, I replayed the conversation, hunting for what I said that sent her running. Then it hit me. *Hell, you're in one now.* The second the words echoed in my head, my gut twisted. How could I have been so fucking stupid? I threw the gearshift into drive and floored it.

I ran into her cabin, not bothering to knock. I stepped inside, scanning the room until I saw her, curled on the floor. Because of me. I hurt her. Then she told me to go home, and my stomach dropped. But when she whispered she wasn't worth it…it damn near broke me.

I meant every word I told her, she's already enough. Because she is. And it's true…I want things I never knew I wanted. Hell, I avoided them. Until her. The knock on the door pulls me out of my thoughts. I grab the pizza and set it on the coffee table.

A few minutes later, she slips out of the bedroom, her hair damp and braided, an oversized T-shirt and pajama pants hanging loose on her frame. Her eyes are still puffy, but she looks softer now, calmer. The second she's close enough, I pull her into my lap. She settles against me, her head tucking under my chin. I press a kiss to the top of her head and hold her tighter. "Do you have plans tomorrow?"

She lifts her head. "No. I'm free for the next few days until the products for the salon get here."

"How about we spend the day together tomorrow?"

"Don't you have to work?"

"No. I've got the day off."

"I'd like that." She smiles, then it fades. "Are you going home tonight?"

"Not a chance."

She giggles, and the sound makes the knot in me finally ease.

"You want to know what we're doing?" I ask, hoping I can keep lightening the mood.

She perks up. "Yes."

"I was thinking we could go for a ride."

"Like a road trip?"

I chuckle. "Something like that."

She sits up straighter, her eyes sparking. "Can we get snacks?"

"Definitely." I laugh.

She rubs her hands together. "Can I control the radio?"

I smirk. "Only if you promise not to play sappy love songs."

She gasps. "Those are the best."

I chuckle. "Okay, two love songs."

She tilts her head. "Five."

"Three and you have to share your snacks with me."

She twists her mouth, pretending to think it over. "Okay…three, I share my snacks, but you have to sing along with me."

"Oh no. I'm not doing that. Keep your snacks, and you can have five."

She laughs, eyes bright. "Deal."

I tackle her, and we roll onto the floor, both of us laughing. She squeals, trying to push me off, but I pin her easily.

"I got the raw end of that deal, Sunshine."

She's laughing so hard she can barely breathe. "You did."

I give her a quick kiss. "Come on, we've gotta be up early."

We eat and work together to clean up the mess, and once everything's straightened, she locks the door and cuts the lights. We head to her room, crawl into bed, and she snuggles in close.

"Sunshine, if I wake up in the morning and you're not here, I'm spanking your ass."

She giggles. "In that case, I'll be in the kitchen."

I shift onto my side and wrap an arm around her. "Don't test me, Raelynn. I'm not opposed to leaving a handprint on your ass."

She wiggles her butt against me. "Maybe I'll like it."

"Oh, I know you will."

Her laughter fades into a soft sigh as she settles against me. I press one last kiss to her hair, and before long her breathing evens out. I hold her tighter, letting the quiet wrap around us until sleep pulls me under, too.

***

I wake before her, the room still quiet, the first light slipping through the curtains. She's curled up against me. I don't move. I just lay here looking at her. Beautiful doesn't even begin to cover it. I make a silent promise. I'll never do something that careless again. I won't mess this up. Because whatever this is, whatever it's becoming, it's deeper than I ever expected. Deeper than I can even admit to myself. Eventually, I slide my hand down her arm, brushing lightly until she stirs.

She stretches with a sleepy smile. "Good morning."

"Morning, Sunshine." I brush a strand of hair from her face.

She stretches again, rolling closer. "When are we leaving?"

I glance at my phone. "About five minutes."

She scrambles out of bed. "That's not enough time!"

I laugh. "I'm kidding. We've got about an hour."

She glares at me, fighting a smile. "Not funny." Then she clutches her chest. "I think I hurt myself."

I roll out of bed and grab her arm. "Does it hurt?"

She bursts out laughing. "No." With a playful sway in her step, she saunters out of the room, still laughing.

I stand there, shocked and impressed. "Not funny, Raelynn," I call out echoing her words.

Her laugh carries from the living room. "Yes it was."

I grab my phone and head to the kitchen. She's already starting the coffee. "Go get ready, Sunshine. I'll make breakfast." I slap her ass on the way by and she giggles, heading for the bedroom.

I crack eggs into the pan, bacon sizzling beside them. While it's cooking, I text Judy, asking if she'll watch Fifi for the day. Her reply comes quick; with an 'I'd love to.' A few minutes later, I set everything on the island.

Raelynn bounces out of the room dressed warm, makeup on, hair pulled up. We eat quick, then we're out the door twenty minutes later. We make two stops; the first my place so I can change, then Cranberry Ridge Grocery for snacks.

Back in the truck, she tucks her legs under her and spreads the snacks across her lap like it's a feast. The sight pulls a grin out of me. She looks so damn cute.

She pops a chip in her mouth and holds the bag toward me. "Want some?"

"Only if you promise not to hog all the good ones."

"Define good ones."

"The folded ones."

She gasps. "Those are mine."

"Guess I'll have to wrestle you for them."

She laughs, cranking the radio. The first notes of some old love song fill the truck, and she belts it out like we're on stage instead of an empty road. I shake my head, but damn if I don't end up singing along.

Two hours stretch out easy, snacks, music battles, her feet tapping the dash. She thinks this ride's just to kill a day off, but I know where we're headed. I've been planning it since last night. And if it makes her half as happy as I think it will, keeping it a surprise is worth it.

I turn down a long stretch of road, the trees thinning until a big sign comes into view. Regional Air Base.

Raelynn whips her head my way, eyes wide. "What, oh my gosh, oh my gosh! Are you taking me in a plane?" She bounces in her seat, snacks spilling to the floor, and I can't help but chuckle at her surprise.

"I said we were going for a ride, didn't I? Thought we could use a little adventure."

She mouths 'oh my gosh' again, pressing a hand to the glass as she stares out the window like she just discovered Christmas came early.

I pull up near a hangar and park. She's already jumping out, brushing crumbs off her lap. She bounces on her toes while I lead her inside, both of us signing in at the desk. We step back out, and I walk her toward the AT-802 sitting on the tarmac. Her eyes widen as we get closer.

"This one's used for wildfire suppression," I explain, running my hand along the side. "Carries water or fire retardant in that tank there."

I walk her around it, checking the wings, the landing gear and the control surfaces. She trails close, listening carefully, asking questions here and there, her curiosity fighting with the nerves written all over her face. When her fingers twist together, I reach down and take her hand. She squeezes back, holding on as we keep going with the inspection.

I help her climb up into the seat, buckle her in and settle the headset over her ears. She fidgets with the cord, eyes darting over the controls like they might bite. I climb in beside her, strap myself down, and pull on my own headset.

Her fingers drum against her leg, her shoulders tight, lips pressed together. I flip a couple of switches, then lean back, speaking into the mic. "Do you trust me?"

Her head pops up in my direction, eyes wide. She nods fast, almost too fast.

I chuckle. "You can talk, Sunshine. I can hear you."

She blows out a breath. "Maybe I shouldn't have eaten so many snacks."

I laugh, shaking my head. "You'll be fine. I'm right here the whole time."

Her smile wavers a little.

"If you get scared, just look at me. Not the sky, not the ground, me. I won't let anything happen to you."

She exhales slowly, shoulders loosening a little, and gives me a small nod.

I flip the radio switch and call the tower, getting clearance. A moment later, the reply crackles through my headset, clearing us for takeoff.

I glance at her, giving her hand a quick squeeze. "That's our green light, Sunshine. Ready?"

Her throat works as she swallows, then she gives me a small, brave but shaky, "Yes."

I ease the throttle forward, the plane rolling across the tarmac. We line up with the runway, the nose straight ahead. I flick another switch, gauges coming to life, and glance her way again. "Here we go."

The engine roars, and the runway rushes beneath us. Raelynn grips the armrest, shoulders tense, eyes locked straight ahead. "Just a few more seconds." The nose lifts, wheels leaving the ground, and she presses back into the seat, holding on tight.

Her lips part like she's about to say something, but she bites it back, forcing herself to stay quiet. I glance over, and even with the scared look on her face, there's grit there, too. She's holding it together, braver than she gives herself credit for.

I level the plane, the climb easing into a smooth glide. Raelynn finally peels her eyes off the dash and looks out the window. Her shoulders drop, the tension slipping away. "It's beautiful."

Below us, Colville National Forest spreads out in a patchwork of color; deep greens fading into gold, orange and fiery red. To the east, a river winds along the edge of the trees, catching the sunlight like a ribbon of silver. A few minutes later, a lake comes into view, its surface mirroring the blaze of autumn around it.

I tilt the plane slightly, pointing. "That's the cabins. And right there, that's the farm."

Her hand lifts to the glass, fingertips brushing it like she could reach the view. I ease us into a slow circle, dropping lower so she can see it all closer. The cabins are tucked against the trees, lining the lake. The farmhouse stands solid with the fields stretching out beside it. From up here, it looks like something out of a painting.

Raelynn lets out a sigh I can hear in my headset. "Reed…it's amazing."

I circle us once more, then level out and guide the plane farther east. She leans toward the window, eyes wide as the landscape opens up ahead.

Cranberry Ridge comes into view. Small clusters of buildings, the church steeple rising above them, the water tower gleaming in the sunlight. From up here, the town looks peaceful, tucked between rolling hills streaked with red and gold.

"There it is," I tell her. "Cranberry Ridge."

Her smile spreads, like she's memorizing every inch of it. "It looks like a postcard."

I point. "There's your salon."

Her face lights, eyes glued to the spot.

I tip my head toward another block. "There's the fire station."

She leans closer to the window, following my line of sight.

"And just over there, that's The Sweet Spot."

She presses her forehead to the glass, taking it all in.

We circle once more before I point the nose back toward the airfield. The runway comes into sight, and I glance her way. "Landing's the only part that gets a little rough, but I promise, it'll be okay."

She doesn't hesitate this time. Her eyes find mine. "I trust you."

"Good," I say, giving her a quick grin before focusing forward.

The runway stretches ahead as I ease the throttle back. The nose dips, wind rushing louder against the fuselage. The ground rises fast, wheels skimming once, bouncing us lightly before catching hold. Raelynn's hand grips the armrest again, but she doesn't flinch away. The plane rumbles as the tires bite into the pavement. A little jolt, then the roll smooths out, speed bleeding off until we're gliding down the strip. A few seconds later, we're taxiing back toward the hangar, the engine easing. I bring us to a stop near the hangar, cut the engine, and slip off my headset. She does the same, still wide-eyed.

"Sit still, I'll help you out." I climb down and round the plane, then pull myself back up to her side. Unbuckling her straps, I step down and hold out my hand. She takes it, sliding out of the seat. The second her feet hit the ground, she throws herself into my arms. Her lips crash against mine.

When she finally pulls back, she's grinning. "Thank you. That was…completely terrifying. And I want to do it again." She laughs against my chest, still buzzing from the rush.

She kisses me again. I glance down at her, cheeks still flushed from the flight, eyes bright with wonder. As we step off the tarmac, I'm already planning the next adventure…because one day like this with her will never be enough.

31

The Great Escapes

Raelynn

We step into the empty hangar, the echo of our footsteps bouncing off metal walls. Reed starts pointing things out, tools on a workbench, another plane tucked in the corner, but I barely hear him. My pulse is still racing, my whole body still buzzing. I stop walking. He turns toward me, mid-sentence. I grab his shirt and kiss him. Hard.

He kisses me back, his hand finding my waist. The kiss is fast, hungry, nothing like the careful way he kissed me last night. This is different. This is adrenaline and relief and maybe a little bit of recklessness.

He pulls back, his voice thick. "Raelynn." A warning.

I push anyway, sliding my hands up his arms, feeling the solid strength under my palms. His jaw ticks, eyes burning as he glances around the hangar. Without a word, he grabs my hand and pulls me into the far corner, behind a plane draped with a heavy cover. The fabric hangs dense, shielding us from anyone who might walk in.

I step back into him, my chest against his, tilting my chin up. "I need you."

His hand slides up my back, fingers gripping the nape of my neck, the other pressing low against my spine, holding me there. His voice drops. "If I fuck you in this hanger baby, everyone will hear you screaming my name."

"I don't care." My answer comes out breathless, because it's true.

His mouth crashes down on mine, a fierce, claiming kiss. His tongue brushes against mine, pulling me under until I can't tell where his breath ends and mine begins. The taste of him floods through me as his hand tightens at the back of my neck, holding me still.

His mouth tears from mine, and he pulls me deep under the plane's cover, shadows wrapping around us. He steps closer. "This won't be slow, Raelynn. I'm going to fuck you fast and hard. I'm going to need you to keep quiet."

The heat rolling off him making it impossible to speak. I shake my head.

A smirk curves his mouth. "I don't think you can be quiet." His hands trail up my hips, fingers gripping at the hem of my shirt and pulling it over my head.

His gaze pins me where I stand, heat sparking in his eyes. "Slowly." His voice thick with command. "Take off your clothes."

I obey, moving slowly. I slide one piece away at a time, never looking anywhere but him, letting him see that I'm not afraid of his demand, that I want this.

A quiet groan rumbles from his chest as I slip out of my panties. I straighten, heart pounding, watching as he peels his shirt over his head. God, he's so hot I can't stop myself. My hand drifts to the button of his jeans.

He doesn't stop me. Just watches, eyes dark, chest rising harder now. I can tell he's biting back the urge to grab me, to take over, every line of his body wound tight with restraint.

Just as I start to inch his jeans down, his hand clamps over mine. In one swift move, he spins me around, my back pressed tight to his chest. His fingers sweep my hair to one side, and then his mouth is on me, sucking and nipping a trail from my neck to my shoulder. I can't help it, a small moan slips out.

"Shhh," he murmurs against my skin. One arm snakes around me, sliding lower, while the other lifts my shirt to my lips, holding it there. His voice is a growl in my ear. "Bite down, Raelynn."

I open my mouth and bite down on the shirt.

"Good girl." His praise rumbles through my body.

His hand slips between my thighs, fingers teasing, and my head tips back against his chest. He pulls in a sharp breath, his lips brushing my temple. "You're so wet for me."

His fingers circle fast over my bud, pleasure rising, the tension already coiling tight in my stomach. Then his other hand snakes up, firm around my jaw. "Not yet, baby. You don't get to fall apart until I'm buried inside you."

I nod, biting down on the fabric stuffed between my teeth, but my body betrays me. My legs begin to tremble, muscles tightening as the edge rushes closer. Just when I think I can't hold it back, his touch disappears, leaving me straining against the shirt.

"I wanna feel you come on my cock."

A desperate sound escapes against the fabric. His name slips out anyway, broken and pleading, muffled through the cotton. I try to twist toward him, but his grip holds me in place.

His voice is commanding against my ear. "Not like that. I'm going to take you from behind, hard and fast. Keep that pretty mouth around that shirt, you hear me?"

I shake my head, and he grabs my neck, kissing it, pushing me down until I'm bent completely over. His hand leaves my neck, trailing down my spine, while his other clamps hard around my hip. I feel him line himself up against my opening, then he growls, "Bite."

He slams into me in one hard thrust. My body jolts forward, but his grip keeps me locked in place. A muffled cry tears into the shirt, the sudden stretch overwhelming and raw. He holds still at first, buried deep, his grip firm on my hip. Waiting. Testing. My body trembles until instinct takes over and I push back against him.

He starts slow, each movement sending pleasure through me until the restraint snaps. "Raelynn." His thrusts turn hard, fast, relentless, the rhythm so precise it steals my breath. His hand snakes around me, fingers sliding between my thighs until they find my swollen nub, stroking in time with every drive of his hips.

The shirt muffles my cries, but it's useless against the sounds clawing their way out of me. My body tightens around him, every nerve on fire, and his fingers don't let up.

He groans, the sound rough and deep against my skin. "Shhh, baby. I don't want someone else to hear what's mine."

I bite down harder, my teeth sinking into the fabric, but it doesn't stop the helpless whimpers vibrating in my chest. The pressure coils tighter, winding me up until my whole body trembles.

My muscles clench around him, and I know I can't hold it off much longer.

He releases my hip, and his hand crashes down on my ass with a loud slap. "Let go for me, Raelynn." He growls.

The command rips through me, and I do, my body seizing, clenching hard around him as the release crashes through me. My pleasure breaks against the fabric in my mouth, heat flooding every inch of me. He shudders behind me, a raw sound tearing from him. His pace falters, then he drives deep one last time as he follows me over. He slows, dragging out the last of our release, before pulling me up and spinning me into him. Our chests heave together as he holds me close.

Just as he opens his mouth to say something, we both hear it, the echo of a voice carrying through the hangar. We freeze. My eyes go wide, but he presses a finger to his lips, signaling me to stay quiet. In a blur, he snatches up my clothes and helps me dress, quick and clumsy, the sound of footsteps growing closer as he pulls his shirt back on. We move fast. He grips my hand, tugging me toward the opposite side of the plane.

"Hey!" a voice shouts behind us.

We take off running, laughter bubbling up between us as we stumble through the exit. He yanks open the truck door, and we scramble inside. The second the engine roars to life, he guns it. We tear down the road, breathless and laughing like teenagers caught in the act.

We can't stop laughing, replaying every second of our great escape all the way back to my cabin. The second we're inside, he doesn't waste time. He lifts me off the floor and carries me straight to the bedroom. Dinner is forgotten. This time there's no rush, no need to hide, just him taking his time, and me giving in to every second of it.

***

Reed leans down, lips brushing mine in a goodbye kiss that's far too slow for someone running late.

"Go," I whisper against his mouth, smiling when he finally pulls away.

He lingers a little longer, then heads out the door. I watch him through the window until his truck disappears down the road.

Grabbing my keys, I snag my bag from the counter and head into town. Today I decided to decorate the salon for Halloween. If I'm going to make this place mine, it's going to need more than just chairs and mirrors, it needs a little fun, a little me.

I park at the salon and decide to walk. My first stop is Main Street Brew, one block away. Just as I'm about to step through the door, a man on the sidewalk catches my attention. Bradley. My stomach dips, but he doesn't see me. I slip quickly inside, the bell above the door jangling a little too loud for my nerves. I order a large latte with a double shot of espresso, tapping my card on the counter while the machine hisses to life. With my cup in hand, I thank the barista and step back out into the cool air. Bradley's gone, so I start the two-block walk to The Crafty Cottage. People mill in and out of shops, smiling, carrying bags, enjoying the morning. I take a sip of my drink and try to soak it in.

That's when I notice a man standing across the street, staring at me. He's in a black hoodie, the hood pulled up. I turn away, lifting my cup to my lips, but when I glance back, he's still there. Still watching. My pulse kicks up. I quicken my pace,

291

glancing over my shoulder. Now he's a little closer, phone pressed to his ear.

I push through the door of the craft store and steal one last look outside. He's gone. *Get it together, Raelynn. You're out here freaking yourself out over some guy minding his own business.* I shake it off and grab a cart.

If I'm going to decorate the salon, I want it to be cute. Not the kind of stuff that makes kids cry before their haircut even starts. Pumpkins with silly faces, friendly ghosts, black cats that look more mischievous than menacing. I toss them into the cart one by one, already picturing the window lined with smiling jack-o'-lanterns and little bats dangling from the mirrors. By the time I hit the checkout, I'm humming along to the faint music playing overhead.

I push out the door, arms full of bags, instantly regretting not driving. But the salon is only three blocks away. By the time I hit the first block, my arms are already aching. I stop, shifting the bags against my hip. When I glance left, my stomach drops. The man from earlier is standing across the street, a black hoodie pulled low, camera raised. The second he notices me watching, he lowers it. He's too far away for me to make out his face, but close enough to send a chill down my spine.

I start walking faster, the plastic handles biting into my fingers. When I look again, he's moving, too, crossing the street, heading straight toward me. My pulse spikes. I fumble for my phone and hit Reed's name.

"Hey, Sunshine."

"Reed." My voice comes out shaky. "There's a man. He's following me."

The warmth drains from his tone, turns hard. "Where are you?"

"I'm walking toward the salon. About a block away."

"I'm on my way. Get inside and lock the door."

"Okay," I whimper.

"Raelynn." His voice drops, firm enough to root me in place. "Don't open that door for anyone but me."

"He's close." My breath hitches.

"Hurry, baby," he urges, and I hear the slam of his truck door through the line.

I reach the salon door, fumbling with my keys, too terrified to look behind me. My hands shake so badly I almost drop them. Finally, the lock turns. I stumble inside, bags spilling to the floor.

"I'm in."

"Lock it."

I twist the deadbolt with trembling fingers. "It's locked."

"Now go to the back. I'll be there in one minute."

I sprint into my office, my pulse thundering in my ears. Peeking out the doorway, I watch the glass front, holding my breath to see if he walks by or stops. Nothing.

Then Reed's truck barrels into the lot and stops on a dime. He's out and jogging for the door.

"I'm here," his voice rumbles through the phone I forgot was pressed to my ear.

I hurry to the front, hands trembling so bad I can barely twist the lock. The second I get it turned, he shoves the door open, and I practically launch myself into his arms.

32

The Burden I'll Take

Reed

I back her deeper into the salon, one hand still around her, the other reaching to throw the deadbolt again just to be sure. She's trembling so hard I can feel it shaking through me.

"I need to check outside." I try to ease her grip, but she clings tighter, her hands knotted around my neck. I swear I can feel her heart slamming as hard as mine. I press my hand to her back, torn between the need to sweep the lot and the need to keep her anchored right here in my arms.

"Please don't go," she begs, her voice breaking.

I let out a slow breath, my hand sliding up her back, keeping her pressed tight to me. "I'm not going anywhere."

I glance toward the windows, every instinct in me screaming to look, to make sure the street's clear. But the way she's clinging, I know what she needs more than anything is me. So, I stay.

I keep my arm around her until the trembling starts to ease. "Tell me what happened."

She nods, but every few words her eyes dart past me toward the window. Each time, her voice falters.

"Raelynn." I step in closer, shifting until I'm right in her line of sight, blocking the glass. My hands come to her shoulders, firm but gentle. "Don't look out there. Look at me."

Her wide eyes snap up to mine.

"Good. Stay right here with me. Tell me everything."

Her gaze flicks toward the window again, but I tighten my grip on her shoulders, bringing her eyes back to mine. "Start at the beginning."

She swallows. "I saw Bradley outside the coffee shop this morning. But…I don't think he saw me. I went inside fast, and when I came back out he was gone."

My jaw tenses, but I don't interrupt.

"Then, at the craft store…" She shifts, arms crossing over herself. "There was a guy in a black hoodie. He was just…watching me. Talking on his phone. And then…he disappeared."

Her voice thins to a whisper. "On my way back, he was standing across the street. Hood up, camera in his hands, taking pictures. When he saw me looking, he lowered it. And then…" She shudders. "Then he started walking toward me. Didn't even look where he was going. Just…straight at me."

I feel her shaking again under my hands, and it takes everything in me to keep my own expression calm. To not let her see the storm inside me. "You did good calling me. Did you see his face?"

She shakes her head. "No…his hood blocked it."

Before I can say another word, a sharp crack splits the air, followed by the crash of glass shattering. The sound ricochets through the salon. Raelynn screams, and I move without thinking, wrapping her up, pressing her against me as shards rain down. My body takes the brunt while I hold her tight.

Rage surges hotter than the sting of glass against my skin. I push her back gently. Raelynn's cry rips through the air, but I can't hear past the roar in my head. I fling the door open so hard it rattles.

A silver car fishtails out of the lot, tires screaming as it tears down the street. My hands curl into fists, blood pounding in my ear. I slam the door shut and spin back to her. "Go to the office and call the police."

Her head shakes, tears brimming. "No…come with me."

"Raelynn." My voice cracks through the air loud. "I said go in the office and call the police!"

Her eyes widen. I drag a hand down my face. "Baby, I need you safe. Call. I'll be right out here."

She finally turns and hurries into the office, the door clicking shut behind her. I yank my phone from my pocket and punch Luke's number. He answers on the second ring.

"Hey, what's up?"

"I need you at Raelynn's salon. Now. And call Miles and Dylan, tell them to get here fast."

"Five minutes." He hangs up the phone.

I shove the phone back in my pocket and start pacing, boots grinding over the shattered glass. This was Bradley. I know it. Raelynn saw him, then a man in a black hoodie, and a silver car tearing off. Then it hits me…the silver car. The same one that cut her off before, the one that caused her accident. My gut twists, fury burning hotter. That wasn't chance. That was him. He could've killed her that day. He's been circling, pushing and today, he brought it straight to her door.

As I pace the floor, my eyes land on the rock lying in the middle of the broken glass. I crouch down, pick it up and see a piece of paper wrapped around it. My pulse spikes as I peel it free and unfold it. **Go back to where you came from.**

My hand shakes once, then I crumple the note and shove it deep into my pocket. The rock hits the floor with a heavy thud when I throw it down. And my anger climbs higher.

My jaw locks so tight it aches. I need to check on her before I put my fist through a wall. I push the office door open, trying to calm myself, and find her standing in the middle of the room, tears streaking down her face.

I step inside and cup her cheeks in my hands. "I'm sorry I raised my voice. I just…"

"I know," she cuts in softly. "It's okay."

Her arms slip around my neck. I hold her there, grounding both of us. The distant sound of sirens edges closer. I press a kiss to her temple before guiding her toward the door.

"They're going to want a statement. Don't leave out a single detail. I've got a few things to handle, but I'm not leaving you."

"Okay," she whispers.

I brush a quick kiss to her forehead just as the police push through the front door.

Just behind the police, Luke shows up in his work suit, Miles and Kinsley right behind him with Dylan trailing close. Kinsley's face crumples the second she sees the broken glass and police officers. Miles grips her shoulders, murmuring for her to stay calm. She doesn't listen, she rushes past me straight to Raelynn giving her statement.

I jerk my chin toward the side of the building, motioning for the guys to follow. We move around the corner, far enough that Raelynn and the cops can't hear. I lay it out, Bradley, the man in the hoodie, the silver car. They stay quiet, but I can see it, the anger rolling through them, same as mine. I tell them about the silver car, and that it's probably the same one that ran Raelynn off the road, and their expressions harden. I yank the note from my pocket, hold it up and now we're all pissed.

"This isn't a coincidence." My voice is stern, leaving no room for doubt. I meet each of their eyes in turn. "And not one word of this gets back to Raelynn. She doesn't need that weight."

Miles grinds out, "Then teach her to shoot. Hell, teach all the girls."

Luke nods once, already calculating. "My place. Tomorrow. I'll order dinner, make it look like fun, not training."

Dylan speaks next, voice clipped. "I'll board up the window today."

I turn to Luke. "Think you can get cameras installed at the salon and the cabins?"

"I'll have them in by tomorrow morning," His eyes cut to me. "But I'm putting one at your place, too."

"Fine. Do it."

We all shut our mouths when a police officer approaches, notebook in hand. "Reed, did you see anything?"

"No," I lie, jaw tight. "My back was to the window."

The cop sighs like he's already checked out. "Well, chances are it's kids messing around. Happens this time of year…Halloween pranks, you know."

I shake my head but bite my tongue.

Luke doesn't. "What I'm hearing, is you don't want to do your job and actually investigate."

The officer shoots him a look, lips pressed thin, then turns and walks off without another word.

Dylan turns back, shaking his head. "You know, a guy who throws a rock through a window in broad daylight's got some balls. You need to be careful."

Miles nods. "He's right. She probably shouldn't be left alone."

Luke smirks. "She can stay with me."

I shoot him a look sharp enough to cut through steel.

He chuckles, shaking his head. "Fucking with you."

Miles lets out a laugh. "You got it bad, don't you?"

"Yes," I snap, then glare at him. "Shut up."

Dylan glances at Luke, a sly grin spreading across his face. "Looks like it's you and me, now."

Luke swings and punches him in the arm. "Don't ever say that again."

I can't help but chuckle.

The cops finally clear out, and the girls make their way over. Miles tucks Kinsley under his arm, protective as ever, while

Raelynn slides in against me, her arms wrapping tight around my waist.

Dylan, like a dumbass, throws his arms out toward Luke like he's asking for a hug, earning him another solid punch in the arm.

Rubbing at the spot, still laughing, Dylan says, "I'll be back to board up that window."

Luke claps me on the back and heads off. "I'll see you tomorrow." Kinsley and Raelynn hug quick before Miles pulls her close again. He gives my shoulder a firm pat, and together we watch them all leave.

When the lot's finally empty, I glance down at Raelynn still clinging to me. "Come on, Sunshine." I brush a strand of hair from her face. "I'll help clean up the glass. Dylan will be back in a bit to board it up."

We head back inside. She starts gathering her bags while I grab the broom and begin sweeping glass into a pile. A few minutes later Dylan comes back, boards up the window, and waves on his way out.

Raelynn bends to pick up the rock, turning it over in her hand. "You think it was kids that threw this?" She holds it up, eyes flicking to mine.

I can see it, the doubt creeping in. The part of her that's wondering if she overreacted, if she imagined half of it. I hate it. I hate that Bradley's gotten her questioning herself. But I also don't want to scare her with the note in my pocket or the silver car that ran her off the road.

"It's possible." I watch her closely. "But don't doubt yourself about the man following you. You saw him, Sunshine. That wasn't in your head."

Her grip tightens on the rock, eyes darting toward the now boarded window. I want to tell her everything I know, everything I suspect, but not today. Not when she's already shaken to the core.

"Hey." My voice pulls her out of her thoughts. "I took the rest of the day off. What do you say we order some food and slum it on the couch watching movies at my place?"

The corners of her lips twitch up, a flicker of relief breaking through the tension. Exactly what I wanted.

Her brow lifts. "Slum it?"

"Yeah," I grin. "You, me, sweatpants, greasy food, corny movies. Real high-class evening."

"High-class, huh?"

"The highest."

She laughs. "Sounds like a plan."

"Good. But fair warning, if you pick some cheesy rom-com, I'm mocking it the whole time."

"Then I'm definitely picking the cheesiest one I can find."

"Bring it on, Sunshine."

We finish picking up, and she tosses the rock into the trash. On the way out, I tell her, "Luke invited everyone over tomorrow for dinner."

"That'll be fun."

I hate keeping this from her. But after today it's better to let her think it's just food and company, while we make sure she's protected. We climb into the truck, and I wait until she's buckled before firing it up. "Luke's coming by in the morning to put some cameras up at the salon and the cabins."

Her brows pinch, but I flash her a quick grin, downplaying it. "Just for peace of mind."

Cameras aren't just for peace of mind, they're for proof, for protection. For when Bradley pushes again. She doesn't need to carry that burden today, but I'll damn sure carry it for her.

33

Bullseyes and Bumblebees

Raelynn

The cameras are already up, one at the salon, another at the cabins. I spotted the one on the electric pole facing the property as soon as we pulled in. I don't love the idea of them watching over everything, but I can't deny they make me feel better. Since yesterday morning, I haven't felt this secure, like maybe I don't have to keep glancing over my shoulder. Reed's proof of that, too. He's stretched out on my couch, scrolling through his phone. After spending the night and this morning tangled up in him, the sight settles me even more.

I'm in my bedroom finishing up when Reed calls from the couch, "Sunshine, we're gonna be late."

I grin at my reflection. "Then I guess you should've kept your hands to yourself this morning."

"Not a chance. I'd make us late all over again for that."

I laugh, grabbing my bag. "I'll be done in five minutes, Hotshot."

Five minutes later, Reed pops his head through the door. Before he can say anything, I stand. "I'm ready, keep your pants on."

He leans against the frame, eyes dragging over me. "Sunshine, the only reason they're still on is because we're already late."

I swat at him, laughing as he dodges back with that smug grin. We head out the door together, and ten minutes later we're pulling into Luke's driveway.

It's my first time seeing his place, and I can't help but stare. The house is massive, like something out of a magazine, with a lawn so perfect it looks groomed by hand. Everyone's cars are already lined up in the driveway, and we're clearly the last ones to arrive.

As we approach the front door, it clicks twice, then swings open when Reed pulls the handle.

"What was that?" I whisper.

"Oh, it scanned me. Auto-unlocks."

"That's crazy," I murmur.

Reed just laughs.

When we step inside, Luke's already at the door. "About time." He grins.

Reed jerks a thumb toward me. "Blame her."

Luke chuckles, and I shoot Reed a look, fighting the smile.

Luke steps back, holding the door wide. "We're in the kitchen. Don't bother with your shoes, I've got plans for us outside."

We follow him down the hall. The ceilings stretch high above us, the space open and bright, white furniture giving it a clean look. By the time we reach the kitchen, everyone's gathered around the massive island. A chef moves quickly behind the counter, a skillet hissing as he sears thick cuts of steak. The air is rich with the scent, savory, smoky, a hint of butter and garlic riding the steam that curls up toward the ceiling.

Kinsley spots me first and pulls me into a hug, Naya right behind her. Reed smiles before heading over to where the guys are gathered near the back door.

Naya squeezes my hand. "Judy called and told me what happened yesterday. Are you okay?"

"Yes. Reed hasn't left my side." I glance his way, he's already looking at me. I shoot him a wink, and the smirk that spreads across his face makes my stomach flip.

Turning back to the girls, Kinsley gestures between the two of us. "I like this. He's good for you."

Heat rushes to my cheeks, and I duck my head. "He really is…amazing."

Kinsley starts, "Do you…" but Dylan's voice cuts through the kitchen. "How about a little target practice?"

Before I can even blink, Judy appears from nowhere, clapping her hands together. "That's a wonderful idea!"

Dylan crosses his arms, grinning. "Bet Reed's the first one to miss."

Reed barks a laugh. "You kidding? You're the one who couldn't hit water if you fell out of a boat."

Luke smirks. "Nah, my money's on Miles. Man's got arms like a lumberjack but the aim of a toddler."

Miles just shakes his head. "Save the trash talk for when one of you actually hits something."

Judy steps in. "Alright, enough chest-thumping. Let your aunt show you how it's done."

I lean closer to Kinsley and Naya, whispering, "I've never shot a gun before."

They both shake their heads at the same time. "Me either," they say in unison.

We file outside, the guys leading the way, bumping shoulders and still running their mouths like it's a competition before it's even started.

Naya leans closer, grinning. "My money's on Judy."

We glance over, and sure enough, Judy's already slipping a pair of shooting gloves onto her hands, a little smile playing at her lips like she knows she's about to prove every single one of them wrong.

The lawn stretches and at the far end several bullseye targets are set up with a long table nearby with a few guns laid out.

Luke gestures toward the table. "Ladies first. We'll show you how to hold your gun and how it works, then you can take your shots." His tone has shifted, no more jokes, all business now.

Miles steps up beside Kinsley, Reed moves to my side, and Dylan heads over to help Naya. Luke and Judy hang back, arms folded, watching closely as the guys start walking us through it.

Reed steps closer, reaching for one of the handguns on the table. He checks it, sets the magazine aside, then places it carefully into my hands.

"First things first, always treat it like it's loaded," he says, his voice firm. "Finger stays off the trigger until you're ready. Got it?"

I nod, my palms already slick, but I do what he tells me.

"Good. Now, see this?" His hand covers mine, guiding me to the small switch on the side. "That's the safety. Keep it on until you're set to fire."

I glance up at him, struck by how serious his face is, the focus in his eyes. "Why are you so serious about this?"

His gaze flicks from the gun back to me. "Because I don't want you shooting yourself, Sunshine."

This doesn't feel like fun anymore, not like some casual target practice to pass the time. It feels like training. I follow his lead as he shifts my feet apart and nudges my shoulders into place. His hand brushes lightly along my arm, guiding the barrel toward the target. "Like this," he murmurs, showing me how to square my stance, how to hold my breath before the shot.

Kinsley goes first, everyone watching as Miles shows her where to hold and when to squeeze the trigger. She fires three rounds, each one hitting the white around the target. Her eyes go wide and she bounces back, laughing nervously. "That was crazy scary but exhilarating at the same time."

Naya steps up next. She squeezes off three shots, one catches the very bottom of the target, the other two land in the white. She exhales hard, shaking her head, but still smiling.

Then it's my turn. My pulse kicks up, adrenaline buzzing through my veins. Reed steps up beside me. "Breathe in, then hold. You got this."

I nod, trying to block everything else out. I pull the trigger, the crack splitting the air. The shot lands at the bottom of the target. My shoulders jolt, but relief washes through me. *That wasn't so bad.* Feeling a little braver, I adjust and fire again. The next two shots smack the top of the target, and a grin breaks across my face as I set the gun back on the table.

"Nice shots." Reed presses a kiss on my cheek.

I lift my hands to show him, they're shaking. He chuckles. "It's normal, you know." He leans down. "Did you know adrenaline heightens arousal?"

I laugh, shoving his shoulder. "You're ridiculous."

The guys take their turns next, each of them hitting the red in different spots. Dylan lets out a satisfied grunt when his cluster lands close together, Luke smirks at his grouping, and Miles just nods like it's no surprise he nailed his. Reed's shots are clean and sharp, controlled like he's been doing this his whole life.

Then Judy steps up. She doesn't fuss with her stance or overthink it, just lifts the gun, takes aim and squeezes the trigger. One shot. Dead center.

She sets the gun down like it's nothing. "See how easy that was?"

The guys all groan at once.

Dylan throws his hands in the air. "No way. She's got the sights rigged."

Luke shakes his head, fighting a smile. "Or maybe you just suck."

Miles crosses his arms and smirks like he already knew.

Reed just laughs under his breath. "Face it, boys, she smoked us."

The guys are still grumbling when Judy strolls past, patting each of them on the chest. "Let's eat. I'm hungry."

I can't help it; I laugh out loud. Leave it to Judy to drop a bullseye and then walk away like it was nothing.

The girls trail after Judy into the house, still talking about her perfect shot. I fall in step with them. "Where did you learn to shoot?"

She smiles faintly. "I was taught many years ago." Her eyes drop to the floor, and for a moment there's a flicker of sadness that we all catch.

Naya jumps in quickly, lightening the mood. "So…I was thinking we should all go to the Halloween party."

Judy perks up. "The one at the community center?"

"Yeah." Naya grins. "Adult-only, all-you-can-drink, mixed drinks. The works."

Kinsley claps her hands together. "Miles will hate it, but we're in."

"I'll go," I say. "I just don't know if Reed will be busy."

Naya's grin widens. "That man would follow you anywhere."

I laugh, glancing over my shoulder at him. He looks up from the table, catches my eyes, and I can't stop the smile that spreads before I turn back around. In this short time, he's shown me so much patience, understanding, protection and excitement. Life. I can feel it, this pull, this rush every time Reed looks at me. It's not just attraction anymore. I'm falling for him, hard.

Kinsley nudges me, laughing. "You've got heart eyes right now."

"Oh, shut up." I chuckle.

We head back inside, the girls still laughing under their breath. The dining room table is already set, and the chef is just placing the last dish in the center, a steaming platter that fills the room with the rich smell of roasted garlic and herbs. The guys file in right behind us, pulling out chairs as everyone settles around the long table. Plates and bowls get passed down, the clatter of silverware mixing with low voices and the occasional laugh.

Somewhere between the bread basket and the mashed potatoes, the talk circles back to the Halloween party. Luke's already groaning about costumes, Naya's insisting it's mandatory, and before I know it Dylan's pointing his fork at Reed and me, declaring we'll end up in matching costumes. Luke throws in Tarzan and Jane just to stir the pot, which has Kinsley doubled over laughing and Miles groaning about loincloths. Dylan only eggs him on harder, the table buzzing with laughter until my cheeks ache from smiling. Judy, cool as ever, slides in with a grin and reminds everyone the Autumn festival is tomorrow and the perfect place to grab costumes. The girls are instantly on board, already buzzing about vendors and food trucks. The guys one by one admit they can't go because of work, shifts, responsibilities. Miles huffs like the weight of the world's been dropped on him. "Fine. I'll take the girls."

The cheer that follows makes him scowl, but there's no hiding the twitch at the corner of his mouth.

I sit back for a second, just taking it in. The laughter, the teasing, the way everyone folds into each other so easily. For the first time in a long time, I don't feel like an outsider looking in. I feel comfortable here, like I belong. I glance over at Reed. *He's the reason I feel this way.*

After dinner and a little more teasing, we say our goodbyes with quick hugs and a round of "see you tomorrows." Then Reed and I slip out, heading for his truck.

Once we're on the road, the conversation shifts to costumes. I grin. "So, what if I pick something out for you?"

He cuts me a look, half-smirk, half-serious. "I don't care what you pick, Sunshine, as long as you don't give the guys a reason to make me the butt of their jokes."

I bite back a grin. "Fine, then I'll pick something cute."

"Cute?" His brow arches, amused. "How about handsome? Rugged? Hell, even scary. Not cute."

"Fine, nothing cute. How do you feel about tights?"

He side-eyes me, deadpan. "No tights."

I burst out laughing, already plotting. By the time we pull into his driveway, I've thought of something even worse. As soon as we step inside, I kick off my shoes and glance at him with a wicked grin. "I think we should go as a bee and a flower. You'd make a great bumblebee."

His brows shoot up, then lower into a glare. "You wouldn't."

"Oh, I would." I tease, biting back a laugh. "Stripes across your chest, and maybe a little stinger on your butt…adorable."

He lunges, tackling me playfully onto the couch, both of us laughing as I squeal under him. In one quick motion, he rolls me facedown, his body pressing firmly against mine. Heat sparks when I feel the hard press of him against my ass, his breath hot against my ear. "Maybe, a stinger would look better on your ass."

A gasp slips out of me, my body squirming instinctively against his. "Don't even think about it."

His chuckle rumbles against my back. "Sunshine, you're not helping your case, squirming against me like this."

I stop squirming. "Okay, fine." I laugh. "No bumblebee."

He rolls me back over, his mouth crashing onto mine with a hungry kiss. "Knew you'd see it my way."

This is the side of a man I never knew I needed, the one that makes me feel lighter, like maybe happiness really is this simple.

34

The Line I'll Cross

Reed

The light edges through the blinds, landing across the bed. Raelynn's asleep beside me, her head against my arm, hair spilling across the pillow. I've never been in love, wouldn't even know what the hell to call it if I was. But lying here, I can't shake the thought that this is what it's supposed to feel like.

I'll have to call Judy later. She's the one who stirred this up in the first place. Usually, I'd be upset with her for butting in. This time…she might've actually done me a favor. I ease my arm out from under her and slide out of bed.

I grab my jeans off the chair and head for the back door. Fifi bolts as soon as I let her out. I start a pot of coffee, then take a quick shower. When I step back into the hall, towel slung around my waist, I hear the faint clatter of pans. Raelynn's in the kitchen, hair a little messy, trying to find where everything is.

"Good morning."

"Morning. I was going to let you sleep."

She crosses and kisses me. "I wanted to make breakfast before you left."

I slide an arm around her. "Let me get dressed and I'll help."

I leave her with the pan and head for the bedroom. Pull on jeans, a clean shirt, boots. The usual.

Except nothing about this feels usual. She's in my kitchen like it's hers, and somehow it fits. Feels easy. Natural. I stop for a second, hands braced on the dresser. I've never felt this way about anyone. Never wanted to. But with her? I'd do just about anything to keep this. To keep her.

The kitchen smells like coffee by the time I step back in. She's at the stove with bacon already going, so I grab a pan and crack eggs. Between the two of us, breakfast comes together quick. We sit down with full plates and steaming mugs.

"I'm heading home after this," she says, taking a bite. "I gotta get cleaned up and ready for the Autumn festival."

I nod, sip my coffee. Miles will be there. He'll keep her safe. I trust him with that. Doesn't mean I'll stop thinking about her.

"Remember, no cute costumes."

She giggles, points her fork at me. "Got it. Nothing cute."

I lean back in my chair. "When I get out, I'll meet you there."

Her whole face lights up as she tries to hide her smile. "Okay. I'm going to call today about getting that window fixed."

"No need. Dylan knows a guy; he's already heading over to replace it today."

Her eyes soften. "You already did it?"

"Yes, Sunshine. You've got a grand opening coming soon. Can't have people walking into a half-finished place."

She sets her fork down, pushes back her chair and comes around the table. Sliding into my lap, she settles against me, eyes locked on mine. "Why do you do so much for me?"

I meet her gaze. "Because if it's important to you, then it's important to me."

The words sit between us. I want to say more. The truth is, I think I might love her. But I keep it to myself, at least for now.

She leans in, arms looped around my neck. "Thank you…for everything. It's not just what you do, it's how you care."

I hold her close, and the thought pushes in again. *I really need to talk to Judy.* I kiss her once, slow enough she knows I don't want to let go, then lean back. "I've gotta get to work."

She stands, grabs her bag and grins. "Alright, go save the world. I'll be the one eating too much kettle corn."

At the door, I give her a look. "Save me some of that kettle corn, Sunshine."

She laughs, bumping my arm before heading out. I follow her to the car. She steps in, waves once before backing out. I stay there until her taillights disappear down the road. Then I pull out my phone, scroll to Judy's name, and hit call.

She answers. "Hello, honey."

"Hey, Judy." I clear my throat, lean back in the seat. "Can I ask you something?"

"You can ask me anything, honey."

"How would you know…hypothetically…if someone was in love?"

She's quiet for a beat before answering. "You know when their joy feels like yours. When their hurt cuts deeper than your own. Love shows up in the little things, wanting to see them safe, wanting to make life lighter for them, even if no one else notices. It's when their laughter fills you up. That's when you know, Reed."

I don't say a word at first. She doesn't know it, but she just spelled out exactly what I'm feeling. After a moment, I clear my throat. "Yeah…I think I understand."

"Is that how you feel, honey?"

I let out a slow breath. "Yeah. I think it is. But what if it's too early? What if she's not ready to hear that? When do I know it's the right time?"

"Love isn't about finding the perfect time, Reed. It's about being honest and trusting that the right person will meet you there."

I start the truck and ease out of the driveway. "And how do you know if she's the right person?"

Her smile carries through the line. "That's the part you can't be told, honey. You just know."

"Thanks, Aunt Judy."

"You're welcome, sweetheart."

Well, that didn't help much. I don't "just know." I guess if she wants more, she'll let me know. Until then, waiting's the safer bet.

I pull into the station, park the truck and head inside. The guys are already gathered around the table, waiting on the chief to hand out assignments.

Tommy eyes me as I walk in. "Morning, Davison. You look like you're somewhere else."

Jose smirks. "Yeah, he didn't even hear us say good morning."

I drop into a chair without answering, still stuck in my own head. The chief comes in with his clipboard. Chairs scrape, the room settles, and he starts running through assignments. I hear the words, but they don't stick. My mind's back on Judy's advice. *Pull it together, Reed. You've got work to do.*

The chief finishes up, and everyone scatters. I get to it, ignoring the guys. The morning moves fast, with a couple of calls, nothing major, then extra cleaning around the bays. When lunch rolls around, I'm still moving, keeping my hands busy so my thoughts don't get the better of me.

My phone buzzes in my pocket. Luke's name flashes on the screen.

"Reed! The silver car just passed by Raelynn's salon. Slow. Too slow."

"Is it there now?" I'm already moving toward my truck.

"No, but I have an idea where it's going."

"Where?!" I rip open my truck door and jump in.

"I'm pretty sure it's headed for the cabins. I'm on my way."

"So am I." I glance at the time. No one should be there, but it doesn't stop me from getting pissed.

The engine roars, the speed climbing quick, the road a blur under me. Luke's words hit again. *The cabins.* The thought of that silver car pulling in, prowling around where she sleeps, where she's supposed to be safe, rage boils so hot it drowns out everything else. Every turn I take is sharper than the last, every mile shorter. If that car's there…if he's there…I don't give a damn about cops, laws or consequences. If he's there, I'll fucking end him.

My phone rings again. Luke. "The car's at the cabins. Where are you?"

"Two minutes out. Luke! He's mine, you hear me?!"

"Don't lose your head, Reed. We'll handle it, but not if you charge in half-cocked."

My grip tightens, every muscle itching to fight. "He fucked with the wrong woman. I'm not letting this go."

Luke's voice sharpens. "It's pulling out of the cabin drive."

I scan the road ahead, and there it is. "I see it!"

The silver car guns it, tires spinning as it hits the pavement.

"Stay with me," Luke says.

"I'm not letting him out of my sight."

I slam the accelerator, the truck leaping forward as we close in from opposite directions, two headlights locking on the same target.

The silver car darts off the main road, turning hard down the first side street.

I crank the wheel, following close. A glance in the mirror, Luke's right there, too, both of us lined up on his tail.

The car picks up speed, weaving down the narrow road. I push harder, keeping close on his bumper while Luke stays close behind me.

"Take the left side," I snap into the phone. "I'll go right. We'll box him in."

"Got it."

I gun the truck, pulling up alongside the car as Luke closes the other side. The driver swerves, desperate for space, but there isn't any left.

"Now!" I jerk the wheel just enough to crowd him over. Luke does the same, hemming him in tight. The bastard panics, loses control. Tires screech, metal grinds, and the car skids off the asphalt, crashing into the ditch.

I slam the brakes, heart pounding, every nerve in my body screaming to tear the door open. Luke's truck jerks to a stop just behind me, and we're both out in seconds, boots hitting the pavement hard. I stride up to the driver's side and yank the handle. Locked.

Through the glass, I get my first good look at him. Mid-thirties, scruffy beard, ball cap pulled low, sweat slicking his temples. He jams the gear shift, wheels spinning uselessly in the ditch, mud and leaves kicking up.

I explode, my fist drives through the window. Glass shatters, spraying across the seat and over him. He yells, throwing an arm up, but I'm already reaching in, grabbing a fistful of his shirt.

"Get the fuck out of the car!"

I drag him halfway through the broken window, his legs scrambling uselessly against the floorboard. Luke's there in a second, yanking the door open from the inside, the two of us hauling him out onto the ground.

With his shirt bunched in my fist, ready to swing, Luke's grip clamps down on my arm. "We need information first."

My nose flares, rage barely contained, but I don't move.

Luke crouches low, voice steady but sharp enough to cut. "You've got one chance. Give me answers, and fast… or I'll step back and let him kill you."

The man's eyes go wide, chest heaving as his gaze flicks from Luke's calm stare to me looming over him, fists still clenched and ready. The man lifts his chin, trying to square his shoulders even from the ground. "You don't scare me."

Luke lets out a short laugh, cold and humorless. "Wrong answer." He steps back.

I don't hesitate. My fist crashes into his face, snapping his head sideways, blood already spilling from his nose.

Luke crouches back down, his tone smooth but deadly. "You want to try again?"

The man spits blood, eyes darting between us. His bravado drains quick. "Alright, alright. I'll tell you."

Luke leans back on his heels, then rises, giving me space. "Good. Then talk." He steps aside.

I take his spot, crouching low, my shadow falling over the bastard. I yank him closer, my fist still in his shirt. "Start talking! Why are you following her?!"

He swallows hard, shoulders jerking like he's debating whether to lie or give it up. "I'm a private investigator. I was paid to follow her."

"And why did Bradley hire you?"

His eyes widen, the name hitting harder than any punch. His mouth works, stammering around the words. "I…I don't."

I jerk him closer, my patience gone.

Luke crouches just enough for the man to catch his stare. "Careful now. He already broke your nose. Don't make him break more."

He glances between the two of us, weighing his options, and realizing fast he doesn't have any.

"Okay…okay. All I know is he wants her out of town."

The words hang heavy, fury clawing up my throat at the thought of Bradley pulling strings from a distance, trying to shove Raelynn out of her own life.

Heat burns through my veins. "And is running her off the road part of Bradley's plan?" The words come out bitter.

The man flinches, hands flying up like they might shield him. "No! That…that was an accident! I wasn't paying attention, I swear!"

"And the rock through the salon window?" My words are edged in fury.

He stammers, words tumbling out. "I…I don't get paid until she leaves. I'm sorry, I thought it would be the fastest way."

That's it. My fist connects with his jaw before I can even think, the crack echoing off the trees. He sprawls sideways in the dirt, groaning, blood running fresh down his chin. I drag him upright, shoving him against the side of the car. His eyes are glassy, fear pouring off him, but it doesn't slow the rage pounding through me. My arm pulls back, ready to break him apart, when Luke steps in and catches me by the elbow. I jerk away and drive my fist into his nose again anyway, blood spraying across the shattered glass. The fucker screams, clutching his face. I rear back again, vision burning red, but Luke yanks me back hard, both hands locking on my arm before I can land another.

"Enough, Reed." His voice is calm but firm, cutting through the buzzing in my ears. "We need him talking, not unconscious."

The man groans in the dirt, blood pouring between his fingers, and I stand there breathing hard, every muscle screaming to finish what I started.

Luke glances at me. "Let me take it from here."

I shake my head once, before finally stepping back. My fists clench at my sides as I fight to keep control.

Luke steps forward, standing over him. "Where are you from, and what's your name?"

The man groans, rolling to his side, one arm still clamped over his bleeding nose. "Spokane. My name's Victor."

Luke tilts his head, eyes narrowing. "You're not lying, are you, Victor?"

"No…it's the truth."

"Well, Victor," Luke says evenly, "consider this a reminder not to come back here again. Us country boys handle things different around here." His boot drives into Victor's ribs, the crack followed by a choked cry.

I step forward, ready to drive my boot into Victor's face, but Luke moves in front of me. "We have to go. Now!"

The meaning cuts through, and I force myself to shake my head, swallowing the rage. "Meet me at the farm." We break off, heading for our trucks. Both engines roar as we peel out, leaving the scene before anyone shows up.

At the farm, we slip inside. I head for the sink, washing the blood from my hands before pulling one of Miles' plain black hoodies over my shirt. Luke waits in the kitchen, phone to his ear.

When I step back out, he lowers it. "Text Raelynn. Tell her you're on your way. I already wiped the cameras. Go, and call me later, I want to do some digging on this guy."

"Thanks, man." I clap his shoulder.

"Brothers," is all he says as we both head out the door.

35

Four Girls, One Pack Mule

Raelynn

Miles' truck feels smaller than it is with all of us crammed inside. He's at the wheel, Kinsley in the front seat beside him, and I'm wedged between Judy and Naya in the back. The three of us are shoulder to shoulder, laughing so hard the whole truck rocks.

"Costumes," Naya says, fanning herself. "We need something guaranteed to drive Miles and Reed out of their minds."

"Robin Hood and Maid Marian," I chime in, grinning. "I already brought up tights to Reed he said 'no way in hell' to tights."

Judy bursts out laughing, clutching my arm. "Oh, I'd pay money to see that boy in tights. Lord help us."

Kinsley twists in her seat, eyes dancing. "Or we could just keep it simple. Beauty and the Beast. You'd make a perfect Beast, Miles."

Miles only shakes his head, giving her a side-eye that makes her laugh harder.

Naya wiggles her brows at me. "Okay, fine. Then Reed can be a unicorn, and Raelynn can be his fairy sidekick."

I groan. "Reed would kill me if I picked him out a unicorn costume."

Miles glances in the mirror, with a wicked smile. "It'd be the best night if he was a unicorn." He actually chuckles.

That sets Judy off. She's laughing so hard she wipes at her eyes. "Oh, I think you might be right, Raelynn."

The truck finally rolls into the festival grounds, and the second we crest the hill, Kinsley and I both lean forward at the same time.

"Holy…" she breathes.

"Shit," I finish for her.

The field stretches wide, transformed into something out of a movie. Food trucks and vendor tents line the edges, spilling into rows that twist and curve through the grass. Fire pits glow here and there, smoke drifting up into the crisp air, carrying the scent of burning wood and cinnamon candles. Hay bales and corn stalks frame the paths, and everywhere I look people in costumes wander, arms loaded with antiques, decorations, and bags of who-knows-what.

Miles parks, and the second he cuts the engine, Judy claps her hands together. "Well, girls, let's go shopping."

We all pile out, laughter and music carrying across the field. For a moment I just stand there, taking it in, wondering how this little town manages to make everything feel larger than life.

We don't get far before the smell of spiced cider pulls us in. A booth with steaming cups waits just inside the main row, and Miles doesn't even protest when Judy steers him toward it.

"Four hot ciders," Judy says, already fishing for cash.

The woman behind the counter smiles. "Five. He looks thirsty, too." She nods toward Miles.

Kinsley grins and passes him his cup. "You're stuck with us, might as well drink like us."

He shakes his head but takes it anyway.

We're sipping, the steam curling into the cool air, when another vendor catches our eye. A woman with trays of bracelets steps forward, each one glinting with tiny charms and beads.

"They're handmade," she says warmly. "Pick one out, you'll always remember today."

Naya's already reaching. "Well, now we have to."

In minutes we're all sliding them onto our wrists, laughing as Judy insists hers makes her feel twenty years younger. I grab an extra, holding it up. "This one's for Mel. She should be here with us."

Kinsley's smile softens, and Naya nods. "Next year, all five of us."

We clink our cider cups together like a toast, then drift right into the rows of tents. We start down the row, hitting the first tent, an antiques booth stacked with everything from chipped teapots to tarnished lanterns.

Naya reaches into a crate and pulls out a strange-looking contraption, holding it up by the handle. "Okay, Mrs. Encyclopedia, what's this?"

Judy doesn't even blink. "That's a medical tool. Used for pelvic exams back in the day."

Naya's eyes widen, and Kinsley nearly chokes on her cider. I slap a hand over my mouth, already laughing.

Miles takes one look, mutters something under his breath, and walks away from the booth.

The three of us lose it, doubled over while Naya gingerly sets the thing back down like it's radioactive.

By the time Miles circles back, we've moved on to a case of old coins and stamps. Kinsley leans close to the glass. "It's wild to think people actually used these every day."

Naya squints at a faded envelope. "And paid how much for a stamp? A nickel?"

"Three cents," Judy corrects.

We wander further down the row and stop short at a section stacked with brittle plastic Halloween masks from decades ago, vampires, clowns, witches with jagged teeth. Their colors are faded, the eyeholes too wide, the expressions frozen in something between a grin and a snarl.

"Okay," I mutter, picking up a cracked clown face. "This is officially nightmare fuel."

Naya shudders. "Imagine kids running around in these. No wonder horror movies exist."

Kinsley laughs, holding up a crooked pumpkin mask. "Tell me this doesn't look like it came straight out of a crime documentary."

Judy just waves a hand. "Oh, we wore those every year. Nobody thought they were creepy back then."

The three of us glance at each other, and Naya mouths, "yeah, right."

We move on from the creepy masks and step into a tent glowing with warm light. Shelves and tables are stacked with candles in every color, jars of wax lined up like soldiers. The second the scent hits, pumpkin spice, apple cider, something that smells suspiciously like a bakery, every one of us perks up.

Kinsley stops short, pointing at a handwritten sign. "Oh my god. It's a buy one, get one free sale."

Before I know it, the three of us practically mow Miles down in a rush for the nearest table. He throws his hands up like he's dodging traffic while we dive headfirst into the jars, unscrewing lids and shoving scents at each other.

"Smell this one!" Naya says, waving something labeled Frosted Maple Pancakes under my nose.

"This is a dangerous place," I mutter, already balancing two jars in my arms.

Judy lifts one up, eyes shining. "Ooo, this one smells like book pages. I have to have it."

Miles leans against the entrance, smirking as he watches us practically clean the place out. Under his breath I catch, "I'm gonna end up carrying all this shit."

That sends the three of us into another fit of laughter, juggling jars like it's a competitive sport.

By the time we stumble out of the candle tent, each of us has four jars tucked into bags, which means Miles is instantly loaded down like a pack mule. He takes the bags without a word, rolling his eyes, and trailing behind us.

The next tent opens into what might as well be heaven, a full-blown candy shop. The sweet smell hits first: caramel apples lined up on sticks, bags of kettle corn still warm, roasted almonds sugared and steaming, trays of fudge cut into neat squares.

Naya clasps her hands dramatically. "Forget the candles. This is the real jackpot."

Kinsley's already pulling me toward the apples. "We're getting at least two of these."

Judy sighs happily, drifting toward the fudge samples. "Now this is my kind of booth."

Miles shifts the mountain of bags in his arms. "Grab me one, too."

Kinsley rolls her eyes but hands the vendor extra money. When she presses the caramel apple into his hand, she grins. "You're not fooling anyone. You've got a bigger sweet tooth than the rest of us combined."

He just smirks around a bite of caramel, not bothering to argue.

We hit half a dozen more tents, each one worse for Miles' arms. By the time we've collected scarves, handmade soaps, and a bag of kettle corn the size of my head, he looks like he's training for some kind of farmer-strongman competition. Not that he complains, just smirks when Kinsley tosses in "one more thing."

Eventually the path opens into a massive tent that feels like a food court dropped in the middle of the festival. The air is thick with the smell of grilled sausage, barbecue, fried dough and hot cider. Strings of orange lights crisscross the ceiling, tables packed in rows beneath them. We scatter, each of us coming back with something different. We eat and talk and laugh until my stomach aches from more than the food. I have to admit, today has been pretty perfect. The only thing missing is Reed.

I glance at the time, wondering what Reed's doing right now. Probably buried in work, same as always.

Kinsley leans closer. "When's his shift over?"

I sigh. "He's got a few more hours still."

She pats my leg under the table, a quiet comfort.

Before the moment can get too heavy, Naya claps her hands together. "I think the next two tents are costumes and decorations."

Judy's already on her feet. "Then what are we sitting here for?"

We gather up our things, weaving toward the next row. The tent is a riot of color, witch hats dangling from hooks, racks of costumes crammed so full they spill into the aisles, shelves stacked with rubber bats, fake cobwebs and glowing jack-o'-lanterns. At the back, a row of little fitting rooms waits, curtains half pulled.

Naya squeals, grabbing a feathered mask. "Okay, we're trying stuff on. No excuses."

Kinsley already has a glittering crown balanced on her head. "Miles, you're next. You'd look amazing as a vampire."

He doesn't even look up from where he's holding our bags. "Not happening."

Judy snickers, shoving a pirate hat onto my head. "Oh, let him sulk. He's no fun."

I laugh as Naya drags Kinsley toward the fitting rooms, both of them juggling costumes in their arms.

Naya's the first to commit, pulling a black leather catsuit from the rack. She holds it up against herself with a wicked grin.

"Oh, this one's mine." And honestly? With her curves and black hair, it looks like it was made for her.

Judy twirls a Queen of Hearts costume in her hands, the skirt flaring out with stiff red fabric. "This is perfect!"

Kinsley digs through another rack, then turns with a smirk. "If you're a football player," she says to Miles, holding up a jersey and shoulder pads, "then I'm your cheerleader."

Miles actually chuckles.

"Mermaid and pirate," I say with a grin. "I'll tempt him from the ocean, and he can drag me onto his ship."

That sets Judy off. "Lord have mercy, child."

Kinsley laughs. "Okay, that's officially the hottest costume combo here."

We finish loading up on accessories, crowns, plastic swords, glittering masks, before finally spilling out of the tent, arms full and cheeks sore from laughing. We drift toward one of the fire pits scattered around the field. The flames crackle bright against the cool afternoon air, the smoke curling up into the sky. We circle close, warming our hands while the bustle of the festival carries on. I stare into the fire, the heat soft against my face, and the thought sneaks in before I can stop it. This year I'm not just tagging along to some Halloween party, pretending to enjoy myself. I'll be going with someone who actually wants to wear a couple's costume. *Are we a couple? Is it official?* The fire pops, sparks lifting into the daylight, and the questions burn right along with it, leaving me smiling on the outside but tangled up underneath.

"So," Judy says, breaking through my thoughts, "where to next? The drink tent, or I heard there's a new handbag tent this year."

Miles groans, rolling his eyes. "Of course there is."

The girls laugh, and just as we start to drift away from the fire, my phone buzzes in my pocket. I pull it out, and my heart skips when I see his name.

Hotshot: On my way. Got out early.

A smile spreads across my face before I can help it. "Reed's coming. He got off early."

Kinsley grins, bumping my shoulder.

Miles exhales like a man being rescued. "Oh, thank God."

36

The Cost of Protection

Reed

I drive toward the festival grounds, telling myself to calm the hell down before I get there. Easier said than done. My pulse is still running hot, like the chase hasn't ended.

I flex my fingers then glance at my hand. The scrapes across my knuckles are raw. It's a good thing Luke was there. He pulled me back before I went too far, before I did something I couldn't take back. Now I've got the mess written all over my hands, and when she sees them, I'll have to lie. The thought alone knots my stomach. I don't want lies between us. But I can't let her know what happened today.

She's probably laughing with the girls right now, cider in her hand, cheeks flushed from the cold. Meanwhile, I'm running through excuses instead of just looking forward to seeing her. I draw in a few deep breaths, trying to compose myself before pulling into the lot. Miles' truck is easy to spot, parked near the edge. I slide in beside it, kill the engine and climb out.

I can hear the sounds of the festival in parking lot: laughter, music, vendors calling out. I follow the path in and halfway down. I catch sight of them. Miles is loaded down with bags, the girls each holding one and sipping on their drinks.

A chuckle slips out at the sight of poor Miles.

Raelynn sees me first. She smiles and meets me halfway. I bend close, lowering my voice. "Before you say it, yes, I missed you."

She giggles, eyes bright. "I missed you, too, Hotshot."

I press a quick kiss to her lips, then we head back to the group. I reach my hand out to help Miles with the bags and Raelynn's eyes drop, and her smile fades. *Shit. That didn't take long.*

She drops her bag and grabs my hand. "What the hell happened?"

I kiss the top of her head, forcing calm into my voice. "We were practicing for training day tomorrow, and my hand got banged up."

"Did you have someone look at it, Reed? This is bad."

"It's fine, Sunshine."

But the damage is done. Naya and Kinsley are crowding in, eyes locked on my knuckles like vultures circling.

"Reed, some of these are deep," Kinsley says.

"Maybe they've got a first aid tent here," Naya adds, already scanning the festival like she's about to flag someone down.

I need to stop this tidal wave before these girls have me strapped to a stretcher getting chest compressions. "Girls, I cleaned it, and I'm letting it air out. I'm up to date on my shots."

They all hesitate, then ease back, finally convinced enough to let it go. I glance up and catch Judy with her arms crossed tight, Miles' jaw ticking hard. *They know.* I shoot them both a sharp look, my warning clear: keep your mouths shut.

I clear my throat and turn toward the girls. "So…what's next?"

"Purses," Naya answers without hesitation, and the three of them practically skip off.

Judy lingers long enough to pin me with a we-are-going-to-talk-about-this look before trailing after them.

I reach out and take a few bags from Miles. Once the girls are far enough ahead, his voice drops. "Training, my ass. Your knuckles took a beating because you gave a beating."

I can tell he's mad, not at me, but at the fact he wasn't there.

"Luke was there," I answer quickly, cutting him off before he works up steam. I give him the short version of the story, enough for him to know what went down.

We step into the purse tent and hang back near the entrance while the girls scatter down the aisles, fingers already skimming over leather straps and shiny buckles.

Miles shifts the bags in his hands, keeping his voice low. "Did you guys take care of the problem?"

"Most of it," I admit. "But Luke's still digging."

He nods once, eyes tracking the girls as they laugh over something a few tables down. Then he turns back to me. "You need to be careful. You don't know this Bradley guy. Not really."

I shake my head once and turn toward the girls as they walk up with another plastic bag in their hands. I force a smile, slipping back into their rhythm before Raelynn can catch the weight still hanging on me.

Judy sighs, pressing a hand to her back. "Well, my poor old feet are starting to hurt. I think that's our sign to call it a day."

Everyone agrees, and we start heading back toward the trucks, arms loaded down with bags. After hugs and goodbyes, I load Raelynn's bags into the truck. Before I close her door, I lean down. "Let's get you warmed up. I want to take you somewhere."

She smiles up at me, eyes curious. "Where?"

I chuckle. "It's a surprise."

I close the door and my phone vibrates. Pulling it from my pocket, I glance at the screen. A text from Luke.

Luke: Did a quick sweep over Raelynn's car for a tracker. Found one. Didn't destroy it, moved it onto a police cruiser instead.

Heat spreads through me, but a smirk edges at my mouth anyway. *Smart bastard.*

I slip the phone back into my pocket and climb into the truck. The engine rumbles to life, heat kicking on. I glance over at her, that smile still on her face.

"You ready?"

"Yes. So, are you going to tell me where we're going?"

"Nope." I pull out of the lot, glancing over at her. "So, how was your day?"

Her face brightens. "So good. We shopped half the tents, bought way too much, and poor Miles carried almost everything like a champ. He never complained once."

I laugh under my breath. "If he didn't complain, then he liked it."

She grins, then her eyes flick to my hand resting on the wheel. The smile slips. "What about your day? And how did you hurt your hand?"

"Training," I say without missing a beat. "We were wrenching a hose onto a hydrant, my hand slipped, and I smacked it against the side of the damn thing." *The lie just keeps getting bigger.*

Her brow knits as she studies my knuckles. "Does it hurt?"

I shake my head, forcing a small smile. "No, baby. It doesn't hurt."

We pull into the salon parking lot, and I point toward the front. "Got something to show you."

Raelynn hops out, eyes going wide when she sees the new window. She runs her hand lightly over the glass before turning back to me. "It looks like it never even happened."

"Dylan's guy is good. Matched the shade of the other panes so it all blends."

She slips her arms around me, hugging tight. "Thank you."

I kiss the top of her head. "This isn't the surprise."

Her brows lift as I take her hand and lead her down the sidewalk. We stop in front of a storefront with indigo-painted trim. Studio Indigo.

Her fingers squeeze mine. "I've been wanting to go here!" She practically starts bouncing.

I push the door open and let her step inside. Raelynn stops just past the threshold, her mouth parting as her gaze sweeps the room. The gallery walls are lined with paintings, landscapes bursting with color, portraits so detailed they almost look alive, abstracts that pull the eye deeper the longer you look. The space smells faintly of oils and wood polish, soft music humming in the background.

She drifts forward slowly, leading me along by the hand. At each piece she pauses, leaning in, tilting her head, whispering little observations I don't quite catch but love hearing anyway. Every step lights her up more.

Watching her like this, happy, unguarded, lost in the art, it reminds me of what Judy said this morning: "You know when their joy feels like yours." And she's right. Seeing Raelynn like this, it feels like the happiness is mine, too.

She moves to the next piece, still buzzing with excitement. When her hand flies to her mouth, a soft gasp slips out.

It's her drawing. The charcoal sketch she gave me, my motorcycle parked at the scenic overlook, the ridge and treeline stretching wide behind it, the day I took her for a ride. Framed, mounted, hanging on the wall where it belongs.

Her eyes are glassy with shock, like she can't quite believe it's real. I step up beside her, keeping my voice quiet. "I wanted people to see what you can do. So, I talked to the owner, showed them your work. They didn't hesitate."

Her eyes dart to mine, before slipping back to the piece on the wall.

"You're damn good. Everyone deserves a chance to see what I already know."

She turns toward me, tears sliding down her cheeks. I brush them away with my thumb before she steps into me. I hold her close, until she finally pulls back. Her eyes shine as she whispers, voice trembling. "Thank you…for believing in me more than I ever believed in myself."

I reach past her and peel a slip of paper from the wall beneath the frame. She blinks fast when she reads the little plaque underneath.

Raelynn Newberry — Happiness.

She laughs softly, wiping at her cheeks, joy and tears colliding all at once. "I can't believe you did this for me. I love it. It means more than I can even say."

I press a kiss to her forehead, and after a few more minutes wandering the gallery, we step back out into the cool air. Our hands find each other's easily, swinging between us as we head back toward the salon.

The whole time she's glowing beside me, my mind keeps dragging back to the lie. I told her a story about training when the truth is I lost control. Beat a man bloody because I couldn't hold back. And if she knew, would it scare her? I stop next to the truck and turn her to face me.

Her smile drops when she sees the serious look on my face. "What's wrong?"

"I have to tell you something, but I need you to listen before you react. Can you do that?"

She shakes her head, body tensing at my words.

"First…I told you before I never wanted a relationship…"

Her hands fall away from me.

"Let me finish, Sunshine. That's not true anymore. Because I want one with you. And because of that, I need to tell you that…I lied to you."

Her voice drops to a whisper as she takes a step back. "About what?"

The look on her face guts me, fear, hurt, and something that looks a hell of a lot like doubt. I never wanted to put that there. My hands twitch with the urge to pull her in, but I shove them into my pockets instead.

"There was more to the rock that went through your window. A note was tied to it. I didn't tell you at the time. It was from Bradley. Today, Luke and I tracked down the guy in the silver car. He admitted he's a hired PI. Bradley paid him to follow you, to scare you off. He wants you out of town."

She steps up to me and pulls my banged-up hand from my pocket. I search her eyes, and I can see the hurt in them.

She lifts my hand. "What about this?"

"That's what it cost, Sunshine. And I'll pay it again if it keeps him from coming near you."

She lets go of my hand and steps back, her eyes holding mine.

"I understand why you kept it from me. But Reed, I'm not the same girl you met and that's because of you. You've shown me how to live, and I'm not letting anyone take this…" She gestures around us, then back to me. "Away from me…No more secrets."

Her words cut through every excuse I've been holding onto. I let them sink in, the truth of them pressing down until I can't look anywhere but at her. "I can't promise I'll stop trying to protect you. That's who I am. But I promise no more secrets."

Her shoulders ease, the tension slipping away. "Good. Because whatever it is, I'd rather face it with you than be kept in the dark."

I hook an arm around her waist and pull her back to me. "There's one more thing."

She tilts her head up, waiting.

"I think it would be safer if you stayed with me."

Her chin lifts, her voice quiet but sure. "Then I'll stay."

What I don't say… what I can't say yet… is that I don't want her anywhere else. Not for a night. Not for a minute.

"Let's go get your things."

We climb into the truck and head toward the cabins. After a mile or so, I glance over at her. "So, what costumes did you pick out for us?"

Her lips twitch. "Unicorn and fairy."

I snort. "Yeah, because nothing says firefighter like a unicorn horn."

She laughs, leaning against the seat. "You'd look cute, though."

"Cute's not the word I'm going for," I mutter, but I can't help but grin.

She laughs, the sound soft but wicked enough to make me glance over. "Relax, Hotshot. I didn't get you a horn."

I arch a brow. "Then what?"

She pulls her knees up a little on the seat, grinning. "Mermaid and pirate."

"Thank God," I deadpan. "I always wanted to be a mermaid."

She bursts out laughing. "You're the pirate!"

I smirk, keeping my eyes on the road. "Good. I was worried about how I'd look in seashells…but I can't wait to see them on you."

She giggles, shaking her head. "Are you flirting with me?"

"Yep. Is it working?"

She laughs, eyes sparkling. "Maybe it is."

"Better get used to it, Sunshine. You move in, my flirting doubles."

37

The Pirate and His Siren

Raelynn

I blink against the thin streak of sunlight slipping through the curtains and roll toward the nightstand. My phone screen lights up…11:03 a.m. We really did it. Packed every last box, hauled it all into his place, fell asleep the second our heads hit the pillow after putting everything away.

I carefully slip out from under the blanket, not wanting to wake him. He looks good when he's sleeping, all rough edges smoothed out, jaw slack, one arm slung over where I was a second ago.

I pull my hair into a messy knot and head for the kitchen. A quick scan through his fridge and pantry is enough to pull a plan together, and before long I'm whisking eggs in a glass bowl, ready to make omelets.

The sound of footsteps makes me glance up, but before I can turn, his arms slide around me from behind. His mouth brushes my shoulder. "Good morning."

I lean back against him, smiling. "Good morning. Did I wake you?"

"No." His voice is rough, still wrapped in sleep.

A smile tugs at my lips as I tilt the bowl. "I'm making you breakfast before you leave for training."

He releases me just long enough to pour himself a mug of coffee, leaning one hip against the counter as he watches me. "You want to go with me?" He takes a slow sip.

"I can't, I need to get ready for the Halloween party tonight."

He checks the time on the stove and quirks a brow. "Sunshine, we've got hours before the party."

"I'm going to need hours. It's part of the costume."

He gives my ass a quick smack on his way past. "You worry about that costume, Sunshine. I'm gonna shower and get ready for training."

I roll my eyes, though the grin on my face betrays me. "Bossy."

He just winks over his shoulder and disappears down the hall, coffee in hand.

I pause, fingers brushing the rim of the bowl as the whisk stills. My chest tightens, a different kind of warmth spreading through me. He had my sketch hung in an art studio. He's protected me when I needed it most. He moved me in without a second thought. Had my window fixed before I even asked. All of it, because he cares. *He has to love me, right? How could someone do all this and not?*

By the time he comes back out, the table's set and the omelets are still steaming. He's in uniform now, fresh from the shower, hair still damp, a shadow of stubble roughening his jaw. The sight of him like that sends a little jolt through me, my pulse skipping like it always does when he looks this good.

He sits down across from me, fork in hand. "Didn't shave. Figured I'd lean into the stubble, look more like a pirate for the costume tonight."

"You'll make a good pirate. And…it's kind of hot." I reach over and run my fingers across his jaw.

He smirks, catching my hand and brushing his thumb over my knuckles. "Good. Then I'll save my best 'arrrs' for my mermaid."

I laugh, shake my head, and pick up my fork again. "So…what's the training for today?"

"Every year we run drills the day before Halloween. It's practice, but it's also prep. Because Halloween night, things get wild. Everyone's on call until morning."

"Do you normally get called in?

"No. I normally work it, but I took it off this year."

I take another bite. "Why did you take it off?"

A smirk lifts the corner of his mouth. "So, I could spend it with you."

I look down at my plate with a smile I can't fight. "I'm glad you took it off."

That's love. Has to be.

We finish eating, and I walk him to the door. He leans down, pressing a quick kiss to my lips. "I'll see you in a few hours."

I rise up on my toes, kissing him again. "Good luck."

He pulls the door open, glancing back at me. "Lock the door behind me."

"I will." I shut it gently, but before I can take a step, it swings open again.

"Lock it, Sunshine."

I laugh, shaking my head as he pulls it shut. This time I walk over and slide the deadbolt in place. From the window, I watch him climb into his truck, wishing I could go with him, but then a different rush takes over…excitement. I turn up the volume on my Bluetooth speaker, music filling the quiet house, and head down the hall to start getting ready for tonight.

I set everything out on the dresser and take my time painting scales across one side of my face. Hours slip by as I layer and blend, each one shaded just right until they almost shimmer like the real thing. My eye makeup is dramatic in teals and purples, lips a soft pink. I add a dusting of glitter around my eyes and across my chest, catching the light every time I move.

The lock clicks at the front door, and I hear the quick patter of Fifi's paws as she races to greet him.

"Don't look!" I call out from the bedroom. "I want it to be a surprise."

His laugh carries down the hall. "Alright, Sunshine. I'll take a shower."

"Your costume's already in the bathroom," I shout back, smiling to myself.

A few minutes later, the water kicks on. I turn back to the mirror, working gel into my hair, scrunching until it has that wild, just-stepped-out-of-the-water look.

I hear his footsteps in the living room, followed by a low groan. "I'm not wearing this parrot on my shoulder, Sunshine."

A laugh slips out, and I freeze, careful not to ruin the paint before it dries. "Don't make me laugh, you'll wreck my makeup!"

His chuckle drifts down the hall.

I thread a few seashells through my hair, then check the mirror one last time before slipping on the purple seashell top and teal pencil skirt, patterned with fish scales to match the ones painted across my face.

I take a deep breath, nerves kicking up as I smooth my skirt and step out of the bedroom. My bare feet carry me down the hall toward the living room where he's standing with his back to me, tucking in the hem of a baggy pirate shirt. The ridiculous parrot is perched on his shoulder, a red bandana tied across his forehead.

He glances up as I walk in. For a split second, his jaw drops before he quickly recovers with a crooked grin. "Holy shit, Sunshine!"

My eyes trail down him. The top three buttons of his shirt undone to show off his chest, his hair still damp and messy in that perfect way. He strides over, hook in hand, and when he stops in front of me, his gaze sweeps me from head to toe.

"You look stunning, baby." The cold curve of the hook grazes across my stomach as his eyes darken. "We could always stay home."

A giggle slips out as I step back, shaking my head. "Oh no. This took me hours, we are going. You'll just have to wait to dig your hook into me until after."

His grin turns wicked. "I'm digging more than my hook into you later."

"I'm counting on it," I murmur, then turn and walk to the door. I know he's watching, so I bend slowly to grab my shoes, making sure he gets a perfect view of my ass.

He groans behind me. "Tempting me now, Raelynn. You're gonna get yourself dragged to the bedroom."

I giggle and straighten, knowing full well he'll keep that promise and I'll gladly let him.

He strides over, slips on his boots and pulls the door open. I grab my jacket and start past him, but he leans down, voice dark. "You know I'm not opposed to fucking you in public."

My cheeks heat, but I toss him a look over my shoulder. "I'll behave myself in public if you do."

His grin is pure sin. "Yeah…not happening."

We pull into the lot at the community center, the place buzzing with life. People in every kind of costume are making their way inside, laughter and music spilling out the doors. Reed takes my hand as we step in, and I slip out of my jacket at the coat check before he leads us further inside.

The first familiar faces we spot are Kinsley, bubbly in her cheerleader costume, pom-poms shaking as she talks animatedly with Naya, who's sleek and feisty-looking in a black cat suit.

We walk up, and both girls lose it when they see me. "Oh my god, Rae, you look fantastic!" Kinsley gushes.

Naya lets out a sharp whistle, pointing at my chest. "Damn, girl."

Heat floods my cheeks, but I laugh. "Thanks. You both look great." And I mean it, Kinsley looks cute and full of pep, and Naya's giving off pure sexy, fierce energy. Kinsley senses the nerves I'm trying to hide and grabs my hand. "Let's go get some drinks." She starts pulling me away.

I turn and smile back at Reed, and he shoots me a quick wink before I'm swept off.

We pass Dylan, who's decked out as a lumberjack with a fake ax slung over his shoulder. "Ladies," he greets us with a grin before heading toward the guys near the back.

At the bar, Judy breezes by in a Queen of Hearts dress, her crown tilted just right, red lips bright against her smile. She looks adorable, skirts flowing as she disappears into the crowd.

Naya orders us each a mixed drink called Rotten to the Core. She hands them out, and Kinsley and I cringe at the color. "It's brown."

"Trust me," Naya laughs.

Because we do, we shrug, clink glasses and toast. "To friendship."

We drink, and my eyes go wide. "That's delicious, it tastes just like a caramel apple."

Kinsley hollers over the band that just started up. "These are the kind of drinks that sneak up on you!"

I nod, nerves still fluttering in my chest, and take another long drink. The sweetness chases some of the jitters away, replacing them with a welcome buzz of excitement.

I turn and take in the room, letting my eyes sweep over the crowd. The community center looks nothing like itself tonight.

Black and orange streamers twist across the ceiling, cobwebs stretch from wall to wall, and glowing jack-o'-lanterns line the stage where the band is playing. Strings of purple lights snake around the doorways, casting everything in a soft, eerie glow. The scent of popcorn drifts through the air, mixing with laughter and music.

Costumes fill the space in every direction, witches with pointed hats and glittery capes, vampires with dripping fangs, and a pair of ghosts draped in bedsheets with eyeholes cut crooked. A group of firefighters dressed as cowboys cluster near the bar, while near the dance floor, a couple dressed as Frankenstein and his bride sway together, green makeup and all. That's when I see Luke dressed as an army soldier making his way across the room.

Naya flips her hair over her shoulder, eyes sparkling. "I'm going to enter the women's costume contest."

Kinsley immediately looks at me, her grin mischievous. "We could get Miles and Reed to enter the couple's contest."

By the time we make our way back across the room, Reed's eyes are locked on me the moment I walk up.

"You want to enter the couple's costume contest?" I ask, tilting my head.

He leans down, pressing a soft kiss against my lips, careful not to ruin my makeup. "Whatever you want, baby."

My confidence flares, bold and certain. "We're going to win."

"Damn right we are."

Kinsley squeals when Miles agrees, bouncing on her toes as she grabs my hand and Naya's, dragging us toward the sign-up sheet.

"Let's get another drink!" Naya calls as we head back.

I glance down at my half-full cup, then shrug. "What the hell." I tip it back, finishing the rest in one swallow.

Kinsley bursts into laughter and follows my lead, tossing hers back, too. She wipes her mouth and leans close. "You think Judy can make us more of that hangover potion?"

Naya nearly doubles over laughing. "God, I hope so."

Fresh drinks in hand, we head back to the floor just as the music kicks up, lights spinning across the crowd. Together we dive in, the beat wrapping around us while we dance.

A prickle crawls up the back of my neck, the kind that says eyes are on me. I try to keep my smile in place as I sway with the girls, scanning the crowd. Plenty of people are watching the dance floor, a clown leaning against the wall, a couple of cowboys by the bar, a king and queen near the stage. My gaze drifts further until it lands on Reed and Miles. Both of them are looking our way.

I shake it off, forcing myself to turn back to the girls, laughing and spinning until the song finally fades out. The next track drifts in, softer, meant for couples, and bodies start pairing off across the floor. I turn, planning to make my escape, and nearly run into Reed. His grin is crooked, but his eyes are serious as he dips into a half bow, holding the hook out like a hand. "Dance with me, my siren."

I slip my fingers around the curve of his hook. My lips curve as I tip my head. "You know what happens to the pirate in the siren story, right?"

He leans closer. "Then I'll gladly drown."

He pulls me flush against him. The music slow around us, couples swaying all around, but it feels like the whole room disappears.

"Careful, siren," he murmurs, hook tracing lightly along my hip. "Pirates are known for taking what they want."

I lean up, brushing my lips close to his ear. "Careful, pirate…sirens don't just lure their victims, they drown them in pleasure first."

We dance until the song ends, and then Naya bounces up, throwing her arms around both of us. "Ugh, I hate being single. Let's get a drink."

I laugh, letting her pull me along, Kinsley right on our heels. At the bar, we order a round of shots, tossing them back in unison. We burst into laughter when a couple wanders by dressed as a taco and a bottle of hot sauce, clearly made for each other.

The bartender stops back over, sliding fresh drinks our way. "These are from the guy over there."

We glance where he points, but it's no help, a vampire, a doctor and a wizard are all clustered together, watching the room.

"Happy Halloween," Naya declares, clinking her glass before taking a sip.

Kinsley and I shrug and do the same. From there, the night blurs into drinks and dancing, trips back to the bar, the music pulsing through us for what feels like hours.

But then it hits me again, that prickle at the back of my neck. The weight of eyes I can't shake. My smile falters, and I lean toward the girls. "I've got a bad feeling."

We stop, the three of us scanning the room. Nothing jumps out.

"Maybe it's the drinks," Naya offers with a playful shrug.

We all agree and try to keep moving, but I can't shake it. My gaze drifts again, and there he is, the same clown I saw earlier, still leaning against the wall. When I look his way, he casually lifts his glass and takes a sip.

I quickly glance away, heart thudding, but curiosity makes me peek again. This time he's chatting with a girl dressed as a fairy, tiny wings glittering at her back.

I know I'm probably overthinking it, but I tell the girls anyway. We slip off the dance floor together, heading toward the guys.

38

The Words We Waited For

Reed

The girls make their way across the room, but the second I catch Raelynn's face, my stomach knots. Something's off. I step forward and grip her shoulders gently. "What is it?"

She shakes her head, trying to brush it off. "It's probably nothing…but I keep getting this feeling someone's watching me."

The girls fill us in on the weird vibe and soon we're all scanning the room, eyes darting over costumes that make it impossible to tell who's who.

"There's no sign-in sheet," Luke mutters. "No way to track who's here in costume."

I nod, then look down at her. "I'm glad you told me, Sunshine. It's late already. You want to get out of here?"

Her brows pinch. "Are you sure?"

I lean close, pressing a kiss to her temple. "Baby, I've been ready for hours to get you home."

She giggles and some of the tension eases.

We say our goodbyes, and Kinsley squeezes Raelynn's hand. "I'll let you know if you win the contest."

At the coat check, Raelynn keeps glancing over her shoulder while they pull her jacket from the rack. I hate it. She shouldn't have to feel like this, shouldn't have to wonder who's watching. And for the first time, a knot of dread twists in my chest. Maybe Bradley's plan is working, because who wants to live with fear hanging over them?

I grab her hand and lead her out, scanning the lot as we walk, but there's nothing. Just shadows, cars and the hum of traffic.

By the time we make it home, she's tipsy, but smiling again. I park the truck, circle around to her side and open the door. She stumbles, and I catch her against my chest.

She laughs. "That was close."

I scoop her up, her laughter spilling against my neck. "I think it'll be faster this way."

Her head drops to my shoulder, makeup smearing against my shirt. Inside, I unlock the door and carry her to the couch, setting her down gently before turning back to close and lock up.

When I return, she's fighting with her shoes, cheeks flushed from drink and effort. I kick off my boots and chuckle. "Sit back, I'll help."

She leans against the cushions, watching me while I crouch down and tug her heels free. Then I head to the bathroom, run a washcloth under warm water and bring it back. Settling beside her, I tilt her chin and wipe her face clean.

Her hand lifts, holding mine. "I had a lot of fun." She yawns.

I set the washcloth on the table and rise, helping her to her feet. "Let's get you to bed, Sunshine."

We step into the bedroom, and I grab one of my T-shirts off a hanger. She sways a little, fumbling with the clasp on her seashell top. I walk over, catch her waist and spin her slowly. Brushing her hair over one shoulder, I unclasp the top and ease the zipper down the back of her skirt. Both pieces slide to the floor in a soft heap.

When she turns back, the heat in her eyes nearly knocks me flat. I lean down, claiming her mouth leaving no doubt how badly I want her. When I pull back, I slide my T-shirt over her head.

"As tempting as you are right now…" My jaw tightens when her fingers slip under the collar of my shirt, nails scraping lightly across my shoulder. I catch her hand, holding her gaze. "I want you to remember every damn thing I do to you and right now I don't think you will."

"Fine," she says with a sly smile.

Before I can react, she turns and slips off her panties, my T-shirt barely covering her curves. My tongue swipes across my lips as I fight the urge to grab her right then and there. She glances back over her shoulder with a grin. "Good night, Hotshot."

She crawls into bed, making damn sure I get a perfect view of her ass. I follow, pulling the covers over her before leaning down close, my mouth brushing her ear. "Tomorrow, I'm going to fuck you until you beg me to stop."

She giggles, rolling onto her side. I press a kiss to her cheek. "If you can remember I said that."

Another yawn slips out as she snuggles deeper into the pillow. "Challenge accepted, Hotshot."

I laugh under my breath, hoping she really does remember. Crossing the room, I strip out of the costume and pull on a pair of sweats. When I finally slip into bed beside her, she's already out, a soft snore rumbling past her lips.

I slide closer, wrap an arm around her waist, and let sleep take me, too.

***

The bed's empty when I wake. I roll out of bed and follow the sound of soft music drifting from the kitchen.

"Good morning," she sings, glancing over her shoulder at me.

"Good morning." I rub my a hand over my jaw. "You're awfully cheerful this morning."

She grins, flipping a pancake before sliding a mug of coffee toward me. "Today's Halloween. I want to put decorations on the porch and carve your pumpkin before tonight when we pass out candy."

Watching her this happy wakes me up faster than the coffee ever could.

She flips a pancake in the pan with a practiced flick. "Go sit, breakfast will be ready soon."

I side-eye her with a grin, but head to the table and drop into a chair.

"Oh, and by the way," she calls from the kitchen, voice dripping with laughter. "I'll never beg you to stop."

Her laugh rings out, and I can't help but laugh with her.

A moment later she walks in and sets a plate down in front of me before taking her own seat. She points toward the pumpkin sitting on the floor by the table, one I didn't even notice until now.

"Is that the pumpkin we got at Holland Farm? The day Judy wasn't feeling good?"

I laugh, shaking my head, because I'd completely forgotten to tell her. "Yeah. About that…"

Her brows knit. "What's so funny?"

I rub the back of my neck, already grinning. "I know I said no more secrets, but I forgot all about this one."

She leans forward, eyes narrowing playfully. "Spill your guts."

So, I do. I tell her everything, how Judy set the whole damn thing up from the very first day. How when she was drunk with the girls and I showed up because Judy called me. The same night she called me Hotshot for the first time.

Raelynn stands, clearing our plates, but she's still listening as I go on. I tell her about tearing down cabin two and why she just happened to be there carving pumpkins, about the motorcycle ride Judy all but shoved her into. About how she called me for the inspection when I wasn't on duty.

She stops beside the pumpkin on the floor and lifts it onto the table, her smile growing as I keep unraveling the story. "Overbidding at the silent auction just to win the firefighter date, knowing she was going to send you and I was the prize. Tricking the girls into the kissing booth by pulling the sign down so you'd wander right in."

Her eyes widen, surprised but amused. "Wait… did she smash my window out?"

I laugh, shaking my head. "She said that was a happy coincidence."

Raelynn bursts out laughing as she spreads newspaper across the table and sets the pumpkin in the middle of the table, her smile widening. "And here I thought it was you chasing me."

I laugh, shaking my head. "Hell, I couldn't figure out what was going on. Miles finally told me to talk to Judy."

She tilts her head, brows lifting. "How did he know?"

I chuckle, reaching for the carving knife. "Apparently that's how him and Kinsley got together."

She laughs, shaking her head. "It's fine… even though you didn't chase me. I love you anyway." She freezes, her smile faltering as her eyes flick up to mine, when she realizes what she just said.

I stand there stunned, the air knocked right out of me.

"I… I did…" she stammers, like she wants to reel it back.

Before she can, I'm already moving. I cross the room in a few quick strides and cup her face in my hands. She blinks, surprised by how fast I closed the distance, her eyes searching mine.

"Say it again," I whisper, my thumb brushing her cheek.

She hesitates, then straightens, squaring her shoulders. "I love you."

The breath I've been holding breaks free as I lean down and kiss her, pouring everything I feel into it. When I finally pull back, my lips still grazing hers, I whisper, "I love you, too."

I lift her and she wraps her legs around me, clinging tight as I brush my lips over hers. "Again, Sunshine."

She giggles against my mouth. "I love you."

Her words light a fire in me. I carry her down the hall, her lips moving against mine, stealing every step.

"What are you doing?" she asks between kisses.

"I'm going to make love to you for the first time."

In the bedroom, I set her on her feet, but she doesn't back away. Instead, she looks up at me with a bold spark in her eyes. "No… I want to make love to you."

I nod, understanding. She wants to lead this time.

She rises onto her toes, kissing me slow, then deeper, her tongue brushing mine. Her hands slide across my chest, nails skimming my skin. I groan against her mouth, and she smiles into the kiss, pushing me back step by step until I hit the edge of the bed.

Her fingers hook into my waistband, guiding my sweats down until they fall away. She eases me down, a light push to my chest until I'm stretched out flat. My fists knot in the sheets, every muscle tense, fighting the urge to take over.

She leans up over me, her hair brushing across my skin, her lips tracing a slow, taunting path down my body tasting, sucking. My breath catches, when she lingers lower.

"Sunshine…" The word breaks rough from my throat, a warning that I'm about to lose it.

Then, she pauses just as I feel her breath on my hardness and looks at me. Her tongue flicks out as she pulls my cock into her mouth. My eyes slam shut, jaw tight, as every nerve in my body lights up. The rhythm she finds is slow, her hand wraps around me working the same pace as her mouth. Her tongue teases in ways that leave me shaking, every breath ragged. My hands shoot to her hair, gripping.

She hums her approval, the vibration jolting through me. "Fuck, Realynn." Every ounce of my control stripping away.

I feel it building, too close, too fast. With a sharp breath, I grip her shoulders and pull her off me before I can lose it. My chest rises and falls hard, breath ragged.

She smiles, before she crawls up and straddles my hips. She peels my T-shirt off her body, tossing it aside. My hands immediately find her hips, sliding upward, fingers tracing the curves I can never get enough of. I lean forward, pulling her hard nipple in my mouth, sucking and teasing until her back arches and a gasp escapes her. I drag my lips lower, then back up, slipping her gently between my teeth before kissing higher, over her chest. Her fingers curl into my hair, holding me there, urging me on. I pull back just long enough to kiss her mouth again. She presses me down against the mattress, her body covering mine. Her lips trail over mine as she shifts, reaching down between us. I suck in a breath the second her hand wraps around me, guiding me to her opening. When she sinks down, inch by inch, a groan rips from my chest, raw. The feel of her, hot, tight, taking me so slow I can barely stand it, has every muscle in my body strung tight.

She settles fully onto me, sitting flush, her chest rising and falling fast. A soft sound slips from her lips as she pauses, adjusting to the stretch. My fists twist in the sheets, jaw locked, every nerve burning with the need to move, to claim, but I force myself still.

God, the way she feels wrapped around me like this, it's heaven and torture all at once. I've never felt anything so consuming.

She leans down, hovering just over my lips, her breath warm against me. "I love you," she whispers.

I cradle her face in both hands, forcing her eyes to stay on mine. "I love you, too."

The words linger between us as she begins to move, slow at first, her hips grinding into mine. A low groan escapes me, my grip tightens on her waist as I move with her, letting her set the rhythm. My thumb slips between us, circling gently over her sweet spot. The sound she makes…soft, broken and her head falling back as she moves…is enough to burn me alive.

She rides me harder, every motion dragging me closer to the edge. My hand locks around her hip, guiding her, holding her tight as I move with her. Every muscle in my body trembles under the strain of holding back. Watching her like this…taking me, loving me, every inch of her body and heart poured into the moment. It undoes me. A growl rips from my throat as release crashes through me, my hips surging up to meet hers. She cries out, her body tightening around me, falling apart with my name on her lips.

She collapses against me, her body still shuddering as the last waves roll through her. I hold her tight, then roll us onto our sides, keeping her close.

Her breathing is ragged, lips parted, eyes heavy-lidded as I brush the damp strands of hair from her face. I press a slow kiss to her mouth, lingering there.

"You're mine now," I murmur against her lips.

Her eyes soften, a tired smile curving as she whispers back, "I was already yours."

39

A Perfect Halloween, Until…

Raelynn

I lean against the kitchen counter, spoon in hand, watching him on the porch. He's got a strand of little bats stretched between his hands, hanging them across the railing. My heart does a little flip just seeing him like this, his hair messy, his jaw still rough with stubble, shoulders broad beneath his hoodie as he reaches up.

I turn back to the stove, giving the chili another stir, the scent of tomatoes and spices filling the kitchen. For the first time everything feels simple. Good. Normal in the best way. This morning plays in my head, when he told me he loved me, too, the look in his eyes when I made love to him. I never thought I'd have someone like him.

The door creaks open and he steps back inside, brushing his hands together. "Bats are up."

"What time does trick-or-treating start?"

"About two hours." He steps into the kitchen.

I wipe my hands on a dish towel, then head into the dining room. The carved pumpkin sits in the center of the table, and I pick it up carefully, carrying it back to him. "It still needs a candle."

He arches a brow at me. "I don't have a candle."

I laugh, shaking my head. "Reed, I was living in a cabin. I don't have one that small either."

He chuckles, leaning in to kiss my cheek. "I'll head to Cranberry Ridge Grocery. Grab a few candles…and candy while I'm at it."

As he turns, I swat his ass with the dish towel. "Get the full-size bars. We want to be the cool house."

"You realize if I buy full-size, we'll have a line out the door till midnight."

"It'll be great!"

"Yeah, great," he mutters with a chuckle as he heads out the door.

Once it clicks shut, I turn the heat down on the chili and hit the bathroom to take a quick shower. My hair's still damp when I braid it over one shoulder, then I pull on jeans and a hoodie before hurrying back to the kitchen to check the pot. I decide now's as good a time as any to call Judy.

I grab my phone, punch in her number. "Hello, Raelynn!"

"Hi, Judy."

"How's your Halloween going?"

I lean against the counter. "It's been perfect. And I hear that's because of you."

Judy laughs softly on the other end, no hint of shame in it. "Well, I suppose I did meddle a touch. But I only ever wanted to see you happy and I knew Reed was the one to do it."

I let out a laugh of my own. "A touch of meddling? Judy, you practically wrote the script."

She chuckles, sounding far too pleased with herself. "Well, someone had to."

My voice softens. "Thank you, Judy. You were right…he's perfect."

"You're welcome, honey. And if he ever acts up, you just give me a call."

"I don't think I'll ever have to."

"Good girl." Her voice warms with satisfaction. "Happy Halloween, Raelynn."

"Happy Halloween, Judy."

We say our goodbyes, and the line clicks off just as the front door opens. Reed steps inside, arms loaded down with bags. He sets the bags on the counter, and my eyes go wide as I peek inside. "How many did you buy?"

He smirks, unloading stack after stack of full-size bars. "I don't know. But my guess? Once the news gets out, every kid in town will be here."

I rub my hands together with a grin. "I can't wait."

He laughs as I practically bounce into the kitchen to grab the biggest bowl I can find. Together, we start emptying the candy into it.

I heft the overstuffed bowl and carry it to the front door, setting it on the little table by the entryway. Turning back to him, I grin. "You want to help make cornbread?"

He smiles, sarcasm dripping from his words. "There's nothing I'd rather do."

I laugh, shaking my head as I head back into the kitchen.

He follows, rolling up his sleeves before taking his place at the counter beside me. "Where do you want me?"

I giggle, handing him the mixing bowl. "I'll mix, you measure."

We work together, measuring and mixing until the batter comes together. I slide the pan into the oven and set the timer before glancing over at him and laugh. "How on earth did you get cornmeal on your elbow?"

He grabs a towel and wipes at his arm with a playful scowl. "Did you see the way you were mixing? Stuff was flying everywhere."

I shake my head, grinning. "Oh no, don't blame me. I'm not the one stirring with my elbow."

He lets it go with a playful huff, and we spend the next few minutes wiping down the counters and sweeping up the stray dusting of cornmeal. When the timer dings, I pull the cornbread from the oven, the golden crust filling the kitchen with a warm, sweet smell. Reed grabs bowls and spoons, and together we plate up chili and cornbread before settling at the table.

We've just started eating when a loud knock rattles the door, followed by a chorus of, "Trick or treat!"

I jump out of my seat, nearly spilling my spoon, while Reed chuckles at me. I hurry to the door and swing it open to find two little girls in princess dresses grinning up at me. I drop full-size candy bars into their bags, and their eyes go wide.

They glance at each other, giggling, then race down the steps. I catch the whispered words as they run to their parents. "We need to tell everyone they've got full-size!"

Reed chuckles from behind me. "I might need to head back to the store."

We barely make it back to the table before the next knock rattles the door. Then another. And another. Before long we're taking turns, trading off between bites of chili, handing out candy to a steady stream of kids, astronauts, ghosts, mummies, cowboys, even a couple of cartoon characters I can't place. Laughter and voices fill the night, their costumes flashing under the porch light as they dart away, already comparing their prizes.

I'm laughing, too, right up until I glance down the sidewalk. My smile falters. A massive wave of kids is heading our way, a sea of costumes spilling down the street.

I look at the bowl, then back at Reed, panic creeping in. "I think we need more."

His eyes cut to the nearly empty bowl, then to the mob of trick-or-treaters closing in. Without a word, he snatches up his keys like he's headed out on a call. "I'm on it."

I watch as he bolts for the truck, climbing in and starting it up. He eases it down the street, careful and slow, threading his way past the oncoming flood of kids.

I lean against the doorway, the emptying bowl clutched in my hands as the line of kids starts to form on the porch. My stomach knots, every one of them is about to find out the "cool house" ran out of candy.

Out on the road, Reed's taillights vanish down the street, and I can't help a shaky laugh. He doesn't do anything halfway, not work, not love, not Halloween.

The line at the porch grows, chatter and giggles carrying through the door, when headlights sweep back across the drive.

Relief floods me as Reed pulls in, climbing out with both arms loaded down with bags. He comes in through the back door and dumps the haul straight into the bowl I've set on the counter.

"I cleaned them out," he says, a little out of breath, like he'd just saved Halloween single-handedly.

I grin. "My hero. But it's your turn now."

He groans but grabs the bowl and heads for the porch. I follow, standing beside him as kids dart away from the steps, cheering over their candy and racing for the next house.

A group of teenage girls come up next, their giggles giving them away before they even reach the porch. The second they get a good look at him, their eyes go wide. One leans toward the others, whispering not nearly quiet enough, "He's so hot."

I can't help but chuckle, and he just shakes his head, dropping candy into their bags.

"Happy Halloween," he mutters, straightening up. Then he passes the bowl back to me. "I'm done. Your turn."

I take the bowl with a grin, tilting my head toward the sidewalk where three more groups of girls are lining up. "Maybe it's not the candy they're here for, Hotshot."

His eyes narrow, and I thumb over my shoulder at the cluster of whispering girls still sneaking glances our way. He groans under his breath, running a hand down his face. "Great. Just what I needed, teenage fan club."

I laugh, nudging him with my elbow before turning back to the line of trick-or-treaters.

A little boy in a firemen costume, shuffles up next, his plastic helmet slightly crooked and a red coat hanging off his tiny shoulders. He peers up at Reed with wide eyes. "You're a firefighter!"

Reed bends down to his level, bracing his forearms on his knees. "I am. And I've gotta say, your costume is way better than my uniform."

The boy's grin nearly splits his face. Reed leans closer, his voice warm. "You come by the station sometime, and I'll let you climb up in the truck. Deal?" The boy bobs his head so hard I'm afraid his helmet might topple off, then races down the steps yelling to his parents about the fire truck.

I press a hand to my chest. *I think one of my ovaries just exploded.*

Reed straightens, watching the little boy run off with his parents, and reaches for the bowl again. "I think I can handle a few more."

I smile as I pass it to him. "Go ahead, hero."

He shakes his head, but there's the faintest curve at the corner of his mouth. He takes his place at the door, handing out candy as a steady stream of kids pours up the steps; fairies, zombies, superheroes, every costume imaginable. Eventually the crowd thins and the last of the rush tears down the steps, racing toward the next house. We both let out a breath at the same time.

"I think that's most of them."

He's right. After that it's just a trickle, a lone witch with her dad, a pair of twins in matching dinosaur suits, a teenager who looks too old to be out but lights up anyway when Reed drops two full-size bars into his bag.

I arch my brows. "Two?"

He shrugs. "Yeah. There are a lot worse ways for a teenager to spend a night."

"You've got a soft spot," I tease.

"I've got a soft spot for you."

We sink onto the porch steps together, the bowl balanced between us. A few more kids wander up here and there, their costumes rustling as we drop candy into their bags. The night has slowed, the street quieter now.

I lean into him a little, watching the glow of jack-o'-lanterns flicker across the neighborhood. "You know…this might be the best Halloween I've ever had as an adult."

He pulls me closer. "Me too."

A cool breeze whips around the house and I shiver. He notices instantly, rising to his feet and holding out his hand. I slip mine into his, and he pulls me up.

"Let's go in and warm up. Maybe finish that chili we started on."

"My god, that sounds good right now."

He laughs. "It really does."

"How much time's left for trick-or-treating?"

He checks his phone. "Thirty minutes."

We head inside, and I start ladling fresh bowls of chili, the steam curling into the air. I've just set one on the counter when a sharp alarm splits the air, rattling through the house.

I jump, heart pounding, and Reed is already moving. "What is that?"

"Fire alarm." He yanks on his boots and snatches up his keys.

I hurry after him. "Reed…"

He spins back long enough to press a quick kiss to my lips. "I have to go, Sunshine."

"Be careful," I whisper, watching as he bolts out the door.

The engine roars to life, tires spitting gravel as he peels down the drive, red lights cutting through the dark.

It's probably just a false alarm, I tell myself. He said it happens a lot on nights like this.

I pull the door closed and head back to the kitchen, tidying the counter and rinsing the bowls. The sound of the door opening pulls me from the sink, a smile tugging at my mouth. I dry my hands and move toward the living room.

"False alarm?" I call as I round the corner.

But when I step into the room, it isn't Reed. I freeze, my pulse spiking. "W-what are you doing in here?"

40

The Call Before the Fall

Reed

I race toward the station. My heart's still hammering, but it's all instinct now, the shift from home to work, from man to firefighter.

Other trucks and cars are pulling in as I round the corner, crew members piling out and sprinting for the open bay. I swing into my spot and barely kill the engine before I'm running inside with them.

"Structure fire!" Chief's voice cuts through the noise, sharp and commanding.

Turnout gear hangs in rows, and in seconds it's madness, jackets yanked down, boots thudding on concrete, helmets snapping into place. I grab mine, shrug into the heavy coat, and pull the straps tight.

I snatch the set of keys for the engine. Four guys are right on my heels, climbing in as I haul myself into the driver's seat. The bay doors rumble open, cold night air rushing in. I slam the truck into gear and roll out, lights flashing, siren wailing. In the side mirror, the second truck pulls onto the street close behind us.

"Address?" I bark, eyes locked on the road.

"East side, Maple and Third!" Tommy rattles it off, already checking the map screen.

Across town. I push harder on the gas, siren screaming through the night.

From the back, Leo leans forward, yelling over the noise. "It's Dusty's Diner!"

Jose twists in his seat, frowning. "The place closed early today for Halloween."

I glance at Tommy. "Radio Chief. Tell him the location and have him get a hold of the owners, find out if anyone's supposed to be there."

"On it." Tommy snatches up the mic, pressing it to his mouth as the siren wails. "Dispatch, Engine One en route to Maple and Third, Dusty's Diner. Can you confirm with the owners if anyone should be inside?"

Static crackles, then the dispatcher's voice fills the cab. "Copy that, Engine One. We'll reach out to the owners and advise."

A dark column of smoke rises into the night sky, flames shooting up from the back near the kitchen. I flick on the spotlight, cutting across the empty lot as we roll in.

I park hard, engine rumbling down, and the second truck pulls in beside us. Both crews are out in seconds, boots pounding the pavement, voices raised over the crackle of fire. The crew falls into step, each man knowing his role, hoses uncoil, gear slamming into place.

The fire spreads fast, chewing its way along the roofline. A window bursts with a sharp crack, glass raining across the lot as black smoke pours out in thick waves. The rush of oxygen feeds the flames, sending them surging higher, brighter.

We push toward the front, heat washing over us as the fire spits and growls inside the diner, daring us to come closer.

Behind me, the second crew swings the aerial ladder into place. Its hydraulics groan as it lifts, nozzle swiveling down. A jet of water hammers the roof, steam exploding into the night.

At the door, Tommy's already there, Halligan bar in hand. He wedges it tight against the frame, muscles straining as he forces the metal inward. With a sharp crack, the door gives way.

"Go!" I bark, and Mason and I surge forward, masks down, line ready. Smoke billows out, thick and choking, but training kicks in. I drop low, dragging the charged line with me as we push into the glow of the fire.

Inside, the smoke swallows everything. My mask hisses with each breath, heat pressing down in waves. A muted scream breaks through the noise, faint but undeniable.

I freeze, hand going to my radio. "I hear someone."

"I hear it, too," Mason answers, his voice tight through the mask.

"Turn your headlamp on."

We both click them on, beams slicing through the thick haze. "Where are you?" I shout, voice muffled by gear but carrying.

Nothing. Just the crack and spit of fire.

We push deeper, scanning every corner the light touches. Then it comes again, not a scream this time, but soft, broken sobs.

Mason's head snaps toward the sound. "That way."

The noise pulls us to the side office. I reach the door and shove it open. Smoke billows out, thick and choking, rolling low across the floor. Through it, I spot her, crumpled near the desk, motionless.

"Hold the line," I order to Mason, already moving.

He plants his boots and braces, keeping the nozzle steady as I drop low and push through. The heat licks at my gear, smoke swirling as I reach her. Her body is slack when I scoop her up.

I stay crouched, weight balanced, keeping her shielded as I make for the exit. Mason moves with me, backing out, hose hissing in his grip, fighting the spray as it kicks and bucks. Together we push toward the glow of the open door. Leo is already waiting just outside, gloves up. I shift her weight and pass her into his arms.

"Get her on air."

"Got her," he answers, moving fast toward the medics.

Tommy's already at the rig, hauling out the oxygen tank, while the wail of an ambulance pierces the night. I glance back toward the diner where Mason's still holding the line at the door. The third rig swings into the lot, siren cutting as it circles around back to secure the rear. I head straight for the door.

"Let's move!" I shout as I rejoin Mason, taking the nozzle and leading us in. The fire greets us immediately, snarling and spitting, smoke curling so thick my headlamp barely cuts through.

I key my radio. "Engine One inside. Keep your eyes open, there could be more victims."

A reply crackles back: "Copy that. Search and rescue still priority."

The line hisses as we push forward, the water cutting a path but barely taming the heat. Mason stays tight at my shoulder, the hose jerking between us as flames claw higher, rolling along the ceiling.

We clear the restroom first, door kicked open, light sweeping across empty stalls.

"Clear!" Mason calls, and we move on.

The dining room is worse, chairs overturned, flames chewing through the booths. Smoke swirls heavy and black, choking out everything above waist height. I scan fast, headlamp cutting through table legs, praying I don't find anyone still inside. Nothing moves but the fire.

We push into the kitchen, water hissing against metal, steam blasting back in our faces. Mason fights to keep the line steady as I swing my light into every corner, the cook line, the prep tables, even the walk-in cooler. The heavy door hangs open, but it's empty.

"Clear," I say into the radio.

We press on, deeper into the back storage closets, shelves stacked with boxes, flames licking through cardboard and paper. Mason sweeps the stream over it, beating the fire back enough for me to yank the doors wide one by one. All empty. We move fast, methodical, every muscle burning from the weight of the gear, but there's no stopping.

One closet after another, empty. No voices, no movement, nothing but the groan of the building and the roar of fire. I give Mason a sharp nod and we push back, swinging the stream wide.

The smoke thickens, pressing down hard, every breath loud in my mask. Water rains from above as the aerial crew hammers the roof, the spray breaking through charred shingles and pouring inside. Steam blasts back at us in waves, the heat pushing against my gear, every inch of fabric tested.

We keep at it, sweeping the line side to side, pushing the fire into the corners and beating it down. Slowly, the roar dulls, flames shrinking to smolder and hiss. What was an inferno minutes ago begins to sag into wet black ruin.

"Containment starting," I say into the radio.

The reply comes through the static: "Copy, Engine One. Keep it fixed."

I tighten my grip on the nozzle, shoulders burning from the strain, refusing to let up. The flames shrink with every pass of the line until they're no more than stubborn embers clinging to corners and rafters. The roar fades, smoke rolling heavy but thinner now, the worst of it beaten back.

"Knockdown complete," I call over the radio.

"Copy that," Chief answers. "Start overhaul."

Fresh crews move in behind us, tools in hand, pike poles, axes, thermal cameras, tearing into walls and ceilings, hunting for hidden fire. Mason and I step back, dragging the hose out of their way.

By the time we hit the doorway, the night air feels clean against the heat still radiating off my gear. I peel my mask up, take my helmet off and pull in a deep breath. Mason does the same, both of us bent over for a second, sweat stinging our eyes. We drop onto the bumper of the engine, letting our weight settle while the others carry on inside. The aerial still drips overhead, water raining down the blackened shell of the diner. Sirens have gone quiet, replaced by the steady chop of axes and the crack of splintering wood as overhaul begins.

Mason and I sit in silence for a beat, the weight of the call still pressing on us, when Chief steps up. His face is streaked with soot, eyes sharp but tired. "The victim's en route to the hospital. She's conscious now, talking to the medics."

Both Mason and I lean back against the truck, relieved no one was killed tonight.

"Good job." Chief nods before turning away, heading back toward the smoldering shell of the diner to oversee the overhaul.

I drag a glove over my face, helmet dangling from my other hand, the night air cool on my skin. For the first time since the alarm sounded, I let myself exhale.

The relief lasts all of thirty seconds. Headlights sweep the lot, too fast, and a familiar truck barrels in. Brakes squeal as it jerks to a stop, and Luke jumps out. One look at his face and my stomach drops. I'm already on my feet. Mason pushes up, too, but I step toward Luke, meeting him halfway. My jaw's tight, braced for the words.

"What is it?"

Luke's voice is urgent. "A silver car just passed the salon. Then the cabins. I think it might be headed toward your place next."

"Fuck!"

"I'll drive," Luke snaps, and we're already running for his truck. I drop the helmet to the ground and climb in. The second my door slams shut, Luke floors it, tires spitting as we tear out of the lot.

I yank at my straps, shedding heavy gear piece by piece, tossing it into the backseat. My phone's already in my hand. I call Raelynn. Straight to voicemail. "No, no...come on, pick up." I jab at the screen again. Still nothing.

"Faster, Luke." My eyes are locked on the dark stretch of road rushing under us.

He pushes the truck harder.

I call her again, and again it rings out. My pulse is hammering now, every second dragging like an hour.

"Luke…is it at my house?"

"I don't know. That was an hour ago. I monitored it on video until the car went out of range. I think it could be near your place now."

My phone's already back to my ear, calling Raelynn again. No answer.

"Come on, Sunshine. Pick up."

Luke whips into the driveway and kills the engine. We're both out before the truck fully stops. The front door is hanging wide open. I shove it farther, almost afraid of what I'll find inside. The end table is on its side, lamp shattered. Fifi cowers under the coffee table, trembling. Raelynn's phone lies on the rug, screen glowing with missed calls…mine.

Behind me, Luke's already on the phone with the police, but his voice is drowned out by the pounding in my head. I move through the living room fast, into the kitchen. Bowls are smashed on the tile. A dining chair is on its side, another shoved halfway across the room.

"Raelynn!" My voice tears out of me as I sprint down the hall. I rip through the bedroom…empty. The spare room…nothing. Bathroom…door open, lights off. She's not here.

Luke steps up beside me as I grip my hair, my chest heaving.

"Reed…you need to see this."

He holds out his phone. One look and my life shatters.

On the screen, it's me, running out the door to the fire call. Raelynn stands in the doorway, watching me leave. She lingers a second, then turns back inside.

Minutes later, a black van eases into the driveway, lights off, moving like it doesn't want to be seen. My hands fist, but I can't look away. A man in all black climbs out. Hood up. He walks straight up the steps and right through the unlocked door. For a long stretch, nothing. Just the house. Silent. Still. Then the door bursts open. My heart slams against my ribs. Raelynn fights like hell, kicking, punching. She twists in his grip. He's got her around the waist, dragging her. She almost breaks free, slipping from his hold. But he jerks her back, pressing a cloth over her face. Her body goes limp.

"NO!" The roar rips out of me. My fist slams into the wall. Pain shoots through my knuckles, but I don't care…I want more, need more, something to break under my hands. "She was right here!" My voice cracks, fury boiling so hot it blinds me. I pace, fists clenched, every muscle screaming for action. "I left her for three fucking minutes!"

Luke grips my shoulder hard. "Reed stop. We'll get her back. But you've got to hold it together."

I shove his hand away, eyes burning. "He took her right out of our home! He walked in here and took her! I swear to God, I'll fucking kill him!"

41

Dragged Into Darkness

Raelynn

The doors open, cold air spilling in around him. He doesn't move right away, just stands there with his hood up, one hand still on the knob. For half a second, I think he's a late trick-or-treater. But then he steps closer, and the entry light shines across his face. Two black eyes, a split lip, a bruised chin. My stomach twists. Recognition slams into me. It's him, the one who's been following me. The one Reed and Luke tracked down. The one Reed beat.

I take a step back.

His hand lifts. "Don't make this harder than it has to be." He moves forward again.

"You need to leave. Reed will be back soon." The lie slips out quick, because I have no idea when he'll be back.

The man chuckles, a sound that makes my skin crawl. "I know where your boyfriend is."

Shit. My pulse spikes, heat rushing through me. "What do you want from me?"

"I don't want anything from you," he sneers. "But my boss does." He lunges.

I spin and bolt for the kitchen. My phone's on the counter, I just have to reach it. My fingers stretch for it, but pain yanks me backward. He catches me by my braid, whipping me around so hard I stumble. Instinct kicks in. I twist with the motion and my fist connects with his face, straight into his already broken nose.

He grunts, dropping my hair, both hands flying to his face. "You bitch!"

I tear away, sprinting toward the dining room. My foot catches a chair and I shove it behind me, knocking it over to block his path. It barely slows him. He shoves the chair aside with a snarl and charges. I weave around the table, heart hammering. I make it back into the kitchen. My phone…if I can just…My hand closes around it, but before I can lift it, he clamps the back of my neck. The impact slams me into the counter, hard enough bowls shatter across the floor.

"Let me go!" I thrash, phone still clutched in my hand, but he's stronger. He jerks me away from the counter and drags me, feet kicking, into the living room.

He throws me down hard, the impact rattling through my bones. My phone skitters across the floor, screen flashing as it lands just out of reach. I claw toward it, desperate, but he's faster and yanks me back.

My feet kick wildly, catching the end table. The lamp smashes into pieces beside us. I scream, the sound ripping from my throat, but his hand slams over my mouth, muffling it into nothing. He hauls me up and drags me toward the open door. I see a black van parked in the driveway. *No. No, I can't let him get me in that van.* Panic fuels me. I thrash harder; kicking, twisting, punching. My fist lands against his battered face, and he grunts, grip slipping. I drop to my knees, hope flaring, but it doesn't last. He catches me again, arms locking around me, and this time a cloth presses hard against my face. I pull in a ragged breath, fighting, clawing at his wrist. The world blurs…black edges closing in. And then nothing.

***

Cold seeps through the floorboards, biting into my side as I stir. The weak light overhead flickers, throwing long, uneven shadows across bare wooden walls. My head pounds as the memory slams back piece by piece…the door, the van, the cloth clamped over my face. A shiver runs through me. My wrists jerk, but a rope cuts into my skin, pinning my arms behind me.

I drag my gaze around the room. Rough planks, warped with age. A single cracked window leaking pale moonlight. Dust thick in the air, cobwebs laced into corners. Rusted bed frames line the wall, springs broken and mattresses torn apart. It feels abandoned, like an old hunting cabin or something left to rot years ago. Every sound stands out: the drip of water, the creak of loose siding, the groan of wind working through the cracks. I swallow, throat dry, heart hammering, the panic trying to claw its way up.

I stay still, straining to hear, terrified he might still be here. Slowly, I start working my wrists but the rope bites deeper. I glance around the room, weighing my chances. I roll to my side, trying to push up onto my knees. A shadow cuts across the floor. Before I can react, he steps in front of me and shoves me flat again, his hand hard on my shoulder. "If you get up, I'll tie your legs, too." He's holding a rag to his nose, his voice muffled, thick with pain.

"What do you want from me?"

"I told you already."

My pulse spikes. "What does Bradley want from me?"

He cackles and strides across the room. Planting himself at the door, he leans back against it, blocking any chance of escape. "I'll let him tell you. Now shut the fuck up."

I shift onto my side and roll into a sitting position, leaning back against the cold, rusted frame of an old bed. He takes a step toward me, and the words tumble out fast. "I'm not getting up."

He narrows his eyes but stays where he is.

I sit there, forcing my breathing to settle, mind racing. *Running's impossible with my hands bound. Fighting would be stupid.* My fingers brush behind me. The bed frame has a jagged piece of metal sticking out. My heart skips. Slowly, carefully, I adjust, rubbing the rope against it. The frame rattles with the motion. I still, pulse rising, eyes flicking to him. He hasn't noticed. I try again, moving slower this time, each scrape measured.

My gaze drifts around the room, memorizing what I can. On the left, an old table sits crooked with a chair slouched beneath it, both coated in dust, tucked under a boarded window. In the middle of the room stands a big iron wood stove, its pipe leading up through the ceiling

"Does the stove work?"

His head jerks toward me, suspicion in his eyes. "Yeah. Why?"

I hug my knees closer, letting the lie slide from my lips. "I'm freezing."

If it works… maybe the smoke could be seen. Maybe Reed would know where to find me.

I keep my movements slow, rope scraping against the sharp edge of the bed frame. My eyes stay locked on him, every muscle braced in case he notices.

He huffs, muttering under his breath, and crosses to the door where a stack of old wood is piled. He scoops an armful and drops it by the stove, the logs hitting the floor with a crash that echoes through the cabin. The sound covers me, and I work faster, dragging the rope hard against the jagged metal. Fibers strain, heat burning into my wrists, but I don't stop until the clatter of wood quiets. He crouches, stacking the logs inside the stove, then strikes a match. The flame flaring as he tosses it inside. With a slam, he shuts the stove door and stands, wiping his hands on his jeans.

I force myself back into stillness. When he turns, his eyes rake over me. "Anything else you need?" His voice drips with sarcasm.

I swallow hard, lifting my chin just a little. "No."

His boots scrape across the floor as he crosses back to me. Rough fingers clamp around my chin, forcing my head up.

"I'm stepping outside to take a piss." His breath is hot against my face. "If you move, I'll give you more chloroform again. You got it?"

Chloroform. The word flashes through my mind like a blade. My stomach knots. I nod quickly.

He squeezes harder, his nails digging into my skin, then shoves my face so hard I topple sideways. My shoulder smacks the floor.

I drag myself upright, my pulse racing and glare up at him. "Coward. Hiding behind Bradley's orders."

His expression shifts from hard to ugly. In two strides he's over me, and the back of his hand cracks across my cheek. Pain explodes across my face, and I hit the floor again.

"Keep your fucking mouth shut."

A grunt slips out as I push myself back up. My cheek burns where he hit me. Tears sting my eyes, but I blink them back, refusing to let him see me cry. The door bangs shut behind him, and his footsteps fade outside.

I pull myself straighter against the bedframe. My wrists burn as I drag them harder, faster against it. With each scrape, the fibers give the faintest shift. I grit my teeth and work harder. I don't stop, not even when my arms shake.

The hinges creak, the door swings open and he steps back in. My muscles clench, waiting to see if he noticed anything. But he doesn't move toward me, just returns to his post by the door, leaning against the frame.

I start working the rope again, each scrape tearing at my skin. The fibers snag, then give. My pulse stutters. One more drag and then the tension breaks. The rope slips loose, falling behind me onto the floor. I keep my arms tucked close, wrists pressed as if they're still bound, biting down the urge to gasp.

His phone rings, sharp and sudden. I hit the bed frame hard, and metal rattles behind me. His gaze snaps to me as he lifts the phone to his ear. "Yeah. She's here. Hurry up." He hangs up. The air feels thinner, like the walls are closing in. Bradley is almost here. I force my expression blank, mind racing. My hands are free, but he's between me and the only exit. I just need a plan. Some way to pull him from that door.

That's when I see it…a little mouse skittering along the wall. My throat goes dry, then I let out a bloodcurdling scream, pitching it high and desperate. I stumble to my feet, arms tucked behind me like I'm still bound. "A mouse!" I shriek. "It touched me…it's over there!"

He curses under his breath and lunges forward, scanning the floorboards. His eyes narrowing as he searches. I inch toward the door, breath shallow, heart in my throat. *Just a few more steps.*

He pauses and his head snaps down.

Shit.

The rope I left lies in plain sight on the floor. His head jolts up, his eyes cut back to me, furious. But I'm already moving. I hurl myself at the door, shoving it open with my shoulder, slam it shut behind me and run.

It's pitch-black, only the faint glow of the moon breaking through. A second later the door crashes open behind me. I know I can't outrun him. I drop to the ground, flattening myself in the tall grass and weeds, praying the shadows hide me.

He barrels past, crashing through the brush in the wrong direction. I wait until the sound fades, then shove myself up, staggering forward on shaky legs. The tree line looms ahead, under the moonlight. I push for it, every step fueled by desperation.

"Stop!" he bellows, the sound tearing across the dark.

I risk a glance over my shoulder. He's gaining on me, every step of his long stride devouring the space between us.

If I make it to the trees, I have a chance. The line of dark trunks looms ahead and I push harder, willing my body not to give out before I reach them.

42

When Silence Screams

Reed

Her phone's still glowing on the rug, screen flashing with my missed calls. My chest caves at the sight. *She tried to reach me. I wasn't there.* I snatch it up, gripping so hard the edges bite into my palm, then shove it into my pocket before it shatters in my hand.

Something dark glints near the kitchen. I move fast, drop to a crouch. A single drop of blood stains the hardwood floor. My stomach twists, rage choking me. *She fought.* I can see it now; the chair shoved halfway across the room, bowls shattered on the tile. Silence presses in, so heavy it roars. For a second I swear I hear her voice, echoing off the walls, calling my name. Fifi's whine cuts through the silence. She's wedged under the table still, trembling, like she watched it all happen. *Even the damn dog knows I failed her.* My fingers curl around the leg of the overturned chair, ready to hurl it through the wall, through the window, anything to drown out the sound in my head.

Luke's hand clamps down. "Don't! It's evidence."

The word stings worse than the fire under my skin. *Evidence.* That's all it is to him, a piece of a puzzle. To me it's proof she fought hard enough to bleed.

He peels the chair from my grip. "We'll find her."

My hands won't stop shaking. "We have to, Luke."

"We will. The police are on their way. Dylan and Miles, too. I already texted them."

I can't wait. Every second feels like she's slipping further away. The walls close in, the wreckage pressing down until I can't breathe. I bolt for the door. I slam through it, my eyes searching for something to break. My hand closes around the pumpkin sitting on the porch…the one she carved this afternoon. I lift it, ready to smash it against the steps, to watch it explode the way I feel inside. But the memory stops me cold. Her laugh. Her hands. That stupid crooked grin she was so proud of. My grip shakes. I set it down hard, my breath ragged, anger clawing for a way out. There's nothing I can destroy that won't feel like destroying her. The fury has nowhere to go. My fist slams into the porch post, wood splintering under the hit, pain screaming up my arm. It barely registers. Nothing breaks loud enough. Nothing breaks like I need it to.

Dylan's truck skids to a stop at the end of the drive. He's out before the engine dies. "What's going on?"

Luke's right behind me holding Fifi. "It's better if we have backup, Reed."

I know he's right, but it doesn't matter. Standing here, useless, feels like burning alive. I start pacing, hands clawing through my hair.

Luke fills him in fast, details I can barely process. My ears are ringing, every nerve screaming for action. Dylan's face goes hard, jaw set.

Miles' headlights sweep the drive, Kinsley in the passenger seat. They're both out in seconds.

"What happened?" Miles demands, eyes already hunting. Beside him, Kinsley's pale, wide-eyed, bracing for an answer she doesn't want to hear.

Luke doesn't sugarcoat it. "She was dragged out and drugged. They took her."

Kinsley's scream splits the night wide open. She folds, knees slamming the dirt, hands clawing at the ground. The sound guts me, and my hand slams against the porch rail to steady myself, but it's useless. Her pain mirrors mine, raw and endless, but she's got someone to catch her. Miles pulls her up, shields her, tries to block the hurt. I turn away, dropping my head against the porch rail. I can't look at them without seeing Raelynn, without aching to hold her the same way. For the first time in my adult life, tears slip free. Shame burns hotter than the grief. *I never should've walked out that door. I never should've left her standing there, watching me leave. I should've turned back, should've checked the lock, should've done something. Anything. Instead, I handed her over without a fight.* That thought rips through me, jagged and merciless, and I hate myself more than I hate him. I wipe them away hard and push off the railing, fury building until it's the only thing holding me upright.

"Everyone shut up!" The words tear from me as I cut across the yard, heat rolling off every step. "A man in a black van took her. Luke tracked a silver car. So, why the hell is the car circling the salon and cabins while the van's the one that grabbed her?" My throat burns, rage scraping raw, but it's more than anger…it's panic in disguise, clawing up my chest until it feels like it might rip me apart.

"Decoy," Luke answers flatly.

Dylan nods. "Then we need to find the silver car."

Miles pulls his keys from his pocket, presses them into Kinsley's hand. "Get Naya and Judy and go home."

"No!" She jerks back, shaking her head. "I'm going with you!"

"The hell you are!" His voice is firm, unmovable.

She squares up, ready to fight him right there in the yard. Luke cuts in. "Kinsley, if you want to be useful, go get them and head to my place. The security system will let Judy in. Once you're there, call me. I'll have the three of you watching surveillance feeds." He passes her the trembling dog.

Miles nods hard. "Fine. But once you get there, you don't leave. Do you understand me?"

"Yes." Her voice wavers, anger barely contained as she grips the keys tighter tucking the dog under her arm. She turns without another word and the truck roars to life, headlights slicing through the dark. A second later she's gone.

Red-and-blue lights roll down the road in waves. Cruisers slam to a stop, doors flying open, radios barking orders that sound too calm for the storm tearing me apart. Uniforms spill into my yard, eyes scanning, hands already reaching for notepads. Procedure. Reports. Statements. All while Raelynn's out there, drugged, dragged, and God knows what else.

My boots tear lines into the dirt as I pace, jaw clamped so hard it threatens to crack. Dylan and Miles answer their questions, trying to give them what they need, but all I hear is wasted seconds. One cop scribbles like it's just another line on a page. I want to rip the pen from his hand and snap it in two. They don't feel the clock the way I do. Every tick is another mile between me and her. If I wait on them, I lose her. And that's not fucking happening.

I yank Luke aside. "How do we track down the van?"

"I already have my guys working on it. But it's going to take time."

"We don't have time."

A uniform cuts across the yard, stopping in front of us. "What do you know?"

"Nothing," I snap. "We know fucking nothing."

His eyes shift to Luke. "What about you?"

Luke glares at him. "I know what I need to know."

The officer bristles. "Stay out of this, both of you."

"Go do your job, Terry. So, I don't have to." Luke counters.

His mouth opens, ready to bite back, but he just shakes his head and turns away.

Dylan and Miles join us as the police push through the front doorway.

Miles steps close. "What's the plan?"

"You and Dylan track the silver car. Luke and I will take the van." My voice leaves no room for debate. He took her from me and that mistake will cost him everything.

Luke's phone buzzes. He glances at the screen, then answers and hits speaker.

"We're here," Kinsley says.

"Go in through the garage," Luke directs. "Head downstairs to my office. I already sent instructions to the printer with a code.

You're looking for a silver car. The license plate number is on the printout. Report back to Miles and Dylan."

"Okay." The line clicks dead.

Luke tucks his phone away. "Both vehicles were headed northwest. We start there until we hear back."

Through the windows, I catch glimpses of uniforms drifting from room to room, jotting notes, murmuring into radios. *Yeah, I'm not waiting on them.*

We move to split off, but Miles plants himself in my path, eyes locking hard on mine. "I know this pain. Don't let desperation make the choices for you." His voice isn't a warning, it's a memory. I see it in his face, the ghost of what he carries, something he still doesn't talk about. The words slice deeper than I want to admit. My jaw clamps, every muscle screaming to shove past him, to bolt blind into the night and tear the bastard apart. Miles doesn't wait for my answer. He doesn't need to. He already knows I've lost it.

Luke turns to Dylan. "Start at the cabins. That's the last place I saw the car."

Dylan nods once. He and Miles climb into the truck and tear off down the road.

Luke tosses me his keys. "You drive. I need both hands free to stay connected to my guys."

The metal digs into my palm when I catch them. My chest feels like it might split in half, a storm pulling me one way, fear the other. I shove into the driver's seat and fire the engine. It growls under my hands as I slam us onto the road. Too fast. I ease back, scanning headlights, side streets, every shadow like Raelynn might be hidden there. Every car I pass feels like it could be the one carrying her further away.

Luke's phone buzzes. He answers, puts it on speaker. Miles' voice fills the cab. "The girls spotted the silver car headed north. We're about two miles behind it."

"Where?" My grip locks on the wheel so tight my arms shake.

"North on Old 23."

Luke cuts in, clipped. "We need information, not a body."

"I got it," Miles snaps back before hanging up.

I stare down the dark road, headlights washing over empty pavement, heart slamming against my ribs. And I know exactly what's running through my brother's head. When they catch him, there won't be much left.

I keep searching, but I can't concentrate. No matter how hard I try, my mind keeps going back to the video. She was dragged from our home, her fight stolen from her by force. I know she's scared out of her mind, wondering if I'm coming.

Luke's phone buzzes again, snapping me out of it. He answers and puts it on speaker.

"It's not him," Miles snaps, frustration sharp in his voice.

"What do you mean it's not him?!"

"We just chased down some poor teenage kid," Miles huffs. "Scared the shit out of him. He said he bought the car from some guy named Victor two days ago."

Luke cuts in fast. "My guys are calling now. We'll call back." He ends the line, immediately answering another call, pressing the phone tight to his ear. Silence stretches, every second chewing me raw.

I can't take it. "What?! What the hell is it?!"

Luke types something into the GPS, the screen glowing blue in the dash. "Property Bradley purchased two weeks ago. Ten miles away."

My foot slams the gas. Hope and something darker surges back through me.

43

Run, Hide, Fight

Raelynn

The second my feet break into the treeline, the world swallows me whole. It's nearly pitch black, the canopy above devouring what little moonlight slips through. I veer left, hugging the edge, catching faint flashes of the clearing beside me. I can't go too far in. I know what happens if you get lost in these woods.

Branches claw at my face as I push forward, every crack of a twig sounding like a flare giving me away. My breath saws in and out, loud in my ears, impossible to quiet. I slip behind a tree, press my back to the bark, and freeze. The night holds still with me, until his voice tears through it. "Raelynn!"

Slowly, I bring a hand to my mouth, trying to smother the puff of white that gives me away in the cold. He's close. I peek around the tree. His back is to me, shoulders shifting as he scans the dark. Then he starts to turn. I duck back fast, bark scraping my cheek. Leaves crunch under my feet from the movement. *Damn it.*

"I hear you," he growls, steps pounding closer. "Run if you want, Raelynn. You won't get far. And when I catch you, you'll wish you'd stopped when I told you to."

I push off the tree, weaving hard through the trunks. A wide pine looms ahead, its heavy branches sweeping the ground. I pick up speed and slide feet-first beneath it, curling tight against the trunk. The earth is damp and cold against my body as I curl up tighter.

I close my eyes and pray. I pray that Reed finds me. *Does Reed even know I'm gone?* Panic twists deeper. I don't know how long it's been since the rag hit my face, since the world went black. Minutes? Hours? Time doesn't feel real anymore. For all I know, he's still on the fire call. My thoughts stop short, when I hear footsteps.

"You can't outrun me," he snarls, his boots crunching past just feet away. I clamp down harder, hoping the sound of my heartbeat doesn't give me away.

Then the ground shifts. He drops, arm shooting under the branches. Fingers clamp around my ankle. A scream rips out of me. I kick wild, heel smashing into his face. He grunts, cursing, both hands flying up as he doubles over.

"Bitch!" he roars. "Hit me in the face again, and I'll break your fucking arms!"

I scramble backward, needles grinding into my palms. I roll to my knees, crawling fast out the other side. He's still on the ground, clutching his face. I don't wait to see more. I run, my feet slipping in the dirt before I get traction. This time I don't stop, not even to breathe, pushing harder until the trees thin at the edge.

A heavy branch lies broken on the ground, dead leaves still clinging to it. I throw myself down beside it, yanking it across my body, pulling the brittle weight over me like a shield. My chest heaves under the cover, every muscle screaming to stay still.

That's when I feel it…tiny legs skittering across my skin. Crawling up my arms. Across my neck. Bugs. Dozens of them. Hundreds maybe. My body twitches, every instinct screaming to shake them off, to scream, to move. A sharp sting bites into my hand. Another at my throat. My teeth clamp down hard as I fight the urge to cry out. If I move now, he'll see me. If I don't, I'll go mad under this crawling swarm.

Tears burn hot in my eyes, slipping sideways into my hair. Through the lattice of leaves, I watch his boots move past, every step a threat. He lingers, head turning, scanning the dark. My whole body seizes, lungs locked tight as the bugs keep crawling, keep biting. Finally, he drifts further away, his shape swallowed by shadow.

I can't take it anymore. My body jerks, shoving the brittle branch aside. Dead leaves scatter as I claw at my skin, swiping and shaking until the crawling fades. My breath tears out of me in harsh bursts, chest rising and falling like it might break open.

Then his voice cuts through the trees, close enough to freeze me all over again. "I'll hunt you till sunrise if I have to! You can't hide forever."

He's not chasing me…he's hunting me. And he won't stop.

I spin in a circle, eyes darting through the trees. What would Reed tell me to do? *Run. Hide. Fight.* The words pound in my head like his voice is right here.

Run…I'll never outrun him.

Hide…he'll sniff me out sooner or later.

Fight…I'll lose.

I swallow hard, forcing my mind to steady. If I were Reed, I'd play it smart. Make him think he's ahead when really, I'm behind. Heart hammering, I crouch low and start doubling back, retracing my steps in the shadows, praying he keeps pressing deeper into the woods while I slip the other way.

For a few precious moments, hope flickers. The sounds of his footsteps fade, swallowed by distance. Maybe I've fooled him. I move faster, weaving through the trees, already picturing freedom.

He steps from behind a trunk without a sound, like he's been waiting, like he knew exactly where I'd run. I skid to a stop, feet slipping in the dirt. My body pitches backward, and I hit the ground hard, knocking the air from my lungs. His footsteps thunder toward me. Adrenaline surges. I scramble up, legs burning as I launch forward again.

I don't hear him anymore. The footsteps, the snapping branches…gone. The quiet presses in until I can't stand it. I glance back. Nothing. He isn't there.

When I face forward again, a hand explodes out of the dark, cracking across my face. White light bursts behind my eyes as I'm knocked backward, skull slamming against the ground. The world tilts, the forest spinning around me, then drops into black.

***

When I come to, I'm moving. My body jostles with every step, slung over his shoulder like dead weight. The sway of his stride makes me nauseous, bile clawing up the back of my throat. Every step jars my ribs, my skull pounding from the blow. I force my eyes to stay open, and the world tilts with the motion, stars above, then dirt, then shadow, flipping in sickening rhythm until I have to squeeze them shut again.

I'm no longer in the woods. Panic surges when I see it…the same building I fought my way out of. The sight guts me. *Not here. Not back here.* If he locks me inside again, my chances shrink to nothing. I thrash, kicking, fists slamming against his back, screams tearing from my throat.

"Put me down!"

I bite hard through the fabric of his shirt, teeth sinking into his shoulder blade.

He roars, twisting, and then I'm airborne, thrown to the ground like a bag of sand. Pain rips through me. I scramble to rise, but his hand whips across my face. The hit snaps my head sideways, and I drop limp to the dirt, copper flooding my mouth.

He stands over me. "You bite me again, and I'll break every tooth out of your mouth."

He hauls me up like nothing and slings me back over his shoulder. My body aches, my head spinning, but I make a choice right then. No matter what he says, no matter how many times he hits me, I'm not giving up. I just have to be smart. If I keep hurting him, he'll keep lashing out, and I need to last long enough for Reed to find me.

I force my eyes open, scanning the dark as he carries me. My best guess is we're at an old lumber mill. The main building is gone, only burned-out ruins left behind, but the bunkhouses are still standing, warped and crooked.

We pass a massive, rusted pulley system, cables drooping like dead vines. I twist suddenly, grabbing for it. The metal bites into my palms, sharp enough to cut, but it wrenches my weight just enough, I slip from his shoulder and crash onto my hands and knees.

I try to push up, desperate to run. His hand fists in my hair before I can rise, yanking me back so hard my neck screams. A cry rips free as he drags me upright again. He spins me, his grip shifting to my face, fingers digging into my cheeks. His eyes are wild, breath sour against my skin.

"You're only making this harder on yourself," he snarls, shaking his head.

I force a laugh, bitter and sharp. "Harder for me…or for you?"

His jaw snaps tight. He doesn't answer, just snatches my arm in a bruising grip and hauls me forward. My feet stumble, scraping against the dirt as he drags me the rest of the way to the bunkhouse.

The door creaks open and slams behind us. The air inside is stale, heavy with dust and rot. He yanks me across the room, shoving me down hard to the floor. Rope scrapes my skin as he jerks my wrists and ankles together, pulling the knots until they burn.

He crouches low, his face inches from mine. "Because I don't want to hear your fucking mouth again." A filthy rag comes out of his pocket, and before I can twist away, he ties it hard across my lips. Cutting off the scream, I try to spit in his face. He shoves me over, and I land on my side, cheek pressed to the dirty floorboards.

I lie still, weak and useless…the opposite of how Reed makes me feel. But I feel it. I'm slipping back into who I used to be…no one. Powerless.

Tears sting as I shut my eyes, and my thoughts turn to him. *I know he's out there, tearing the night apart to find me. I can almost feel it, the weight of his fury and the force of his love. He won't stop. He can't.* I roll onto my side, facing away from the man still standing guard, doubt seeping in like poison. *What if Reed doesn't find me? What if he gives up? What if he decides I'm too much to fight for No.* I shove the thought down. He told me he loved me. He asked if I trusted him…and I do. With everything in me, I do. He'll come for me. I know it.

I lay there for God knows how long before I hear it…a car crunching over the dirt outside. Headlights sweep across the bunkhouse, spilling through the broken window and gaps in the siding. The man doesn't move from the doorframe. I don't roll over. I don't want to see Bradley's face when he sees me like this.

My thoughts spin, frantic. *Why? Why me? Why my building? Why go to all this trouble…for a damn building? He had me drugged, dragged, beaten…for property?* None of it makes sense.

A chill cuts deeper than the cold floorboards. What else will he do to get what he wants? Beat me until there's nothing left? Kill me? Or worse…go after the people I love just to watch me break?

My thoughts turn to them. *Reed. My dad. My friends. If he can take me from my own home, what's to stop him from reaching for them, too?*

44

The Wrong Choice

Reed

The speedometer climbs, engine roaring like it shares my pulse. Headlights slice through the dark, bending with every curve, trees blurring into nothing. Every nerve in my body strains forward as if I can drag the miles out of my way by sheer force.

Luke's quiet beside me, eyes locked on the GPS, fingers flying across his phone. His calm feeds my rage…like he's a stone wall while I'm one spark away from igniting. I can't stop picturing her hurt, crying, her head flopping from whatever they gave her. Every second feels like it's carving another scar I'll never get rid of.

"Eight miles," Luke says the screen glow painting sharp lines across his face.

Eight miles. An eternity and a heartbeat away.

One mile later, headlights flare in the mirror. Dylan's truck swings out behind me, staying tight on my bumper. A rush hits my chest. *These men…my brothers in every way that matters, are here. Not for glory. Not for credit. For me and for her.*

"Turn right up ahead," Luke breaks into my thoughts.

I yank the wheel, tires shrieking, the truck tilting like it might roll. Gravel spits, dust chokes the dark.

"We can't help her if we're all dead." Luke grips the handle.

I don't answer. Because if I don't get her back, I'll die anyway.

My phone vibrates against my leg. I dig it out, nearly dropping it before pressing it to my ear. "Yeah."

"Reed, it's Frank." Her dad's voice cracks. My chest caves.

"Yes, sir."

"You heard anything?"

"Not yet, sir." My throat works, but the words scrape out raw. I want to stay locked on the road, on what's ahead, but this is her dad.

"You have to find my little girl. Bring her home safe. She's all I have left."

"I'm trying, sir."

"Just call me Frank. And Reed?"

"Yes, Frank."

"Make them pay."

"They won't walk away from this."

The line clicks dead.

I shove the phone back into my pocket, air stuck in my throat. He's trusting me with everything he's got left in this world. Trusting me to bring his daughter home. That weight should crush me, but it doesn't. It turns to fire, scorching through my veins, burning away doubt until there's only one truth left. I'm going to keep that promise. No matter what it costs.

"One mile," Luke says, eyes on the GPS. "Make a left. And slow down this time."

I huff out my annoyance but ease off the gas, the engine dropping to a low growl.

"Cut your lights, we're almost there." Luke types out a text.

I flick the switch. Darkness falls over the road, the truck gliding forward like a shadow. A heartbeat later, Dylan's headlights vanish behind me.

Luke points toward the shoulder. "Park here. We should go on foot from this point."

Gravel crunches under the tires as I ease the truck to a stop. My hands stay clamped on the wheel for a moment, fighting the urge to floor it straight through whatever's ahead.

Behind us, Dylan pulls in tight, engine cutting off a second later.

I shove the door open, step out and roll my shoulders like I can shake off the fury pressing down on me. Luke stretches his neck, a quiet exhale slipping past his teeth. Just small motions, but I know what it means…we're bracing, setting ourselves in stone for what's coming.

"Keep an eye out for Raelynn." My voice is low as Miles and Dylan step up beside me. "But Bradley? He's mine."

They don't argue. Just give quick nods.

We slip off the shoulder and cut through the trees until the yard opens up ahead. A small one-story house with detached garage sits in the clearing, every damn light blazing. Just past the house sits two large sheds.

Luke leans close, voice dropping to a whisper. "Satellite images show three entrances…front, back and side."

"Luke, take the side. Miles and Dylan, the back. I'll go through the front."

They peel off without a word. Miles glances over his shoulder and gives me a quick nod. I return it, jaw tight, then push forward.

The grass is damp as I cut across the yard, every light from the house glaring against the dark like a spotlight. Too bright. Too exposed. My fists ache with the need to smash through the front door. My pulse kicks harder, ears straining for anything…her voice, a cry, even the scrape of movement. But there's nothing but the hum of the porch light and the thud of my own heartbeat.

I cross the porch one step at a time, every nerve ready to snap. To the left of me, I catch the faintest outline of Dylan and Miles slipping toward the back, Luke ghosting along the side wall.

The porch looms, boards creaking under my boots as I climb the steps. I pause listening but no voices carry through the glass. No movement. Just silence.

I plant my foot firm, turn my back to the door. Then I drive my heel straight into it. Wood splinters under the force, the frame giving way with a crack that rattles through the night. The door bursts inward, slamming the wall hard enough to shake the glass in the windows.

The same noise echoes from the side and back entrances a second later, a chorus of breaking wood and crashing hinges as the others force their way inside.

I storm through the living room…bare walls, a couch, nothing else worth a damn. The kitchen's the same. Empty. Down the hall, I rip the doors open to the bedrooms one after another. Nothing.

"Clear," Miles calls.

"Nothing," Dylan snaps.

Basement door waits at the end. I take the stairs two at a time. Concrete walls, bare floor. Empty. I come back up to the others drifting into the living room, all of us standing there in silence.

"I'll check the garage," Miles mutters, heading out the back.

"I've got the sheds," Dylan adds, peeling off through the kitchen.

Luke and I stand in the middle of a hollow living room. It feels like failure.

She's not here. Bradley's not here. We burned miles of road, wasted time we don't have, chasing shadows while he's got her God knows where. Every minute gone is another chance he's breaking her down, another chance I won't get back. The reality burns in, violent and unshakable, until all that's left is the need to destroy.

I lunge forward, grip the edge of the coffee table. I rip it off the ground and hurl it. It crashes against the wall, splintering apart, the crash echoing through the empty house like gunfire. My hands keep moving, grabbing anything I can reach; lamps, chairs, a picture frame sending them flying until the room looks as gutted as I feel. No one stops me. Luke stays planted in the doorway, silent. Miles and Dylan hover just inside, watching with faces hard but eyes that don't flinch. They let me burn, let me break, because they know this isn't just fury. It's failure, bleeding out of me piece by piece. When there's nothing left to throw, I stand among the shattered pieces. My lungs dragging in air is the only sound left.

Dylan breaks the silence first. "What's the plan?"

The answer claws up my throat…*I don't know*. The scream almost rips free, but headlights sweep across the windows, flooding the house with white before they do.

We all drop low. I stay bent, moving toward the front door. Luke follows me, Dylan and Miles slip to the back.

The floor groans as we ease outside. The car rolls into the garage, engine cutting out. A door slams shut, and the man rounds the corner. I glance at Luke, shake my head once, silently telling him it's Bradley.

We spring forward, closing the distance quickly. My hands hit him first, slamming him back against the car. Dylan and Miles round the corner at the same time, sealing him in. Bradley thrashes, twisting hard, trying to wrench free. I slam him tighter against the car, Luke locking his arm. His fight falters the second he sees all four of us circling him.

"Let me go!" he shouts, voice cracking under the weight of panic. "Don't you know who I am?!"

The words rip something dark out of me. Same tone, same arrogance as the first time we crossed paths in the sub shop.

I lean in close. "I don't give a fuck who you are."

His eyes widen, recognition snapping into place. He remembers. He knows exactly who I am.

Bradley jerks against my grip, breath ragged. "What do you want?!"

My jaw locks. "Where is she?!"

"I don't know!" he snaps, eyes darting away.

I yank him forward, then drive my fist into his gut. He folds with a cough, gasping for air. "You better start talking!"

"Fuck off!"

Luke steps in without a word and cracks him across the face. The sound of bone breaking is crisp. He hunches forward blood gushing from his nose.

I grab a fistful of his shirt and haul him upright. My face is inches from his. "I don't think you understand what I'll do to you if I don't get her back."

Blood runs down his chin as he spits, eyes burning with defiance. "I'm not telling you shit!"

My hand tightens and I drag him out of the garage to the driveway. I kick his legs out and he drops hard to his knees. "If you don't start talking, this is where you'll die."

Luke's phone buzzes. He glances at the screen, then nods once to Miles. Without a word, Miles steps up beside me as Luke peels away, answering the call.

Miles lowers himself, his voice normal, like he's just stating fact. "We won't stop him. We'll let him kill you right here, and then we'll help bury your body."

Bradley's face twists, blood dripping from his nose, but there's a flicker in his eyes…fear. But he makes the wrong choice. "Go to hell!"

My fist pulls back, ready to drive into him again when Luke steps up, eyes locked on Bradley. His voice cuts through the night. "Bradley, I see you don't value your own life. But do you value your mother's? Sara Manchester. 2431 Pine Street."

Bradley freezes, the color draining from his face. Before he can spit out another lie, Dylan steps up, voice rough with impatience. "Just kill her…we're wasting time."

Bradley buckles, panic flashing across his face. "No, no, don't hurt her. I'll tell you everything."

Luke's phone rings again. He steps back, but before he answers he turns his head toward Bradley. "Let's hope they didn't already do it."

"I said I would tell you everything!" Bradley yells after him, desperation gurgling through the blood in his throat.

"Send it," Luke says into the phone. He ends the call, then turns back and walks up to Bradley, who's bracing like he already knows bad news is coming.

"It's too late," Luke mutters, and drives his fist down. Bradley crumples, out cold.

"Luke…" I snap, but he cuts me off.

"I know where she is. Get in the truck."

We bolt down the driveway, back to where we left the trucks. I slide behind the wheel and fire the engine. "You didn't kill his mother, did you?"

Luke shoots me a look. "I Googled her. I wouldn't hurt an old lady."

Relief rushes through me, but it's thin, gone as fast as it comes. All that matters is Raelynn.

Luke's phone lights up. He answers and taps speaker.

Dylan's voice blasts through. "You didn't kill his mom, did you?

"Jesus Christ! What kind of monster do you guys think I am?"

"Oh, thank God," Miles mutters in the background.

"Just follow us." Luke hangs up the phone.

I glance at him. "What's going on? Where is she?"

His eyes stay fixed on the road ahead. "You're not going to like this."

The words hit harder than a fist. Pain and fear roll through me, flooding every vein until it's all I can feel.

45

Obedience is a Cage

Raelynn

I hear footsteps approaching. The hinges groan as the door swings open. A tear slips down my face, impossible to stop, but I refuse to give him the satisfaction of seeing me cry. I keep my back to him not wanting to see the smug look on his face.

"It's about time," the guard mutters. "She's a feisty bitch."

Another voice answers, one that freezes me to the floor. "She's not feisty. She's my wife."

No. My whole body goes rigid. That voice can't be real. I roll slowly, brows pinched, heart skipping hard. *It can't be.*

But then he steps into the strip of light cutting across the floor, his smile curling like he's been waiting for this moment all along.

Jacob.

My stomach twists, bile crawling up my throat. The last fifteen years slam back into me all at once. His voice. That smile. My body reacts before my brain can catch up, my shoulders curl in, eyes drop, breath shallow. The same old routine. The girl he trained me to be. Weak. Obedient. His.

But in the back of my mind, Reed's voice cuts through. The way he looked at me, the way he made me believe I was more than this. Strong. Worthy. Alive. That's who I want to be. That's who I am now. *Right?*

"Still so stubborn," he murmurs, crouching close enough that I can smell the cologne I once knew too well.

His hand comes under my chin, fingers tilting my face up. For a second, his touch is almost gentle, until his expression twists, turning ugly fast. He surges to his feet, anger rolling off him in waves. I flinch back.

"What did you do to her face?!" he shouts, spinning toward the man at the door.

I cower against the floorboards as Jacob rips a gun from his waistband and aims it straight at him.

The guard throws up his hands. "Look, man, she fought…she escaped!"

Jacob strides across the room, pressing the barrel hard into his chest. A whimper slips out through my gag, a broken sound, begging him to stop even though I know it won't matter.

He turns his head, eyes cutting back to me, then back to the man. His tone shifts, mocking. "Well, Victor, it looks like my wife forgives you…so I guess you get to live." Before the relief can land, Jacob hauls back and slams the butt of his gun across Victor's face.

I squeeze my eyes shut, the crack of impact dragging me back through years of his cruelty. Nights when his anger turned everything into punishment. Moments when I believed I deserved it. The memories press in, choking me.

Victor crashes to the floor, clutching his face, blood slipping between his fingers.

Jacob crouches beside him, a twisted calm settling over his features. He pats Victor's shoulder like they're old friends. "Now…go get the supplies out of the car."

Victor stumbles to his feet, hand still pressed to his bleeding cheek and rushes out the door without looking back.

I stay curled on the floor, heart pounding so hard I can feel it in my throat. This is who Jacob is…always has been. Cruelty dressed up in control. And every time he shifts from rage to calm, it terrifies me more than the violence, because you never know when it's coming.

He slides the gun back into his waistband and turns toward me, the storm already gone from his face. What's left is worse…a practiced calm, the mask of a good husband.

"Look at you." He crouches in front of me. His fingers work at the knot until the rag slips from my mouth. "There. Better? You can breathe now."

The gesture should feel merciful. Loving, even. That's how he wants it to look. But I know better. Every small kindness from him always came with a price. Every gentle word was just a hook, setting me up for the next blow.

I wet my lips and keep my head down. "Thank you."

His voice dips lower. "Did you try and run, Raelynn? Did you escape?"

My body trembles, as words shake out of me, thin and useless. "I…I didn't know it was you."

His hand clamps around my chin again, tilting my face up until I have no choice but to meet his eyes. The softness is gone, replaced by that old, familiar steel.

"You ran." His voice is quiet but slicing all the same. "You tried to get away from me. From your husband. Do you know what that means?"

Shame burns through me, even though I know better, even though I hate myself for it. My mouth opens, but nothing comes out.

"It means you're guilty, Raelynn. Guilty of betraying me. Guilty of forgetting who you belong to."

My shoulders curl tighter, my voice breaking small. "I'm sorry."

"Louder." His grip bites harder into my jaw. "Say it like you mean it."

"I'm sorry!" The words tear free, and I hate how they sound…how they feel like chains sliding back around me.

The door creaks open, breaking the moment. Victor stumbles back inside, arms loaded with bags and boxes. He dumps them on the table without a word and heads out again for more.

Jacob releases me slowly, satisfaction curling at his mouth. He doesn't need to say it, I already know. He thinks he's got me right back where he wants me. He stands, crossing the room and turns back, arms spread like he's offering me a gift. "I brought all your favorite things." He means…his favorite things. Always his.

"I thought, since you like the cabin life so much…liked it enough to move away from me…I'd buy you a cabin. What do you think, babe?"

The words are like a slap. *Babe. I hate it.* I always have. It's his way of branding me, shrinking me small enough to fit his world. I keep my eyes down, swallowing the bile that rises. "I love it. Thank you."

He smiles and walks back over to me. "I'm so good to you. Now you're going to be a good wife and help me set up our new home." He crouches, fingers working at the ropes until my wrists and ankles are free. Then he jerks me to my feet, his hand clamping down on my shoulder, pulling me closer until I can feel his breath. His eyes bore into mine. "Are you going to be a good wife?"

I nod quickly.

He yanks me closer, pressing his mouth to mine. The kiss is hard, demanding. When I don't respond, he rips back, his jaw ticking, fury flashing. For a heartbeat, I brace for the blow. But he doesn't strike. He just lets me go, turning away like I'm not worth it.

He strides to the table, tearing open one of the boxes. "Look what I brought you." He pulls out a blue and white dress. The one I purposely left behind the day I walked away from him. He loved it on me. That's the only reason it's here. He holds the dress out for me to take. I stare at it. My fingers twitch but don't move. The silence stretches too long.

His patience snaps. In a flash, his hand is at my throat, squeezing just enough to steal my breath. I choke, my hands flying up to his wrist. "Put on the fucking dress." His eyes blaze down into mine. The fabric dangles between us, his fist shaking with fury as he shoves it harder against my chest.

Every instinct screams to rip it apart, to throw it in his face. But fear drags me back into the girl I swore I'd never be again. My hands close around the fabric, trembling. His grip loosens, fingers slipping from my throat, but his eyes never move from me. He doesn't have to say it, the message is clear. Now.

I move quickly, clutching the dress tight against my chest with one hand, fumbling with the other to strip away the clothes I'm in. Heat creeps up my neck, shame burning under my skin as I keep the fabric pressed to me, trying to hide what I can.

He just watches. Like he's savoring every twitch of hesitation, every shaky movement I make. When I finally slide the dress on, I don't even have the chance to reach for the zipper. His hand clamps my shoulder, spinning me around. I flinch as his fingers trail up the fabric, then pull the zipper slowly up my back.

His palm drifts higher, brushing the braid over my shoulder. "You know I don't like braids." He tugs the band free, loosening my hair until it spills around me. His hand lingers for a second before he steps back, a smile cutting across his face. "You look beautiful."

"Thank you," I whisper, keeping my eyes down.

The door swings open. Victor lumbers in, arms loaded with the rest of the bags and boxes. He drops them in front of the table with a thud. For the briefest second, his gaze flicks to me, and something flashes there…pity, maybe. It twists in my chest, a hope I can't afford.

But then he turns to Jacob. "Where's my money? I did what you asked."

He pulls an envelope from his jacket and tosses it onto the table. "Don't come back."

Victor snatches it up. My throat aches with the scream I bite down, the plea begging to tear out of me…*Take me with you. Please.* But I know better. So, I stay quiet. Obedient. Just like Jacob wants.

As Victor slips out the door, Jacob turns back to me, his grin spreading. "Ok, let's make this house a home." He chuckles.

I smile at his stupid joke, the kind he trained into me years ago, thin and fake. "Of course."

He digs into the boxes, pulling things out one by one, blankets, pillows, canned food, candles, pots and pans. He places each item in my hands and points where he wants it. I move like a puppet, setting everything down exactly how he says, nodding when he corrects me. It goes on and on until every box is empty, every corner filled, every piece of his world arranged the way he wants it.

On the outside, I look calm. On the inside, I want to die with every step, every order, every smile I have to fake. *Please, God. Don't let this be my life again. Don't let me stay here long enough to use any of this. Please let Reed find me before I disappear back into this cage.*

He claps his hands together, eyes sweeping the room. "Look what I created for us, babe. The perfect getaway."

I nod, my fake smile locked in place. "Perfect."

"I'm starving. Why don't you make us something to eat?"

"Of course." I cross to the stack of canned food, every step heavy. "What would you like?"

"Surprise me." He sinks into a chair, leaning back like a king watching his servant.

My fingers shake as I choose a can of chicken and beans. I grab the opener and press it to the tin, turning the handle, but it sticks and fights me. My jaw tightens. I try again. No use.

He notices. He always notices. The chair scrapes against the floor, and my whole body freezes as he rises. In seconds, he's behind me, his arm snaking around my waist. His hands trail down my arms, guiding mine like this is some tender moment. The can finally cracks open under his grip.

His breath warms my ear. "I missed you." His lips brush against my neck before pressing a kiss there.

I swallow the vomit in my mouth and force the words out. "I missed you, too."

I spoon the chicken and beans into a pot and set it on the wood stove. The metal pops and hisses as the food warms, the smell thick in the stale air. When it's ready, I plate it carefully and set it in front of him.

He picks up the fork, takes one bite, then looks at me. "Aren't you going to eat with me?"

I shake my head, forcing my voice quiet and even. "I'm not hungry."

The fork clatters against the plate. And he whips the whole thing to the floor, food splattering across the boards. His chair scrapes back hard. "We can't even have a nice meal together?" His voice rises as he stalks toward me.

I throw my arms up, covering my face, bracing for the blow I know is coming. My body folds small, every nerve screaming to disappear, to survive.

But in the dark behind my hands, another thought pushes through…Reed. The way he touches me like I'm unbreakable. The way he looks at me like I'm his whole damn world. He would never let me shrink like this. Never let me forget who I am. I hold onto that thought like a lifeline, even as Jacob moves closer.

46

Failure Has a Sound. I Heard It.

Reed

The look on Luke's face tells me his words are going to sting. I brace for it. "Tell me what you know, Luke."

"She's about thirty minutes out," he says, eyes still on the glow of his phone. "Best I can tell, they've taken her to an old lumber mill. Deep in the forest. Place hasn't been used in decades."

The bottom drops out of my chest, a cold rush flooding in and leaving nothing to hold onto. *Thirty minutes might as well be thirty years.* Pressure builds in my veins, pushing me harder, faster.

"How do you know she's there?"

Luke doesn't flinch. "Because that's where Jacob Trenton has her."

The name sounds familiar, but I can't place it. "Who?"

Luke finally turns his head, his face carved from stone. "Her ex-husband."

The words tear through me, so brutal I can barely breathe. They rattle around my skull, turning everything red, choking me. My pulse hammers, my body so charged I don't know if I can hold it together long enough to get there.

The screen on the dash lights up, the GPS starting to count down the miles.

"How the hell does Jacob have anything to do with this?"

Luke exhales. "I started by digging into Victor. When I couldn't make a connection between him and Bradley, I shifted my focus."

"What did you find?"

"Bradley had a few emails and texts from an unknown number…messages about Raelynn's building. I traced it. Found it tied to a property purchased a week ago."

My grip tightens. "And what does Victor have to do with that?"

"I went back to his records. The same number popped up again."

"Then who the hell owns the property?"

"When I pulled the deed…Jacob's name came up."

Suddenly, all her little tells make sense. The way she folds in on herself sometimes, like she's trying to disappear. The way she flinches if I move too quickly, even when all I'm doing is pointing at something. The guilt in her eyes when she couldn't let herself be with me, like she was betraying some twisted vow he carved into her. The way her head tips just slightly, scanning over her shoulder as if something…or someone…is always there. How she brushes off compliments, cheeks coloring like she can't believe they're real. How she looked at me when I told her I loved her, eyes shining with something deeper than joy. Relief. Fear. Hope, all tangled together. And it all comes back to him. Jacob Trenton. The fucker who put those scars in her bones. The man who made her feel like she didn't deserve to be loved, who left her convinced she was nothing more than a charity case. Now he has her again.

Luke continues before my blood boils over. "Best I can tell, Jacob tried to buy the building to force Raelynn to fail and run back home. When she refused, he hired a PI to scare her off. But she still didn't leave. So, they came up with a plan to take her when you were away."

"The fire," I grind out.

Luke nods.

She stayed because she wanted to live her life, on her terms. She refused to crawl back to him, even when she was scared. She was building something new…because she loves it here…because she loves me. And when he couldn't own her, he stole her.

"There's one more thing. He's a cop. Which makes him even more dangerous."

The steering wheel shakes under my grip. "He spent years breaking her down, and now he thinks he can do it again?" My voice rips through the cab. "I'm going to kill him, Luke."

Luke finally looks my way. "I know."

My gaze drops to the GPS, taunting me with the truth. Five minutes. That's all we've been on the road. It feels like hours, time dragging its feet while she's out there with him. Every second is like torture I can't escape.

Luke breaks the silence. "My guys have eyes on the property. About twenty minutes ago, a black van left. We should be coming up on it in one mile."

I sit taller. "It's Victor."

Headlights cut through the dark, bearing down on us. "That him?" I grit.

Luke's gaze flicks to the screen, then the road. "Yeah. And try not to kill us."

The van draws closer. I jerk the wheel hard, swinging into its lane. The van swerves, loses control, and slams nose-first into the ditch, smoke billowing from the engine.

I stomp the brake, truck lurching to a stop. Both doors fly open. Luke's out first; I hit the ground right behind him. Dylan and Miles pile from their truck, closing fast.

I drop into the ditch and rip the driver's door wide.

"Fuck!" Victor yells, throwing up a hand.

I don't give him the chance. My fists crash down, one after another, slamming him back into the seat. No words. No mercy. Victor's head snaps with every blow, his body starting to sag under me.

Strong arms lock around my chest, yanking me back.

"Let me fucking go, Miles!" I roar, thrashing to get to Victor again.

Luke plants himself in front of me. "He's just the messenger."

"He put his fucking hands on her!" I snarl, fury vibrating through every muscle.

Miles tightens his hold. "He did. And now he's going to prison with a fucked-up face."

Dylan hauls Victor out of the van, limp and bloody, dragging him over and propping him against the tire. He crouches low, his voice a steady growl. "We're going to ask you some questions. If you value your life, you'll talk."

Victor shakes his head, blood running down his jaw.

"Go walk it off, Reed," Luke snaps. "We'll take care of this."

"Go!" Miles echoes, shoving me back a step.

I drag both hands through my hair, gripping hard like I can rip the anger straight out of my skull. My chest heaves, every breath fire. I pace the road, trying to pull myself together, but all I see is him dragging her out of the house and drugging her.

I spin back, storming toward Victor. "There was blood on the floor at my place. Was it hers?"

Victor's head jerks side to side, frantic, swollen lips spilling words. "No…it was mine. She…she punched me in the face when I grabbed her."

For a split second, pride flickers…then it vanishes, wrath taking its place. She shouldn't have had to fight him. And now she's facing worse.

Luke asks, "How many people are there?"

Victor wheezes through split lips. "Just one. Jacob."

Miles presses, "Is she hurt?"

I hold my breath, bracing for the answer.

"She was fine when I left her, I swear."

Fine when he left doesn't mean fine now.

Miles doesn't let up. "What's he planning to do with her?"

I step forward, needing to hear it from his mouth. His eyes lift, locking on mine.

"I don't know. I didn't know he was like this. I swear, I wouldn't have delivered her if I knew."

The words twist like a knife. *He handed her over and now wants pity?*

Luke crouches next to him. "And yet you didn't do anything to stop it."

Victor ducks his head. "No."

"Why?" Dylan asks.

Victor swallows. "Because I was paid to look the other way."

Money over her life. I can barely keep from breaking him all over again.

Luke doesn't give me the chance. "Who started the fire at Dusty's?"

Victor shakes his head. "Not me. Jacob had Bradley start it…said it would draw you out, keep you busy while I delivered her."

The confession hits like a hammer. They torched Dusty's, risked lives, just to buy themselves time to take her.

Luke presses. "Is there anyone else working for him?"

Victor lifts his shoulders weakly. "I don't know. But he forked over a lot of money for a cop's salary."

That's all I need to hear. "Miles, Dylan…you two stay here. Call the police but wait 20 minutes. Give us a head start to get there before they arrive."

I bend low, getting in Victor's face. "If I find out you're lying, I'll have these two finish what I started."

His swollen eyes widen, but I don't wait for an answer.

We head for the truck. Stones crunch under my boots, every step faster than the last.

"Don't leave me here!" Victor's voice cracks behind us. "Please…let me go…"

Dylan's hand whips across Victor's face. "Shut up," he snaps, shoving him back against the tire.

I don't look back. I climb in, slam the door and turn the key. The engine growls to life, vibrating through my chest. Luke's already in the passenger seat, silent, watching me like he knows nothing he says will cool me down.

The road unrolls in front of us, the truck eating up the distance, but it's not fast enough. It'll never be fast enough. My hands are locked so tight. I've been angry before; at fires, at wrecks, at the unfairness of death, but never like this. Never this wild, this close to coming apart.

And I know why. It's her. Because I love her. Because I need her. Because the thought of losing Raelynn is like ripping the air from my lungs. She's the one thing I can't afford to fail. And I don't care what waits at that mill. I'll tear it down beam by beam if I have to. Nothing's keeping me from her.

Luke calls out turns, guiding us down back roads that twist deeper into the trees. I barely hear him. Every mile we cover, my sanity slips further. I tell myself to calm down, to focus, to believe I'll find her and bring her home…but doubt rears its ugly head, whispering what ifs I can't shake.

I'm so lost in my own head that it jolts me when Luke says, "Turn left. It's two miles down this trail."

The path is narrow, trees closing in on both sides. Branches claw over the hood, dead leaves scattering under the tires. Tire tracks shine in the headlights, fresh against the dirt.

Luke checks his phone. "When the trail opens into a clearing, there should be two bunkhouses still standing. The one on the right has smoke coming from the stack."

I nod, jaw locking hard, teeth grinding as I ready myself for the fight waiting ahead.

"I think Victor was telling the truth," Luke adds still looking at his phone. "I don't see movement. Pretty sure he's alone."

The trees thin, and the headlights fan out over the clearing. The beams sweep across weathered siding, lighting up the bunkhouse on the right. I crank the wheel and pull in but stop short the second I hear it…her voice.

"Reed!" Raelynn's scream rips through the night. "No! Reed!"

I'm out of the truck before the tires stop rolling, heart slamming against the walls of my chest.

"Reed!" she cries again, the sound tears me in two.

"Please! No! Reed!"

I sprint across the clearing, her voice cutting through the dark, pulling me forward with every step.

BANG!

A gunshot explodes from inside. The sound stretches the world into slow motion. Her pleas cut off, swallowed by the echo.

For a second, the world caves in. My life…everything…gone with that sound.

"Raelynn!" The roar tears out of me, ripped from someplace deeper than my lungs.

Luke shouts behind me, trying to stop me, but I keep running, straight into the fire.

47

This Is It

Raelynn

His footsteps thunder closer, pushing fear deeper into my bones. I squeeze my eyes shut tighter, bracing for it. The hit comes fast. His backhand slams across my face, the sting exploding through my eye as I hit the floor hard.

Before I can think, his hand clamps around my arm, yanking me upright. His face twists with something almost soft. "I didn't want to do that. I'm sorry. You just make me so mad."

Tears slip down my cheeks, and he watches them fall…studies them…like it pleases him.

"I'm sorry," I squeak.

"Good." His tone softens more, satisfied. "Now go clean up the food."

I scurry across the room, grab a rag and drop to my knees, scrubbing at the mess he made. My hands shake as I wipe beans and chicken into the cloth, my tears dripping into the stains. The humiliation presses heavier than his hand ever could.

When I finally dare a glance up, he's sitting in the chair, watching me. His voice is calm, almost casual. "When you're finished cleaning that up, we'll cook a new dinner and eat together. Like a married couple should."

My stomach knots, but I force the words out, just the way he expects. "That sounds…nice."

His smile stretches, satisfaction gleaming in his eyes. "That's my girl."

I keep my head down, scrubbing harder. *I hate him.*

When the floor is finally clean, I drag myself back to the stove. I open another can with hands that won't stop trembling, heat it, plate it. He sits there the whole time, finger tapping against the wood, the rhythm of his impatience. Every tap digs deeper into my nerves.

When I finally place the plates down, he rises like he's civilized, pulling out a chair for me as though this is some kind of date. "Sit," he says smoothly, waiting until I do before settling across from me.

He eats, watching me between chews. I force myself to take a few mouthfuls, then push the food around my plate, spreading it thin so it looks eaten. My stomach rolls with every swallow.

"This is nice," he says after a moment, his tone light. "Almost enough to make you forget about that fire boy you've been staying with."

I still, fork stiff in my hand. My silence is the wrong answer…I can see the anger starting to gather in his eyes. "It does," I blurt, forcing a smile that makes my lips shake. "I love you."

His expression smooths, satisfied, but bile burns the back of my throat. Inside, I'm screaming. Disgust curls through me, thick and bitter. I hate myself for saying it, for feeding him the words he wanted. Each one tastes like poison, a betrayal not just of Reed, but of the woman I've fought so hard to become.

He pushes back from the table and rises. For a second, I think the storm's about to break again. Instead, he lowers himself to one knee in front of me, his hand slipping into his pocket. When it comes back up, the food I just ate threatens to come back up with it. My wedding ring. I left it behind the night I finally walked away. He holds it out between two fingers, his smile curling like this is some kind of proposal. "You forgot something, babe."

The glint of gold feels heavier than any chain. My fingers twitch, but I keep them locked tight in my lap.

"Go on," he coaxes. "Put it back where it belongs."

I don't move. My body refuses. All I can do is stare at the ring.

His smile vanishes. His hand lashes out, snatching mine so hard my knuckles crack. He rams the band onto my finger, the metal biting as it scrapes into place.

"There," he mutters, gripping my hand like a vice. "Right where it should be."

His eyes burn into mine, and then his voice shifts back to fake gentle. "I forgive you, Raelynn. For your little affair. For forgetting who you belong to." His lips twitch like it's mercy, like it's love. "We'll start over. Renew our vows. Make this official again."

I nod faintly, my face calm, but inside I'm screaming. Every word is poison. *Forgive me? For surviving him? For finding someone who made me feel alive?* My stomach knots so tight it hurts, but I keep my expression blank. Pretend. Survive. That's all I can do.

He stands and jerks me to my feet, his gaze locked on mine. "Repeat after me. I, Raelynn, will never leave again. I will never fuck another man again. I will only ever love my husband."

The words hang heavy between us. My throat closes. My head shakes before I can stop it. "No."

His fist slams into my stomach, folding me in half. Air rushes out of me in a broken gasp as pain radiates through my body.

"Say it!" he snaps, his grip biting into my arm.

Tears blur my vision, my voice shaking as I force the words past my lips.

"I, Raelynn, will never leave again." *I'm already gone.*

"I will never fuck another man again." *He's right. Only Reed.*

"I will only ever love my husband." *And that isn't you anymore.*

His smile is triumphant. He looks at me like I've been conquered all over again.

I cling to the truth…every word he made me say is a lie.

His smile lingers as he yanks me closer, one hand clamped around my waist. His breath whispers against my cheek. "Now tell me you love me."

The words stick, but I choke them out anyway. "I love you."

His eyes soften like he believes it, like the lie erases everything. "I love you, too." He presses his mouth to mine, hard, before pulling back with a grin. "Dance with me."

Before I can answer, he crosses to the table, digging through a box until he finds a small speaker. He powers it on, taps his phone and a familiar melody spills into the room. Our wedding song.

He strides back and pulls me into his arms, swaying us across the floor like this rotting cabin is a ballroom. His hand presses into my back, forcing me to move with him, while the lyrics I once thought were beautiful scrape across my skin like knives.

I keep my eyes down, counting each step, every second feeling like an eternity. But in the back of my mind, I hold on to Reed. The way he protects me, like nothing in this world could touch me as long as he's near. How he would never raise a hand to hurt me. The way he loves me, with kindness, with patience, with a gentleness that steadies me when I need it most. Reed would never force me to do anything. With him, the choice has always been mine. That's real. That's mine. Not this prison. Not this man.

Jacob spins me once and pulls me back in. He smiles smugly, certain I'm his again. I let him believe it, because surviving means pretending. But inside, I'm clinging to Reed, and it's the only thing keeping me from falling apart.

The song ends and he stops swaying. He brushes the hair from my face, his eyes drilling into mine. "You know what I expect from my wife."

His hand slides up my leg, and my body stiffens. I jerk back from his touch.

Anger flashes across his face. My pulse spikes. I scramble for an answer, forcing the words out fast. "I'm really tired. It's been a long day."

His jaw twitches. I brace for the explosion. But then his expression smooths, his smile pulling tight. "Come. Let's sit. We can talk about our future while you rest."

I nod quickly, letting him guide me back toward the chair. I sink down, folding my hands in my lap like the dutiful wife he wants.

I know what he really wants. The way his hand slid up my leg, the way his eyes burned…it's only a matter of time before he forces me into his bed.

Please, Reed. Please find me. Please don't let him touch me.

He leans back in his chair, eyes roaming over me. "You know what I expect, Raelynn. A real marriage. No more running, no more disobedience. You'll keep the house, wear the ring, stand by me. You'll be the wife you should've always been." His smile widens, and my stomach knots. "And in our future, there won't be anyone else between us. Just you and me. We'll share everything again, meals, a home, our bed."

I keep my head bowed so he doesn't see the horror in my eyes. I need space, any space at all. "I'll be a good wife," I murmur. "I'll clean up our dinner dishes."

He leans back, grinning like it was his idea all along. "There you go. See how nice this is? Just like old times. You and me, the perfect pair."

I rise, gather the plates and carry them to the counter. I keep my back to him as I start cleaning, letting the motions of washing and wiping hide the fear inside me.

I'll do what I have to in order to survive. I'll nod, obey, play the part he wants if it keeps me alive long enough for Reed to find me. But I won't give him that. I won't let Jacob touch me. I would rather die than betray Reed that way.

I can almost hear what Reed would tell me if he were here… 'Do whatever it takes. Just live.' I bite down hard, swallowing the tears that threaten to rise. Maybe Reed would forgive me if I gave in. But I won't forgive myself. Not for that.

The plates clatter softly as I stack them, rag damp in my hand. I force myself to keep moving, to stay small, invisible. Then his presence fills the space behind me. His arm wraps around my waist, pulling me tight against him. His breath warms my hair as he lowers his mouth to my ear. "You smell so good. God, I've missed you."

My body locks, every muscle screaming.

He turns me in his arms, dragging me against his chest. His eyes burn down into mine, hungry. "Come to bed with me. Make love to me."

This is it. I reach back, fingers scrambling across the counter for anything, anything I can use. My hand brushes the edge of a fork. I grip it tight, curling my fingers around it like a lifeline.

My pulse hammers so loud I can barely hear the words leaving my mouth. "No! I'm never going to make love to you…because I don't love you!"

For a heartbeat, silence hangs heavy between us. Then he explodes.

I drive the fork into his chest with everything I have. His snarl rips through the room as he pulls back, fury twisting his face. He yanks the fork out and hurls it across the room.

Before I can move, his hand slams into me, throwing me to the floor. My palms sting as I hit the boards. I scramble, trying to push myself up, but his boot comes down hard against my stomach, pinning me to the ground. He leans over me, spit flying as he growls, "If you can fuck another man, you can fuck me."

I thrash beneath him, nails clawing at the floor, desperate to break free. But he's too strong. He drops to his knees beside me, one hand clamping around my throat as the other pulls a gun free and sets it on the floor. His other hand goes to his belt buckle. I scratch, kick, scream, "No!"

He bends low, his voice venom. "You're nothing but a whore, and I'm going to treat you like one."

The leather slides free, he rips his belt off, then his fingers tear at the fabric of my dress.

Headlights flood through the cracks in the cabin walls, spilling across the floorboards. Jacob stills, then chuckles darkly. "That must be the fire boy. Maybe if I kill him, you can finally give yourself to me." His hand stretches toward the gun.

"Reed!" My scream rips from my throat. *I know it's him. I know he's here.*

"Please…no!" I beg, twisting, reaching with everything I have. My fingertips brush cold steel. I grip the gun a second before Jacob's hand closes over mine. We struggle; the gun caught between us. His weight crashes down, fury pouring from him as he snarls. I fight, scream, push with everything I have.

Then…BANG!

A light flashes…then the sound of thunder explodes through the cabin, and the world tilts sideways into silence.

48

She Didn't Move

Reed

I charge the last steps, shoulder down. The wood buckles under my shoulder, the door slamming inward with a hollow crash. My eyes sweep the room in a blur. Raelynn is on the floor. Her dress torn, blood soaking into the fabric at her stomach. Her hand trembles against the boards, her gaze fixed on the ceiling, wide and empty. Jacob kneels over her, his shadow swallowing her.

He shot her. God, no…he fucking shot her.

The gun lies on the floor beside him, close enough to reach. I bolt across the room, terrified that if he picks the gun back up, he'll finish her.

I kick the gun hard, sending it skidding across the floor. I grab Jacob by the collar and haul him upright, my fist cocked, ready to cave his face in…then his body sags. Dead weight drags against me, and that's when I see it. Blood spreading across his chest.

My head whips back to Raelynn. The blood soaking her dress isn't hers. It's his.

Jacob chokes, mouth twisting in pain as his eyes roll back. I shove him aside, willing him to die right there, and drop to the floor beside her.

"Raelynn…" Her name slips out broken.

She doesn't move.

My eyes race over her, scanning every inch. One eye swollen black. Her lips split, blood at the corner. A bruise lining her jaw. Her dress torn. A tear slides down her temple, dripping to the floor. She's in shock.

Carefully, like she might shatter, I take her hand in mine. "It's over."

Nothing.

I slide an arm around her shoulders and lift, turning her gently until she's facing me. I hold her steady, supporting her weight, forcing her eyes toward mine.

But it's like she's looking through me.

"You're safe, Raelynn." My chest tightens, the words catching.

Nothing changes.

I lean in closer, pleading. "Come on, Sunshine. Look at me."

Her lashes blink twice, faint, at her nickname.

"That's it, Sunshine," I whisper, my forehead almost touching hers. "I'm here."

She blinks again. And again.

I guide her hands up, placing them on my shoulders. "Feel me," I murmur, willing her to come back to me.

For a long, aching second nothing happens. Then her fingers twitch once against my shirt, the smallest spark of life. Her grip tightens, just barely, but enough.

"That's it," I breathe, covering her hands with mine. "Hold on to me."

Her lips part, dry and trembling. "Reed." Barely a whisper, but it's her.

My chest caves with relief, tears burning the corners of my eyes. "Yeah, Sunshine. I'm here. I've got you. You're safe now."

I cup her face gently. My thumbs brush the tearstains on her cheeks. "I love you. You hear me? I love you.

Something shifts in her gaze…like the fog finally starts to fade. Her eyes lock on mine for the first time, really seeing me. She leans forward, her weight pressing into my chest, her arms weak but reaching.

"I love you, too," she breathes, her voice breaking.

I wrap my arms around her and hold on, finally letting myself breathe.

Then a ragged voice cuts through the room. "Get away from my wife."

She pushes back from me and slowly stands. Her legs shake, but she forces them steady, limping across the room until she's standing over him.

Her voice cuts through the silence. "Repeat after me." She pauses stepping closer.

"I, Jacob, will die with no control."

"I, Jacob, will die unloved."

"I, Jacob, will die on this floor."

She pulls a ring off her finger and lets it fall. It clinks against the floorboards in front of him, spinning like a top. He watches as it wobbles, then falls flat. His eyes linger for a moment…then they close for good.

Her hand trembles at her side, so I reach for it, curling my fingers gently around hers. "Come on, Sunshine," I murmur, guiding her toward the door. "You don't have to see him anymore. Not ever again. Let's get you out of here."

She lets me lead her, one step at a time, until the night air hits her face. Her voice is so quiet I almost miss it. "Am I…am I going to jail?"

I stop just outside the door and tip her chin up, forcing her eyes to mine. "No, Sunshine. You survived. That's all you did. You survived."

Luke is standing a few feet away, phone pressed to his ear. He glances up as we step into the clearing, his gaze flicking to Raelynn before he finishes the call. The distant wail of sirens grows louder. I ease her into the passenger seat of the truck. Her eyes are glazed over but are holding on me now, clinging to my presence.

Luke steps up, sliding his phone into his pocket. "I'm having my guys pull everything, texts, property records, surveillance. It's all getting sent straight to the police chief. You've got nothing to worry about."

Headlights sweep the clearing as Dylan and Miles pull in, their truck grinding to a stop. A beat later, red and blue lights flash against the bunkhouse as a dozen cruisers flood the clearing.

I plant myself by the door of the truck, one hand braced on the frame, keeping myself between Raelynn and the madness unfolding around us.

Cops swarm the property, guns drawn, yelling commands. They rush in, clearing the building, finding Jacob's body inside. Two officers bound toward us. I turn, blocking the view from Raelynn. I know she's not ready for what's coming.

Luke tilts his head toward the cops. "I'll buy you some time. Take care of her."

Then he steps into their path, voice commanding. "I already sent the chief evidence, messages, records, property deeds."

I watch as one of the officers lifts his radio, calling it in to confirm what Luke's saying.

I turn back to the truck. Raelynn whispers, "I killed him." Tears streak down her bruised face. Her gaze drifts past me, fixed on nothing, locked somewhere I can't reach. "There's something wrong with me," she murmurs. "I should feel bad…guilty…but all I feel is relief." Her body shakes, a steady tremor from the cold air and adrenaline wearing off. She doesn't blink. Doesn't move. Just stares into the distance.

I take a step closer, cautiously, not wanting to spook her. When I'm close enough, I lower myself down, crouching in front of her, drawing her eye back to me before I speak. "You didn't do anything wrong, Sunshine. What you did was survive. That takes strength most people don't have."

"You found me…you came for me."

"Nothing was going to keep me away."

She searches my face. "How did you find me?"

"I had a lot of help from them." I tip my chin toward the guys, all standing with the police now. Red and blue lights flash across their faces.

"I'll tell you everything, Sunshine. But first, you're going to have to give a statement. I'm sorry I can't protect you from that…but it has to be done."

She nods faintly, voice barely above a whisper. "I understand."

"I'll stay with you. I promise." I push to my feet and open the back door of the truck. My turnout jacket lies across the seat. I grab it and drape it around her shoulders, the heavy fabric swallowing her. As I settle it into place, her hand rises, and her fingertips brush my face with a touch so gentle I still.

Her eyes meet mine. "I'm ready to talk with them. I want to go to home."

"Okay," I murmur, brushing a strand of hair from her face. "I'll go get them."

I bring her fingers to my lips, and she takes a slow inhale, shoulders rising as she pulls the air in deep. When it leaves her, she sits taller, pulling my jacket tighter around her frame. I force myself to let go and step away from the truck, watching her straighten against the weight of it all. Crossing the clearing, I find the officers waiting with Luke. "She's ready to talk, but the second she's done, we're leaving. Understand?"

They nod, falling into step beside me as we head back toward the truck. When we reach her, she lifts her chin, fragile but stronger now, pulling herself upright, readying herself. The officers kneel a few feet away, notebooks in hand. Medics push past them, checking her vitals and cleaning the cuts, but she doesn't shrink from their touch. Luke hangs back, giving her space, while I keep myself near enough that my shoulder brushes the door, a silent reminder she's not facing this alone.

Her voice wavers at first, but she doesn't back down. She tells them about being taken, about waking up in that cabin, about the way she ran through the dark and was dragged back. She names Victor, tells them how he delivered her straight into Jacob's hands. My jaw clenches so hard it aches. I want to tear Victor apart all over again, but I keep my eyes on her, letting her see I'm with her through every word. And with each detail she forces out, I feel it, like she's reclaiming a piece of herself, determined she'll make it through this.

She goes on, her gaze dropping to her lap, but her words don't falter. She tells them what Jacob did…the commands he barked, the vows he forced from her lips, the dress he shoved on her. My chest burns, fury and helplessness twisting together, but underneath it I catch something else. The more she lays it out, the more I can feel her pulling free of him, piece by piece, refusing to let his control be the last word.

Her voice tightens, but she pushes through, describing what he was about to do. My stomach knots, heat rising behind my eyes, because I can see it…her terror, his hands on her. Then her gaze lifts, locking on mine with a clarity that cuts straight through me. "He was going to kill Reed. That's why…I fought for the gun. That's why I pulled the trigger."

The truth slams into me, but not just the danger. It's the fire in her voice, the certainty. She didn't just save herself. She saved me, too. Because no matter what waited on the other side of that door, nothing would've stopped me from breaking it down. Nothing. Jacob would've killed me and did whatever he wanted with her.

I can't take another second of them scribbling in their notebooks while she bleeds out the truth. I step forward, blocking their view. "She's done." My tone leaves no room for argument. I turn back to her, and the moment my arms open, she comes into me.

Her arms circle my waist, her face pressing against my chest. I hold her tight, kiss the top of her head and breathe her in. "I love you," I whisper into her hair.

Holding on with a quiet strength that's all her own she says, "I love you, too."

Behind me, Luke steps up, slipping his hand into his pocket. He presses his keys into my hand. "I'll get a ride back with Dylan after I finish giving them our side of it."

She doesn't hesitate, pulling her legs into the truck. I shut the door gently, circle around and climb in. She watches out the window as the first hint of sunrise bleeds across the horizon, then turns back toward me. The bruises can't hide the determination in her face.

I ease the truck onto the road. For a while, neither of us speaks. Her hand finds mine on the console, fingers lacing tight, and she doesn't let go. After a few miles, she shifts closer, her shoulder brushing mine. Every breath she takes feels intentional, like she's proving she's still here, still choosing her own future. I keep one hand on the wheel and the other wrapped around hers, driving us both out of the dark.

The best place for her is cabin five. I want to take her straight home, but I can't. Right now, that house is a crime scene, and I don't want her facing it until it's been cleaned. When we finally pull up, the sky is gray with morning. As I open her door, she takes my hand and steps down on her own. Together we walk up the path, the cabin waiting in the quiet dawn. Inside, I guide her to the bed, and she lowers herself onto it with a long breath. I pull the blanket over her legs, brushing a strand of hair from her face. She catches my wrist before I can move away. Her eyes are tired but clear. "Stay with me," she whispers.

"I'm not going anywhere." I sit beside her, leaning back against the headboard. She shifts closer, curling into my side, her hand pressed flat over my chest like she's reminding herself of my heartbeat. I wrap an arm around her and hold her there, breathing her in. We don't speak. We don't need to. She watches the sunshine of a new day spill across the window, and I watch the only Sunshine that matters…her.

49

This Is What Surviving Looks Like

Raelynn

It's been a week, and if one more person tries to "check in" on me, I might freak out. Kinsley and Naya have practically set up camp in my living room, tag-teaming between baking, cleaning and glaring at me every time I so much as leave the room. Judy has apparently decided the best therapy for trauma is a steady stream of casseroles and pies, which explains the five extra pounds currently hanging out on my hips.

And the phone calls. Mel rings four times a day, her voice always bright and cheerful, asking how I'm doing, if I'm eating, if I'm sleeping. Two more from my dad, who's insisting I move back in with him until I'm "back to myself." Reed isn't any better. He is convinced I can't be trusted to cross the street alone.

The ridiculous part? I can't even be mad about it. Annoyed, yes. Smothered, absolutely. But mad? Not when I know every single one of them has gone out of their way to make this so much better. They didn't let me fold in on myself, not even on the days I wanted to. Instead, they kept me moving, kept me busy and helped me pour everything into getting ready for tomorrow…the grand opening of my salon.

It's nearly 9:00 P.M. when I abandon yet another one of Judy's pies on the counter and walk back into the living room.

Reed's herding Kinsley and Naya toward the door like he's corralling toddlers instead of two grown women.

Kinsley digs her heels in. "Make sure she actually eats dinner tonight, not just pie."

Naya folds her arms, glaring at Reed. "And make sure she rests. No sneaking back to the salon for a 'quick project.'"

Reed gives them both a look. "I think I can handle it."

"Mm-hmm," Kinsley says, clearly not convinced. "We'll be back later to check."

"Tomorrow morning, too," Naya adds, wagging a finger at me like I'm grounded.

Finally, the door shuts behind them, and Reed locks the dead bolt. He crosses the room and drops onto the couch. "Sunshine, your friends are driving me crazy."

A laugh bursts out of me before I can stop it. "You're all driving me crazy."

Reed clutches his chest in mock horror. "Me?"

"Hotshot, I'm pretty sure I can take a shower by myself."

He chuckles, as he leans back. "That's not for you, Sunshine. That's for me." He winks.

I roll my eyes at his lie, and plop down beside him. "I'm excited…but nervous about tomorrow. What if no one shows up?"

He rubs my knee. "It's going to be great, Sunshine. You've worked your ass off. The whole town's been waiting for a salon." His mouth quirks into a smile. "But…I'll admit, I'm going to miss this. Sitting around, having you all to myself."

"Me too," I murmur, then push to my feet. I walk toward the bedroom, knowing full well his eyes are tracking every step. At the doorway, I stop, glance back and in one slow move, pull my shirt over my head.

Reed sits upright, gripping the couch.

Keeping my eyes locked on his, I pop the button on my jeans and ease the zipper down. "I know one thing that'll make these nerves disappear," I tease softly. "Unless you'd rather I handle it myself…" Before he can answer, I slip into the bedroom, laughing.

The sound of heavy footsteps follow instantly. "No need to handle it yourself, Sunshine. I'm at your disposal."

***

I watch from the middle of my completed salon as Reed hangs the Grand Opening banner outside. On the wall to my left, the name I chose waits beneath a draped cloth, ready to be revealed. I never let Reed see what I picked, and the secret makes my chest flutter with anticipation.

I turn slowly, taking it all in, the polished floors, the fresh paint, the chairs lined up in perfect rows. I can't believe how far I've come. My salon. This isn't just a building. It's proof. Proof that I fought my way back, that I'm still here, still me, still ready to live my life on my own terms.

Getting here wasn't easy, late nights, paint in my hair, second-guessing every choice. And then that night…darkness pressing in, fear clawing at me, trying to convince me I'd never make it to this point. But here I am. Standing in my dream. And nothing…no one…is going to take this away from me again.

The door swings open, and Reed steps inside, a streak of dust on his shirt from the banner. "Fifteen minutes, Sunshine. What's left?"

I smile at him…this man. The one who picked me up, dusted me off and kept me going when I thought I couldn't. "I just need to sweep and set up the refreshment table." I glance toward the empty street. "But…I'm worried. No one's here yet."

He crosses the room and wraps me in his arms, pressing his chin lightly to the top of my head. "They'll be here." He pulls back and spins me. "Now go get your table done." Then he smacks my ass.

I giggle and head toward my office where the boxes of cookies and drinks are waiting. My chest tightens, doubt slipping in as I start arranging cups. *What if no one shows up? What if all this really was for nothing?*

From the other room, I hear him call out, "Stop overthinking it, Sunshine. They'll be here."

A laugh bubbles out of me despite myself. He knows me too well.

I keep my hands busy, lining cookies on a tray, setting out cups, anything to keep my nerves from chewing me alive. When I finally glance at the clock, my heart skips…it's one minute to opening. Wiping my hands on a towel, I step out of the office…and pause completely caught off guard by the view.

Through the front window, a crowd stretches down the sidewalk. And right there, among them, is Reed. He must have slipped out the door while I was in the office, giving me my moment.

My eyes sting as I walk toward the front. The first person in line is my dad, pride written clear across his face. Next to him stands Reed, smile firmly in place, and beside him Kinsley with her phone held high, Mel's smiling face beaming through the screen. Judy waves, Naya practically bounces with excitement, and even Miles, Dylan and Luke are there, grinning like they wouldn't miss this. And behind all of them are faces I don't recognize. A couple dozen people who came anyway. People who chose to be here. For me.

My chest swells as it all hits at once. These aren't just customers. They're my people…my family, my friends, my neighbors. The kind of people who show up when it matters.

I grip the handle and pull the door open. Cheers erupt instantly, clapping and whistles echoing down the street. My dad is the first to step forward, pulling me into a hug so tight it nearly lifts me off my feet. Then Reed's arms are around me, steady and warm, and after him come Kinsley and Naya, Judy with tears in her eyes, Mel blowing kisses through the phone. Miles, Dylan and Luke hang back a second before stepping in, each giving my shoulder a solid pat and a quiet "congrats."

Soon the chairs are full, people mingling with drinks and cookies, checking out every corner of the place. A line forms at the desk, and I'm scribbling names into my book. Appointments fill one after another, page after page, until I'm booked solid for the next four weeks.

Finally, the last name is written down. I snap the book shut, my hand aching but my heart so full it could burst. I cross the room, weaving through clusters of neighbors and friends still chatting.

"It's time!" Judy's voice rings out, cutting through the noise like only she can. Instantly, the room quiets, all eyes swiveling my way. I step up beside the wall, my pulse quickening as every gaze in the salon turns to me. My hand lifts, hovering just above the cloth draped over the sign.

For a moment, I let myself soak it in. This isn't just about a name on the wall. It's about every late night, every doubt I pushed through, every scar I refused to let define me. It's about family, friends, and the man who never let me forget I was worth fighting for.

With a breath, I grip the edge of the cloth and tug it free.

Sunshine Salon

The gold letters gleam against the fresh paint, and the room erupts; cheers, clapping, laughter filling every corner.

Through it all, my eyes find Reed. He steps forward from the crowd, weaving his way toward me, and I can't stop the smile that breaks across my face as I watch him come closer. "That's perfect, Sunshine," he murmurs against my hair, holding me close while the applause swells around us.

Bit by bit, the cheers fade as people start to trickle out, offering hugs and congratulations on their way to the door. The salon quiets, just my closest circle left behind.

Naya claps her hands together, a mischievous grin spreading across her face. "Alright, enough of the polite stuff. Time to turn this party up." She digs into one of her bags and produces not one, but two bottles of wine.

The girls cheer. The guys groan.

Luke jerks a thumb toward the door. "Fireside?"

Dylan nods immediately, but Reed hesitates, his eyes flicking to me. "I don't know. Maybe I should…"

"I'll be fine," I cut in quickly. "Go. Have a beer with the guys."

He lingers, clearly torn, until Miles claps him on the shoulder. "Stop hovering. She'll survive without you for an hour."

Reed shoots him a look, but I catch the corner of his mouth twitch before he finally sighs and relents.

"Don't worry, Hotshot. I've got Judy here. We've all seen her shoot," I tease.

We both glance her way. She smiles sweetly and waves.

Reed chuckles, shaking his head. "You're not wrong." He kisses me quick, then follows the guys out the door.

When I turn back, Naya is already pressing a glass of wine into my hand. "To fresh starts," she declares.

"Fresh starts," we echo, clinking our glasses together.

Kinsley grins wide, eyes sparkling. "And to new beginnings…I got approved for my new building!"

The room erupts with laughter and applause, all of us buzzing with her news.

Mel's voice bursts from Kinsley's phone screen. She's holding up her own glass from the other side of the video call. "And I'll be moving there in two weeks…just in time for Christmas!"

"You'll love Cranberry Ridge at Christmas," Judy chimes.

We all cheer and toast to Mel's news. "To Cranberry Ridge at Christmas!" We toast.

The pizza shows up, and we don't even bother with the tables. We pile onto the floor, legs crossed, paper plates balanced on our knees, laughing between bites and sips of wine. Exactly an hour later, the door swings open. Reed steps inside, the chill of the night trailing in with him. That's when I feel it…surrounded by these girls and the man I love...the happiness I deserve.

Resources

If you or someone you know is experiencing abuse or struggling with depression, please know you are not alone. Support is available.

National Domestic Violence Hotline (U.S.): 1-800-799-SAFE (7233) | thehotline.org

National Sexual Assault Hotline (U.S.): 1-800-656-4673 | rainn.org

988 Suicide & Crisis Lifeline (U.S.): Call or text 988 | 988lifeline.org

For readers outside the United States, please seek local hotlines or resources in your area.

Author's Note

Thank you for returning to Cranberry Ridge and stepping inside Cabin 5. Writing this story felt like opening a new door in the series…one that was a little heavier, a little messier, but also full of healing and hope.

This was a story about two very different journeys colliding…Raelynn, still carrying the weight of her past and learning how to heal, and Reed, convinced he didn't want love until she changed everything. Writing them reminded me that sometimes the heart knows what we need long before our head catches up.

Thank you for joining me for Raelynn and Reed's journey. I hope Cabin 5 made you feel seen, made you smile, and maybe even made you believe that no matter how dark the past gets, there's always light ahead. There's plenty more coming from Cranberry Ridge (and yes, Judy's probably already meddling in it).

With gratitude,

P.L. Wellisley

Acknowledgments

Writing a second book doesn't feel any less surreal than the first. If anything, it feels even more special…because it means I get to keep building this world, these characters, and sharing them with you.

To my readers: thank you. Every message, every review, every time you picked up Cabin 6 and came back for Cabin 5…you gave me the encouragement to keep going. I hope Raelynn and Reed's story touched you in the way writing it touched me.

To my family and friends, thank you for your patience, your cheering, and for never questioning the hours I disappear into Cranberry Ridge. To those who read early drafts, helped with edits, proofread pages, or simply listened while I sorted through ideas…you made this story stronger, and I couldn't have done it without you.

And finally, to anyone carrying scars of their own: this book is for you. May you find hope, laughter, and light in unexpected places…just like Raelynn did.

Endlessly grateful,

P.L. Wellisley

Books by P.L. Wellisley

<u>Cranberry Ridge Series.</u>

Cabin 6 – Kinsley & Miles' story

Cabin 5 – Raelynn & Reed's story

Cabin 4 – Coming Soon

Cabin 3 – Coming Soon

Cabin 2 – Coming Soon

Cabin 1 – Coming Soon